Praise for the writing of Cl

Club Shadowlands

"*Club Shadowlands* is a superbly crafted story that will dazzle any BDSM fan and have them adding it to their must read list!"

— Shannon, *The Romance Studio*

"…I was so taken with the characters in the club from the beginning that I wanted to finish reading this in one sitting. I did enjoy it very much, so much I can say that those that love BDSM romances should check it out."

— Lainey, *Coffee Time Romance*

A Reviewer Top Pick! "There's continuous action with varying degrees of BDSM, which move the story along quite quickly. Ms Sinclair did a nice job of sensualising her characters…"

— *Night Owl Romance*

Dark Citadel

"Cherise Sinclair is an author to watch in the BDSM genre, gifting us with complex characters and sizzling scenes, making readers like me begging for more!"

— Victoria, *Two Lips Reviews*

"Cherise Sinclair starts out using subtle skill to bring the reader into this exciting lifestyle. *Dark Citadel* is a decadent delight and an immensely satisfying read."

— Priscilla Alston, *Just Erotic Romance Reviews*

LooseId®

ISBN 13: 978-1-59632-879-2
MASTERS OF THE SHADOWLANDS
Copyright © June 2009 by Cherise Sinclair
Cover Art by Christine M. Griffin
Cover Layout by April Martinez
Publisher acknowledges the authors and copyright holders of the individual works, as follows:
CLUB SHADOWLANDS
Copyright © January 2009 by Cherise Sinclair
DARK CITADEL
Copyright © April 2009 by Cherise Sinclair

Printed in the U.S.A. by
Lightning Source, Inc.
1246 Heil Quaker Blvd
La Vergne TN 37086
www.lightningsource.com

Author's Note

This book is fiction, not reality and, as in most romantic fiction, the romance is compressed into a very, very short time period.

You, my darlings, live in the real world and I want you to take a little more time than the heroines you read about. Good Doms don't grow on trees and there's some strange people out there. So while you're looking for that special Dom, please, be careful.

When you find him, realize he can't read your mind. Yes, frightening as it might be, you're going to have to open up and talk to him. And you listen to him, in return. Share your hopes and fears, what you want from him, what scares you spitless. Okay, he may try to push your boundaries a little -- he's a Dom, after all -- but you have your safeword. You *will* have a safeword, am I clear? Use protection. Have a back-up person. Communicate.

Remember: *safe*, *sane* and *consensual*.

Know that I'm hoping you find that special, loving person who will understand your needs and hold you close. Let me know how you're doing. I worry, you know.

Meantime, come and hang out with the Masters.

Cherise
cherisesinclair@sbcglobal.net

Contents

CLUB SHADOWLANDS

Chapter One

Jessica Randall scrambled out of the water-filled ditch, her heart hammering. Frigid rain slashed through the dark night, drenching her face and clothing. Gasping for breath, she knelt in the mud, surprised to have made it to the bank in one piece. She glanced over her shoulder and shuddered. Alligators loved to hang out in Florida ditches. A few moments more and she could have been... She stifled the thought with a shudder.

Hands shaking, she scrubbed the water off her face and pushed to her feet.

As her fear diminished, she peered through the darkness and could barely see her car. Poor little Taurus, nose down with water roiling around the hood.

"I'll be back for you. Don't worry," she promised, feeling like she was abandoning her baby.

Once on the narrow country road, she pushed her tangled hair out of her face and looked each way. Darkness and darkness. Dammit, why couldn't she have an accident right in someone's front yard? But no, the nearest house was probably the one she'd passed about a mile back. She headed that way, stopping to glare at the pool of water where her car had aquaplaned right off the road. The armadillo, of course, was long gone. At least she hadn't hit it.

Head lowered, she trudged down the blacktop toward the house, getting wetter and wetter. Hopefully she wouldn't trip on something in the darkness. Breaking her leg would be the final straw in a day that had been a disaster from start to finish.

Number one mistake: meeting at a halfway point for their first date when the man lived miles and miles outside of Tampa.

He sure hadn't been worth the trip. She'd have found more excitement auditing business accounts. Then again, he hadn't appeared all that impressed with her either. She grimaced. She'd recognized the look in his eyes, the one that said he really wanted tall and slim, an Angelina Jolie type woman, no matter that her posted picture portrayed her quite accurately: a pint-size Marilyn Monroe.

So far, she'd have to say finding a guy through the Internet rated right up there with back-country shortcuts, her second mistake of the day.

Aunt Eunice always swore things happened in threes. So would braking for an armadillo be considered her third mistake, or was there another disaster lurking in her near future?

She shivered as the wind howled through the palmettos and plastered her drenched clothing against her chilled body. Couldn't stop now. Doggedly, she set one foot in front of the other, her waterlogged shoes squishing with every step.

An eternity later, she spotted a glimmer of light. Relief rushed through her when she reached a driveway studded with hanging lights. Surely whoever lived here would let her wait out the storm. She walked through the ornate iron gates, up the palm-lined drive past landscaped lawns, until finally she reached a three-story stone mansion. Black wrought iron lanterns illumined the entry.

"Nice place," she muttered. And a little intimidating. She glanced down at herself to check the damage. Mud and rain streaked her tailored slacks and white button-down shirt, hardly a suitable image for a conservative accountant. She looked more like something even a cat would refuse to drag in.

Shivering hard, she brushed at the dirt and grimaced as it only streaked worse. She stared up at the huge oak doors guarding the entrance. A small doorbell in the shape of a dragon glowed on the side panel, and she pushed it.

Seconds later, the doors opened. A man, oversized and ugly as a battle-scarred Rottweiler, looked down at her. "I'm sorry, miss, you're too late. The doors are locked."

What the heck did that mean?

"P-please," she said, stuttering with the cold. "My car's in a ditch, and I'm soaked, and I need a place to dry out and call for help." But did she really want to go inside with this scary-looking guy? Then she shivered so hard her teeth clattered together, and her mind was made up. "Can I come in? Please?"

He scowled at her, his big-boned face brutish in the yellow entry light. "I'll have to ask Master Z. Wait here." And the bastard shut the door, leaving her in the cold and dark.

Jessica wrapped her arms around herself, standing miserably, and finally the door opened again. Again the brute. "Okay, come on in."

Relief brought tears to her eyes. "Thank you, oh, thank you." Stepping around him before he could change his mind, she barreled into a small entry room and slammed into a solid body. "Oomph," she huffed.

Firm hands gripped her shoulders. She shook her wet hair out of her eyes and looked up. And up. The guy was big, a good six feet, his shoulders wide enough to block the room beyond.

He chuckled, his hands gentling their grasp on her arms. "She's freezing, Ben. Molly left some clothing in the blue room; send one of the subs."

"Okay, boss." The brute—Ben—disappeared.

"What is your name?" Her new host's voice was deep, dark as the night outside.

"Jessica." She stepped back from his grip to get a better look at her savior. Smooth black hair, silvering at the temples, just touching his collar. Dark gray eyes with laugh lines at the corners. A lean, hard face with the shadow of a beard adding a hint of roughness. He wore tailored black slacks and a black silk shirt that outlined hard muscles underneath. If Ben was a Rottweiler, this guy was a jaguar, sleek and deadly.

"I'm sorry to have bothered—" she started.

Ben reappeared with a handful of golden clothing that he thrust at her. "Here you go."

She took the garments, holding them out to keep from getting the fabric wet. "Thank you."

A faint smile creased the manager's cheek. "Your gratitude is premature, I fear. This is a private club."

"Oh. I'm sorry." Now what was she going to do?

"You have two choices. You may sit out here in the entryway with Ben until the storm passes. The forecast stated the winds and rain would die down around six or so in the morning, and you won't get a tow truck out on these country roads until then. Or you may sign papers and join the party for the night."

She looked around. The entry was a tiny room with a desk and one chair. Not heated. Ben gave her a dour look.

Sign something? She frowned. Then again, in this lawsuit-happy world, every place made a person sign releases, even to visit a fitness center. So she could sit here all night. Or...be with happy people and be warm. *No-brainer.* "I'd love to join the party."

"So impetuous," the manager murmured. "Ben, give her the paperwork. Once she signs—or not—she may use the dressing room to dry off and change."

"Yes, sir." Ben rummaged in a file box on the desk, pulled out some papers.

The manager tilted his head at Jessica. "I will see you later then."

Ben shoved three pages of papers at her and a pen. "Read the rules. Sign at the bottom." He scowled at her. "I'll get you a towel."

She started reading. *Rules of the Shadowlands.*

"Shadowlands. That's an unusual na—" she said, looking up. Both men had disappeared. Huh. She returned to reading, trying to focus her eyes. Such tiny print. Still, she never signed anything without reading it.

Doors will open at...

Water pooled around her feet. Her teeth chattered so hard she had to clench her jaw. There was a dress code. Something about cleaning the equipment after use. Halfway down the second page, her eyes started blurring. *Damn it all.* This was just a club, after all; it wasn't like she was signing mortgage papers.

Turning to the last page, she scrawled her name.

When Ben returned, he checked the papers for her signature, handed her a towel, and showed her into an opulent restroom off the entry. Glass-doored stalls along one side faced a mirrored wall with sinks and counters.

She glanced in the mirror and winced: short, pudgy woman, straggly blonde hair, pale complexion now blue with cold. Surprising that they'd even let her in the door. Dropping the borrowed clothing on the marble counter, she kicked her shoes off and tried to unbutton her shirt. Her hands were numb, shaking uncontrollably, and time after time, the buttons slipped from her stiff fingers. She couldn't even get her slacks off, and she was shuddering so hard her bones hurt.

"Dammit," she muttered and tried again.

The door opened. "Jessica, are you—" The manager. "No, you are obviously not all right." He stepped inside, a dark figure wavering in her blurry vision.

"Permit me." Without waiting for her answer, he stripped her out of her clothes as one would a two-year-old, even peeling off her sodden bra and panties. His hands were hot, almost burning, against her chilled skin.

She was naked. As the thought percolated through her numb brain, she jerked away and grabbed at the dry clothing. His hand intercepted hers.

"No, pet." He plucked something from her hair, opening his hand to show muddy leaves. "First a shower."

He wrapped a hard arm around her waist and moved her into one of the glass-fronted stalls behind where she'd been standing. With his free hand, he turned on the water, and heavenly warm steam billowed up. He adjusted the temperature.

"In you go," he ordered. A hand on her bottom, he nudged her into the shower.

The water felt scalding hot against her frigid skin, and she gasped, then sighed as the heat began to penetrate. After a minute, she realized the door of the stall was open. Arms crossed, the man leaned against the door frame, watching her with a slight smile on his lean face.

"I'm fine," she muttered, turning so her back was to him. "I can manage by myself."

"No, you obviously cannot," he said evenly. "Wash the mud out of your hair. The left dispenser has shampoo."

Mud in her hair. She'd totally forgotten; maybe she *did* need a keeper. After using the vanilla-scented shampoo, she let the water sluice through her hair. Brown water and twigs swirled down the drain. The water finally ran clear.

"Very good." The water shut off. Blocking the door, he rolled up his sleeves, displaying corded, muscular arms. She had the unhappy feeling he was going to keep helping her, and any protest would be ignored. He'd taken charge as easily as if she'd been one of the puppies at the shelter where she volunteered.

"Out with you now." When her legs wobbled, he tucked a hand around her upper arm, holding her up with disconcerting ease. The cooler air hit her body, and her shivering started again.

After blotting her hair, he grasped her chin and tipped her face up to the light. She gazed up at his darkly tanned face, trying to summon up enough energy to pull her face away.

"No bruises. I think you were lucky." Taking the towel, he dried off her arms and hands, rubbing briskly until he appeared satisfied with the pink color. Then he did her back and shoulders. When he reached her breasts, she pushed at his hand. "I can do that."

He ignored her like she would a buzzing fly, his attentions gentle but thorough, even to lifting each breast and drying underneath.

When he toweled off her butt, she wanted to hide. If there was any part of her that should be covered, it was her hips. Overweight. *Jiggly.* He didn't seem to notice.

Then he knelt and ordered, "Spread your legs."

No way. She flushed, didn't move.

He looked up, lifted an eyebrow. And waited. Her resolve faltered beneath the steady, authoritative regard.

She slid one leg over. His towel-covered hand stroked between her legs, sending a flush of embarrassment through her. The full enormity of her position swept through her: she was naked in front of a complete stranger, letting him touch her...there. Her breath stopped even as disconcerting pleasure moved through her.

He glanced up, his eyes crinkling, before moving his attention to her legs. He chafed the skin until she could feel the glow. "There, that should do it."

Ignoring her attempt to take the clothing, he helped her step into a long, slinky skirt that reached midcalf—at least it covered her hips—then pulled a gold-colored, stretchy tank top over her head. His muscular fingers brushed her breasts as he adjusted the fit. He studied her for a moment before smiling slowly. "The clothes suit you, Jessica, far more than your own. A shame to hide such a lovely figure."

Lovely? She knew better, but the words still gave her a glowy feeling inside. She glanced down to check for herself and frowned at the way the low-cut elastic top outlined her full breasts. She could see every little bump in her nipples. *Good grief.* She crossed her arms over her chest.

His chuckle was deep and rich. "Come, the main room is much warmer."

Wrapping an arm around her, he led her out of the bathroom, through the entry, and into a huge room crowded with people. Her eyes widened as she looked around. The club must take up the entire first floor of the house. A circular bar of darkly polished wood ruled the center of the room. Wrought iron sconces cast flickering light over tables and chairs, couches and coffee tables. Plants created small secluded areas. The right corner of the room had a dance floor where music pulsed with a throbbing beat. Farther down, parts of the wall were more brightly lit, but she couldn't see past the crowd to make out why.

Her steps slowed as she realized the club members were attired in extremely provocative clothing, from skintight leathers and latex to corsets to—*oh my*—one woman was bare from the waist up. A long chain dangled from…*clamps* on her nipples.

What in the world? Wincing, Jessica glanced up at her host. "Um, excuse me?" What was his name, anyway?

He stopped. "You may call me Sir."

Like the Marines or something? "Uh, right. Exactly what kind of club *is* this?" Over the music and murmur of voices, a woman's voice suddenly wailed in unmistakable orgasm. Heat flared in Jessica's face.

Amusement glinted in the man's dark eyes. "It's a private club, and tonight is bondage night, pet; I thought you'd have realized that from reading the rules."

Just then, a man in black leathers walked by, followed by a barefoot woman with her head down and wrists cuffed. Jessica's mouth opened, only no words emerged.

One eyebrow raised, the manager waited patiently. She could feel his hand pressed low against her back, like a brand.

What had she gotten into? "Bondage?" she managed to say. "Like men making *slaves* of women?"

"Not always. Sometimes a woman dominates the man." He nodded to the left where a man dressed in only a loincloth knelt beside a woman. The woman wore a skintight latex vest and leggings with a coiled whip attached to her belt.

"And domination can range all the way from an entire lifestyle, twenty-four/seven, to just a fun bout of sex. Many women fantasize about having a man take charge in the bedroom." He stroked a finger down her flushed cheek. "Here the fantasy is real."

Something inside her tightened at his words, a fascination mixed with shock. *Take charge*—what exactly did that mean? Then the memory swept through her of how he'd touched her naked body, how he'd simply…taken charge, and she couldn't keep from looking at him.

His dark eyes were intent on her face, as if he could read her reactions as easily as she would read a client's books. She felt telltale redness rise in her cheeks.

"Come," he said, smiling, his hand moving her forward. "Let's get something warm inside you—"

Inside her? Like the thrust of a man's—She jerked her mind away. Good grief, she'd been here five minutes, and her thoughts were in the gutter. A smart person—and she was that if nothing else—would make a polite retreat right about now.

"And then you can decide if you want to hide in the entryway or stay here with the grown-ups."

Even as her spine stiffened, she realized how easily he'd played her, and she glared at him.

His lips quirked.

As they approached the circular bar, the bartender abandoned making a drink to come over. He looked like a Great Dane with shaggy hair, all bone and muscle, even taller than...*Sir.* She frowned over her shoulder at the manager. *What the heck kind of name was Sir?*

Chapter Two

"Something hot, Cullen, for Jessica. Irish coffee with lots of Irish." As Zachary gazed down at the little intruder, he had to smile. She had a lovely body with lush hips wide enough to cradle a man in softness and full breasts begging to be savored. Her skin was fair, and her eyes the color of spring leaves.

And right now, those eyes were wide as his grandmother's favorite supper plates. How she'd read the rules and not understood the nature of the club, he couldn't comprehend. He really shouldn't have let her in, signature or not, but her helplessness had brought out all his Dom instincts to protect and nurture.

"A hot drink would be wonderful," she told the bartender.

Zachary's eyes narrowed; she was still shivering a little but much improved.

The toweling off had helped, as had her dawning embarrassment when he'd handled her. Although in her mid- to late twenties, she was obviously not accustomed to being touched so intimately. Her blushes had left him with a growing desire to touch her even more thoroughly, to explore her body, and discover her responses.

But he hadn't been able to ascertain if she would welcome his attentions or not. As for if she was a sub… The votes weren't in on that yet either. However, once she moved past the initial shock of seeing the club, he'd be able to look into her mind and see if the sight of domination excited her.

The night was yet young. If he sensed desire in her thoughts, he would enjoy laying her soft, vanilla-scented body out across his bed, restraining and opening her for his pleasure.

"Master Z." One of his newer dungeon monitors stopped beside him, his bony face worried. "Could you arbitrate for a minute?"

"Certainly." Zachary glanced at Jessica. "Do you need an escort to the entry or will you be staying?"

Her mouth—pretty pink lips that would look quite lovely around his cock—pursed as she glanced around the room. He sensed her misgivings vying with her intense curiosity. The curiosity won. "I'll stay."

"Brave girl."

The creamy Irish coffee burned all the way down, starting a little fire inside her. *Heavenly.* When the bartender came back, Jessica had finished and was gazing sadly into the already empty cup.

"Ready for more?" he asked.

Heck, her purse was in the car trunk and would be there until a tow truck pulled her car out. "No, thank you. That's all right."

He leaned an enormous arm on the bar and frowned. "You obviously want another. What's the problem?"

What was it with these guys? "Are you and your boss mind readers or what?"

His laugh boomed, drowning out the music. "Master Z's the mind reader; I'm just observant."

His statement was a little too straightforward for comfort. Surely, the manager didn't read—*nah.* "I left my purse in the car, so no money."

"Not to worry. You're the owner's guest tonight." After a minute, the bartender set a steaming mug in front of her. "There's a two-drink limit, so I made this one plain coffee."

"But I've only had one drink."

He grinned at her. "You haven't been here before. You may well need more alcohol after a bit."

Now why did that sound so ominous? She sipped the drink instead of inhaling it, and this time the warmth filling her was from hot coffee and not potent alcohol. She set an elbow on the bar, sighing as the cold released its last grip. When she saw Sir again, she'd have to thank him for the drinks.

So, he was the owner of this place, not the manager. No wonder everyone jumped at his requests. Then again, she hadn't known he was the owner, and she'd let him strip her naked and that wasn't like her at all. Somehow he'd been in control from the moment he walked into the dressing room. *Master Z,* the bartender had called him; that fit all too well. She stiffened. *Bondage* club... Did that mean *he* was into tying people up?

The thought made her squirm. How could she ever face him again without turning red? She sighed, realizing she probably wouldn't see him again anyway. After all, he was way out of her class. Too good-looking. Too self-assured. With that touch of silver in his hair and laugh lines around those smoky gray eyes, he was definitely a man, nothing like the boyish types that seemed to be everywhere. And he had those lean, rippling muscles...um-hmmm.

But what really attracted her was his air of sheer competence, like whatever he did, he'd do better than anyone else. She sighed, shook her head. Duh, Jessica. A guy's nice to you, and there you go, getting all enthused.

But to her slender mother's disgust, she'd never had the trim, perky body that men liked, and Master Z would know that since he'd seen her in all her naked glory. Considering his appearance, he could have any woman in this place. Hell, any place. Yeah, she would just avoid him and not make an even bigger fool of herself.

Turning on the bar stool, she checked out the room. A *bondage* club. Now this presented her with an adventure she'd never imagined. Nothing like this existed in the tiny town where she'd grown up. And in Tampa, she'd never ventured to try anything so exotic. Shoot, her idea of adventurous was volunteering at the animal shelter.

She grinned. While here, she might as well widen her knowledge base. Aunt Eunice would be delighted, and her mother would be horrified.

But nothing thrilled her more than learning something new. Where to start?

The people dancing appeared to be having fun, although she'd never been at ease on a dance floor, at least not sober. Give her a business or social occasion, and she felt right at home. Make it a man-woman interaction, and she tensed up like a businessman being audited.

As she watched, her eyes widened. Some of the gyrating out there would have the participants arrested anywhere else. One young man with a serious hard-on whirled the woman into his arms and then pressed so close that only the fabric between them prevented insertion.

She took another sip of her drink and realized the dancers were just too provocative for comfort. Like that one couple. The man moved his woman where he wanted her. He touched her when he wanted, even put her hands on him...there.

With an effort, Jessica dragged her gaze away, tried to watch the other couples on the floor. And focused on a big man in skintight rubber jeans that bulged with a thick erection. He pulled his bikini-clad woman to him, tangled his hands in her hair and tipped her head back to take her lips. He kissed her slowly. Thoroughly.

Jessica blinked, realized she was pressing her thighs together. *Whoa, time to stop watching the live action.* Here she'd thought she could call herself fairly experienced. Sure, she was small-town raised, but she'd lived in Tampa long enough to have had several lovers. Not that she was all that good at the sex stuff. Really, making love was rather overrated, at least for her.

She grimaced, remembering the last time and how she just couldn't stop thinking about everything and anything. Did he think she was fat? Would he see how her stomach pouched out? Should she move her hips faster? Would he like his balls touched or not? Sex was just too stressful.

After finishing her coffee, she glanced back at the dance floor. Heck, that woman out there looked like she was getting more from one kiss than Jessica had ever gotten from the whole *insert-dick-move-around* shebang. And now, the man had his hand on the woman's bared breast, was actually toying with her nipple. When his fingers tightened in what looked like a painful pinch, the woman's knees sagged.

Damn, but just watching was getting Jessica overheated. Her own nipples burned. Furtively, she glanced down. No bra. Her nipples poked out like someone had glued pencil erasers to her chest. Turning back to the bar, she crossed her arms over the traitorous flesh and willed them to go down.

The bartender looked at her, a hint of amusement in his eyes. He lifted his thick eyebrows at her cup.

She shook her head. No more alcohol, and she was definitely warm enough. Time to go walkabout and cool off.

Sliding from the bar stool, she headed away from the dance floor toward the rear of the room. People crowded the tables and couches; the murmur of conversation increased as she moved away from the music. The place looked almost like a normal bar if she ignored what people wore…and the hands-on stuff. She edged past a table where a woman knelt at her guy's feet. He stroked her hair like a pet cat.

Jessica frowned. The owner had called her *pet*. She did not— *really* did not—want to think about what he'd meant by that. Especially since thinking about *him* made her think of that couple on the dance floor. What would it be like if it were Sir touching her, holding her against his… *Oh, girl, do not think that way.*

Halfway down the room, she neared one of the places on the wall that was lit with brighter sconces. Now she could see what it was. She blinked in horror. There was a naked woman strapped to a wooden X on the wall. *A live woman, not a statue.* Jessica's feet didn't want to move even though she knew she was staring.

Okay, okay. This was really like a strip bar; naked women doing stuff. But the woman was *tied* there, her legs open, breasts free. Everyone could see her.

She instinctively started to go to the woman's aid, then stopped and scrutinized the people watching. No one appeared concerned. A man in shiny black latex jeans and sleeveless shirt stood within the roped-off area busy with some small metal things in his hands.

Jessica made herself study the woman on the cross thing. Eyes focused on the man in latex, the brunette wasn't hurting; her squirming movements seemed provocative.

Had that woman *wanted* to be tied and naked? Biting her lip, Jessica tried to imagine what kind of person would surrender such power to someone else, even so far as being tied up. Not someone like herself, that was for sure. She'd fought her way up the business ladder, could hold her own in social circles, was an assertive, independent woman.

So why was she finding this so fascinating?

Why did this place feel like her dreams come to life, only more erotic than anything she'd ever imagined? Her face flushed as she remembered Sir saying, *Many women fantasize about having a man take charge in the bedroom.* Surely he hadn't been able to tell that she was one of them?

She looked at the woman again. What would that be like? Heat swirled through her at the thought of being there herself, wrists lashed... *No, that was totally wrong. Keep moving.*

She threaded through the spectators, past the roped-off area. Most of the members were in couples or groups, and Jessica felt conspicuously alone.

And underdressed, even if she wore more than a lot of the women. But her full breasts jutted out against the tight shirt, bouncing with her movements. This wasn't the sixties, for heaven's sake, and she never went without a bra. Not in public. Conservative accountants didn't wear stuff like this. Or go without panties either. The silky feeling of the skirt sliding against her bottom, the caress of cool air against her private areas was disconcerting, especially in this sex-charged room.

People brushed past, leaving perfume, cologne, and musk in their wake. A couple went by, the man leading the woman with a leash strung to a collar around her neck, and the scent of sex permeated the air around them.

Look at that. The way the man had the leash wrapped around his fist, the way the woman followed... Jessica touched her neck. Her core actually burned as shockingly wanton thoughts filled her head: a man's hands buckling a collar on her, touching her. A man—*Sir*—doing anything he wanted to her.

Across the room at the bar, Zachary smiled, enjoying the wide-eyed innocent. When she touched her neck, he hardened, knowing exactly what was in her mind. Her emotions were so strong, he could almost see as well as feel them.

"Lost your little sub, Z?" The bartender set a glass of Glenlivet down.

"Not lost. Released to explore."

She reminded him of a kitten freed from the kennel, faring forth on a new adventure, ears forward, tail held high. She was definitely a brave little ball of fluff. He had watched her stop in front of the St. Andrew's cross, felt the shock radiate from her.

Unlike most people, she had strong, clean emotions. Curiosity. Courage to explore something new. Shock. Worry and sympathy for someone she thought might be hurt. The ability to think before reacting.

And now...*arousal.* Other emotions might be more satisfying, but few were as enticing as awakening desire.

"She's a cutie," Cullen commented. "Apparently not used to seeing public displays. She was watching the dancing, especially Daniel with a sub, and she kept turning red."

Zachary sipped his drink. "Then it should be interesting when she reaches the back of the room."

Cullen laughed. "You have a twisted mind, boss. Do you have plans for her tonight?"

"Perhaps. She's fascinated by the Dom/sub couples." Would the kitten scamper back to safety?

"Wish I could just mosey through a woman's mind like you do."

"According to the subs you've had, you do quite nicely without the talent." Smiling, Zachary turned to check the room, but the little innocent had disappeared.

This was like being Alice in a very twisted Wonderland, Jessica decided, one where all the characters had only sex on their minds. She'd been propositioned by a woman, by a fat man, by a couple trolling for a threesome. Then she'd struck up a conversation with a really cute guy, and suddenly he knelt at her feet and wanted—

"You want me to whip you?" she repeated in disbelief. Surely there were laws about whipping people?

He had big brown eyes, full lips. The chain and leather harness displayed seriously ripped muscles. He nodded vigorously. "Please, Mistress."

Jessica rolled her eyes. "Sorry, but I'm not into pushing guys around." Well, not unless they'd messed up their accounts, or forgotten to save their travel expense receipts. But order a guy around in bed? Major chill factor there, even without adding a whip into the business. *Ugh*.

He looked so disappointed, she patted him on the head before turning away. He tipped his head back to rub his cheek against her hand like an oversized cat.

This place was *so* strange.

Turning away, she continued her tour with only a touch of trepidation. After all, it couldn't get much worse than women hanging on walls, right?

Farther down, another small area was roped off, and Jessica stopped with a quick breath of astonishment. Damn, the guy had been serious about the whipping stuff. Face against the wall, a naked woman hung from shackled wrists. A short, muscular man wearing only studded black leather pants stood behind her slapping a thin cane into his open palm. Testing it. With a whooshing sound, the wooden stick smacked against the redhead's bare buttocks. The sound made Jessica cringe even before the woman's high shriek.

Jessica took a step forward, her stomach queasy. This wasn't right, shouldn't be allowed. Another step, pushing past the observers, and she'd reached the ropes defining the area. She bit her lip. *Stop and think*, she told herself.

The man had paused, and…the woman was laughing, her voice sultry, obviously more excited than hurt despite the red mark streaking her skin. Glancing back over her shoulder, the redhead wiggled her butt at the cane wielder in an invitingly lewd fashion.

All right. The woman obviously wanted to be hit. Hurt. This was way too strange; definitely not fantasy material. Jessica eyed the cane.

"Ouch," she said under her breath.

A man standing next to her smiled. His beefy build in glossy black PVC clothing made him look like a tank.

"Sounds to me like you'd like to participate," he said, his hand closing around her arm. "There's an empty St. Andrew's cross farther down."

She gasped. "No. No, I'm not—"

He dragged her away from the crowd as she tried to pry his fingers off her arm. Dammit, was she going to have to scream or something? Would anyone in this bizarre place even notice? Screams were happening everywhere. Dear God, all sorts of bad things could happen without anyone realizing. Her hands went sweaty as fear shocked through her. Then anger hit. This was not going to happen.

Planting her feet, she hauled off and kicked him in the knee.

"Shit!" He jerked her off balance, and she landed on her knees in front of him. "Bitch, you'll regret defying me," he growled. He grabbed her hair, fingers tightening until tears filled her eyes.

Chapter Three

"Let me—"

"Let her go." A figure loomed behind her assailant. The owner. Sir himself. Jessica's fists opened as relief filled her.

"Consensual is the operative word here, and she's not consenting," Sir said in that deep, smooth voice.

The jerk spun around, still holding her by the hair. "She did. You should have seen her watching the whipping. She wants it."

"Actually, she doesn't. She has no interest in being whipped and no interest in you." Sir's hand closed around the fingers wrapped in her hair, and a second later, she was free.

Her legs were shaking too badly for her to rise. Hugging herself, she huddled in place. Another man appeared, this one with a yellow badge on his leather vest. "Problems here?"

The jerk pointed at Sir. "He interrupted my scene."

"Did you just accuse Master Z of interrupting a scene?" The bouncer sounded shocked. "Master Z?"

"She's unwilling." Sir held out a hand to Jessica, and she grasped it. His hand was hard, muscular, and he pulled her to her feet so easily it was frightening. "Are you all right, little one?"

She drew in a breath and nodded. If she tried to talk, her voice would come out wussy, so she'd just keep her mouth shut.

"Come here." Master Z wrapped an arm around her, tucked her into his side. He was so big, she felt tiny next to him. Tiny, delicate. *Female*.

The jerk's grab at Jessica was intercepted by Master Z, and then the bouncer had him by the collar.

"Mark him down for a month's suspension and to repeat the entire training class if he wishes to return after that," Master Z told the bouncer. "He apparently wasn't paying attention."

"He didn't even talk to her—he doesn't—" the jerk protested.

Dragging him away, the bouncer said in an annoyed voice, "Master Z not only owns this place, asshole, but he always knows what subs want. Always."

Jessica shivered. The man had called her a sub; that would be the term then for the one being bossed around. Why was she thinking about terminology now? She managed to inhale, start breathing again. He called her a sub. There was no way that she was a sub. God, she needed to go home.

Master Z chuckled. "Rough day, huh?" He wrapped his arms around her, holding her firmly. His hand pressed her head into the hollow of his shoulder. *Comforting. Safe*.

She gave a half laugh and a shudder. "He was going to wh-whip me. And no one would have realized..." She evened her voice. "Thank you."

"My pleasure." He just stood there, holding her, letting people flow around them like water around a boulder. Unconcerned. Nothing seemed to bother this man.

"How did you know I didn't want that? Wasn't just...playing or something? You don't really...know—"

"I know, kitten." His voice rumbled through his chest as he stroked her hair. His appealing scent—light citrus mingling with a man's unique musk—made her want to burrow closer.

But she couldn't get much closer; she was plastered against him like wallpaper. Her breasts were mashed against his hard chest, her hips cradled against his. He felt good against her. Too good, and hadn't she wanted to keep her distance from him?

His other hand was low on her back in the hollow above her buttocks. And she wasn't going all stiff at being touched. But he'd had his hands on her already, she realized, flushing as she remembered how he'd dried between her legs. She hadn't even known his name.

She still didn't know his name. She pushed herself back and looked up.

With the light behind him, his eyes were almost black as he studied her. His lips curved and a crease appeared in his cheek. "You need a drink and a chance to catch your breath." He released her from his arms and held out a hand. "Come."

Should she? She considered her options. Go with him or try to walk back through the bar on unsteady legs, getting hit on every few seconds. Well, that was easy. She put her hand in his.

Still smiling, he led her to the bar. "This time you may choose your drink."

She hesitated. *Water or alcohol?* Water would be smart, but a drink would definitely help the shakes. And somehow the fear had burned off any alcohol from before. "A margarita. Thank you."

"Cullen," Master Z said, his voice somehow carrying past all the conversations, maybe because it was so deep. The bartender glanced over.

"A margarita, please."

Ignoring the other people waiting, the bartender made her drink and set it in front of her. He smiled at her escort. "Definitely a pretty pet, Master Z."

"I'm no pet." Jessica scowled. "What kind of derogatory term is that, anyway?" She tried to slide onto the bar stool but couldn't quite manage. Wobbly legs, short—why couldn't her parents have been tall? Then she wouldn't look so much like a dumpling with feet.

Sir grasped her around the waist and set her on the seat, taking her breath away with his effortless strength and the feel of his muscular hands through the thin fabric she wore.

"Not derogatory," he said, standing close enough that their hips brushed. "It's an affectionate word for a sub."

"But I'm not a sub. I'm not into that at all. I hated what that man wanted to do. Being whipped... Just the thought makes me sick."

He tucked a strand of her hair behind her ear, his fingers leaving a tingle in their wake. "It's a rare person who would enjoy being assaulted by a stranger."

"Huh." The shakes were lessening, and her brain was starting to work again. "So a submissive person doesn't just go belly-up when some guy orders her around?"

He grinned, a flash of white teeth in a darkly tanned face. "Hardly. Just as with any relationship, a Dom/sub relationship has attraction"—he stroked a finger down her cheek and her breath stopped at the intense look in his eyes—"and trust."

Pulling her gaze from his took effort, but she managed. She wasn't comfortable at all with the way her senses had woken up, as if he'd plugged her into an electrical current. Turning, she rested her elbows on the bar top and concentrated on her drink, trying to ignore the way her body felt, the way he affected her. Hmmm, her reaction was probably from him saving her. She'd read something about that. Okay, fine.

Be cool, continue talking, girl. "What kind of trust?" His scent came to her again, appealingly male.

He curled his hands around her bare upper arms and turned her toward him. With one hand, he tilted her chin up until his gaze trapped her. "The trust that your master knows what you need and will give you what you need, even when you aren't always sure."

The words, the sheer certainty in his rich voice, sent heat stabbing through her, a wave of need so potent she quivered inside.

As if he could see into her head, he smiled slowly and whispered, "The trust that lets a woman be tied down and spread open for her master's use."

Her mouth dropped open as she took a hard breath, the image of herself naked, spread-eagled on a bed with him looking down at her was more erotic than anything she'd felt before.

He cupped her cheek, leaned forward, his breath warm against her ear as he murmured, "And your reaction to that shows you are a submissive."

She jerked away from him, away from the heat growing inside her, and the awareness of his body so close to hers. "No way. I really am not."

Time to change the subject. She cleared her throat, her voice husky when she asked, "So, what's your name, anyway? Does everyone call you Master Z?"

He merely smiled at her and picked up the drink the bartender had left for him. His big hand engulfed the glass. When his lips touched the glass, his eyes met hers, and she could almost feel those lips closing over her mouth, over her breast... *Jeez, Jessica, get a grip.*

He set the glass down, and then, as if he'd heard her thoughts, he took her face between his hands and brought his mouth down on hers. Her heart sped up, but it was the way he held her in place that sent hunger searing through her veins. His lips were firm, knowledgeable, teasing a response from her. A stinging nip made her open her mouth, and he plunged in, his tongue stroking hers.

Everything inside her seemed to melt. A burn started between her legs, and her hands curled around his muscular forearms in an effort to keep herself upright.

With a low laugh, he took her wrists and put her arms around his neck. Nudging her legs apart, he moved between them. Hand on her bottom, he slid her closer until her mound rubbed against his thick erection, the thin material no barrier at all. When she gasped at the pleasure surging through her, he simply took the kiss deeper, his grip implacable.

By the time he pulled back, she was trembling all over; her hands dug into his wide shoulders so tightly her fingers ached. The room seemed to throb in time with her whole lower half.

His eyes crinkled when she just looked at him, unable to speak. Cupping her cheek, he sucked on her lower lip, drawing it into his mouth, his tongue sliding across it. And when he released her, a wicked smile told her that he was thinking of putting his mouth elsewhere. Her nipples tightened into hard buds.

"Master Z?" A different bouncer approached, his manner tentative. "Could you check this out? Just take a second?"

Sir's gaze kept Jessica pinned in place as his knuckles rubbed against her aching breasts. She managed to not moan, somehow, but she might as well have, considering the glint of laughter in his eyes.

"I have to attend to something," he murmured. "Will you be all right?"

She huffed out a breath. "Oh, sure."

It was good—very good—that he had to leave her; in another minute, she'd have been willing to do anything he asked, and in this place, that could be really bad. She let out a shaky breath.

His lips curved. "Don't consider yourself safe yet, pet. I'll be back soon."

Master Z—no, she wasn't going to be calling him *master* anything out loud, no matter how well he kissed—glanced at the bouncer. "Show me."

Zachary followed Matthew, one of the dungeon monitors. Not bad timing, actually. She needed time to absorb what he'd said, time to grow tantalized by the thought of being taken. She was definitely attracted, not only to the idea of domination, but to him personally. When he'd spoken of taking her for his pleasure, he'd not only felt the flare of excitement in her mind, but heard the deep breath she'd taken, seen the increasing pulse in her neck. And her reaction to a simple kiss was so heated, he'd had to control himself to not lay her out on the bar top and bring her to a screaming orgasm right then.

He couldn't remember the last time he'd been so drawn to a woman. Just watching her walk through the room with her firm stride, her chin up, he'd felt the compulsion to take her, to have her for his own.

An assertive woman. He wasn't surprised that the sub, Joey, had assumed she was a Domme. From a distance, he would have assumed the same. But up close, when he touched her, she yielded completely, even when her reaction confused her.

Everything about her appealed to him, from her lush little body to her logical mind…and the passion that kept breaking loose from her stringent control.

And she was pushing his own control to the breaking point. So, let her wander some more. Think some more. All the choices needed to be hers, right up until she handed the right to him.

Matthew stopped at one of the farther stations. A sub was tied down over a spanking bench. Her Dom had his cock shoved into her mouth, and she was crying, protesting.

"One of the observers was worried," the dungeon monitor said, "but the sub hasn't used any safe word or gesture."

Zachary tilted his head, his eyes on the sobbing woman, letting her feelings slide into him. He grinned. "It's part of the scene and her favorite activity. No worries."

Matthew clapped Zachary on the arm with a laugh. "Good enough. Damn, life is easier when you're here, boss. Sorry if I interrupted something with that little newcomer."

Biting her lip, Jessica gazed after Sir. She'd been more turned on by kissing him than by having sex with someone else. How did he do that? Affect her like that? There was something about him…not just his words…even his walk was powerful. Controlled. Back in college, she'd been to a karate exhibition where some of the black belts had that aura, an unsettling mixture of danger and discipline. She wasn't the only one who he affected, either. Club members moved out of his way; the women turned to watch after he passed.

Just like her.

And he'd called her *little one.* She frowned. If another man labeled her that, she'd cut him down to size, so why had her insides melted when Sir did it? Oh, she was in deep trouble here.

After he disappeared into the crowd, she turned back to finish her drink. Trying to ignore the seductive music, she smiled at the two men who took seats beside her, exchanged introductions, and was soon in a heated conversation about tax laws.

One of the men, Gabe, had a presence about him almost like Sir. His confidence and the commanding look in his eyes gave her a funny sinking feeling inside.

The bartender's gaze had that effect on her too, she realized, as Cullen wandered back to their area. He shook his head at Gabe. "Uh-uh. Z's."

Gabe frowned. "Now there's a pity. Well, Jessica, if you ever find yourself fancy-free, I'd enjoy getting to know you better."

"I—" Unable to think of a proper rejoinder, Jessica nodded politely and watched Gabe walk away. She turned to Cullen. "What is this 'Z's' stuff? He's not my owner, dammit."

His grin flickered so quickly she almost didn't see it. "No, love, he's not. I just thought I'd save Gabe some effort. I've seen you with Master Z; Gabe doesn't stand a chance."

Jessica glared and turned her back on him. Like she was so obvious.

She wasn't, was she?

Of course not. Putting her chin up and Sir out of her mind, she smiled and opened conversations with the members around her. Strange conversations at times. One man had long chains fastened to his belt. In fishnet tops and latex shorts, two men, obviously gay—or would that be bi?—checked her out for a threesome. A woman, in skintight red latex and matching gloves to her elbows, owned a bookstore and was fun to talk with, but her heated gaze was disconcerting.

When the woman moved away, Jessica glanced around the room. Her nerves had settled. She should continue exploring since her tame world sure didn't include anything like this place. Why did she find some of this stuff so…arousing?

Uncomfortable as the admission was, she needed an answer. She'd never been one to hide her head in the sand, after all.

And this time she'd be prepared for jerks. She could also use Master Z's name as a conjuring tool: *Don't mess with me or Master Z will make you disappear.* Yeah, that might work.

Grinning, she slid off the bar stool and set out. She received two more propositions in the first twenty feet; one man was worth a second look. He had that same confidence—strength—as Master Z and Gabe. But somehow, Sir made every man in the room seem weak, unfinished. She thought of the way he looked at her—all his attention on her, not on the music or other people or planning his evening or even his next sentence. To be the focus of that intensity was heady.

And then, of course, came the question she really didn't want in her mind: *What would it be like to have all that attention on her in bed?*

She blinked and refocused her own attention to the here and now, not in visualizing Sir with his clothes off, with his big hands wrapped around her wrists and his mouth...

Argh. Stop. Look. Walk. At one of the well-lit stations, a person was tied on what must be that St. Andrew's cross the jerk had mentioned. This time the shackled person was a male whose female boss was whipping him in horrible places. Completely appalled, Jessica stared for a moment, pulling her legs together in reaction. No, she didn't want to watch this—no way. Hurrying past, she could only think, *These people are crazy.*

She passed two women talking together on a couch. The woman in a black catsuit was telling the other, "Your safe word is banana. Can you remember—"

And what would a safe word be?

The farther she got from the entrance, the more the lighting changed, growing ominous. Ah, some of the flickering wall sconces had red-tinted bulbs.

At the end of the room, open double doors led into a wide hallway. A lot of people were milling around in there, and the noises made Jessica's stomach twist: screams, the sound of a whip, begging. Too intense. She wasn't going down that hall.

Not that she could escape all the uncomfortable sounds. As she headed toward the other side of the room, high-pitched screams rose above the hum of conversation. In a roped-off area, a burly man with tattooed arms was whipping a little brunette tied on a sawhorse-like table. The poor woman was shrieking, "Stop! Stop, please, stop!" He didn't stop. People stood outside the ropes, not doing anything. *Damn them.*

Fury seared through her like wildfire. Her sister had been beaten like that during her marriage; Jessica had suspected abuse, but hadn't acted. She would this time.

Coming up behind the man, she grabbed the whip out of his hand. "You perverted asshole, let her up, or I'll show you what it feels like!"

The man's bulldog face flushed red, and he took one step forward, then stopped, hands closing into fists at his side. Turning to a spectator, he snapped out, "Fetch me a monitor." Spinning back toward Jessica, he snatched at the whip.

Jessica punched him right in the face, knocking him down, shocking herself. Aside from karate classes in college, she'd never hit anyone. But, hey, the punch had worked.

The brief thrill disappeared as he slowly got to his feet. *Very not good.* Her mouth went dry. She backed up a step, her heart hammering against her ribs.

His eyes were maddened; his fist rose as he stepped forward.

"Stop." Master Z's compelling voice. The man halted, and Jessica sucked in a relieved breath. Everyone turned as Sir strode into the roped-off area. He glanced at her then the man. "Explain, Master Smith."

"We were in the middle of a scene, and this crazy woman comes roaring out of the crowd, screaming, grabs my whip, and damned if she didn't punch me." Rubbing his reddened chin, the man's lips curved a little. "It's almost funny, but still, she ruined our scene."

Master's Z's gaze turned to her and she winced at the grim look in his eyes. "Jessica, explain."

"She was screaming and yelling, 'Stop, stop,' and he was whipping her. No one was doing anything." Feeling like a child called on the carpet, she held out the whip. "I took it away from him."

"What is your sub's safe word?" Sir asked the bully.

"Purple."

"Did she use it or the club safe word?"

"Nah. She wasn't anywhere close. We been together three years, and she's only used it twice. I'm pretty careful that way, Z."

"I know you are." Master Z turned back to her, his brows together in a frown. "Did you actually *read* any of the rules that you signed?"

Jessica flushed, looked down. "Uh...no."

"I'm sorry for that, and even sorrier that you will be punished for what you thought was a good deed."

Chapter Four

Her mouth dropped open. Punished? "But—"

"A scene is planned in advance, Jessica, and much anticipated. Furthermore, each sub has what we call a safe word, a word to use if they get too frightened or the pain is past what they can stand. The safe word is never, never *stop*."

Jessica licked dry lips. "You're saying she didn't really want to be saved? She—but look at her back; she's all red."

The people outside the rope laughed. "If I picked up a whip and started hitting you with it, yes, that would be abuse, and it would hurt." Master Z took the whip from her hand. "However, when someone is aroused, within the context of a sexual moment, then the pain can heighten a person's responses and pleasure. These two both enjoy this activity. Their enjoyment—and the scene they'd planned—has been destroyed by you."

People who like being hurt. Okay, she'd seen that already. The club had rules—rules were good—and she'd screwed up big-time in this strange world. Time to apologize, extricate herself gracefully, and retreat.

Sitting in the entry looked more and more attractive, and she was going there right now, Master Z or no Master Z.

Now released, the whipped woman joined the bully. The tiny woman's whole body trembled, and the man put an arm around her, incongruously tender, considering the way he'd wielded that whip.

Jessica sucked in a breath, looked at her. "I'm very sorry. I thought you were being hurt, and well... Please forgive me."

Master Z raised his eyebrows at the man.

"No, Z, I'm sorry. I can see this is a pet of yours, and she didn't do it on purpose, but she screwed up our scene." He kissed the top of the woman's head. "Ruined the night for us. We got club rules for this, and I want them enforced."

"It is within your rights, Master Smith." Master Z sighed and clasped Jessica's wrist in one firm hand before continuing, "Here is my judgment. I will discipline, allowing you to participate. I will stop when I am satisfied both punishment and repentance have been achieved. Since she is a newcomer and not in the lifestyle, that must be taken into consideration for intensity and duration."

Master Smith frowned, and then his face cleared. "Guess that'll do."

Sir turned, motioned to a barmaid, and pointed to the bench where the whipping had taken place. "Clean that, please."

A spray bottle and paper towels came from a tiny shelf on the wall, and the barmaid quickly cleaned the bench.

What did he mean by *punishment?* Jessica's gaze went from the bench to Master Z. She was getting a really bad feeling about this. "Listen, I apologized, and I'll leave now."

His grip didn't loosen. "Jessica—"

"You are *not* going to whip me." She tried to pull her arm away. "You can't—"

She tried to punch him.

Smiling slightly, he caught her fist in one hard hand. When she yanked at her hand, he let go, stepped behind her, and pinned her arms to her sides.

Lifting her, he placed her facing the bench.

"Not a whip," he said mildly, as if he were continuing a conversation. She could feel his body all along hers, and despite the fear, she noticed.

As he pulled Jessica's lush body tighter against him, Zachary could feel her reaction in both her body and her mind. Fear, yes. But arousal still lingered, which surprised him at first. Then again, even a perfectly straight person would be turned on by the Shadowlands; for a submissive—even a novice—the activities in the room would be an erotic dreamland.

And had turned into a nightmare. He should never have let her in here, and guilt carved at his gut like a dull knife. But perhaps he could make this easier for her, not that she'd understand his actions or how arousal could change the quality of pain.

Keeping her pressed against him, he nuzzled her neck, breathing in her warm vanilla scent. She shivered.

"You aren't ready for a whip," he whispered, his lips brushing her ear, feeling how both fear and excitement heightened inside her. "I doubt you would ever enjoy that pain."

Without decreasing the pressure over her arms, he moved his hands up to cup her breasts. If she weren't attracted to him, weren't aroused, this would be reprehensible behavior, but her nipples pebbled under his touch. Ignoring the crowd accumulating behind them, he focused on bringing the heat out in her. Her breasts were soft and round, heavy. She could undoubtedly feel the warmth of his hands through the thin top.

She could feel the heat of him through her shirt as his thumbs rubbed her nipples, sending blazing sensations searing through her body.

"Stop it," she hissed, squirming in his unyielding grasp. Her heart pounded with fear, yet she was all too aware of his hands on her, of how his larger body held her in place so easily. It was Sir who had her in his arms, Sir who made her feel safe, only there was no safety here.

She felt something close around her ankles. "Hey!"

The man and the whipped woman were kneeling on each side of her. She tried to kick at them and couldn't move her legs. They'd strapped her ankles to the bench legs.

"Let me go, dammit. I didn't agree to—"

"Actually, you did," Sir murmured. "I have your signature. The penalties for interrupting a scene are spelled out in detail on the third page."

"No way." She tried to wrench free. "Damn you, let me go."

He held her as easily as he would a puppy, his arms around her both comforting and terrifying.

"Master Smith, could you lower the front several inches, please?" Sir said. "And bring the entire bench up another foot." Even as he spoke, he teased her breasts, rolling the nipples, stroking the undersides.

When he moved a hand down to press against her mound, a wave of heat rolled through her. She struggled harder, but she couldn't move away from his attentions, and even her fear couldn't quite suppress the sensations awakening in her. Or was her fear heightening them?

The table was adjusted.

"Jessica, bend over now," Master Z said. She tightened her body to stay straight. Damned if she'd help him in any way.

He gave a huff of laughter, moved one arm down to cross at her hips and bent with his chest against her back, forcing her down on the table. She struggled uselessly, panting with exertion.

Pulling her arms out to the side, he flattened her chest right onto the bench.

Two more snicks and she realized the ever-so-helpful pair had shackled her wrists to the bench legs. Her arms were pulled straight with no give, and she yanked at them uselessly. "No, dammit."

Sir walked around the bench. Reaching under her, he arranged her breasts so they hung down on each side of the narrow bench top.

Jessica tried to move her legs, to raise her body from the bench, but she was restrained completely. Horror rushed through her as she realized, with the bench tilted head down, her bottom was sticking high in the air. She heaved in a panicked breath, yanked at the wrist straps.

"You bastard," she jerked out. "You let me up, or I'll sue you so bad. I—"

"Kitten," he said, stroking her heated cheek. "No one ever does. Lawsuits make headlines, and no one wants to admit they've been here."

Publicity? She choked, bitterness sour in her mouth. She couldn't afford a scandal in her straitlaced accounting world. Her threat of a lawsuit was useless, and he knew it.

"I am sorry, little one. You're going to have to submit and take your punishment." After stroking her hair, he walked over to the wall. She twisted her head, trying to keep him in sight. Her breath stopped. The flickering lights on the wall had concealed what hung there. Canes and whips and paddles and crops. A whimper escaped her, and she strained harder against the restraints.

She could hear people laugh as she struggled. Lots of people.

Hands behind his back, Sir took his time contemplating the devices, and her anguish grew. *No, not the whip, you promised.*

Please not the horrible long, stiff cane. And then he picked up a round paddle the size of a person's head.

"This seems to fit the need," he said. He touched her cheek gently and said, no longer whispering, "Jessica, since you are new to this, I will make it easy. You have permission to scream, to cry, to swear and call names, to beg…even to stay silent. Anything you do will be acceptable for this period of time."

"You jerk, don't you tell me what I can do." She was so angry, so frustrated, so terrified, she felt tears springing to her eyes.

"Jessica, I just did."

He disappeared behind her, and try as she could, she couldn't turn her head far enough to see him. The club members were ranged around the roped-off area, watching. Spectators at a live show. She hated them as much as she hated him.

Someone lifted her skirt and smiles appeared. Her teeth ground together as heat seared her face. She had on no underwear; all of her butt was up and naked in the air where everyone could see.

Sir's voice. "Such a pretty little ass, don't you think, Master Smith?"

"Very nice."

Master Z massaged her buttocks, slowly, gently. He ran his fingers over her bared skin, his touch sensual, growing increasingly intimate as he traced the crease between her buttocks and thighs. Her awareness narrowed to just his touch, and then she gasped as his fingers stroked between her legs, sliding in the wetness there until need slid into her body like hot air through an opened window.

And he moved away, leaving her throbbing.

"I'm not setting a specific number." Master Z's voice. "I will say when to stop."

And something hit her bottom with a horrendous slap. Her legs jerked, and pain seared her skin, shocking pain. She ripped at the restraints as she frantically—*wham!* The burn shot down to her toes. She closed her mouth over the cry; she wouldn't yell or cry, see if she—*wham!* Her bottom was on fire. Another blow, then another, each one raising her to her toes, her body arching on the bench.

And then it stopped. Trying not to cry, she rested her forehead on the leather.

"As the offended parties, please take three strokes apiece," Master Z said, his voice as courteous as if he'd been a fancy waiter.

Jessica shook her head frantically. *No more.* Tears leaked from her eyes, turning Master Z into a blur as he crouched next to her.

"It will hurt less if you can relax," he murmured, wiping the tears from her cheeks.

"Please—"

"You can take more." He reached under the table, cupped her dangling breast. "You will take more." He nodded at someone and *wham!*

A cry escaped her this time. *Wham! Wham!* It hurt so bad, and she sobbed.

With one hand, Sir stroked her back; the other hand held her breast in an intimate grip. His fingers on her nipple—even through the pain she could feel his touch—created the strangest feelings inside her.

Wham. Just one buttock. Another blow on the other. And one smack across her upper thighs that made her scream.

"I'm sorry," she sobbed, looking at Sir, trying to get him to believe her. "I didn't mean to cause trouble; I didn't."

His eyes softened. "I know, little one." He stood, walked toward the end of the table out of her sight. She whimpered. *What was he going to do? No more, please, please, please.*

Something touched her bottom, and she cried out more in fear than pain.

"Pink and tender. Poor kitten," Sir said. His hands caressed her bottom, painful and yet almost exciting. The feeling of need edged back. "Release her. Punishment's over."

A few people in the crowd groaned in disappointment but stopped suddenly as if their complaints had been cut off. The other master and his sub unstrapped her hands; someone undid her legs. Sir grasped her around the waist, lifted her to her feet, and held her steady until she found her balance. Her face was wet, and she wiped tears from her cheeks. Her insides seemed to be shaking harder than her legs.

"This time, deliver your apology on your knees, Jessica," Sir instructed.

Only his hand under her arm kept her from falling over as she clumsily knelt. She looked up at Master Smith and his slave. "I'm so, so sorry I interrupted. And that I didn't read the rules." Trembles made her voice shake. *What if it wasn't good enough? What if—*

Master Smith snorted a laugh. "Sounds repentant to me, Master Z. Apology accepted."

"Are you satisfied, Wendy?" Master Z asked.

The little brunette nodded. "Yes, Sir." Her eyes met Jessica's with a hint of sympathy.

Jessica let her head drop forward in relief. It was over. Her thighs were quivering so hard she wanted to just crumple onto the floor. Tears still dripped down her cheeks.

She felt so lost.

And then Sir bent and effortlessly lifted her into his arms. Head spinning like a tilt-o-whirl ride, she clutched his jacket.

"Shhh, kitten, you're all right," he murmured, and something inside her relaxed. She felt his lips in her hair and knew she was safe.

Zachary found an empty couch in the middle of the floor and settled into it, keeping her firmly in his arms. Guilt was a hard lump in his guts. Never had a kind gesture gone so wrong. He should have made her stay out in the cold entry with Ben, should never have let her into the club.

Dammit, even with her being aroused, there had been no evading the pain or the shock of being spanked.

He gentled his arms around her, settling her head against his chest. "All finished, little one."

She buried her head in his shoulder, choking back her sobs in a way that broke his heart. He could feel her trying to wall up her distress, but between Dom and sub, there should be no walls. She didn't know that yet and wouldn't for a time, even if she wanted to walk this path. She wasn't his sub, but he'd acted as her Dom for the punishment; aftercare was his responsibility.

This was where he would start.

He shifted her in his arms so he could tilt her head up and look into her eyes. "I have you, Jessica," he said quietly. "Let it out."

Her emerald eyes blinked at him. She seemed almost shocked at his words—had no one ever been there for her?—and then tears welled anew. Her head dropped back on his shoulder, and he could feel her shudder with muffled sobs. Her choked words drifted up to him as his warmth and embrace seeped into her.

"In front of people... It hurt... Nobody ever..." Her barriers fell, and she sobbed, shaking as hard as when she'd been chilled from the rain. *Sensitive little one, a sheltered little pet.* It only made him want her the more.

He stroked her hair, murmured gently as she cried; he told her how brave she'd been, how wonderfully she'd apologized, how much he cherished her sharing with him. He praised her courage at trying to save the other sub, how rare it was to find someone willing to act to help another.

He told the truth. Even though she'd been wrong to break up the scene, the bravery of her actions impressed him. The facets of her personality were mesmerizing; from a spitfire to a yielding woman in his arms; from controlled and careful to passionately responsive. She delighted him.

Slowly her crying turned to jerky breaths as exhaustion overcame her.

But after all too short a time, he felt her mind turn on and start burying the pain and hurt under layers of control. Her body stiffened, no longer accepting any comfort.

"I want to leave now," she said in a hard voice.

Oh, he knew this had been coming. "The rain and wind haven't lessened, and you have no car. However, you may stay in the entryway, and no one will bother you."

Her breath hissed out, and she shoved at his arms. "Let me go."

"We will sit here until your legs work on their own. Unless you want me to carry you across the room?"

She stopped immediately. "At least put me down."

"No."

That brought her head up, her green eyes wet like a forest in the rain.

"I have never had to punish someone I just met," he said, letting his own anger show. "Discipline is a trust issue between a Dom and a sub. We do not have that trust between us. To have to perform a scene, a punishment scene like that, was extremely unpleasant. It bothered me to hurt you, Jessica," he growled. "You will let me hold you, and offer me some comfort in return."

Her eyes widened. Earlier, she had understood the damage her heedless actions had created with Master Smith and his sub. Could she grasp the discomfort she had caused him?

He could almost hear that clever mind turning over the events. This was a very smart woman.

And then she whispered, "I'm sorry" into his shirt.

"As am I," he returned evenly, not granting her the grace of forgiveness. Not just yet.

She sniffled a little, edging her way under his defenses. "What do you want me to do?"

"Just sit with me, little one," he sighed. "Until we both recover a bit. You are a comforting armful of woman, and my body likes having you against it."

With his words, her mind opened to more than any lingering pain. He could sense the way her body suddenly became aware of him again, of his hardness against her softness, of his hand stroking her hair, of his scent. Even as she relaxed, she squirmed a little to ease the pain of her sore ass. His cock reacted to the provocative movements. She had the kind of body he enjoyed most: round, soft, and abundant.

As he hardened, she froze, realizing what her movements had incited.

He chuckled, pressed his lips to the top of her head. "I want a kiss, and then I'll take you to the entryway."

"That's all?" she asked suspiciously.

His eyes narrowed, and he stroked his fingers on the underside of her breast, his thumb rubbing the nipple. Her alarm was accompanied by a flare of heat.

"Maybe I should ask for more?" he murmured.

She set her hand over his, trying to pull him away, as successful as a kitten tugging on a human's hand.

"Kiss me," he said.

With an aggrieved sigh, she tilted her head up to him.

This time he would go more slowly. He brushed her lips teasingly, like in his days in Special Ops, scoping out the terrain. Her mouth was soft with a tiny ridge in the center of the lower lip, dividing it into two tiny bottoms. He took the kiss deeper, opening her lips with his own, coaxing her into responding. Under his slow assault, her mouth softened, much like a woman's nipples after she'd come. Still deeper, he invaded her mouth, taking possession.

Her fingers tightened around his hand, so he tightened his fingers around her breast. A gasp. He read in her mind the complex roil of emotions of a woman with growing needs. Heat seared pathways from her breasts to her pussy, and when he sucked her tongue into his mouth, it upped the sensations in her body the way an elevator carries a person to the top.

When her magnificent body quivered with hunger, he drew away slowly before he could be lured into more. A promise was a promise, and she was overwhelmed already. If the chill of the entryway cooled her lust, then so be it. Of course, if her needs and thoughts drove her back into his territory... Well, his imagination had already placed her in his bed, her pussy open to his tongue, his fingers, and then his cock. He would enjoy taking her over and over until her screams of ecstasy left her limp and ready to take again.

He shook his head to ease down a little, then brushed another kiss over the mouth that was almost as sumptuous as her breasts.

"Up, little one." He pushed her to her feet, wrapped an arm around her as her knees buckled. Just to annoy her, to put strength back into her legs—and to see if the punishment was turning to something else—he ran his hand down her ass, squeezed each sweet cheek in turn, remembering the vivid pink that had glowed on her fair skin.

She caught her breath, and, oh, yes, another gratifying increase of heat.

"As I said, pain is a sensation very close to excitement," he murmured, still stroking her buttocks, enjoying her confusion as the soreness twisted into erotic sensation. "If I bit you there, you'd probably come."

Her back stiffened, and she tried to move away. She wasn't used to words tantalizing her desires even as his fingers did her ass.

Without saying more, although he was already thinking of what he'd be saying soon to her, what he'd say when her first wrist was shackled to his bed, he led her out to the entryway where Ben ruled in the cold and barren room.

Chapter Five

The troll guarding the door glanced up as they entered. Sir kissed Jessica's fingertips, nipped one sharply enough to send heat into her fingers and even deeper, and left without speaking.

"Got yourself kicked out?" Ben set down his pen and pushed his papers to one side.

"I didn't want to be in there anymore." Jessica settled onto the floor in the corner farthest from the door and shifted uncomfortably. Hardwood floor, sore butt...bad combination.

He'd hit her with a paddle.

The memory of the pain entwined with the memory of Master Z's hands stroking over her bare bottom, how his fingers had touched her breasts so gently. Her hands closed into fists. What kind of person was she to be aroused by that?

"Do you do that sort of stuff?" she asked Ben, jerking her head toward the door. Not that she really wanted to talk, but her mind kept shifting to uncomfortable places, much as her butt was doing. Trying to take her mind off both, she started finger combing through the tangles in her hair.

"Nope. I'm straight vanilla sex, as they call it. Z prefers that for his guards. We don't get diverted." He fumbled in his pocket, tossed her a comb.

"Thanks." She grabbed a lock of hair to work on. "It doesn't bother you what they do in there?"

He shrugged. "World's full of variety, why not sex? Everything in there is—what's the phrase?—safe, sane, and consensual. Yeah. If they like a little more kink to get their rocks off, it's no business of mine." He grinned, rubbed his jaw. "My brother-in-law is from New Orleans. Doesn't like bland food. If it doesn't bite back, he'll dump pepper sauce on it. Nice guy; just has different taste buds than me."

As he turned back to his paperwork, she stared down at her hands. Different tastes. Did she have different tastes? *Surely not.*

Those people on the dance floor—the ones who had excited her—had been the two couples where the men were obviously in charge. Sir had used a word for that, but she couldn't remember what he'd said.

"What are the terms for a guy in charge and a woman obeying?" she blurted out, and reddened when his eyebrows lifted.

"You're thinking of a Dominant/submissive relationship? Dom/sub. If the dominant is a man, he'll usually be referred to as Master or Sir or anything else he chooses." Ben's lips curled up. "His sub sure isn't going to contradict him, right?"

The smack of the paddle rang in her ears. "Uh, no. Where does *slave* come into it?"

"More often that's a person in a life relationship, where the Dom/sub stuff isn't confined to the bedroom. There's some couples here like that, but for lots of people it's only for sex or playtime."

"So every night this place is filled with…"

"BDSMers? Nah. Saturdays only. Fridays are for the swinging crowd, Thursdays are leatherboys. Sometimes he'll rent the room out for private parties."

"Busy place." Master Z, they called him. So he was a dominant, and he treated her like a submissive. *Submitting to a man.* Even as she rejected the whole idea, her body thrilled at the thought. Dammit, he'd hit her with a paddle until she'd been crying all over the place. Then he had held her as tenderly as a child and let her cry on him.

She shifted again, trying to find some position where her butt didn't hurt. Like that would happen. So would she prefer sex to have a bite? Should she be analyzing this like she would some client's books?

Why shouldn't she take the time to study it?

Okay, then, admit it... Watching the Dom/sub couples had made her hot. Hotter than she'd felt even watching porn on TV with Matt, her last boyfriend. He'd been trying to get her more interested in sex, but the porn had been not only boring, but a turn-off.

Watching that Dom kiss his sub—no, *take* a kiss, allowing no refusal—had been far more erotic than watching a penis pumping into a woman on film. And the way Master Z kissed... Her insides melted at the memory. She shook her head. Thinking about his demanding mouth, those firm lips, would turn her brain to mush. *Think, Jessica.*

But this BDSM stuff was way over the top, wasn't it? She didn't need something kinky to get off. Sex for her was pleasant enough, really it was. Once she got started. And she got off at least half the time. Her orgasms were nice.

She bit her lip. Why did she get the feeling that if she went to bed with Master Z, *nice* wouldn't be the operative word? Because he'd *take* her, not have sex with her. And she figured she wouldn't have any choice in how it would happen or what he'd do.

And just the thought of that sent moisture trickling between her legs. *Oh, God.*

Still drawing the comb through her hair, she realized the strands were free of knots, flowing down to the middle of her back. Now what was she going to do to keep herself diverted? She could hear the people inside the club laughing, talking. The music thrummed with a compelling beat.

She wanted to go back in there. Find out what she was missing. And she was too scared to do it. He'd spanked her, dammit.

A part of her brain pointed out that she'd broken the rules, and he hadn't been happy at all about having to enforce the rules.

Nonetheless, what if she went back and he did something horrible to her?

She didn't even know him.

"Is he a good boss?" she asked, her voice barely over a whisper.

Ben shook his head. "Oh, you've got it bad, don't you? Okay, here's the rundown on Master Z. Been here for years. The club is his hobby. Nothing unlawful, no drugs allowed. Pays his employees on time. Expects his people to be professional. Divorced once, two grown children, not serious with anyone now. Women fall all over him, and in his world, he's known as the best master around. And that's according to the subs, who would definitely know." He gave her a challenging grin. "That what you wanted to hear?"

She flushed and nodded, looking down at her hands.

"Oh, and he doesn't go for the hard-core S/M stuff, whips and beatings and hot wax stuff. If you're hankering after that, he's not your man."

"But—" *The paddle.*

"Not to say if a sub stepped out of line, she wouldn't get punished," he added. "But there's a difference between a spanking kind of thing and getting whipped. Or so I've been told."

"Oh."

Sir was interested in her. She'd seen that, felt his erection pushing against her. He'd be willing to take her to bed. Show her...*things*. The thought made her insides quiver and her core throb.

If she stayed here in the entryway and left in the morning, this Dom/sub stuff would be an itch at the edge of her mind, be whispering to her every time she went to bed with someone. She'd be comparing a *what might have been* with normal sex and never know if reality would have lived up to her imagination. After all, maybe sex with a master would be just another fizzle like so much of her sex life had been.

Could she stand not knowing?

Before she'd really decided—had she decided?—she was on her feet.

"Going back in?"

She set the comb down on his desk. "Don't tell me. I'm dumber than I look, right?"

He grinned. "Braver at least."

* * *

Zachary felt her before he saw her, a compelling mix of desire, fear, and determination, and his own emotions flared up with pleasure. Although he'd hoped, he hadn't really expected her to return, not after such a harsh introduction to the lifestyle. He'd considered joining her in the entry, talking more with her, but had refrained. She should make her decisions without his influence.

Wasn't it ironic that he'd discover an intriguing woman, one where the chemistry between them was like pouring gasoline on fire, and she wouldn't be part of the scene?

But here she was now, resolve and courage uppermost in her emotional fields. She might be innocent as far as alternative sex, but she had an admirable ability to honestly acknowledge her own needs. And the guts to go after what she wanted.

Pity her bravery had brought her to this scene, he thought, trying not to smile as she walked up beside him and froze. A pretty sub with bright red hair was tied to a spanking horse. The angle had been tilted so her ass was high in the air, much like Jessica's had been, Zachary remembered with enjoyment.

He glanced down, seeing Jessica's eyes widen, feeling her shock at seeing the tied sub. And then her imagination was putting her there in the sub's place, with him behind her. Her memory of the paddle was submerged in the arousal searing through her veins at the idea.

The Dom in the scene squirted some lube onto his fingers and now slid two fingers into his sub's perky little asshole. She wailed and squirmed—more from arousal than pain, Zachary knew. But Jessica tightened against his side, so he leaned down.

"These two have a long relationship," he whispered. "He has taken her this way over and over, and she comes screaming every time. They're both enjoying the show they're putting on, Jessica."

She was stiff until his words sank in, then relaxed, gazed up at him. "You're sure?"

"As sure about them as I'm sure that you're not ready to have my fingers sliding into anything except your pussy."

Her sharp inhalation, followed by a shock wave of heat, hardened him like a rock. Yes, the attraction was definitely there. Would the trust that was needed follow?

So when she pushed herself into feeling angry at his blunt words, turned her face up to scold him, he simply took her lips, those soft pink lips he'd been craving since the last time. His arm around her foiled her attempt to step back. He set his other hand along her jaw, keeping her tilted at the right angle to toy with her mouth, to nibble on her succulent lips, run his tongue across the velvety skin and tease until she opened for him, letting him in deeper to discover the secrets inside. When he sucked on her tongue, he could feel her melt.

Her lips seemed to burn under his as he tantalized them both until she flattened her curvy body against him in an effort to get closer. Pleasure indeed.

Reluctantly, he pulled back, taking her arms and setting her away from him. As she blinked, returned to her surroundings, the tied-down sub in front of them received her master's cock with a shriek of delight and then spasmed into a loud and happy orgasm.

Jessica turned a dark red, choked a little. "Ah. Guess you were right about them, huh?"

Grinning, Zachary put an arm around her, steering her away.

They weren't returning to the bar; he was taking her toward the front of the room. Jessica dragged her feet. "Where are we—"

"You've had a long day and probably missed supper," Sir said. "You must be starving by now."

Food? That seemed so…mundane in this exotic place, but the thought set her stomach to growling. "I guess I am a little hungry."

She hadn't noticed before, since it had been on the other side of the bar, but the front corner opposite the dance floor held long tables filled with finger foods. Sir handed her a small plate, and she moved down the table, picking up tiny meat pastries, stuffed mushroom caps, crab canapés. He didn't take anything to eat, just poured them each some iced tea.

"Aren't you hungry?" she asked.

"I ate earlier."

In an unoccupied sitting area, she sat on the couch, and he took a chair. He rarely wasn't touching her, she realized, looking over the coffee table at him and feeling more than physical distance growing between them. She set the plate on the coffee table, increasingly self-conscious.

"So," she said. She was back to feeling awkward in a man's presence; wasn't that weird? "How did you come to own a club like this?"

He leaned back in the chair, obviously at ease, his legs stretched out in front of him. One lean hand held his glass of tea as he contemplated her for a moment. "The lifestyle can be a lonely one, and people turn to the clubs for company. I didn't like some of the abuse taking place in them and wanted to see if I could do better."

She started to pick up a pastry and stopped. How could she eat in front of him? He probably thought she was way too big as it was. When she looked down, her hips and thighs seemed like they were bulging beneath the skimpy skirt. She folded her hands in her lap.

Conversation. They were having a conversation. "Abuse?"

"As with any alternate lifestyle, BDSM can attract unstable personalities. Here, at least, I try to ensure that consensual is more than a catchphrase. But even our screening and training procedures… We still have some problems." His narrowed gaze flickered from the plate to her hands. With a frown, he set his tea down on the table. "Are you no longer hungry?"

She shrugged, feeling gawky and inept. Why couldn't she be all slim and everything, and why did it never bother her unless she was attracted to a man?

He shook his head and smoothly changed seats, joining her on the couch. "Come here, pet." With an unyielding grip, he slid her over until her thighs and shoulders were rubbing against his.

Could he feel the way her hips squished?

"Jessica, I like your body, in case you haven't noticed." He turned to face her, pushing her against the back of the couch.

Slowly he trailed his fingers down her neck, across her breasts, her stomach, and heat flowed into her like a current. She moved uncomfortably when his hand settled on her pudgy hip.

"I like round," he said, holding her gaze with his own as his hand stroked her hip. "I like abundance." His hand moved to cup her breast, and he smiled as the weight settled into his palm. And then he slid her skirt up, and his fingers wrapped around her thigh, moving upward until she squeaked and closed her legs against him.

He bit her earlobe, a tiny jolt of pain, and whispered, "I fully intend to bury myself—very, very deep—in all your softness until you're squirming under me. Until you're panting for release."

God, she was panting now. And the whole world seemed to have caught fire.

Ever so slowly, his hand stroked back down her leg, and then he sat back, leaving her feeling flushed and needy. He didn't put her skirt back, she noticed.

Picking up a mushroom cap, he held it to her lips. "Eat, Jessica," he said. "You are going to need your strength for later."

And when her mouth dropped open at the tantalizing threat, he popped the morsel into her mouth. One warm arm around her shoulders, he continued to feed her, bite by bite, talking in his deep voice about the different people in the club. Cullen, who was a Dom as she'd thought and who went through the subs like wildfire, never took one for more than a couple of nights. Daniel, who'd lost his wife three years past, hadn't been really happy since. How Daniel also liked curvy women. Adrienne, a sub, who'd be disobedient just to get a whipping. Cody wanted to be a twenty-four/seven slave, and Joey was searching for a mistress.

When the food was gone, he smiled down at her. "Feeling better?"

She was, amazingly enough. "Yes. Thank you," she said, meaning more than just the food. She felt comfortable and settled.

"Good. Now tell me why you think your body is unattractive?"

And just like that, she was off base again. Huffing out a breath, she pretended to watch two people walking past. "I don't know where you got that—"

He cupped a hand on her cheek and forced her to meet his gaze. "Don't evade the question, pet. Was it your parents? Men?"

Why did she feel even more naked than when he'd dried her off in the bathroom? She didn't need to talk about this with him—with him of all people.

He waited. Damn him.

"Mom, at times. And there were some men who liked their women to be thin." She shrugged, tried to look away. His hand didn't move. As his thumb stroked her lower lip, he could probably feel it quiver, dammit.

"Well-meaning parents can mess up a person's head, true. And men like that? They should pick skinny women and leave the soft, round ones for men who can appreciate them." He shook his head in disgust. "Sometimes I think our country is filled with idiots."

He really did like her body. The thought was heady, freeing. "You're a nice man," she said.

"Of course I am." His eyes crinkled, and she saw the glimmer of a smile that reminded her of who had fondled her bare butt, had swung a paddle against that same bare butt. His smile widened.

"Ah, right." She rose to her feet, relieved when he didn't stop her. "How about you point me toward the facilities."

When he stood, looking down at her, she felt like that kitten he kept calling her. Like a kitten next to a wolf that wasn't hungry…right this minute. But the danger was there, glinting in those dark gray eyes. She watched him warily when he set his hand low on her back then deliberately stroked the curves of her butt.

She frowned at him.

Before she could even react, he yanked her up against his chest. His hand behind her back held her pinned as his other hand roamed over her bottom—her still tender bottom—so intimately she was embarrassed and aroused all at once.

"First lesson, little sub," he said very softly. "Frowning at your Dom can be risky." One finger traced the crack between her buttocks through the silky skirt material, and she quivered under his touch.

"You're not my—" The carnal look in his eyes froze her tongue. "Um. Right. A lesson. Thanks."

He chuckled and released her, the lack of his warm body against hers like a sudden chill. Shaking her head, she headed for the bathroom, striving for dignity but moving a little too fast to accomplish the effect. She glanced back before going through the door. A man was talking to Sir, but Sir's gaze was on her, a faint smile on his lips.

The sensual flush ran through her right down to her toes.

Chapter Six

Zachary listened to James and his ideas for a scene with his fairly new sub, but his mind was more on Jessica than the conversation. He could tell her thoughts were on him and the way he'd made her feel. She was confused...and very aroused. Excellent.

He turned his attention to James, replayed mentally what the young man had said. New sub, inhibited. Wonderful in private but he couldn't get her off during public scenes.

"Then don't do them," Zachary said. His college-age son would have added a *duh* at the end.

"But I love scening in the club, Z. It's something I don't want to give up. Hell, she may not work out for me after all." James sighed, his unhappiness clear.

Zachary put thoughts of Jessica away so he could focus on the problem. James and Brandy were good together, each meeting the other's needs. It would be a shame for something so minor to cause a division. "You can scene without her reaching climax."

"Yeah, but like that's the whole point of a scene, at least it is for me."

"All right then." Zachary frowned. "If Brandy comes easily when alone with you, then she's inhibited by being on display. If you can bring her to orgasm once or twice in a public scene, she'll probably be fine after that."

"Yeah, that's what I think. She kind of likes doing stuff in front of people...just not getting off."

"A woman is at her most vulnerable then, both physically and emotionally." Zachary glanced at the restroom door. Jessica should be out soon. "James, let me give you a few tips and—"

"Shit, Z, I'm not good with remembering instructions. Can you show me? Do one of your scene lessons?"

Education had always been a priority at the club, and although inducing a public climax wasn't part of the usual training, it was probably a concern to many of the newer Doms and subs. "All right. Next week."

"Cool. I'll make sure I've got the night off." James's grin showed his relief before he nodded toward the restroom. "You know, I've seen your sub before. She visits the animal shelter every week."

James was a vet tech, Zachary remembered. "Doing what?"

"Socializes the animals; you know, walks the dogs, snuggles with the cats. The animals adore her."

"Good to know." A sweetheart, like he'd thought.

"Yeah, thought I'd mention it. She's not the type to boast."

"No." The woman had depths he hadn't explored yet, physically or emotionally.

"Well, thanks for the help, Z," James said. "I'm going to go tell Brandy about next week."

Right after the younger man left, Jessica returned.

Zachary turned to Jessica, savoring her straightforward emotions after the noisy jangle of the young man's. Her mind was so clear; he occasionally could get images rather than just emotions.

Right now, her barriers were back up, her arousal down. She was like hot springs on a high mountain, all that heat covered over with new-fallen snow. Now how long could she make that last, he wondered, amused. "Let's head toward the other side of the room."

The intent look Sir had just given Jessica unsettled her.

In the restroom, she'd had a firm talk with herself as she cooled. She wouldn't make an idiot of herself by getting all hot and bothered. Sure, she wanted to discover more about the bondage stuff, but not to the point of relinquishing all control. "What's on the other side?"

"Just a place to sit more comfortably," Sir said easily. "You have a soft voice, and it's hard to hear you when we're close to the dance floor."

He guided her toward an area filled with small groups of chairs and couches. People were sitting and talking quietly. Well, some of them. They passed a couch where a woman knelt at a man's feet openly playing with his cock.

Jessica turned her eyes away and blushed. "People sure aren't modest here, are they?" she muttered.

His chuckle sent tingles through her. Hell, no matter what he did, she got tingles, as if every skin cell on her body had been sensitized to his touch or voice. Just the feel of his hand stroking her bare arm made her toes curl.

Finding an empty couch, he took a seat, pulling her down beside him. He was so close that his scent wrapped around her as his weight tilted her into him. She clasped her hands together in her lap. "Now what?" she asked in a bright voice.

"Now we get serious." His dark, rich baritone made her stomach quiver. "Why did you come back in?"

The unexpectedness of the question made her insides tighten. Why did he keep asking her these impossible probing questions, dammit? How could she possibly answer this? "I didn't come for…

I was just curious." Curious to see what he could do to her. Her breath quickened.

"Curious to *see*? Or curious *to do*?" He laid one big hand over both of hers.

"Mostly to see." Really.

"No curiosity as to what being restrained *feels* like?"

She grimaced. "I tried that earlier. Remember? The paddle?"

"I do remember, yes." The crease in his cheek appeared, but at least he didn't laugh. "Well, kitten, let's see how you like being restrained...and *touched*." His fingers wrapped around her wrists, pinning her hands on her lap as he cupped her cheek with his other hand.

He kissed her. When his tongue rubbed against hers, warmth filled her. She tried to bring her hands up to touch him only she couldn't, and shock, then heat, ran through her. His mouth moved down the side of her neck, teeth closing gently on the skin, giving her goose bumps.

Again she tried to move. Again his fingers held her in place, and she actually felt herself dampen.

"You have soft skin that begs to be touched," he whispered, licking the hollow in her collarbone. "Nipples that want to be sucked." With his free hand, he ran his finger across the top of her low-cut shirt, stroking the top of her breasts.

She held her breath, wanting him to go further. Not wanting him to. Dammit, she didn't like being so confused.

Smiling, he pushed the elastic top lower until her breasts were half out. His fingertips slid under the shirt to touch one nipple, and it beaded into hardness. Her mouth closed against a sigh, and then she froze as she realized he wasn't looking down, but studying her face, her expressions. As his gaze captured hers, his fingers lightly circled her nipple, around and around, until she could feel need growing inside her, until she was biting her lip.

Too many sensations: the feel of one hard hand restraining her, of his fingers on her body. Urgency filled her as her core throbbed.

"Feels different, doesn't it?" he whispered. ""Do you want more?"

"No." He saw her too clearly, and that was as frightening as how her body was reacting. "No, I don't."

His jaw tightened. "I really do know when you lie, little one. For your comfort, I haven't called you on it before, but now..." His steady gaze pinned her in place. "Now you will be honest with me."

"I—" She shook her head, unwilling to expose her need. Realizing she couldn't lie.

"I think we'll go and satisfy some of your curiosity and some of that need you don't want to admit to." He gave her a level look. "Your answer is 'yes, Sir.'"

Her heart was hammering like she'd been running for miles, and her hands grew sweaty in his grasp. *Do this? Let him...do what he wanted to her?* It was why she'd returned, but the idea was insane. Yet the thought of his hands on her, taking her... She couldn't answer, could only gaze at him helplessly.

He smiled, pulled her to her feet, and led her to a locked door marked *Private* and then into a small room down a hall. With a wave of his hand by the door frame, two wall sconces glowed with soft, flickering lights.

She halted just inside the door, one wrist still in his grip. The throbbing music from the club was a soft murmur in her ears as she looked around. The dark-paneled room held a massive wrought iron bed with a shimmering sapphire cover, an antique armoire, and nothing else. She licked her lips. What was she doing? This was too much, too irrevocable. She pulled against his grip.

"No, Jessica," he murmured. "You're here because you want to be. If you leave, you'll always wonder what could have been."

How did he know that?

Her breath came hard as he led her to the bed, but he simply sat on the edge and pulled her onto his lap, clasping her hand. "First of all, this time between us is simply for pleasure. Trust me to know how to give you that pleasure. Can you do that?" His eyes were intent as if he could see into her soul.

She nodded then stiffened. "You won't whip me...or anything, right?"

"No, kitten." He stroked a finger down her cheek. "You've experienced the worst of the physical punishments I hand out."

Her muscles relaxed slightly. "Okay."

"Second. If you become too frightened or are somehow in pain, your safe word is red. If you use that word, everything stops. It's the equivalent of calling nine-one-one, so don't use it lightly."

A way out. That was good. She realized her hands were cold within his warm grasp.

"But, Jessica." He tipped her chin up to pin her with a hard gray stare. "If you're hurting or frightened, simply tell me." His lips curled up. "If I'm doing my job, I will know; nonetheless, I expect you to share what you feel with me."

Bare her thoughts, her emotions? Could even sex with him be as intimate? Both would leave her vulnerable... This really wasn't a good idea, was it? "Sir, I think—"

"You think too much sometimes," he murmured, releasing her hands to tangle his fingers in her hair. "This is enjoyment, not a college exam." Tilting her head back, his mouth closed on hers in a tender kiss. He kissed her slowly, thoroughly, as if he had all the time in the world. Her skin heated and suddenly she was ready to feel his hands on her, wanted his hands on her. Her fingers curled in his silky hair, and she kissed him back until her head spun.

She hardly noticed when he rose to his feet, his mouth still on hers, when he pulled her to her feet. He stepped back, leaving her out of breath, her lips tingling.

His eyes were dark, his mouth in a firm line as he turned her to face the bed. Bending her forward, he set her hands on the cool silk cover.

"Don't move your hands from where I put them," he said. "Do you understand?"

Oh... It was starting. Her heart gave a hard thud. As her fingers curled the quilt into bunches, she nodded.

"Say, 'Yes, Sir,' so I know you are hearing me."

"Yes, Sir," she whispered, and shivered.

"Very nice." He stroked her cheek. Then she felt his hands on her waist, undoing her skirt. His fingers were firm, sure. When her skirt pooled around her feet, leaving her bare from the waist down, she jerked and started to stand.

"Stay in place, little one." His hand pressed on her back, unmoving until she resumed her position, hands braced on the bed. And then he touched her, massaging her sore buttocks, murmuring in pleasure. "You have a beautiful ass, Jessica. Just right for my hands."

His fingers slid down the crack between her cheeks, touched her folds so intimately that she gasped. "You're wet for me already," he rumbled. He slid his fingers through her wetness over and over until her slit was on fire and her hips squirmed uncontrollably. But she managed to keep her hands still.

"You didn't move. Good girl," he said, and the approval in his voice filled her with pleasure.

"Turn around now." He helped her stand and smoothly pulled her shirt over her head, leaving her completely naked. "Ah, you are a beautiful woman, Jessica," he said, his eyes heating as he took his time looking her over, his gaze as warm as his hands had been.

He really did act like she was pretty. She could listen to that all night.

His warm hands ran up her arms. "Your skin is like expensive velvet, kitten," he murmured before stroking across her collarbone. Her nipples tightened even before he touched them and stroked them with his fingertips into aching need.

"Up on the bed now," he said, his voice deep, smooth. He pushed her ahead of him until she reached the middle. With steady hands, he rolled her onto her back; the way he handled her so easily shocked her. He straddled her, one knee on each side of her waist. She stared up at him. His jaw was strong, darkly shadowed, and his firm lips curved a little in a smile.

He stroked her hair. "Do you trust me not to hurt you, Jessica?"

She nodded, and he waited until she whispered, "Yes, Sir."

"Good girl." His eyes never leaving hers, he picked up her hand and lifted it toward the head of the bed, wrapped a soft strap around it. And then he did the other. So quickly, so easily, and then he moved to lie beside her.

When his eyes left hers, she felt shock sear through her. She yanked against the straps, realizing her vulnerability. *God, what had she done?* She was naked, and he was... She didn't even know him. "No. I don't like this. Let me go."

"Jessica, look at me." He cupped her cheek in one big hand, forcing her to meet his dark gaze. His level, straight gaze. "Trust me to take care of you, kitten. Can you do that?"

Her panic receded a little, even more when he brushed a tender kiss across her lips, nuzzled her temple. She'd never met anyone who affected her like this. She did trust him, far more than made sense. She sighed her acceptance, stopped fighting the ties, although her body stayed rigid.

As she lay there, hands tied over her head, he stood and stripped, not hurriedly, just as efficiently as he did everything, it seemed. Oh, he was as gorgeous without clothing as she'd imagined, his skin darkly tanned, tight over the muscles beneath. Her eyes dropped lower, and she flushed. His erection was huge, thick and hard and jutting toward her, both a threat and a promise.

Following her gaze, he glanced down. "As you can see, I'm looking forward to burying myself in your slick pussy, feeling you all around me."

Her core clutched at his words, as if it had a mind of its own, heating and moistening for his invasion.

After covering himself with a condom, he joined her on the bed. Leaning on one elbow, he caressed her cheek and teased her lips in a soft kiss that quickly turned hot. His tongue took possession, smoothly plunging in and out of her mouth.

And she felt the heat returning as he toyed with her mouth, as his fingers traced up and down her neck, stroking across the tops of her breasts.

Then his hand moved down. "You are like a Christmas present"—his voice was smooth and dark—"gifting me with such tempting pleasures. Your breasts are lovely." He lifted each one, evidently savoring the weight in his hand, running his fingers on the underside, circling each breast until the nipples contracted into hard buds, aching to be touched.

She arched, trying to get closer, and he chuckled.

His fingers closed on her right breast, running over the tiny areola pebbles until they tightened even further. When he drew her nipple into his mouth, his hot, wet tongue drew shudders from her as it circled the peak. His teeth closed and nipped. She gasped. The feeling was just short of pain, sending pleasure jolting down through her like an electric line to her core.

She tried to bring her hands down, wanting to touch him, but the restraints held her tightly. She realized again that she couldn't move; she couldn't stop him from taking anything he wanted. Her breath hitched even as her excitement rose another level.

He moved to the other breast while his fingers kept playing with the first. He took her into his mouth, sucking hard until the nipple stood erect and a dusky red.

"Very pretty," he murmured in approval, and slid down. His mouth pressed against her stomach, nibbling and kissing until she squirmed under his touch, her heart pounding faster with every inch.

He knelt between her legs now, looking at her...her pussy. She flushed. Why hadn't he darkened the room? Sex was one thing; being looked at was another. That area should be private.

Tilting his head, he ran his finger down her stomach to the top of her cleft, and she caught her breath and yanked at her bonds. He eyed her, pushed her leg out a little. Feeling exposed and vulnerable before his gaze, she resisted, unable to help herself.

"I don't think you're going to obey me easily," he mused. "You're too shy."

She had a feeling she knew what was coming. Now he'd restrain her legs. She'd heard about being spread-eagled, legs tied toward the corners. Her breath sped up even as she tried to tell herself it would be fun. At least she knew what was coming.

His eyes crinkled as he smiled at her. "Perhaps not the spread-eagle, then."

Reaching under the mattress, he pulled out a wide strap that was attached to the side of the bed. After wrapping the soft velvet-covered fabric just above her knee, he bent her leg up toward her chest, then out, and pulled the rope tight.

"Hey." Her eyes widened even as he did the same to her other leg and this time she tried to resist, but he was finished before she recovered from the shock. Rather than her legs being straight, he'd pulled her knees up toward her stomach, and outward, tipping her pussy up in the air.

"Now you are open to me," he said, gazing straight into her eyes. "Open for whatever my mouth or cock wants from you." Excruciatingly slowly, he slid his finger down between her folds, taking her wetness and spreading it. "This pretty little pussy is mine to use."

Staring at him, she shivered as her mind went blank. She was bound and more helpless than she could ever have imagined. Her legs jerked uselessly, unable to close, to move. Her usual worries about what to touch, how to move... All decisions had been taken away from her; he made them all. And arousal settled like a warm hand over her whole lower half, and dampness trickled between her legs, revealing her desire to his knowing gaze.

His warm hands ran up and down her legs, massaging the undersides of her restrained thighs. When he stroked the tender crease between her leg and pubis, she shivered. Her core coiled tighter. Leaning forward, he nibbled on her stomach, his breath warm against her skin.

When his fingers barely caressed her clitoris, need exploded within her. She quivered, her entire core burning almost painfully.

"Please," she whispered, not really sure what she wanted.

He raised his head, frowning. "Who?"

"S-sir, please." She needed more, needed something so badly she ached, her insides throbbing, wanting.

"Ah, I like *please*." His big hands curled around her thighs, holding her as tightly as the straps, and his head dipped. His tongue licked into her, and she cried out in surprise, the slick curl of him too quickly gone. But then his tongue found her clit, moving over and around in teasing little flicks, so that her breath almost stopped with each tiny touch. She needed to arch her hips, to press against him, and she couldn't move. She was open and immobile to his touch.

Suddenly he slid a finger between her swollen folds, and into her.

"Ah, ah!" Her tissues were so sensitive, he felt huge inside her. Hot. Her legs shook, straining against the straps.

In, out, one finger, then two, and then his mouth settled on her clit. His tongue stroked, soft then hard, never the same, until every nerve in her body was waiting for the next slide of his finger, the next touch of his tongue. She panted in little hard breaths.

And then, his mouth closed over her clit, and he sucked hard even as he plunged his fingers in and out of her. She screamed as electric spasms shot through her with the brilliance of fireworks. Her insides convulsed around his invading fingers, her hips jerking uncontrollably.

She could still hear her wails echoing in the room when she opened her eyes and realized he'd moved up to lie beside her. His gaze was steady on her face.

"Oh..." she whispered, astonished with herself at her response. Nothing had ever felt like that before, as different from her little pleasant orgasms as an afternoon shower was to a tropical storm.

Her hands were still restrained, and she wanted to move, touch him. She pulled at the wrist straps. "Let me go," she demanded.

He gave her a slow smile. "Soon, little one. But I find I like your hips in this position." He moved on top of her and reached down to touch her pussy. She trembled as his skillful fingers teased her clit, her labia. "You're so very open."

He ran his cock up and down her wetness, setting off little spasms inside her. Staring into her eyes, he thrust slowly, firmly into her, hard and hot and thick, filling her completely. More than completely, deeper than was comfortable in this strange position. She struggled for breath, trying to escape, to move away.

Chapter Seven

Zachary's balls thudded against the little sub's buttocks, a tiny enjoyable jolt, as he sheathed himself to the hilt. She was slick and hot and tight around him. From her body and mind, he could sense her discomfort at his size, and he stopped to give her time to adjust. Her full breasts brushed against his chest, and he leaned down to nibble on one. He doubted he'd ever get his fill of her breasts.

Her pussy contracted around him as he sucked on one succulent nipple then the other, playing with each until he could feel her body responding, wanting more.

He gave her more. Her hips were tilted forward, and he adjusted his movements so each stroke, each exquisite slide into her body, brushed against her clit. Within a minute, she was trembling under him; another minute and she moaned, low and deep, her green eyes blind with passion.

She had so much passion that she'd kept hidden away, and the pleasure of bringing it forth was heady. Ah, but she had more to give. He continued pumping, hard and controlled. With one hand, he released her arms from the bonds. Satisfaction filled him when she grabbed him like a drowning swimmer.

She slid her hands over his back, then her fingers dug into his biceps as he increased the pace and force of his thrusts.

Her breathing was fast and shallow, broken with tiny whimpers, the pleasing sounds of submission. She was very close. He reached down and slid a finger up and over her clit.

Her scream filled the room as her snug pussy spasmed around him.

He let himself go and each intensely satisfying jerk from his cock set her off again and again. Finally spent, he laid his forehead against hers, a little shocked at how overpowering his release had been.

After sucking in a deep breath, he pushed himself up. She didn't move. Her heart was pounding so hard that her breasts shook with each beat. He released her knees, chuckled as her legs slid down, the muscles gone limp.

Rolling to the side, he stayed inside her, savoring the small twitches of her pussy around him. He snuggled her closer, soft and fragrant in his arms. Affection and something more filled him. He couldn't think of when he'd enjoyed sex more or when he'd been so attracted to a woman.

When her breathing slowed, when he could feel her emotions begin to swirl around in her mind, he asked softly, "What did you think of being tied, being opened for my pleasure?"

Her shock at his question, that he would speak of such things, made him hide his grin in her hair. That innocence was such a contrast to her sharp mind, just as her modesty hid the fiery passion beneath. The mixture enchanted him.

"I…hmmm. It's very unusual."

"When was the last time you came screaming?" he whispered.

Jessica gulped. His hand had been stroking her breast gently, like he enjoyed the feel of her skin, and she'd felt well cherished until he asked those questions. Did he actually expect her emotions to be as open to him as her body had just been? She buried her face against his chest rather than answer.

He pinched her nipple, a tiny pain, and her breath caught.

"Answer me, Jessica." His voice had chilled, and when she peeked up, his brows were together.

"Never, okay?" she muttered, annoyed with him in return. *Her orgasms were her business, not his.*

"When we come together like this, you will have no secrets from me," he said, not releasing his gaze. "You will not hide your body or your mind."

She shivered, feeling more exposed than when her butt had been in the air for all to see. His hand ran down her cheek, her neck. "You found being tied down a little scary, a lot exciting, yes?"

Eyes averted, she nodded. *Why did he ask if he knew the answers?*

He watched her for a moment, silently, long enough that she began to worry. Was he planning something else? What else could he do? She shivered as her mind conjured up horrifying...lewd...*tantalizing* images.

"And now you're beginning to wonder what else can happen in this room. In this house." His eyes held a wicked light. His mouth curved in satisfaction as her muscles tightened in apprehension and hunger.

"First, let me clean up a little," he said, and disappeared into the bathroom.

Chilled without him, she sat up, wrapping her arms around herself. Her body was well satisfied, but her emotions... She felt very confused. She had gotten what she wanted, right?

But was her response because of him and how good he was in bed? Or because she'd been tied up? How could she come to terms with her own behavior? That she'd actually let him bind her, and that she'd loved it?

Really, she should go home now, she thought miserably even as she longed to curl back into his arms.

When he came out, he shook his head. "Little sub, you're thinking and worrying again. Time to put you to work."

Work? Scrub the bathroom or—

"Kneel."

She blinked, saw the beginning of a frown on his face, and scrambled off the bed. Even as she dropped to her knees, her mind protested. She was a smart woman, a businesswoman. Surely this wasn't a position she should be in.

Her body didn't agree. She could feel her heart speeding up, her skin becoming more sensitive. Every little fiber on the plush shag rug seemed to caress her legs.

"Very nice." He stood in front of her, stroked her hair. "Take me in your mouth and suck me."

Her mouth dropped open. "But—"

"What do you say?"

He was only half-erect. "Um. Yes, Sir."

He set one finger under her chin, lifted her face. "Have you not done this before, kitten?"

"Twice. I wasn't very good at it," she admitted glumly. Her last boyfriend had been scathing in his comments over her performance with oral sex. Heck, at any type of sex.

Master Z's eyes crinkled. "Why don't you take that warm, soft mouth and put it around my cock. You start, and I'll instruct you as needed."

He liked her mouth. That was enough encouragement for her to grasp him in her fingers. His cock was soft; the head was velvety smooth as she closed her lips around it.

To her delight, he hummed in appreciation. Gently, she moved her mouth over his shaft, feeling him stiffen, elongate. The loose skin tightened around the hardness beneath, and she took her mouth away to stare. Earlier, she'd felt like he'd entered her with something huge; he had.

Chuckling, he stroked her hair again. "Continue, kitten."

At least she'd pleased him enough to get him hard. That was something, right? She slid her lips up and down, wetting him with her mouth.

"Use your tongue," he murmured. "Pretend it's my tongue on your clit. The only difference is in size."

Oooh, she remembered how his mouth had felt on her, how his ravening tongue had licked over her, around... The memory made her wet, made her clit throb. With growing understanding, she tongued the underside of his cock, toyed with the thick veins, then swirled around the head. Taking him fully into her mouth again, she sucked lightly the way he'd sucked on her clit.

His hand tightened in her hair. "Ahhh, that's perfect, Jessica. Now use your hands too."

Hands? Holding his dick with one hand, she pulled her head back and glanced up at him. He moved his legs apart, and his balls swayed, attracting her attention. She'd always wanted to touch a man there, to see what they felt like. With her free hand, she slipped her palm under one, lifting, letting her fingers caress it. So heavy and soft. But she could tell somehow, that although he enjoyed this, she wasn't driving him crazy like he'd done to her.

She really wanted to get him off.

Returning her attention to his cock, she licked her way back up, then grasped him with both hands at the thick base. She squeezed gently and muscles tightened in his legs. Yes! She took him in her mouth again, sliding him in and out, sliding her hands up and down in counterpoint. He grew harder, thicker, and her satisfaction was heady, almost as heady as the need growing between her legs, the desire to have him inside her there.

Her eager mouth was going to be the death of him. Hot and moist. Her awkward movements only made it worse, keeping his attention fully on her and what she was doing. When the urge to pound into her grew overwhelming, he set his hands on her shoulders. "You are very good at this and only going to get better. But I'm not finished taking you yet. On the bed, pet."

She gave him a final swipe with her tongue, glinted a happy smile up at him, and crawled onto the bed. Ah, the princess felt more in control now. He was delighted that her comfort level had increased.

Still, taking her in a mundane fashion wouldn't serve her well. She was a strong woman whose deepest responses apparently came when she was most vulnerable.

The armoire yielded Velcro straps and rope and another condom. He covered himself quickly. As he walked back to the bed with the restraints, he saw trepidation grow in her eyes. He could feel the hint of uncertainty in her mind. She sat with her legs tightly closed; her quickening breath jostled her breasts.

"Give me your wrists," he murmured, and waited patiently through her hesitation. He treasured the way she set her wrists into his grasp. Her trust in him had grown. "Good girl."

After smoothing the Velcro bindings around her wrists, he clipped them together and then slid a rope through the links. Picking her up, he turned her and set her onto her hands and knees. "Don't move, pet," he cautioned, caressing her breast. Her heart thudded under his fingers, the speed increasing nicely.

There was a fine line between fear that would excite and fear that would paralyze the senses. But he could feel her increasing arousal overcoming her apprehension.

He paused for a moment to stroke her hair. It was long enough to wrap around his hand, bringing other diversions to mind. The silky strands were a mixture of gold colors, slipping over her fair skin as he pushed them over one bare shoulder. He nibbled her nape, pleased to see goose bumps appear on her arms. Her body was sensitized, waiting for anything he would do.

After wrapping a wide strap around her right knee, he slipped her bound hands out from under her, leaving her balanced on one shoulder, her head turned to the side. Smiling, he tied her hands to the knee strap.

Her ass was up in the air, displaying her assets nicely. Perhaps someday they'd explore that perky little asshole. For now, he fingered the little dimples beside her spine before setting his hands on pretty cheeks that were still a little swollen from the paddling.

A shiver ran through her body.

Head down, butt in the air, unable to move.

Does this seem rather familiar? she wondered unhappily. Her hands were between her legs, tied to the inside of her right knee. She pulled at the restraints with no success, and the inability to move sent an unexpected tremor of need slicing through her. Apprehension made her heart pound in her chest as she tried to see what he was doing, what he planned. Her skin, even her core, tensed, waiting for his touch.

And then his hands closed on her bottom, and she gasped and shivered. He massaged and stroked her still-tender buttocks, where pain lingered. She shook at the feel of his fingers, the slight pain and excitement rolling together, wetting her between her legs. And she wanted more.

While one hand teased her butt, his other wakened her pussy, sliding into her juices. He ran a gentle finger through her folds and up to play with her sensitive clit. She tried to wiggle, and his hand on her butt clamped down, held her in place. "Don't move, little one."

His finger slid across her pussy, firmly, then teasing flicks, and she could feel her clit swelling.

"Your sweet little clit is just like my cock," he murmured. "Soft until stroked, and now feel how it grows harder. Bigger."

The merciless touching continued until she throbbed with the need for more. When his hand moved away, she moaned.

"I don't want to neglect this area." His sure fingers touched outside her opening then speared through the swollen inner labia into her slickness. She struggled for breath as the sensations spread from just her clit to her whole core. Everywhere he touched grew sensitive and burned with need.

She tightened around his fingers desperately, trying to hold him in as he slid his fingers in and out.

"More," she rasped.

He stopped, removed his hands from her.

Her whole pussy pulsed painfully and she whimpered.

"What do you call me?" he asked patiently.

"Sir. Sir, please touch me."

"Better." Suddenly his mouth was there, where his fingers had been. His slick, hot tongue flicked over her clit, teased her slit with swirling motions that set her to shuddering.

She panted, so close, so close, and then he moved away again, and she groaned, her hands closing into fists.

He chuckled then drove his cock deep into her in one hard surge.

She screamed as her world splintered around her, as she spasmed around his thickness, shuddering so hard her legs weakened. His hands held her in place, gripping her hips and keeping her pinned against him.

He felt even bigger in this position than the other, and now she squirmed, trying to escape. It felt like his cock had filled her completely, was up against her cervix, and she whimpered again, discomfort and desire mingling inside her.

"Shhh, just wait, little one, just wait," he murmured. When he bent over her, his cock shifted inside, driving another gasp from her. He set one muscular arm beside her shoulder to hold himself up, and his other hand played with her breasts. He rolled her nipples gently between his callused fingers until her breasts were tight and swollen, sending carnal messages to her groin.

Her hips wiggled slightly as her pussy shivered around his cock, adjusting to his size. He began to move, each slide in and out making her gasp and then moan as sensations started piling up like mountains on top of mountains. His hand was on her breast, his lips on her back. His cock inside her was big and thick. It sank between her sensitive folds so deep that his balls slapped against her pussy and sent tiny shocks through her.

Slow at first, he increased his speed from a sensuous slide to a hard, forceful pumping. She couldn't move; her hands were still restrained, and she could only take his assault. The feeling of helplessness ran through her, heightening every sensation. Her legs quivered uncontrollably; her whole body shuddered as each merciless thrust sent stabs of pleasure pouring through her body. She was so close again. Her pussy tightened around him, her hands closing into fists.

And then his fingers left her breast, and suddenly he was stroking her clit. With every thrust of his cock into her body, his finger pulsed across her tender clit, over and over.

She screamed as she came harder than before, great spasms inside shaking her like a hurricane, fire streaming through her all the way to her fingertips.

He pulled back, gripping her hips and driving into her as her womb convulsed around him.

"Kitten, you could be the death of me," he growled, and then she could feel his cock jolt as he came hard inside of her. "Thank you, little sub." He nuzzled her neck, her shoulder, before pulling gently out of her. She whined like a puppy from the shocking emptiness.

He disappeared for a second to dispose of the condom.

Eyes closed, she didn't see him, just felt his hands as he rolled her onto her side and released her restraints.

"Come here, little one," he murmured, and pulled her on top of him like a limp blanket. He took her lips in a tender kiss then settled her head into the hollow of his shoulder, and she found nothing in her to resist. His chest was damp with sweat, slick under her cheek, salty on her tongue when she gave it a lick.

Through the muscles covering his chest, she could hear his heart beating in a steady rhythm, nothing like her racing pulse.

His hands stroked her back with shocking gentleness after he'd taken her so hard. Her body felt abused, quivery. *Wonderful.*

Inside her head, she felt the same way. What was happening to her, that a man could treat her like this and she got off on it? Got so off on it that she'd screamed and lost control completely.

She was always in control, dammit; she was an accountant.

"Being in control in bed isn't all it's cracked up to be, especially for a woman," he murmured.

She stiffened a little. *He really did read minds, didn't he?*

"Seems like the world expects you to have to do everything these days: care for yourselves, your families, your children, your jobs… Who takes care of you, Jessica?"

I do, she thought. *Just me.* But being tied up couldn't be considered being taken care of, could it? She frowned, remembering his knowledgeable hands, the way he watched her so closely, how he seemed to know exactly how to push her limits. Was that not being taken care of?

She managed to lift her head up to look at him, only to find his dark eyes studying her. And then he tangled his hands in her hair—just like that Dom on the dance floor had done to his sub—and took her mouth so sweetly, so thoroughly, it was as if she'd never been kissed before.

She was a snuggly one, he thought, listening to her mind fade away and sleep take her. She was draped across him like the softest of teddy bears, her breasts cushioned against his chest, her hips a graceful mound in the low light.

Snuggly and a screamer. Her shock at discovering how far passion could take her had been delightful, and he wanted to hear her low moans, little whimpers, and heady screams again and again. He stroked her hair, soft and silky with a little curl at the ends. Her fragrance surrounded him, a light mixture of vanilla and woman; she'd tasted like peaches on his tongue. He'd never been quite so content just to lie still and savor the afterglow.

The contentment dimmed at the thought that this might be all the time he had with her. She wouldn't be quite so complacent about what had happened here tonight once she returned to her own world.

Her world? He hadn't discovered much about her. What did she do for a living? She wasn't married or involved with someone; she had more integrity than that. Her essential honesty drew him like a moth to a bright light.

In fact, he'd found no one in a long time whose thoughts and emotions had been so engaging. Soothing. Most people were a jumble of raucous feelings, but her mind processed thoughts and feelings in a linear fashion, this emotion, then this one, each clean and simple.

Yet she was intriguing, a puzzle. The easy friendliness she showed to those around her was a decided contrast to her controlled, conservative manner. He wanted to know more.

She roused all too soon, sitting up from him and shaking her silky hair back. If she was on top when he took her, all that hair would rain down on his chest. The thought was tempting. But no, he needed to show some restraint.

He tucked a hand under his head, watching her. She was so graceful and round, and her breasts swayed gently, tantalizingly. He couldn't resist and ran his knuckles along the undersides, circled her nipples with one finger, enjoying the puckering.

"I think... Is it getting close to morning?" Her voice was husky, a little rough, and he smiled, remembering how she'd panted as her climax neared. How she'd screamed.

"It's past dawn, yes."

"I need to... I'm sure it's time to go."

Ah, reality had indeed arrived.

* * *

Someone had actually washed and dried her clothing. How many people did Sir have working here?

Being back in her conservative blouse and slacks seemed to make the evening less real. The club room was quiet now with no music, no people remaining except the bartender.

He nodded at Sir and smiled at her. A nice smile, but she still flushed, knowing what she must look like. Her lips were swollen, her face beard-scratched, her hair tangled. She must look rather well used.

After a moment, she smiled back. *Well satisfied.*

Master Z, with one arm firmly around her, glanced around the bar. "Everyone gone?"

"Yes, sir," Cullen replied. "I'll be done cleaning up in about fifteen minutes."

"How late is it?" Jessica asked.

"Not late, pet." The bartender chuckled. "Early. It's almost eight o'clock in the morning."

She blinked. "I definitely need to get going."

"Of course," Master Z murmured.

Odd how she almost had wanted him to protest. "May I use your phone?"

"No need. I had a tow truck called. And your ride should be here."

After the dim bar, the bright morning light shocked her eyes. In the lingering winds from the storm, low clouds scudded across the deep blue sky. The palm trees lining the long drive swayed while fronds and debris skidded along the blacktop. The air was clear with a salty lash from the nearby gulf, and Jessica inhaled a deep breath before turning to Master Z.

What was the protocol for saying good-bye to someone who'd tied you up? Who'd made you scream as you orgasmed? "Um."

His eyes danced with humor at her awkwardness. Damn him, he was as cool and impeccable as at the beginning of the night. Only the rougher beard growth marred his sleek appearance. He looked like a dangerous pirate dressed for an evening out in London.

She knew damn well she didn't look as good.

"Thank you for rescuing me last night," she said. "And for... Well..." She flushed.

One eyebrow rose and he stepped closer and pressed a kiss to her palm. "For baring your ass and paddling it?" he asked. "For tying you down and enjoying your body and making you come over and over?"

From the searing heat in her cheeks, she knew she'd flushed. Even more disconcerting, her body responded to his words, moistening as warmth pooled in her core. God, she wanted him again.

And he knew, dammit. "It was my pleasure, little one."

He laced his fingers into her hair and took her mouth, his kiss long and lingering with a new hint of tenderness. She sighed when he pulled back.

"Are you going to give me your phone number?" he asked gently, studying her, his eyes steel gray in the morning sun.

"It's—" She stopped. Did she want to continue this? Be the sort of person who did stuff like this? The night was over, and in the light of day, somehow she wasn't comfortable with the idea, even though, just gazing at Master Z, she wanted to drag him back into that little room. And do more...stuff. "I—"

His smile was faint. "I understand. Perhaps it is good you have time to think. I fear you had a rather abrupt introduction to the lifestyle."

Guilt crawled through her at the darkening of his gaze, almost as if she'd hurt him, but surely not. Ben said he had women everywhere, all he wanted. "I don't..." She trailed off, unsure what there was to say.

"I hope you come back, Jessica," he murmured. "You will always be welcome here." He brushed a kiss across her cheek, then turned and reentered the house, making her think of a king entering his castle.

Leaving her with a sense of loss deep in her stomach.

Okay. Get it together. She turned, searching for the tow truck and saw only a limousine in the driveway. Where—"

"Miss Jessica?" The uniformed chauffeur stood beside the car.

A limo for her? All the way back to Tampa? Was Sir crazy? She glanced back at the front door, thought about protesting. She knew she wouldn't win, and she didn't really want to. "I'm Jessica."

Chapter Eight

The following week was fairly normal for Jessica: meetings with clients, working on the computer, wading through poorly kept records and ledgers. But something inside her had changed and apparently was as obvious on the outside as on the inside.

"You look…different," one of her colleagues said when she saw him in the coffee room.

She glanced down at herself. Same old tailored slacks and shirt. Hair in a French braid. Discreet makeup.

"No, not the clothes," he said, frowning. "Just, different. Hey, why don't you join me for a drink after work?"

Too weird. They'd dated briefly and had boring sex. He'd dumped her, which hurt her pride more than anything else. He *was* the office hunk, after all. Now his interest had returned?

"Thanks, but no. I'm pretty busy these days," she said.

"Oh. Okay." Confusion, then shock crossed his face at the refusal.

She was a little shocked too, for she had no interest in dating him again. In all reality, next to Master Z, he seemed insipid. Hollow like a Subway sandwich without any meat inside.

Pining after Master Z was not good.

At night, her tiny apartment felt more lonely than normal as she thought about the difference in her, unsure what it meant. On the plus side of the ledger, she now knew her sex drive was alive and well, that she could have fantastic orgasms just like other women. That change was so new, so mind-altering, she couldn't quite encompass it. She felt...sexy.

But on the minus side... *Well.* Leaning back on the couch, she stared up at the ceiling. Those miraculous orgasms were from being tied up, having a man tell her what to do, and make her do it. Even as she shook her head in disbelief, her body heated, moistened. Ready for more. Wanting more.

Surely she didn't want more bondage stuff. But the thought of never having sex like that again was...was like imagining life without chocolate. She rested her head in her hands.

What was she going to do?

Saturday arrived after seven days of confusion and six nights of erotic dreams. She'd fall asleep, and Master Z would be there, his firm hands holding her in place, his mouth on hers, on her breasts, on everywhere. She'd awaken, panting and aroused, still feeling restraints around her wrists, hearing his low whisper in her ears.

In her spare time, she hit the Internet, researching BDSM. What she discovered hadn't made her any more comfortable.

Now she paced across her living room. Time to decide what to do. Tonight was bondage night. She could return to the club... Or not.

This was just so complicated. She'd insulted him by refusing to give him her number. He'd had her car towed and repaired as if it was nothing. He had subs who adored him. He'd hit her with a paddle and let other people do it too. He'd given her the best sex of her life and made her feel beautiful.

He probably wouldn't even remember her name.

That thought stopped her halfway across the room. What if he looked at her like she were...nobody. Another customer. A one-night stand inconveniently showing up. Her arms chilled, and her stomach felt like she'd swallowed cold oatmeal. Could she bear that?

She shook her head. *No. No, she really couldn't.* All her arguments disappeared in the face of such humiliation. She couldn't go back; he wouldn't—

Her doorbell rang and she frowned. At seven o'clock on a Saturday night, who could be at her door? A pizza delivery to the wrong address?

She checked the peephole—a delivery man—and opened the door. "Yes?"

"Miss Jessica Randall?"

"That's me."

He handed her a soft package. "Have a nice evening, ma'am." He left before she could respond.

Too bizarre. She hadn't ordered anything. After locking the door, she set the package on the glass coffee table and started ripping. Inside the envelope, soft tissue paper wrapped around a…nightie? Taken aback, she held it up. Definitely a nightie in a baby-doll style. A soft pink with a halter top and lacy handkerchief hem. Real silk.

She had never worn anything like that in her life. *What in the*—A card lay in the bottom of the package. Bold black handwriting. *Tonight is lingerie night for the subs. I would like to see you in this and nothing else. Master Z.*

Oh. My. God. Her heart seemed to stutter even as her legs turned wobbly. She dropped onto the couch. He wanted to see her. A thrill ran through her.

And then she frowned. She hadn't given him her number, let alone her address. How had he known where to send anything? Of course. The limousine driver, she'd given him her address. Sneaky, Master Z.

Once again, he'd known how she felt. Some men might have shown up on her doorstep. Her heart gave a hard thud at the thought of seeing Sir. But he wasn't that pushy. Instead, he'd found a smooth way to let her know he wanted to see her. A warm feeling grew in her chest. He hadn't forgotten her.

Now it was up to her.

She scowled down at his gift. *Wear that skimpy thing?* Absolutely not.

She stared at it longer. Then, biting her lip, she stripped and slipped on the top. Cool silk drifted around her body. The halter top lifted her breasts up until they almost overflowed, and the bottom... Well, she'd seen shorter. *Really.* But not much. Although the points of the handkerchief hem dropped in front and back to midthigh, the sides only reached her hips.

She discovered a tiny G-string left in the package and dangled it from one finger. *Wear this? What would be the point?*

She walked over to a mirror. The nightie really did look pretty good on her, didn't it? She twirled so the hemline flirted with her legs. She'd seen less modest outfits at wedding showers. He hadn't sent something that made her look totally slutty.

Actually, she couldn't imagine Master Z sending anything vulgar.

She turned again. If she left her hair down, it would cover up a lot of the cleavage. For the drive, she could wear a coat and leave it in the tiny coatroom. Her hands started to sweat.

Was she really, really considering this?

* * *

Zachary wandered through the club, nodding to the regulars. The place was filling up nicely. Lingerie nights were popular, both with the experienced and the newer crowd. He inspected the theme rooms in the back: the hard-core dungeon, the medical room, the office, the playroom. All were clean and stocked. The dungeon monitors assigned to each area were at their places.

He wondered what Jessica was doing about now. Staring in shock at his gift? Trying to decide what to do? Her confidence in herself and her attractiveness wasn't strong; that might influence her decision. Was she knowledgeable enough about her desires to set her feet on this path?

Clasping his hands behind his back, he strolled back to the main room. *How brave was she?*

* * *

Stomach aflutter with anticipation, Jessica stepped into the entry of the Shadowlands.

Ben glanced up from his paperwork, and a big smile split his heavy features. "Well now, look who's back."

The welcome was sincere, and she smiled at him in return. "Guess so."

"Master Z will be pleased." He flipped through his file box, pulled out the papers bearing her signature. "The boss said, 'This time, read them.'"

She laughed and started perusing the three pages. Several times she stopped to catch her breath at the ways she could have gotten in trouble and the penalties involved. Sir hadn't lied to her about the punishment for messing up someone's scene either. If anything, she'd gotten off lightly.

Ben was grinning by the time she finished. "A little overwhelming?"

"A lot overwhelming," she muttered. If she'd read the forms last week, she'd never have set a foot inside. At least this time she had the benefit of some Internet research.

"Give me your coat, and leave your shoes in a cubby." He nodded at the built-in shoe storage beside the coatrack.

After tucking her shoes away, she took off her coat, feeling like she was stripping.

He gave a low whistle, making her blush. "You look really nice. Go on in now."

The club room was more familiar this time, although the crowd's attire had changed. The female subs were all in lingerie with the males in low-riding bottoms. The Dom types wore dress slacks and shirts, leather or latex. Her nightie was actually one of the more discreet ones. *Thank you, Sir.*

Although most of the members were in couples or small groups, there were singles also. And as she sidled up to the bar, she noticed the interested looks men—and women—cast her way. She noticed her breasts wobble under the sheer silk. Good grief, this was like being naked.

She glanced at an empty St. Andrew's cross and winced. Or maybe not.

The bartender was another familiar face. *Cullen.* He certainly hadn't grown any shorter; the man positively loomed over the customers. She settled herself onto a bar stool and winced as her all-too-exposed butt hit the chilled wood.

Cullen leaned an elbow on the bar to smile down into her eyes. "Little Jessica. I'm very happy to see you again. What can I get you?"

"I'll have a margarita, please."

When he set the drink in front of her, she realized she'd left her wallet in the coat pocket. "My money's in the coatroom. I'll be back in—"

He shook his head. "Nope. Didn't make that clear last time, did I? This is a private club; the members' dues cover their drinks. And you're Master Z's guest."

"That was last time. This time—"

"He's expecting you, sweetie. This time, too." His grin was slow and appreciative as he studied her. She flushed. "He also said if you were brave enough, you'd be a treat for the eyes. As always, he was right."

She actually felt a quiver inside at the appreciation in his eyes.

Glancing away, she realized the tall man next to her was ogling her breasts. With a huff of exasperation and embarrassment, she turned toward the dance floor. Her eyes widened. Leathers and lingerie certainly made for...interesting dancing. The chemises, baby-dolls, and nightgowns offered very little protection against a Dom's hands.

Wetting her lips, she looked away and tried to see if Master Z was around. But what could she say to him anyway? *Hi there, want to tie me up again?* Oh, God, she shouldn't have come. This was too awkward, too embarrassing. She started to slide off the bar stool.

Hard hands grasped her around the waist and set her on her feet.

"Jessica, I am pleased." Sir's voice, deep and dark and smooth, sent a thrill running through her from her head to her toes.

She looked up into his intent eyes, then away, unable to meet his gaze. Chuckling, he held her out at arm's length and studied her. He smiled. "Quite as lovely as I had imagined. The pink suits you."

"Um." He wore a black silk shirt again with some of the buttons open, revealing his corded neck and hard upper chest muscles. She had run her hands over that chest, played with the springy black hair. Her fingers tingled; she wanted to touch him again. Wanted to *be* touched.

"Thank you for the...for the gown," she said awkwardly. The all-too-thin fabric offered no barrier to the heat and strength of his hands.

He rumbled a laugh. "The gown was for *my* pleasure, pet." Pulling her into his arms, he took her mouth in a lingering kiss. When he lifted his head—when her head stopped spinning—she realized he had one arm curved around her waist, and his free hand was rubbing her thong-bared buttocks.

She stiffened, tried to pull away. His grip tightened, tilting her hips into his. Fully erect, he pressed against her pubic area in a way that made her catch her breath.

"I look forward to taking you tonight," he whispered in her ear, "to hearing you whimper and scream as you come."

Heat shot through her so suddenly, so fiercely, she almost staggered. With a deep laugh, he released her and set her glass in her hand.

Cullen had been watching. Now he grinned at Sir. "Feel free to share your pet anytime, Master Z."

To Jessica's alarm, rather than laughing and saying "no way," Master Z inclined his head. "I'll keep that in mind."

Her mouth dropped open. He wouldn't... They didn't... Relief filled her as Master Z curved an arm around her and headed toward the rear of the club.

After a few feet, he stopped. "I almost forgot the rest of your clothing."

From the glint in his eyes, she didn't think he was talking about a concealing robe. "What would that be?"

He held one big hand out. "Give me a wrist."

Oh, God. Asking for a wrist meant restraints, didn't it? A tremor rushed through her and she felt herself dampen. "Now?"

"The only acceptable response from you is 'yes, Sir.'"

She swallowed hard. "Yes, Sir." Even as she placed her left wrist into his hand, warmth pooled inside her.

He unclipped something from his belt, and her eyes widened. How had she missed seeing what he carried? One side of his mouth curved up as he buckled a suede-lined leather handcuff snugly around her wrist.

"Next one."

It was harder to give him her hand this time, knowing what he had in mind. But she did.

With an approving smile, he put the other cuff on her.

She turned her hands over and studied the cuffs. Sturdy leather. The right cuff had one metal ring; the other cuff had another ring hanging from the first.

His intent gaze captured hers and didn't move away as he snapped the rings on the two cuffs together, binding her hands together in front of her. This wasn't in private. She pulled at the cuffs, her breathing increasing when nothing gave. "I don't think I like—"

"Actually, you do," he said, running the knuckles of one hand over her breasts where her nipples had tightened into hard points. When she tried to step back, he merely tucked his fingers around where the cuffs joined and held her in place.

She shook her head as he continued touching her, stroking her breasts.

"What are you feeling now, Jessica?" he asked, as if he wasn't rolling one nipple between his fingers.

"I—noth—" She stopped. *No lies*, he'd said. But...

"Just stop and think about your body, little one. Are you excited?"

Her heart beat quickly. Her breasts seemed to have swelled under his hands. Her private areas were wet and throbbing.

People walked around them; she could hear soft chuckles, but couldn't look away from Sir's intense eyes.

"Answer me, kitten. Do the cuffs excite you?"

"Yes." She felt like such a slut. Kinky sex, that was all she wanted.

He smiled slowly, his gaze heating as he leisurely looked her over. "I like seeing you in them." He touched her neck. "And seeing how they made your heart speed up." He ran one hard finger across her lower lip. "How your lips tremble."

He reached under her skirt and touched her so intimately, she choked. He lifted his fingers to his face, then hers. She could smell herself, so different than his scent.

"I can smell your arousal," he said.

Oh, God.

He chuckled. One hand around her waist, he strode through the crowd nonchalantly, as if he wasn't walking with a woman whose hands were buckled together in front of her. Reading about this stuff was sure a lot different than doing it.

"Where are we going?" Jessica asked, then grimaced. "Um. Am I allowed to talk?"

"Good question." He stopped, pushing her long hair back behind her shoulders. So much for her attempt to hide her cleavage. "Normally a sub would ask permission before speaking. But I want you to ask questions, so…" He ran a finger over the top of her breasts. "For tonight, you have permission to speak freely, unless I give you an order or until I take away that permission. Is that clear enough?"

"Yes, Sir."

His approving smile had the butterflies in her stomach doing loop-de-loops. "As to your first question, I try to do the rounds every hour or so," he said. "I like to keep an eye on the crowd, the activities. I don't believe you've seen the entire club yet, have you?"

"No." Jessica's gaze winced away from a man strapped to a bondage chair. A woman in a metallic blue bustier and leggings was tying ropes around the man's balls. Sweat poured down the man's face and chest.

They'd reached the double doors on the back wall. The area she'd avoided last time. Sir led her down a wide hallway where long glass windows alternated with doors on each side.

Z stopped her at the first window. "This is the office."

She wrinkled her nose in perplexity. Why would he have his office here? And why were people crowded around the window to the room? She edged forward to peek around a man's shoulder. *Oh.*

The room had a desk, rolling leather chair, books on shelves, thick dark red carpeting. Nice office. A man sat behind the desk writing while his secretary—a woman with her hair in a bun, and wearing a tight skirt and white blouse—was on her knees, sucking his cock.

Jessica licked her lips, then whispered to Sir, "Guess it's not your office, huh."

He grinned, a white flash of teeth, then led her farther down the hall.

The next room appeared familiar, and Jessica jerked to a stop. "That's a—"

"A gynecologist's table, yes. This is the medical room."

A man, bare from the waist down, was being assisted onto the exam table by another man in a doctor's white coat. Jessica shivered, remembering the feel of a doctor's hands down there in that private place. *How could that man do that, knowing everyone could watch from the window?*

Even worse, the next room had the window glass slid open. People leaned over the windowsill, watching avidly as a man dripped hot wax onto a woman strapped to a table.

Horrified, Jessica wrenched away from Sir, backed away. Torture. That was torture, plain and simple.

Master Z held his hands out to her, gaze steady. "Jessica."

After a moment, she put her cuffed and chilled hands into his warm ones. He smiled faintly, pulled her into his arms, and held her firmly against his chest like a child.

"The lifestyle runs from a little bondage all the way to severe pain. I avoid subs who need pain like that, for I do not have a liking to dispense it. Can you trust me to know how much or how little pain you would find enjoyable?"

"No pain is enjoyable." She buried her head in his shoulder. "That's just wrong."

"And after your bottom was paddled, how did it feel?" he whispered, running his hand over her bare ass, reminding her of how the pain had mingled with excitement, making her hotter.

She couldn't answer.

He didn't make her, though his gaze was too knowing. He knew how it had made her feel. *Damn him and that mind-reading stuff.*

The next room, darkly medieval with chains dangling from a rock wall, contained only three people. A naked blonde lay face up on a roughly hewn bench, her arms and legs shackled to the floor. A woman slapped the blonde's legs with a flogger while a man sucked on her breasts. Giving thin screams, the restrained woman arched her back, pushing her breasts up.

"The dungeon," Master Z said. "It becomes more popular as the evening goes on, as does the playroom."

The last room was huge. One round high bed, at least three times the size of a king, took up almost the entire room. Five people were in there, twisting and turning in various positions, all entangled together. One woman on her knees sucked on a cock while a man pounded into her from behind. Two men...

Jessica's mouth dropped open as disbelief ran through her, then a thrill of excitement. "How...unusual," she said, her voice husky.

Standing behind her, Sir put his arms around her, one hand cupping her left breast. He kissed her neck, murmured, "Your heart just sped up. Something interest you here?"

"No. Uh-uh." She tried to take a step away from the window, but he didn't move. Holding her with an unyielding arm around her waist, his other hand slipped between her legs and under her thong to the growing wetness there. He stroked her clit with his slickened fingers, over and over, until she squirmed uncontrollably.

"I grow tired of your prevarications, pet." His voice had turned firm. "Answer me."

She tried to close her legs, but his hand was there, spreading her pubic lips open. One finger slid into her, and she jerked as warmth shot through her body. He wouldn't make her—

"I-I... Okay. It... I've never seen that."

"There's more," he growled, obviously dissatisfied with her answer. The finger pushed deeper inside her.

"Sir." She sucked in a breath and gave up. "It's exciting."

"What part did you find exciting?"

"The woman with two men," she whispered, her face flaming hot.

"Anything else?"

Her hips tilted into his hand as he kept up the slow stroking. "People watching."

"Thank you for being honest, kitten." He squeezed her in a brief hug. "I know this is hard to talk about for you. Although we've moved past the days when only the missionary position was acceptable, society still insists sex should be only one man and one woman in private. It's hard to get past that mind-set, especially for someone as conservative as you."

The matter-of-fact logic was steadying, his understanding of her personality even more so. Just then, the man in the room behind the woman shouted his release, and the woman came, her hips jerking frantically.

And Jessica could feel moisture trickle down her thigh.

"Mmm-hmm, I think you're getting past your inhibitions nicely," he said, amusement in his voice. He kissed her neck then released her, leaving her throbbing.

Chapter Nine

They went back to finish their drinks; then Sir ignored her protests and took her out onto the dance floor. The music was slow and romantic. She could do this, especially with Sir holding her warmly against him. He danced like everything else he did, competently with a firm lead.

"How did you get so good at everything?" she murmured, enjoying the soft music, the slow glide of his hand up and down her back. He'd unhooked her wrists, and she savored the feel of his hard shoulder muscles under her fingers.

"You haven't seen me anywhere but here, pet. Your opinion might be a little overstated."

Somehow she doubted that.

"What do you do when you're not here?" He seemed too straightforward to be a lawyer or businessman. Maybe—

"I'm a psychologist."

She jerked back, stared at him. "You?"

He burst out laughing. "That amount of amazement isn't exactly flattering."

"But—" Well, heck, no wonder he read her like a book. "Then you don't actually read minds?"

He pulled her back, nuzzling the hairs at her temple. "Within a short distance, I can actually read minds. Emotions, rather, and limited to what the person feels at that moment." His hands curled under her butt, pressing her against his cock, keeping her half-aroused with his attentions. "Since I work with young children, being able to know what they're feeling is essential."

Sir. Working with children. And she could actually see it; she'd never met anyone more comforting, more able to make a person feel safe.

Still... "I'd have figured some sort of sex therapy, considering...this." She waved her hand at the room.

"Counseling children is my gift to the world." He grinned, rubbed her against his erection until her legs felt weak. "*This* is what the world gives me."

Her body moved into aching need at the feel of him against her mound, the feel of his hands cupping her butt. How did he do this to her?

"Um—" She'd forgotten the question she'd been about to ask.

"And you, Jessica? What do you do for a living?"

Question. He'd asked her a question. "I'm an accountant."

His soft laugh ruffled her hair. "I should have known. You would be a perfect accountant."

"What does that mean?" she asked. Her hands came down from around his neck. She pushed him away enough to frown into his face and move his tormenting hands away from her butt.

He grasped her wrists and put her hands back around his neck. "Leave your hands there, pet," he ordered. And then he put his hands back, only this time he slid his hands under her skirt so he was touching her bottom.

Her feet stopped.

"If you're not dancing, my fingers can do this," he whispered, moving one hand to her front, sliding between her legs, under her G-string. She jolted as his fingers explored her folds. "Dance or enjoy?"

She set her forehead against his chest, shivered as his fingers brushed over her clit. "Dance, please."

When his chuckle rumbled through his chest, she shivered again.

After returning his hand to her butt, he resumed dancing. "As for being an accountant, you're extremely smart, logical, conservative, controlled. You like organization and facts. And, at least when it comes to man/woman relationships, you are more comfortable with numbers."

He didn't even bother to ask her if he was right. He knew he was. "Pretty boring," she muttered.

"Ah, but under all that control is a wealth of passion and a very soft heart," he whispered into her ear. "Not boring at all."

Okay... That was okay then. Satisfied, she snuggled closer into his arms.

She was just full of surprises, Zachary thought, enjoying the feel of her ass in his hands. He wouldn't have dreamed she'd have an exhibitionistic bone in her body, let alone an interest in ménage. He'd enjoy exploring those pursuits with her further.

An accountant. He smiled into her hair, no longer vanilla scented but lightly floral. No heavy perfumes for Jessica. A thought came to him, and he asked, "Do you own anything besides suits?"

She gave him a disgruntled look. "I have a couple of dresses."

He raised an eyebrow.

"Fine. Office attire. But I have jeans too."

"Now that I'd like to see." That curvy ass would look fine in tight jeans. It certainly looked fine in the negligee. The V of the skirt offered flashes of her butt, something he doubted she realized.

The music ended, and the next song started, a fast one for the younger members. Tucking an arm around her, he noticed again how nicely she fit against him.

Maybe she should have a sample of one of her new interests. "It's a nice night out; let me show you the side yard."

* * *

The grass was cool against her bare feet, the warm tropical air scented with night-blooming jasmine. Sir led her away from the door, weaving through tall bushes. Soft lights illuminated the fountains scattered here and there, leaving pools of darkness. The landscaping formed small, secluded areas where Jessica caught glimpses of bare skin in one, heard a low moan from another.

She bit her lip and glanced at Sir. This was just a tour, wasn't it? She'd been anticipating a visit to that little bedroom again; surely they'd be going back there, wouldn't they?

"Ah," Sir said in a low voice. "I think you'll like this spot." He turned into a small area, not as secluded as some, she noticed uneasily. A tiny fountain on one side gurgled like a rocky stream, glimmering with a golden light. On the other side was a long, cushioned bench... No, she realized, a swing, hanging from the huge live oak behind it.

Master Z sat down on the swing. "I'd like you on my lap, pet." And he grasped her around the waist and lifted. "Bend your knees," he said and placed her on her knees, straddling his legs.

"Relax," he murmured, waiting until she lowered her bottom onto his thighs. Smiling, he set the swing in motion then pulled her forward into a kiss.

His mouth slanted over hers, his lips firm and demanding, and she felt herself start down that slide into arousal. When his hand cupped the back of her head, holding her in place for his kiss, her insides melted like hot butter. God, he could kiss.

She would have been happy kissing forever, but she felt his hand behind her neck. Her halter top dropped away, exposing her breasts.

"Hey!" She grabbed the fabric to hold against her. "There are people out here," she whispered frantically. "Don't do that."

He sighed audibly. "Little sub, give me your wrist." He held out one hand.

"Sir." It sounded like a whine even to her. She closed her mouth against further protest and set her hand in his.

Without even looking, he snapped her wrist cuff to the wire of the swing behind his left shoulder, then did the same with her other wrist on his right. She pulled back, started to move her legs.

"No, kitten. If you move your legs, I'll strap them down."

She froze.

"Very nice. Just where I want you," he murmured, cupping her breasts in his warm hands, his thumbs rubbing her nipples.

She could feel the growing dampness between her legs. With gentle hands, he lifted her slightly higher and took one nipple in his mouth. Her fingers curled around the back of the swing as he sucked. Sensation jolted through her. She tried to listen for people coming, but his mouth was so insistent, and when his teeth closed gently on the tip, she sucked in a breath at the exquisite pain-pleasure. Her pussy had started throbbing, and she barely refrained from rubbing herself on his leg.

He lifted his head, his eyes dark in the shadows. Watching her face, he reached under her skirt to stroke between her legs. "Lift your hips up," he told her, his hand pressing upward against her mound, the pressure electrifying.

As she raised herself slightly, he tugged her G-string off one hip and moved the crotch to one side. She almost moaned when he slid his finger through her wetness and started playing with her clit. His fingers were firm, then soft, sliding up and down, and everything in her focused on that spot. And then he took a nipple into his mouth, sucking urgently, his tongue rubbing the nub against the roof of his mouth. She jerked as too many sensations flooded through her, as everything in her tightened, waiting, nearing—

When he moved his fingers, she whimpered at the loss, at the unfilled need searing through her.

"Shhh, kitten." He covered himself with a condom from his pocket. Grasping her hips, his powerful hands lifted her higher until she was balanced on her knees. He slid his hard, thick cock into her and yanked her down until he was buried inside her, filling her to bursting. Her cry shocked her and brought her back to sanity. God, there were people around.

"What if someone comes past?" she hissed, freezing, resisting his hands on her hips. People seeing them... The thought was horrifying and oddly exciting.

He leaned his head back on the swing, the set of his jaw stern. "Listen closely, pet. If you cooperate nicely, then they'll just see you sitting here. If you continue to ignore me, they'll see you naked on your back on the lawn, with your legs on my shoulders and me inside you."

The image made her shiver in embarrassment, yet sent another roll of heat through her, and he could tell.

His grin flashed. "Kitten, you never fail to surprise me," he murmured, laughter in his voice. He started to reach back for the cuffs. *He wouldn't, would he?*

She jerked upward on his cock, the feeling of his sliding within her so erotic, she moaned before whispering, "I'm sorry. Stay on the swing. Please, Sir."

He chuckled, putting his hands back on her hips. He lifted her—and this time she didn't resist—upward until his cock was almost out and then slammed her back down on him, his shaft thick within her, her pussy clenching at the sensation. Up and down, his hands hard on her hips, the pace unrelenting. Her world narrowed to the overwhelming pleasure of him moving inside her as each merciless thrust sent her closer to the edge.

Somewhere she could hear voices, knew they could hear the slap of flesh, the creak of the swing, and she shuddered. His hands tightened on her hips, not letting her slow. Moaning, she closed her fingers around the back of the swing.

And then he leaned her forward and took her nipple in his hot mouth, sucking hard. Angled forward, her next downward movement slid her sensitive, engorged clit across his hard pelvis, and with a set of screams, she broke under the waves of pleasure, bucking against him uncontrollably. Her pussy rippled and contracted around his hard length, setting off his own orgasm, and his hands dug into her hips as he ground himself against her.

Her head bowed as her body went limp. He balanced her with one hand. "Hold on, little one, while I release you."

A second later, unrestrained, she sank forward onto his chest, trembling with aftershocks. Every time the swing rocked, his cock moved inside her, and her insides convulsed again. He kissed her hair, holding her in the way she was coming to love, with his arms firm and tight around her.

"Let me up for a moment, kitten," he said eventually. After disposing of the condom in a concealed receptacle, he resettled her on his lap with her legs together on one side. The swing moved gently; they simply rocked for a while. The fountain gurgled. Footsteps and murmurs came from people walking past their secluded nook.

The air was soft on her bare shoulders, his hand warm as he stroked her breasts. Breasts—she stiffened. Her halter was still loose. Her fingers closed on the material, and then she hesitated, glancing up at him. His lips quirked, and his hand didn't move from her breast. Dammit.

"Compared to what someone saw a few minutes ago, this is nothing."

Those people—Oh God. "Why didn't you stop?" She glared at him.

He tilted her chin up. "Because you heard them too, and it only added to your climax."

With a moan, she hid her face in his shoulder. "What is wrong with me?"

"Absolutely nothing." He let her snuggle back against him. "Each person is different when it comes to exhibitionism. And you knew they'd only get a quick glimpse of what we were doing."

"What about you?" she asked after a minute.

He stroked her hair. "Oddly enough, I don't care one way or another. But a Dom's responsibilities include exploring your needs, both the desires you know about and those you haven't experienced. I think, someday, you might well enjoy being on display—"

She started to protest then remembered the naked woman on the St. Andrew's cross, up there for everyone to see, and felt the slow slide of heat through her.

Sir chuckled. "And I'd enjoy seeing you there."

That thought made her burrow closer. She listened to his heartbeat for a while, slow, even, calming. Had she ever had a man that just liked to hold her? Had she ever been content with just being held? The stillness between them was so comfortable…

Okay, one question from last week was answered. This was more than just BDSM stuff; she wanted Sir himself. She wanted his hands, callused and hard, on her body. She wanted more of his intense eyes, his deep voice, his attention.

Oh, she was in trouble now.

Chapter Ten

Under Sir's amused gaze, Jessica re-tied her halter. Then they wandered back out into the main room, making a slow circle of the bar. Sir knew everyone there, and Jessica couldn't help noticing all the longing looks he got from the women in negligees. *The subs.* Not that he seemed to notice. He kept her close, one hand always on her. Each touch moved to new areas, until her skin grew so sensitive that even the brush of his slacks against her thigh made her shiver.

"Z, I heard you'd requested a bottom for tonight." A tall man in black leather pants and vest leaned against the back of a couch, a darkly beautiful brunette curled at his feet. Jessica remembered seeing the man on the dance floor last week, kissing a different sub. He continued, "Vance is clearing the medical room for your scene."

"Ah. Would you believe I had totally forgotten about the lesson? Thank you for reminding me, Daniel." Sir glanced down. "Jessica, this is Master D. He occasionally works as a dungeon monitor here."

Was this the Daniel who had lost his wife, and who liked soft women? She realized he was gazing at her with overt appreciation. She flushed, knowing her lips were swollen from Z's mouth, and the nightie didn't hide nearly enough of her.

"I'll be happy to watch over Jessica while you're busy, Z," Master D offered with a wicked grin.

She felt Sir's arm around her turn to iron, and his voice was icy, but quiet. "Thank you, Daniel. I don't believe I'll try your resistance in such a way."

Master D blinked, and his eyebrows rose. "Well now... I see."

"Z, my dear." Leading a collared blonde sub on a leash, a pretty woman in a red vinyl catsuit walked up to them. "We're looking forward to your scene. Did you want to use my slave or—" Her gaze ran over Jessica, and she smiled slowly. "That's a pretty morsel you have there. Will you be using her instead?"

Jessica glanced up at Sir, her stomach twisting. He wanted another woman for...for what?

"Thank you for the offer, Melissa. Give me a moment." Sir grasped Jessica's shoulders, turned her to face him. His smile had disappeared. "Little one. Last week, I promised to give a short training scene. I'll be using a sub, but... I don't think you are ready for this, kitten."

She saw the woman's slave staring at Sir with open lust, all but drooling. Jessica's hands tightened into fists. Z was *her* Dom, dammit, at least for now. And he wanted her to let him use someone else. *Put his mouth and*—"I'll be your sub."

"Jessica, you don't realize what this would entail."

Butterflies swarmed into her stomach, making her voice quiver. "It would be in public? In that medical room?"

"In that room. In public. Yes."

"Doing what?" she managed to ask. Maybe she could keep her clothes on.

"That would be up to me, pet." He stroked a finger down her cheek. "Pleasure only, no pain. But the decision is yours."

Could she stand seeing him with someone else? No. "I'll do it. Use m-me." Jessica choked a little on the last word. *Was she insane?*

"Well." He tilted her chin up, studied her face until she had to tuck her lip between her teeth to hide the trembling. "You are still very new to this. Are you certain?"

She gave a jerk of her head. *Yes.*

Zachary frowned as Jessica's feelings washed over him. Her fear was mixed with a possessiveness that pleased him immensely. And he saw that taking another sub at this point would damage her growing trust in him. But the lesson he'd promised James wouldn't be easy for her, although she was perfect for the role.

Her eyes narrowed as he considered, and he could feel her determination. Stubborn little minx. How did she get him into these situations? He sighed.

"So be it." He set an arm around Jessica's waist. "Daniel, Melissa, thank you for your offers."

Daniel grinned. "Your sub seems mighty feisty."

Melissa snorted. "That won't last long." She tugged at the blonde's leash and headed toward the back, saying, "Come, slave, I think we'll watch this."

Z pulled Jessica closer and followed. He could feel the way her legs wobbled and shook his head. He'd probably have to carry her out of the room afterward.

The hallway had filled with people. As Jessica entered the medical room, she realized the windows had been slid open so the audience could hear. They'd be listening to Sir. To her. Oh, God.

She pressed her lips together and straightened her spine. Be brave, she told herself, putting a hand on the exam table for balance. Besides the table, the room held a small sink with a cupboard above it, a metal tray table, a rolling stool, even an upright lamp. Very much like her doctor's office. And, hey, she'd survived pelvic exams before. Breast exams, vaginal exam, speculums—she could handle this.

Sir took a white lab coat from a hook on the wall and shrugged it on, transforming himself into a doctor. Looking oddly correct in the part.

A locked drawer in the cupboard yielded three packaged objects. He set them on the tray table. A speculum maybe? But what were the other two?

Touching her cheek lightly with his fingers, he gave her a warm look, then said, "Undress, please, and climb up on the table."

She glanced at all the people, her heart quailing as she realized everyone was staring at her.

Sir tilted his head at her, his eyes level. Waiting.

She'd told him she could do this; she'd insisted, and so she would.

Her fingers trembling, she undid the halter ties, sucking in a breath as her breasts were exposed. She heard whispers from the people outside the room, and her jaw tightened. She knew what they must be saying. Naked was bad enough; being fat and ugly made it all worse. Her nightie dropped to the floor.

"Stop."

Her hands froze in the process of pushing the thong down.

She realized Sir was right in front of her. He cradled her face in his hands, looking deep in her eyes. "Jessica," he murmured in a low voice the audience couldn't hear, "you are a lovely woman with a gorgeous body. Although there may be some fools who want skinny women, I don't. There are many others here who share my preference and adore your type of body."

He'd said that before, but now, with all these people, he must be ashamed of her. "Are you sure?" she whispered.

Shaking his head in obvious exasperation, he pressed her hand against him, against a rock-hard erection. "This is what seeing you naked does to me."

He liked her body. The glow of that kept her buoyed up as she removed the thong, as she climbed up onto the table. The leather was cold against her bare skin. She glanced at the people crowding the windows and then couldn't pull her gaze away.

With a huffed laugh, Master Z stepped directly in front of her, blocking her view. "Look at me—only at me," he ordered. Her eyes met his, his so very dark and gray, crinkling at her, and she felt better. A little better.

"That's right. In fact, I think we'll blot those people out altogether," he murmured. "Close your eyes."

She hesitated.

He growled, "Jessica."

She swallowed and complied. He put something soft over her eyes, tying it in back—a blindfold—and held her hands firmly when she instinctively reached up to tear it off. After a minute, she regained her control and put her hands in her lap.

"Lie down, little one," he said, moving to a position beside her. One arm behind her back and a hand between her breasts, he pressed her flat onto the table. Her legs dangled off the end. "Are you comfortable?"

No, she wasn't; oh, she really wasn't. She managed a nod.

Silence.

Moistening her lips, she whispered, "Yes, Sir."

He chuckled. "Let me rephrase that so you can be honest. Aside from being terrified and embarrassed, are you comfortable?"

The room was warm enough, the table cushioned. "Yes, Sir."

He took one of her hands, kissed the knuckles. "Very good, kitten. I'm proud of you and how brave you're being. I know this isn't easy." The enjoyment of his praise lasted only seconds, until he said, "Now, being a good doctor, I'm going to make sure you don't move."

Expecting him to put her feet into the stirrups, she was shocked when a strap was cinched across her body, just below her breasts, pinning her arms to her sides. Heart pounding, she yanked at the restraints. She couldn't move. "Sir!"

"Shhh, little one." His hands came down on her shoulders. "Nothing here will hurt you. What is your safe word?"

She could feel little quivers running up and down her whole body as her breath came fast and shallow. He waited, his hands resting on her shoulders, the warmth, his presence so reassuring. He wouldn't hurt her. She was all right, and she was stronger than this. She couldn't back down now and disappoint him. She managed a deeper breath. "Red. It's red."

"Do you trust me?"

She gave a little nod.

His hand cupped her cheek. "Brave kitten."

"This lesson covers one way to introduce a novice to public scening," he said, his voice louder, like an instructor. "In Jessica's case, she is very new, and I'm proud to be awarded her trust. Trust or not, with a new sub, shyness can be difficult to overcome. One type of inhibition is the focus of tonight's lesson.

"We, of course, begin with a breast exam." His fingers lifted her breasts, stroking in circles, massaging. "Healthy breasts, as you can see."

Okay, she was good. She'd been expecting something like this.

His fingers found her nipples, stroked them to hard points, pinching hard enough to make her squirm, never quite hard enough to hurt.

"And sensitive also."

Each pinch woke more nerve endings in her breasts, in her core. She couldn't see him, couldn't see where his hands were, and her skin grew acutely sensitive as if anxious for the next touch of his fingers.

His hands ran down her torso, stroked her stomach. She heard him move from her side toward the end of the table, then the squeak of the rolling stool. She knew what was coming next. Her legs closed involuntarily before she forced herself to relax. A ripple of laughter came from the spectators.

"Because our little sub here is a novice, for her comfort, I will ask for quiet during the demonstration."

The noise of people dropped to whispers. Firm, warm fingers closed around her right ankle, and he ordered, "Give me your foot, Jessica. Now."

She heaved in a breath, let him lift one leg and place her right foot into a stirrup. She gritted her teeth when a strap closed around her ankle, pinning her foot to the cold metal. Dammit, her doctor never used straps—restraints made it way more nerve-racking.

He grasped her left foot. Drawing her legs apart, he set it in the other stirrup. The air felt shockingly cool against her heated tissues. Another strap over her foot. She was restrained—arms, feet. *Blind.*

Her hands closed into fists as she tried not to panic.

And he waited, one warm hand running up and down her calf. "With new subs, the experience of being in a scene can be overwhelming. The embarrassment, even the fear, can keep them from moving into arousal or achieving release. As a result, often the regular amount of stimulation will not achieve its purpose for first-timers."

Her muscles loosened as she listened to his warm, deep voice.

Then he grasped her hips, slid her toward the end of the table. "Positioning is very important with the exam table," he said. "The patient's ass must be well over the edge." He let go.

"And with what I'll be doing, allowing too much movement wouldn't be good." Something was fastened across her lower abdomen. A strap, holding her firmly in that place.

He pushed the stirrups sideways, widening her legs until she was gaping open. *Oh, God.* She could do this. She must. Her legs were shaking uncontrollably.

Something scraped across the floor. A click. She could feel the heat of a lamp between her legs—on her private areas—and she gritted her teeth.

She heard someone move, heard Sir's voice next to her. His fingers stroked down her face, and his lips brushed over hers gently. "Easy, little one, no one will hurt you. Are you in pain?"

She managed to say, "No, Sir."

Then he said, "Start very slowly, softly," and she didn't understand what he meant until hands settled on her breasts. Not Sir's hands.

She arched in the air, shaking her head. "No."

"Jessica." Sir's voice was quiet, but firm. Implacable. "You do not have permission to speak. Can you be silent?"

Gags—she'd seen pictures on the Internet. His voice said he would do that; he didn't lie. She gave a jerky nod.

"Excellent." His steps sounded, moving toward the end of the table. "Continue, please."

The stranger's hands moved, softly stroking breasts already sensitive from Sir's attentions earlier. She tried not to pay attention, to ignore them, but the fingers were callused and excitingly rough against her tender skin. She could feel her nipples tightening in betrayal.

"Very nice," Sir murmured. "And down here, we'll start here with a surface examination. Pretty pink lips." A finger stroked down through her folds, making her jerk in shock. He touched her lower, against her rectum, and she tried to not cringe away. "Healthy little ass, never been used."

His fingers touched her core.

"Good lubrication, nice and slick," Sir announced, then gently pulled her outer lips apart, exposing her more fully. She tried to pretend it was just a regular exam. She'd had them before.

"For those who haven't had their anatomy lessons," Sir said, "this is a pretty pussy. The vagina extends upward from here." A finger stroked her folds, and then slid into her, and she gasped as heat shot through her. She couldn't be getting turned on in front of these people; she couldn't.

He removed his finger, slid back up through her folds. "And this is the clitoris, or clit, extremely sensitive. It must be kept slick with juices."

His finger swirled inside her, making her hips wiggle and then up, up onto her clit, sliding over and around until need tightened inside her.

"Nipples," he murmured, leaving her confused until the stranger's fingers circled her tight nipples, fingering each little pebble, pulling gently until her back was arching.

Sir's fingers were suddenly gone, leaving her empty and needy. "Now, let's go over some methods to overwhelm resistant subs." The sound of a package being ripped open. "I have a fondness for this little toy. Three speeds. Again, sufficient lubrication is mandatory."

A squirting sound then fingers at her asshole. She shook her head wildly, trying not to yell in horror as something was pushed up and into her rectum. Something slick and hard and foreign.

This was no doctor's exam. She strained against the restraints, hands and feet. Nothing gave.

"Are you hurting, Jessica?" Sir asked, stroking her leg. Waiting for her answer.

At his calm voice, she stopped pulling at the straps, tried to think. The thing pushed up in her felt strange. Wrong. Horrible. But there was no pain. "No, Sir," she whispered.

"Honest little one," Sir murmured. She felt his fingers between her buttocks, and the thing moved within her. "I'll set this to slow."

Vibrations started in her ass, the sensation startling. Gritting her teeth, she tried to rub her bottom against the table to dislodge it, to make it stop, only her butt was too far out over the edge, and the stomach strap kept her in place.

"Then we have this little toy," Z said. Another paper-ripping sound. "Personally, I prefer quiet in the center with vibrations front and back. So rather than a vibrating dildo, I often use this. Also on slow."

Something touched her clit, settling so gently onto her that she didn't react at first. Then a tiny hum sounded, and the thing was vibrating right on top of the sensitive tissues his fingers had already aroused. Her hips jerked upward as every nerve in her body jolted into awareness. She moaned.

"Excellent." Z chuckled. The vibrations on her clit somehow made the ones in her ass even more arousing. Between the sensations, she felt his finger stroke around her pussy, teasing her until her inner leg muscles spasmed. "Mouth, please."

Suddenly a hot mouth closed on one breast, sucking her nipple up, tonguing it firmly. She arched with a cry that rang through the room.

"Finally, for the coup d'état, you see the everyday dildo. This one is soft latex with gentle ribbing."

She felt just the touch of teeth on her nipples, the vibrations in her, on her clit. Her core tightened. She was shaking, coiled tightly, hurting, needing just that little more to send her over—only she didn't want that. Orgasming here, in this room? She didn't want to lose control in front of these people. *No, no, no.*

Panting, she started going through the multiplication tables in her mind. *Eleven times eleven is one hundred twenty-one. Concentrate, dammit.* She felt the horrible urge to climax recede.

Sir chuckled, murmured, "Well, there's a stubborn sub."

To her surprise, the vibrations stopped on her clit, stopped in her rectum. The mouth left her aching nipples, leaving them wet, the air cool.

Sir was silent; only his hand running up and down her calf let her know he was there.

Was she done? Was it over? Her head spinning, she sighed in relief, then started to worry. Sir had obviously wanted more than just a medical exam-type scene; he'd wanted her to have an orgasm. Here, in front of all these people. And now he'd be disappointed in her. The thought hurt, but she just couldn't—

Then the vibrations started up again, now hard and fast on her clit, in her ass. A hot, wet mouth closed on one nipple while fingers pinched the other. Gasping, she went rigid, shot back into shocking arousal.

And then something hard and thick slid into her vagina, engorging her as it was thrust in and out, pushing her tissues harder against the vibrations on each side. Her hips jerked uncontrollably as it slid in and out, and suddenly every sensation combined all over her body. She couldn't stop it. Bright lights exploded behind her eyes as massive spasms enveloped her. She screamed, screamed again and again, her body jerking as her vagina contracted and billowed around the hard intrusion in her body.

Everything seemed to go dark, still for a moment. Then she realized people were cheering, applauding. She gasped and jerked as the dildo was removed, leaving her empty. The vibrators had stopped; gentle hands removed them from her sensitive clit and asshole. She lay limply on the table, her heart hammering. Hands gently stroked her breasts. She could feel Sir's rough cheek against her tender inner thigh, then his lips.

"As you can see," Sir said, "the vibrators are an excellent tool for novice play; the combination of the three will compel an orgasm that a shy person would inhibit otherwise.

"And"—his fingers began to stroke her down below, one finger sliding between her swollen folds—"once that barrier is broken, the next climax is easier to induce."

The finger, two fingers, set up a hard stroking into her pussy, curling up and hitting a spot where she suddenly felt need flowing over her, her hips jerking in time.

"A woman can easily come again if you find the G-spot. And, of course, in this position, her clit is nicely available."

As the fingers inside set up an urgency, a coiling she couldn't evade, Master Z's mouth settled on her clit. His tongue ran over her; his lips closed around her as he sucked her clit into his mouth. She bucked uncontrollably against his mouth, yanking on the restraints with a high scream as he forced her into a long, hard orgasm.

He stroked her inside and out until her muscles were too weak to spasm further before withdrawing his fingers. The stool squeaked as he rose. "And that brings this lesson to a close. Come and talk with me later tonight if you have questions."

The sound of the whispers diminished until the area was quiet, and Jessica could hear her own gasping breaths.

"Easy, kitten, it's over. You'll be free in a moment."

Heart pounding, trembling all over, Jessica couldn't seem to move as Sir unfastened the straps on her feet and arms. When he pulled the blindfold off, she blinked in the light and focused on Cullen's face. *Cullen?*

"You, sweet sub, have lovely breasts," he rumbled, planting a hard kiss on her lips, and then walked out of the room.

Her shaking increased as Master Z helped her to sit up. Without speaking, he wrapped a thick, soft blanket around her, picked up her nightie, and carried her out into the noisy bar.

Chapter Eleven

Zachary found a fairly deserted corner and settled onto a couch with his shaken little sub in his lap. Club members walked past, occasionally nodding with a smile, none speaking. James gave him a grin and a thumbs-up.

Jessica still hadn't spoken when he leaned back with her huddled against his chest.

"You were wonderful," Zachary murmured, holding her firmly in his arms, letting her return to the world in her own time. "I'm very proud of you, little one."

She was shivering, a continuous trembling through her whole body, and he wrapped the blanket tightly around her, settling her more comfortably against him. He rested his cheek on top of her head, content to relax with her. For a Dom, the intense focus required for a scene, especially with someone so new, was exhausting but exhilarating at the same time.

For a sub... Forced past her inhibitions, Jessica had given freely of her responses, holding nothing back. Yet for someone with her personality—modest, controlled, reserved—to be so abandoned in front of strangers would be a shock to her very system.

If she needed to spend the rest of the night just being held, then so be it.

As her trembling slowed, she could hear a slow thudding in her ear, more real than the music playing elsewhere. The fragrance of citrusy soap mixed with a man's musky scent surrounded her, and she realized her cheek rested on skin and springy chest hair. There were arms around her.

She blinked, feeling snuggled and warm. Safe. A blanket covered her from toes to shoulders, hiding her from others. Her gaze lingered on the people walking past, people who glanced, but didn't speak.

She just lay for a time, unable to get her thoughts to gather quickly enough to want to move. She was in her *happy place*, her little nephew would have said.

Sir—and it was Sir, she recognized his scent and his arms—didn't seem to be in any hurry to leave. Eventually, she managed to pull in a deep breath and lift her head.

His hand stroked up and down her arm. "Welcome back, little one," he murmured, his voice sending a funny quivering through her. She could feel his lips touch her hair.

She pushed herself up a little, turned so she could watch him, feeling like she was seeing him for the first time. He was so...male, so in control. He had lines at the corners of his eyes; his beard-shadowed jaw was strong, his face lean and hard. Black eyebrows quirked up now as she touched his chin. When his lips curved up into that faint smile of his, she ran her finger across his lower lip, noting the velvety softness overlaying the firm. Very much like him, so smooth on the surface, but unyielding—demanding—underneath.

"I don't remember leaving that room." Her voice was hoarse, a little raw, and she frowned. "I don't remember a blanket."

He lifted his hand from her shoulder to caress her face. "When a sub experiences something so intense, it's not unusual for her to retreat inside, into her own head. We have blankets in all the rooms."

"Oh." Wow. But being held like this was wonderful. She let her mind drift back to what had happened, the helplessness, the sensations that had grown more and more overwhelming until she couldn't stop herself from coming. She remembered Cullen's hands, mouth on her. She shivered.

People watching.

She stiffened a little. "You told them how to handle a novice... How did you know I'd let you...?"

"I didn't, pet." He brushed her hair back from her face. "Both Daniel's and Melissa's subs are new to public scening."

"Oh."

Lowering her head, she whispered into his shoulder, "I was so embarrassed."

"I know." His hand cradled the back of her head; his steady heartbeat under her ear was comforting. "I could tell. You were also excited by it."

She stiffened. Surely not. All those eyes, staring at her, at her naked breasts, her... A shiver ran through her. *Damn him for knowing.* "A little, maybe."

"Mmmhmm."

"You let...let someone else touch me." The shock of that still reverberated through her.

"I did. Why do you suppose I would allow that?"

What was this, a test? But she was too comfortable, too exhausted for outrage. Why did he? "To give me more... stimulation?"

"Good." He kissed the top of her head. "That was one reason. But I might not have taken that method with a different sub. Why you?"

He had done that just for her? But... She froze as the answer came to her. "Because of the way I reacted at the playroom. The two men."

"You were aroused at the idea then. And once you moved past being horrified, you were aroused by Cullen's hands on you."

Oh, God, she had been. "Doesn't that bother you? To share?"

He huffed a laugh. "I find I am more possessive with you than normal. But what kind of a master would I be if I know you want to experience something, and I don't make it happen?"

He'd done that for *her?* She felt his arms around her as she thought about it. How it had felt when Sir's hands had been on her and another man's mouth on her breasts. A disconcerting hint of arousal unfurled inside her. She'd liked having two men. Oh, she had. How many bewildering revelations about her was Sir going to uncover?

"Am I supposed to say thank you?" she grumbled.

"Eventually, I think you will," he said, a hint of laughter in his voice.

"Why Cullen?"

"You like him, pet. Having a true stranger touch you might have been too much to deal with afterward. At this point in time."

And the unstated promise of more curled her toes and wiped out any words she could think to say.

"I was pleased you felt brave enough to volunteer, kitten. And I'm very pleased with you. You trusted me enough to let go, to take care of you; that is the building block for everything." He kissed her so gently; she felt tears in her eyes. "It's unusual for circumstances to toss a person into this so quickly. You're a strong woman."

She huffed out a breath. "I don't feel very strong right now."

"No. And that's why we will simply sit here and watch the world go by for a time."

"We've already been here quite a while," she guessed, watching his eyes for confirmation. "Shouldn't you be out and checking on things?"

He bundled her back against his chest, his voice a rumble in her ear. "You, pet, are more important than things."

And he held her.

* * *

Eventually she sat up again. "I'm ready to move."

"And so you shall." He folded the blanket back from her shoulders.

Cool air brushed over her naked breasts, and she squeaked, covering herself. With a low laugh, he picked up her nightie and slid it over her head. After fastening her halter top behind her neck, he adjusted her breasts with sure hands, as if he had the right to touch her so easily.

"You're blushing again." He held a finger to her cheek, eyes narrowing. "After everything I did in the—"

She put her hand over his mouth, trying to silence him.

"My fingers were in more intimate places than your breasts," he whispered, ignoring her hand. The jerk. "As was my mouth, my lips, and my tongue."

The memory of the way she'd shattered the last time, under just his hands and mouth, sent warmth pooling back into her groin. "You are impossible."

His lips curved under her fingers. "And you were very loud."

Oh, God, she had been. She pressed her forehead into his shoulder, hiding her face. "How can I ever face anyone here again?" she moaned. "They saw—"

He took her shoulders, pressed a kiss to her cheek. "Kitten, many of the subs here have done a public scene."

"That doesn't help." Every private place on her body had been on display.

"Up we go," he said briskly, setting her on her feet. He tossed the blanket over the back of the couch. When she smoothed her too-short skirt down, she realized she wasn't wearing anything at all underneath it.

"I think you deserve a drink, don't you?" He tucked an arm around her as he strolled her to the bar. She really did love how he kept her so close to him, as if he was proud of her.

Cullen was there, and she froze, still a few feet from the bar. He'd *touched* her, sucked on her breasts. Sir's arm urged her forward, but her feet wouldn't move. She looked up at Sir, shook her head.

He sighed; his gaze met Cullen's. Cullen had been watching them. *Oh, God.*

Sir tilted his head toward her, and she tried to back away, but the grip that had been so gentle was now a steel band around her waist.

Cullen came around the bar. She stared at the floor, blinked when his big boots appeared in her field of vision. "Jessica."

She couldn't move. His laugh boomed out. A callused hand caught her chin, forced her gaze up. "Don't panic, love. Since you are Master Z's sub, I can only touch you with his permission, and I can see that won't be happening often at all. He only let me play because you needed the extra sensations to take you over the top."

And because Sir knew that she was turned on by the thought of two men. Surely Cullen wouldn't know that.

He grinned at her, a slash of white in a brawler's face. "I thoroughly enjoyed touching you, pet, but you don't need to run from me. Are we clear on that?"

She nodded, unsure why she'd been so frightened.

"If you'd permit, Z, I'd like a hug from your sub to know I'm forgiven and we're all right again." He stepped back.

Sir murmured, "Permitted," and his restraining arm dropped away.

Cullen held his arms out. Waited. His eyes had that look that Sir's got, the unspoken command.

Okay. She liked Cullen; he'd only been nice to her. And…*okay*. With a breath, she took the one step to him, felt his arms come around her, very different than Sir's, but comforting just the same. He was so tall; her head only came to the center of his chest. He squeezed her once, let her go.

"There." He tapped her cheek with a finger. "All better. Now, what can I get you to drink?"

Chapter Twelve

For the next few hours, Sir didn't try to take her into any of the scene rooms or do more than fondle her and take a kiss, as if he knew she wasn't ready for anything more intimate. Not at this time. They wandered through the crowd, joined people here and there to chat, and avoided the more intimately engaged couples.

They were just like a normal couple on a date, she thought, trying to ignore the way her body felt when close to his and the way his voice could heat the air around her.

"Got a nasty problem in the dungeon, Z." One of the monitors trotted up, his face flushed.

Master Z took two steps in that direction, then stopped and frowned at Jessica.

"Mmmh, not a good place for you." He led her to a nearby sitting area occupied by a trim woman of around forty and a plump blonde about Jessica's age. "Ladies, may I leave Jessica with you?" Sir asked.

"Of course, Master Z," the older woman answered. "We'd be happy to stay with her."

"I can go with you," Jessica whispered to him.

"Not the dungeon, not if there's trouble," he said, pushing her into a chair. To her surprise, he hooked her hands together, then to a long chain on the floor, before giving her a hard kiss on the mouth. He glanced at the women. "Thank you, ladies."

They barely had a chance to smile back at him before he strode away, moving deceptively fast.

Well. Jessica yanked at the chain that was long enough for her to stand and maybe take one step. "Dammit, what did I do wrong this time?"

"You're new, aren't you?" the brunette said.

Jessica nodded.

"My name's Lenora. You didn't do anything. The chain says you've got a Dom already, that you're not available."

"Oh." As relief washed through her, Jessica leaned back in the chair, curling her feet under her. "Thank you."

The blonde leaned forward, her nightgown longer than Jessica's, but the top much tighter and lower. "I've never seen Master Z chain anyone outside of a scene before. He must really like you."

Jessica laughed. "I should be complimented by being chained? I don't think I'll ever understand this place."

"It's pretty strange at first," Lenora said. "But this is the best place in the area to learn. Master Z keeps his eye on stuff."

It was one of the things she found so admirable about him. "So, maybe you can tell me—" She glanced up as a man in fancy red leathers walked up, smiling at her.

"Hello. I haven't seen you before."

His bearing proclaimed him a Dom, but he lacked that special something that Master Z and Cullen and Daniel had. He saw the chain attached to her wrist cuffs and scowled. "Already taken, huh?"

He turned toward the little blonde. "Maxie, come with me."

Maxie shook her head. "I don't want to be with you, Nathan, and I can't leave here, anyway."

His face darkened. "I don't take back talk from subs, especially not cunts like you." He reached down and grabbed her wrist.

Jessica jumped to her feet and realized with her arms chained, a punch wouldn't go very far. She kicked the guy instead, right in the butt.

He dropped Maxie's hand and whipped around. Majorly pissed.

As he advanced, Jessica backed up until the damned chain went taut. Balancing most of her weight on one leg, she got ready to kick with the other foot.

"Stop now." Daniel strode up and yanked Nathan's arm behind him, pushing until the guy went on tiptoe to keep his shoulder from being dislocated.

Nice job, Jessica thought; he made it look so easy.

"Time to call it a night, buddy," Daniel said, his voice easy, his face angry. "Someone will be in touch about your membership." He hauled the man away.

Heart thudding painfully, Jessica sank back into the chair.

Cullen appeared and knelt beside her chair. "You've got to stop beating up on the members, sweetie. For a sub, you've got a real aggression problem." His smile disappeared, leaving his face hard as he scrutinized her. "Are you hurt at all?"

"No. I'm fine." Jessica ran her hands up and down her arms, feeling chilled. She saw the blonde doing the same thing. "Are you all right?"

Maxie nodded. "I can't believe you did that." Her eyes puddled up, and she sniffled. "You could have been hurt. Nathan can be really mean."

Jessica smiled. "Bruises heal. Watching someone get hurt when I could do something to stop it… That doesn't heal so fast." Like the guilt left from her sister. Her mouth tightened.

Cullen rose to his feet. "Maxie, why don't you come and sit at the bar for a while; let me keep an eye on you."

Maxie's mouth formed an O as her eyes went wide. Then she shook her head. "I can't, Master C. We're keeping Jessica company for Master Z."

Cullen's smile was back. "Dedication to duty is a good thing. Come on over when you're free." His eyes glinted with humor. "If you want."

Considering Maxie was almost drooling, Jessica figured the bartender knew quite well how much the blonde wanted. He strode back to his bar, his long legs a fine sight in tight brown leathers.

Maxie sighed.

Giving a cautious look around for any more overaggressive men, Jessica leaned back in her chair. Here was her chance at getting some information from the women's side of the fence. "I don't think Master Z would have been upset if you'd gone to sit with Cullen."

Maxie's eyes widened. "Defy Master Z? Are you insane? You don't talk back to him, do you?" She added hastily, "Don't *ever* talk back to him." The blonde seemed more scared than when Nathan grabbed her.

What made Maxie look like that? "But, Sir told me he never… He only s-spanked—" The word was difficult to even say. "He doesn't whip or anything."

"Oh, I'd almost rather be whipped than—" Maxie's eyes turned to Lenora. "You tell her."

Lenora sipped her drink then pointed with her chin to a tall, muscular redhead in a two-piece negligee who was sitting next to a thin male Dom. "Adrienne there was giving her Dom a bad time. She was basically topping from the bottom, not doing what he said, and creating a ruckus during their scene. Master Z went over.

I don't know what was said, but I've heard she smarted off to him."

Lenora exchanged glances with Maxie, then continued. "His face... You know how he can look so deadly? Well, the Dom was pissed enough to tell Master Z to do whatever he wanted with her. Master Z picked Adrienne up like she was a doll, dumped her on her back on the end of the bar, and strapped her down with her legs V'ed up in the air. And he gagged her too, a good thing since she was swearing a blue streak."

Jessica tried to imagine being treated like that. On the bar? "How humiliating. I bet she never smarted off again."

Lenora shook her head. "Oh, it gets worse. He grabbed some vibrators and dildos, set them on the bar, and announced she was available to anyone wanting to practice getting a sub off. Anyone."

Jessica felt her own eyes going wide. "You mean...?"

Maxie nodded and almost whispered, "I think every Dom in the place took a turn. Adrienne came so many times that she could only moan for the last few."

Oh, God. Jessica wrapped her arms around herself. "He just left her there?" What kind of a monster was he?

"No, he wouldn't do that. Master Z's death on leaving a bound sub unattended." Lenora glanced at the bar. "He sat right there at the bar, sipping a drink and watching. He stopped a couple of the Doms when they got too rough. When he let her free, she couldn't even stand. But she sure apologized."

Maxie snorted. "She's been real polite ever since, you know?" Her grin faded. "But see, I don't want Master Z mad at me for anything. Uh-uh. I'm staying here like he asked."

Jessica couldn't keep her gaze from the bar. She noticed that the heavy wood ceiling rafters had chains dangling from them. God, she'd thought the medical room was bad.

"I think I'd die," she whispered with a shudder.

Lenora's gaze was on a group of three Doms sitting at a table, and it took a second before she responded. "Well, Adrienne likes the whip and cane. She was acting out partly to get herself whipped, and that was the problem. But Master Z found a punishment she'd do anything to avoid again. He's really scary that way."

"But he's sure something in bed." Maxie sighed, her eyes half-closing.

Jessica's head whipped around. He'd had sex with Maxie? A hard lump formed in her throat. "He's...uh, enjoyed a lot of the women here?" Her face heated when Lenora gave her a knowing look. She nodded.

"Oh, he's had a lot of us," Maxie said, then pouted. "But he never takes anyone for more than a night. Neither does Master D."

"And Master C doesn't go more than two nights, so don't get your heart set on him, dummy," Lenora said to Maxie in a dry voice.

"Oh, I won't," Maxie said and wiggled. "He's too intense for me long-term, but I'm wanting a little intensity tonight."

Trying to get the image of Sir and Maxie together out of her mind, Jessica looked toward the back of the room where someone was shouting. Two of the dungeon monitors were dragging a man toward the front. Face cold, Sir walked behind them.

Screaming curses, the guy kicked and struggled and suddenly broke free of the monitors. He charged at Sir.

Jessica gasped and jumped to her feet.

Sir knocked a punch to one side, and buried his fist in the guy's gut. The man folded like a jackknife, face purpling as he tried to get his breath. Shaking his head, Sir handed him back to the monitors, waved them off, and headed toward Jessica.

Considering the lethal expression on his face, she wasn't sure whether to run and hide or just whimper. She glanced at her cuffs.

Running wasn't going to work. She tucked herself back into the big chair.

But as he approached, the deadly stillness disappeared. His eyes warmed when she tried smiling at him. He set a hip on the arm of her chair and pulled her close. And, oh God, that was just where she wanted to be.

"Lenora, Maxie, thank you for watching out for Jessica," he said, his voice calm as if hadn't just punched a man. "I see you did a good job."

"Well, there was one little thing that happened," Maxie said, a quaver in her voice as she visibly steeled herself to tell Sir everything. Oh, hell. What if he decided Jessica had been out of line? Or decided to go after Nathan and beat the hell out of him?

Jessica shook her head frantically at Maxie then realized Sir's gaze was on her, and his gray eyes had chilled to silver. She froze.

His hand curled around her nape, holding her firmly in place. And damned if the feel of his hand on her, even the look in his eye, sent such potent need through her that she shivered.

"Continue, please, Maxie." Sir's voice was softer and much scarier.

"It's just… Well, Nathan came over, and he didn't bother Jessica, Sir; he saw she was chained, but he wanted me to go with him." She gazed at Sir with trepidation and whispered, "I said no."

"You have the right to say no to anyone here, pet. You know that."

Maxie's sigh of relief was audible and Sir's lips quirked. "He grabbed me anyway and called me a name, but Jessica kicked him."

The hand on the back of her neck tightened painfully before he loosened his fingers. Ruthless eyes pinned her in place. "Did he hurt you, kitten?"

"No. Daniel—I mean, Master D—hauled him away, and Cullen made sure we were okay. We're fine; we're all fine. Really."

His lips definitely curved, although the chill in his gaze was slow to fade. He let go of her neck and stroked his knuckles over her cheek. "I think later we'll discuss your need to shelter other women, Jessica."

Oh, hell, that wasn't a subject she really wanted to talk about. She frowned at him. Damn psychologist mind reader.

He tilted her chin up. "Did you just frown at me?"

She could hear Maxie's gasp and Lenora's hiss of concern.

"No. I didn't." She tried to smooth her face and ended up frowning at him anyway. "Really."

He laughed, deep and full, and the two women simply sat there and stared.

"You know, I think it's your fault that tonight has been so unsettled. I fully intended to have you pinned and squirming underneath me again, long before this, but Murphy's Law shattered that plan quite well."

Her mind played his words back twice before she realized what he meant. She felt herself turn red. And hot. And aroused at the image he'd set into her head: his body on hers, holding her down and—

"Z! Could you check this over?" One of the dungeon monitors who had been escorting the wild man beckoned.

Sir sighed. "Excuse me, ladies." He headed for the group huddled around the bar, but had to stop when a woman knelt in his path. A gorgeous blonde with a golden tan, slender and toned, with a perfect figure that the skimpy blue nightie didn't conceal at all. Sir spoke to her, said something, and the woman raised her face, gazing at him with a mixture of lust and appeal. No man could turn that down.

Jessica felt her heart thud into the ground at her feet.

Sir touched the woman on her head, stepped around her, and joined the men. Well, at least he hadn't taken her up on her offer right there. At least, being a gentleman—bondage and paddles notwithstanding—he probably wouldn't abandon Jessica for the woman tonight. Not tonight.

Her chest hurt, and she rubbed her sternum. She shouldn't be surprised. And she'd undoubtedly enjoy the rest of the evening. Wishing for more than this night from Sir was stupid.

She glanced at the other two women and saw sympathy on their faces. Damn. She turned back to watch Sir, enjoying the way all the men listened when he spoke. Nobody interrupted Master Z, did they?

He turned to take a paper the monitor handed him, and Jessica gasped. His black shirt was torn across his shoulder, the skin underneath covered in blood. Below that the shirt sagged wetly, though the red didn't show. "He's hurt."

And nobody was doing anything about it. Jessica pushed to her feet, tugged at the chain. "He's bleeding. Let me free."

Lenora's brows drew together. "We can't do that, you know."

Jessica growled. "You let me loose right now!"

Maxie's eyes went wide.

"You're an idiot," Lenora muttered as she released the chain, and Maxie unbuckled the ring keeping the cuffs together. Freed, Jessica ran for the bar, shoved her way through to the front, and slapped her hand on the top to get Cullen's attention.

He turned, gave her an astonished stare.

"Sir's hurt," she snapped. "Do you have a first-aid kit?"

He glanced at the end of the bar where Sir stood, then pulled a box off a shelf. "Go for it, sweetie."

Jessica grabbed the box and turned to fight her way out, only the people had moved aside, leaving a path between her and Master Z.

Intent on reading the paper, he didn't even notice her until she seized his arm and tore the ripped shirt from the wound.

"Jessica, what—"

"Don't move," she ordered. A slash, deep and nasty. Her head spun for a second. Blood so wasn't her thing. Then she set the first-aid kit on the bar, and ripped open a gauze packet. "You're bleeding, dammit."

He glanced down at his shoulder, shook his head. "Drugs and whips don't mix well."

"He whipped you?" Shock brought her eyes up to his.

"He tried. Considering he's still heaving his dinner out in the parking lot, I don't feel too badly about it. Serves me right for not being more observant." He touched her cheek with gentle fingers. "You were worried about me."

She dropped her gaze. Putting gauze on the cut, she applied pressure. "This probably needs stitches, Master Z." She risked a look up at him, realizing it was the first time she'd actually called him *Master* out loud.

His dark eyes burned, pinned her in place. He knew. He ran a finger across the top of her breasts and smiled when her nipples peaked. "Cullen," he said, without looking away from her.

"Master Z."

"I'm going to let my little sub finish her bandaging job upstairs."

Jessica's heart gave a hard thud.

"Please take charge of the club," Master Z finished, glancing at the bartender.

"Yes, sir." Cullen's grin flashed at Jessica.

Chapter Thirteen

Zachary tried to put his arm around his sub, but she took his hand and set it against the gauze covering his wound and ordered, "Hold that there."

He shook his head. From a submissive to a spitfire in five easy minutes. The contrast was startling. Compelling. Her concern spilled through him like warmth from the sun.

Until now, he hadn't realized he'd been cold.

Stunned into silence, he unlocked the private door and took her up to the third floor. Flipping on the lights, he waved her in, and got his first-aid box from the closet.

In his kitchen of granite counters and stainless steel appliances, she was like a beam of light with her vivid eyes and pale golden hair. Taking the kit from him, she started rummaging through it.

Zachary poured them both drinks then sat at the round oak table.

She picked up her glass and drank it in one gulp.

He managed not to laugh. "Rough night, kitten?" He poured her another shot, although gulping was hardly the way to drink Glenlivet.

"Take your shirt off."

His eyebrows rose.

Flushing, she hastily added, "Please?"

With a smile, he pulled the shirt off and tossed it into the wastebasket. He glanced at his shoulder. Not bleeding much, not too deep.

Lips pressed together, Jessica washed the slice clean then pulled the edges together with thin adhesive strips. She finished by taping a gauze pad over the wound. "I think that will be all right," she said before dropping into a chair at the table and downing her second shot of scotch.

He checked her work. "Excellent job."

She was still pale, so he poured one final shot and put the bottle away. Any more and she'd be out like a light. "Let's go into the living room," he said, lacing his fingers with hers. She had a delicate hand with small fingers.

Taking a seat in his favorite leather chair, he pushed the oak coffee table farther away and pulled her down to sit on the floor between his legs, her back against the chair. Her pale skin was almost translucent against the dark red carpet.

She turned to him with an insulted expression. "Is this where a pet sits?"

"No…pet." He put a slight emphasis on the word just to see her face flush. "This is where someone sits when they need their shoulders rubbed." His hands closed on her shoulders where the muscles were so tight he had seen the knots from across the kitchen.

"Ohhhh."

The sigh reminded him of her sweet moan when his cock entered her softness. He hardened, considered taking her right there on the carpet. But that wasn't what she needed from him right now. He dug his thumbs into her muscles, felt the loosening.

"Sir?"

"Um-hmm." He moved his fingers to her slender neck, sliding the cool silky hair to one side.

"I'm sorry."

There was a slight quaver in her voice and worry, almost fear in her mind, and he frowned. Sorry for what? She *had* snapped at him, he remembered, or maybe for the way she'd ordered him around? Ah, probably that. She was new to all this.

"Jessica, with some Doms, the slightest misstep will bring wrath down on a sub's head. I don't operate that way. That you were willing to risk my anger to care for me... Kitten, I feel cherished, not angry."

And the feeling was still so unexpected that he was having trouble finding his balance.

"Oh." She took a sip of her drink, wrinkling her nose slightly. Not her favorite drink. He'd have to stock his liquor cabinet with something besides scotch.

Under his fingers, her muscles tightened and he could feel a surge of worry—and outrage—from her. "I heard about the woman you...you put on the bar."

He bit back the laugh, kept his voice soothing. "No wonder you're feeling a little unsure."

"No kidding," she muttered, and he grinned since she couldn't see, and concentrated on working the new tenseness out of her muscles. She was just a bundle of nerves. And here he'd planned to have turned her into a little puddle of goo by now.

Instead he was giving bondage lessons.

Feisty, sensitive little sub. Then again, he'd never enjoyed teaching so much in his life. He wrapped his arms around her.

"Kitten, her punishment was for more than one misstep; she spent the evening deliberately annoying her Dom. And he knew that she'd find a whipping to be a reward."

"But why did she do that?"

"A sub who goes out of her way to be rude is an unhappy sub. She was daring him, practically begging him to take control away from her. If she had confined her actions just to him, I would have simply given him some suggestions. But she took that choice away from me."

His hands returned to her shoulders, easing the last of the tightness, even as his words eased the worry inside of her. She nodded. "Thank you for explaining. It suddenly felt like I didn't really know you at all, you know? Of course, I don't, not really, but—" She grabbed her glass and finished it.

"Mmmmph, there's quite a bit I don't know about you, either." Like why his little sub kept attacking Doms. He pulled her back so he could massage the muscles in front of her shoulders.

"Like what?" she murmured. With her worry abated, her emotions had turned to a warm hum, almost like a purr.

"You've been in the club two nights and attacked a Dom each night to defend someone. Instead of finding a dungeon monitor, you jump right in."

Jessica felt her mind go blank and she tried to sit up. "I... Anyone would do the same, keep someone from being hurt."

"Of course. What makes it so personal for *you*, Jessica?" His hands pinned her against the chair.

"That's—" She huffed out a breath. "Do I get to keep anything private?"

"Well...no." He kissed the top of her head, but his hands, flattened against her chest, didn't move. "Tell me what happened. Who was hurt by a man?"

Pinpoint accuracy. He must be a hell of a psychologist. And she shouldn't have had that last drink; her thoughts were scattered to hell and gone. "My sister. Her husband hit her, beat her up regularly."

"Did you know?" His hands were moving again, soft round strokes, soothing.

"I should have," she said bitterly. "I thought she was a normal newlywed, wanting to be alone with her husband. I believed her when she said she'd tripped on something or had a car accident. I should have known."

"Oh, kitten," he sighed. "Abused women will lie like troopers; they're ashamed, sure they did something to deserve the pain, or they feel that only losers get hurt, or they're terrified of their abuser. Don't blame yourself for not being able to tell. Did your sister get away?"

"Yeah. Once we knew what was going on, we got her out. He's serving time."

"And your sister has scars, doesn't she?" he said softly. "Inside and out and you feel bad every time you see one."

Her throat closed up at the sympathy in his voice. At the understanding. She swallowed, blinked hard. A minute later, she managed to say, "Damn, you're good; are you a psychologist or something?"

He laughed. "At least now when I find a Dom laid out on the floor, I'll know why." He gave her a little shake. "But, little spitfire, if I'm around, let me do it. That's my job."

Somehow he'd drained some of the guilt and warmed her more than the alcohol had. He kissed her cheek, leaned back, and took a sip of his drink. He was still on his first drink, and she was more than a little fuzzy.

Then, his hands returned to the front of her shoulders…and moved under her halter top to stroke over her breasts.

"I-I don't think there are any muscles there," she said, somewhat breathlessly as her body woke up and started clamoring for sex.

"Well, I need to be sure, don't I?" His fingers massaged her breasts lightly. He kissed her shoulder, his day-old beard scratchy, the roughness sending shivers through her. Her nipples tightened, and he noticed, capturing each one between his fingers.

Her body dampened, and she tried to turn, to touch him, but his hands kept her in place, and he nipped her shoulder. "Did I say you could move?" he asked, giving each nipple a pinch, sending shock waves coursing through her.

When he pinned her back against the chair again, heat washed through her. He controlled her so easily. He nibbled under her ear and sucked on her earlobe, and her insides turned molten.

"Then again, I could show you the rest of my home," he murmured, and pulled her to her feet. "I do have a bedroom." He led her toward the back of the house, past the kitchen, and a sound made him stop.

Jessica blinked as a ginger-colored cat stalked through the kitchen.

"Ah, about time. I was wondering if you were going to make an appearance," Sir said to the cat, kneeling to pet it. He looked up. "May I introduce Galahad?"

"Galahad?" she said in disbelief. That had to be the biggest and ugliest cat she'd ever seen, and she'd seem some monsters at the shelter.

"He's a very chivalrous fellow."

Jessica knelt on the floor and held out a finger to be delicately sniffed. In approval, the cat nudged her hand, curveted closer to be petted. "You must be quite a fighter." She frowned at the chewed-on ears and scarred nose.

"He's been with me about five years, ever since I found him raiding the garbage cans. He was big then, has grown even more since."

She would never have picked him as a person who would adopt a stray cat. She didn't know him at all, did she?

"Ben said you were divorced?" she blurted out, then flushed. Yeah, man-woman social skills were definitely not her strength.

"About ten years ago," he said as if her question wasn't unusual. "We married young, when I was in the service. Since I spent most of those six years out of the country, we muddled along well enough until I was discharged. After that, we both tried, but when I entered grad school, she called it quits." He quirked his eyebrows. "Among other differences, she preferred vanilla sex."

He gave the cat a final pat before rising, holding his hand out for Jessica. She let him pull her to her feet.

"And have you been married?" he asked.

"No. Nothing got quite that far," she confessed. "I never—" She stopped; she was not going to tell him that sex had been boring.

His eyes glinted like he'd picked that thought out of the air. Jerk. But he simply ruffled her hair before showing her the rest of his home. An office held a bulletin board covered with photos and letters from his pint-size clients. Framed crayon drawings decorated the walls. "That's quite a collection," she said, touching one photo of a gap-toothed pixie grinning at the camera.

He moved his shoulders. "I've been at it awhile."

And the children meant enough to him that he'd decorate his office with their artwork, she thought, recalling her colleague's offices, filled with business awards, pictures of famous clients, golf trophies.

"Two guest rooms there," he said as they walked down the hall. "And this is my favorite room," he said, showing her a room filled with older furniture, comfortably overstuffed couch and chairs, a giant TV on one wall, a piano in the corner, and a wall of books. She walked over to examine them: Sir Arthur Conan Doyle,

Agatha Christie, Dashiell Hammett, Ross Macdonald. Her eyebrows rose; she had many of the same books. Her imagination presented an image of sitting on his lap, both of them reading and arguing over murders and red herrings.

Finally, he pushed open the door to his master bedroom. Dark blue carpet, mahogany furniture. Tall arched windows open to the night air.

A king-size bed. Her breath caught. Her body roused as if it had been waiting just for this room.

"I think you'll like the furniture in this room." His voice was husky as his hands settled on her waist, warm and hard and—

A rusty meow came from the kitchen.

Sir paused, sighed. "I have to feed him, or he won't stop complaining." He kissed her neck then released her. "The bathroom is across the room if you have need."

When he left, she crossed the room. She definitely had need, now that he'd brought it to her attention. The bathroom was gold and marble with dark green towels. The tub would easily hold two, and the shower could accommodate a football team.

While washing her hands, she glanced in the mirror and gasped. Mascara and eyeliner streaked her cheeks; she looked like a rain-soaked prostitute. She scrubbed it all off, checked the mirror and winced. Even with makeup on, she was just barely pretty; without it...

Scowling at the bare face in the mirror, she snapped the light off and went back into the bedroom. She could hear Sir talking to the cat, his deep voice sparking off flutters in her stomach. He talked to her the same way, she realized. Was she just another pet to him?

Her gaze turned to the bed, and the ugly feeling in her chest grew. How many of those women downstairs had been in his bed? Ben's words ran through her mind: *Women fall all over him, and in his world, he's known as the best master around. And that's according to the subs, who would definitely know.* Lots of subs apparently.

Would that gorgeous blonde be up here tomorrow? Jessica's hands closed into fists, but who should she hit? The blonde? Or herself for being so stupid and letting herself get more involved than she should have? He'd never indicated that he wanted her for more than just sex, after all. And she'd enjoyed the sex, hadn't wanted anything else at first. But every time she learned something about him, she liked him more.

She wanted there to be a *them*, but he didn't feel the same way.

There was no future with him. She walked to the wall of windows and gazed outside. Black clouds were moving in, shrouding the moon and stars in darkness. It would be pouring rain before morning.

She wrapped her arms around herself as unhappiness twisted her stomach. Really, she should leave now; she'd learned the folly of driving on country roads in a storm. And there was nothing for her here.

She glanced at the bed, and her throat tightened. She would hurt even worse if she went to bed with him now, let him make love… No, what they had wasn't *love*, and that was the problem, wasn't it?

"Jessica?" He stood in the doorway. She caught the puzzled look in his eyes, the frown, and then he leaned against the door frame, crossing his arms and waiting. Watching her with an intent gaze. Master Z.

She didn't even know his name, she realized, feeling as if the storm had already started. No, she needed to get out of here before she made a fool of herself.

"I think it's time for me to leave," she managed to say.

His head tilted. "I didn't design my bedroom to make a woman sad, kitten. Or to make her want to run."

"I'm sorry, Sir. It's just… It's been a long night." Her chest hurt so bad she wanted to press her hands to it. "I'm going home now."

"No. You're not."

She blinked. "You can't—"

His mouth curved in a faint smile. "No, I won't push you down on the bed and have my way with you, tempting as I find the thought."

The image sent heat pouring through her veins.

"But I also won't let you leave while you're still under the influence. I wouldn't have given you any alcohol at all if I hadn't thought you'd be spending the night."

"Oh." Well, she probably had drunk more than she should have. But damned if she'd stay here with him. "I'll drive slowly."

His eyes darkened, the muscles in his jaw tightening. "I'll chain you to a wall in the dungeon before I let you leave like this."

The image actually made her dampen, and she closed her eyes. She couldn't stay in his rooms. Or go back to the club and be in that sex-charged atmosphere. "Um. Maybe I'll just go for a nice walk."

He shook his head with a hint of exasperation, then held out his hand. "Come, pet, I have a better idea."

She hesitated.

"No sex involved."

Why did his easy compliance feel so disappointing? "Okay." His hand engulfed hers, warm and hard, and just touching him made her want him more. Oh, this had to stop.

He grabbed a bottled water from the refrigerator, then led her to the back door, and down the steps to the backyard.

She frowned. "This isn't the same area we were in before, is it?"

"That was the side yard; this is the back. This area is only for my use." He tilted her chin up, kissed her. "It's very private."

God, he could kiss. By the time he pulled back, her arms were wrapped around his neck, and she was pressed against him all over. She felt so good in his arms—warm, safe...*stupid.* She shoved him away and took a step back, trying to control her breathing. "No sex?"

He chuckled. "I don't consider kissing to be sex."

"Kissing is sex." She glared at him. If kissing wasn't sex, she wouldn't feel so turned on.

"Since you aren't interested in sex"—he gave her a bland look—"you might as well finish relaxing." He led her past flower beds illumined with solar lanterns to a bubbling Jacuzzi. Heat rose from the water. After setting the bottle down, he pulled her nightie over her head.

"Hey!"

Ignoring her, he unbuckled the leather cuffs that were still on her wrists, then gathered her hair and twisted it into a loose knot on top of her head. Hand on her bare butt, he nudged her toward the water. "Get in."

Options were limited. Fight with him over her clothing or get in where the bubbling water would hide her.

The heat engulfed her as she lowered herself to the seat. The water splashed gently around her shoulders. Her wrists felt light...bare...without the cuffs. She knew he'd removed them to keep them out of the water, but it still felt like he was removing her from his life. She bit her lip, forced a smile. "This feels really nice."

"Good." He studied her face, a frown back on his face, then opened the bottled water, and handed it to her. "Drink this. I don't want you getting dehydrated."

As she sipped the water, he stripped out of his slacks in his usual efficient fashion. Standing on the edge of the Jacuzzi, outlined by the glowing moon overhead, he looked like a god. Tall, shoulders so broad, muscles rimmed in shadow and moonglow.

He stepped into the water and settled himself beside her. After stroking a finger lightly down her cheek, he leaned back, one arm resting on the concrete edge behind her head. An owl hooted from the trees as leaves rustled in the light breeze. The muffled sound of a car door, then a car leaving, drifted back into the yard. As the Jacuzzi burbled softly, Jessica let her head settle back onto the muscled arm behind her. She'd just let her mind clear, show him she was sober, and be out of here within an hour.

Chapter Fourteen

Zachary watched his little sub slowly relax and the night's stress and turmoil uncoil from her muscles. Quite an evening she'd had.

One that had almost ended abruptly a few minutes ago. What had been in her mind up there in the bedroom? He shook his head. The ability to read emotions didn't always help with understanding. She'd felt desire and then confusion and…resolution. Yes, that was it. And then grief.

Grief as she'd said she wanted to leave. No anger at him, no dislike. He was missing some vital step in her reasoning, dammit. But he had gotten one message loud and clear; if she'd left right then, he wouldn't have seen her again.

He picked up her hand, kissed the fingers, and she only sighed. Letting her make such a decision when intoxicated and emotionally frayed… He knew better than that. If she still felt the same way when she woke, he wouldn't stand in her way. Although he'd damned well get her to verbalize the problem.

He *was* a psychologist, after all.

Psychologist enough to know himself and that he didn't want her to go. The opposite, in fact. He'd already known he wanted to see her again, but his thoughts hadn't gone further than enjoying her in the club. But as the evening has progressed, his intentions had changed. And when she'd bandaged him, warming him with her concern, he knew he was doomed. He wanted more from her than a few evenings in the club. She roused feelings in him that he hadn't felt in a long time.

With gentle fingers, he pushed a damp tendril of hair from her forehead. She'd washed the streaked makeup from her face in the bathroom. Did she know how those tear tracks, that evidence of vulnerability, could pull at a Dom? She probably didn't even realize how pretty she was now, her cheeks flushed with the heat, her lips soft and kissable.

After she was half-asleep in the water, he pulled her out, dried her off, and tucked her into his bed, enjoying the way she unconsciously curled into him, soft against his side.

He woke before dawn with the moonlight streaming through the window. She looked just right, he decided, her golden hair spread across the dark pillows, her rounded curves bringing his bed to life. He shook his head, bemused by her presence. The tiny room downstairs was where he took his women; they weren't invited up here to his home.

But unlike many, she hadn't angled for an invitation. He'd wanted her here. Hell, he probably would have tossed her over his shoulder and carried her up caveman-style if she hadn't agreed. She was such a fascinating concoction: the sheer intelligence, the logical mind and reserve that buried the passion underneath. The way her insecurities mingled with that affectionate nature was endearing. Her loyalty to her sister, her courage... She was something, wasn't she?

Even Galahad had given his approval.

He ran a hand down the satiny skin on her bare shoulder and felt himself harden completely. He'd had a half erection all night, ever since she'd screamed in pleasure in the medical room, but she'd needed time to recover, and then whatever had bothered her had come between them.

Now, however... He slid the covers down, baring her. Moonlight gleamed on her breasts, leaving tantalizing shadows beneath. Her waist curved in, then out into lush hips. The darkness between her thighs called to him. His hands traced down her body, touching lightly, his fingers lured into stroking the soft breasts. Her nipples pebbled into points. Her breath quickened. The scent of her arousal drifted to him even as her eyes fluttered open.

Her body felt hot and needy.

Where are my pajamas? she thought drowsily, then more urgently, *Where am I?*

Blinking, she frowned as she remembered the club, Sir. A Jacuzzi. She'd been so sleepy. Was she in his bed?

Her breasts were lifted into hard hands, and she moaned as the intense sensations rippled through her.

"Sir?"

"We're not quite to the sex part," Master Z said. "You may tell me to stop if you want."

His face was above her, the moonlight shadowing its hard planes. He smiled just a little. She was leaving him, she remembered. Wasn't going to do this again. Her heart ached at the thought.

She could call this one last time a way of saying good-bye, right?

"Don't stop," she whispered.

He took a condom from the nightstand and covered himself. "Now, open your legs for me, kitten." His deep voice was rough.

Her legs parted.

"Good girl." His hand touched between her thighs. She was already wet, growing more so as his fingers spread the moisture. One finger stroked her clitoris, sending fiery shocks through her.

She tightened, the heat rising quickly as if he'd already stoked the fire. She lifted her hips into his hand without thinking. He chuckled and she felt her cheeks heat.

How did he affect her this way? She had never been so uninhibited before.

"I like the way you react to my hands on you," he whispered, kissing her deeply, thoroughly, his tongue plunging into her even as he stroked her slit below. The twin assaults left her body shaking with need. He released her mouth only to shift to her breasts, sucking one nipple, then the other, into hard points, and the tugging of his mouth tightened her core.

His fingers continued their slow slide over her clitoris, around and over until each touch sent her closer, until her thigh muscles tightened and quivered.

And then he opened her, positioned himself, and thrust into her. Her swollen tissues flared with his entry. He pinched her clitoris at the same time, the one necessary touch she'd been waiting for, and she screamed, her hips jerking against his as waves of sensation exploded through her, as her womb spasmed around his thick, intruding shaft.

He hummed in enjoyment, moving his hand to her breasts as he slid in and out of her very, very slowly. His thick cock and his fingers on her nipples never let her excitement quite die.

"I didn't think you ever made love in the normal way," she whispered, her voice husky.

He nuzzled her neck. His teeth closed on her shoulder in a light bite. Then he gently tongued the sting. "You miss being tied up already?"

Involuntarily, her pussy tightened around him, giving him the answer she'd never have dared to speak.

"Ah." His teeth flashed white in the dark face, and he captured one wrist, placed it over her head, and then added the other. One big hand easily pinned her wrists to the mattress. "This should do it."

"No restraints?" she managed to ask, realizing she hadn't seen any.

"Don't have any. I don't bring subs up here."

But she was here, she managed to think, and then he increased the force and speed of his thrusts between her legs.

She felt invaded and helpless to do anything. With her arms restrained, her body wasn't hers to control; she had no decisions to make, nothing to do except feel. Each sensation seared through her, the slide of his shaft exquisitely opening her, his hard hand keeping her from movement, his other hand toying with her breasts, plucking and pinching the nipples to just the edge of pain. To just the point where each touch increased her now consuming need.

Then, abandoning her breasts, he set his hand under one of her knees, pushing her leg up, opening her further. He began to pound into her, and the throbbing between her legs became overwhelming. Her orgasm ripped through her, hard and fast, an incandescent flame shooting through her. She moaned as she spasmed around him, as her knee quivered in his hard grasp.

And then his grip tightened as he growled out his own release; the sensations of his cock jerking inside her made her gasp.

"Ah, little one," he murmured. Letting her wrists go, he wrapped his arms around her, pulling her tight against him, his weight full on her and ever so satisfying, his warm breath ruffling her hair. The scent of sex filled the room. She ran her fingers through his thick hair, pressed a kiss to his damp shoulder. *How could she give this up?*

When he started to withdraw, she grabbed his butt, curled her fingers into the hard curve of muscle, and kept his pelvis against her own. "Don't leave."

He kissed her, sweet and slow, before pulling away. "I'll be right back, pet."

A moment in the bathroom, and he rejoined her, pulling her on top of him. It was apparently one of his favorite positions. He played with her buttocks, fondling and squeezing, the movements causing her tender clit to rub against him until she wiggled in his grasp.

He chuckled. "You can go back to sleep now if you want," he whispered, tucking her head down against his shoulder. His musky scent enveloped her; his arm lay heavy across her back and one hand still grasped her bottom. She yawned, sliding down into sleep and safety.

She woke, lying on her back, to find him on his side, propped on one elbow, watching her with those silvery eyes. She was sprawled out with no covers, naked to his gaze. She made a futile grasp at the sheet, but his hand came down on hers.

"Let me look," he murmured, releasing her after kissing her fingers.

Heat washed from her chest to her face, and she knew she blushed from the way his eyes crinkled. She frowned at him. "You're bossy."

"Yes, I am," he agreed, amiably. "And isn't it a shame that you happen to like that."

Huh. Hard to answer that one.

After donning a condom, he rolled on top of her and slid into her with one hard thrust. She gasped as the shock of the sudden entry reverberated through her system.

"All right, pet." Resting on his forearms, he framed her face with his warm hands, forcing her to look at him. "Now that I have your attention, you may tell me what was going on earlier."

His gaze was stern, his hands unyielding. His heavy body pinned her to the mattress with his cock impaling her. There would be no evasion, either mentally or physically.

She swallowed hard. She could get him to release her, she knew, if she demanded to be let free. If she walked out. The thought of leaving brought back the ache in her chest. She didn't want to walk out.

"Jessica," he said softly, "haven't we shared enough for you to trust me with more than your body?" His thumbs stroked her cheeks. She could feel him, hard inside her, not moving, but joining them together in the most intimate of ways.

But she knew how this would end, had to end. He'd lived alone for years. He had eager subs available anytime he wanted. Why would he change for her?

His eyes narrowed. "All that thinking going on. Tell me, pet."

Pet. Anger flared through her, even knowing he'd said it deliberately. She wasn't a damned pet to be taken home and then dumped at the pound if too inconvenient. Fine then, he could hear some truths.

"That woman who knelt in front of you? I don't like knowing she'll be here with you tomorrow."

He looked confused, but she couldn't hold back the next part.

"I don't want you to have other subs, women." And then insecurity welled up in her like an ice bath. What was she doing? Like he cared what she wanted?

She tried to look away, but he wouldn't move his hands or his gaze. The only thing that moved was his cock inside her, just enough to remind her of their connection. "Don't stop, kitten. What else?"

He held her in place so easily, and her wakening arousal set off another spark of anger at her body's weakness and at him for exploiting it. She glared at him. "Just one thing. *Sir.*" She almost spat the word. "There's more between us than just sex, and you'd see it if you weren't so totally blind, dammit."

He blinked at her outburst. Then his lips curved.

"Spitfire," he murmured, his tone pleased.

"I—" God, what had she done? She wet her lips.

His smile widened at her confusion, and he brushed her lips with a gentle kiss. "It so happens that I agree completely."

"You do?" she whispered. There was air in this room somewhere, but she couldn't seem to find it.

Moving a hand from her face, he touched a nipple with one gentle finger, watched it bead into a point. "I do. And I think it's time you gave me your phone number."

Her heart tugged inside her with the rising hope. She shoved it back down, trying to consider his request. Well, not a request, actually. His gaze rose from her breast to spear into her eyes. *A command.*

"What would you do with my number?"

The corner of his mouth rose as he touched her other nipple. "Call you and ask you out to dinner. Talk to you somewhere besides in bed, much as I enjoy having you here."

The air was definitely gone; she couldn't seem to breathe. He wanted more than just sex? Wanted to actually get to know her? Or was this more of the domination stuff, only elsewhere? She hesitated. "Do I call you Sir at a restaurant?"

"No, kitten." Now it was really a smile. "I'm Zachary until we reach the club…or the bedroom."

Her smile equaled his. "I can do that," she said softly as joy filled her.

"However, right now, we're in the bedroom," he murmured, moving hard inside her, "and I do believe you just swore at me." The stern line of his mouth promised retribution and ominous amusement filled his eyes. "Give me your wrists."

Her eyes widened in apprehension even as arousal blazed through her body. "Yes, *Sir.*"

~ * ~

DARK CITADEL

Chapter One

The massive stone building loomed over the extensive grounds like a forbidding castle in some gothic novel. *Club Shadowlands*. Kari Wagner shook her head at the intimidating sight, at the thought of what the evening might hold.

Beginners lessons at a private BDSM club. She'd gone insane. Really. Her mind had rotted completely away. Teaching high school, that's what had caused her lapse in sanity. All those teenagers…

Her date, Brian—or Buck, as he liked to be called—grabbed Kari's arm and pulled her through the front door. She slipped a little, and his grip hardened. "Damn, you're slow."

In the small entry room, a huge security guard stood behind a table, looking so ogrelike he was almost cute. "Good evening, sir, miss."

"Good evening." Kari closed her mouth before she called him Shrek.

He held out his hand. "Papers, please?"

As Buck handed over the doctor's certificates and money, Kari eased her arm away. She'd been attracted to his authoritative personality—so different from the usual men she dated—but he'd never been rough before. Then again, he didn't know how to do this domination stuff any more than she did.

The guard finished looking at the papers and handed them off to another man before saying, "I'll take your jacket, sir. And miss? Please leave your shoes with me now."

"My shoes?" After a glance at the guy to see if he was serious—he was—Kari slipped off her orange sneakers.

The guard patiently kept his hand outstretched until she handed over her Tigger-decorated socks also. A little snort of laughter escaped him. "Thank you, miss."

Buck's pale brows drew together at the sight of the socks. "What the hell are you wearing?"

Kari glanced down at her ankle-length denim dress. "Sorry. It was parent-teacher day, and my last set of parents arrived a half hour late. I didn't have time to go home and change."

"Honestly, Kari, you dress like a five-year-old." He straightened the lapels of his black suit.

"Well, I used to teach kindergarten after all." She laughed. "But my high-school students like my clothes too." Besides, even if she'd had time to change, what would she have worn to a BDSM club? Some weird lacy corset thing? Surely they'd dated long enough for him to know her better than that.

"Well, folks, have a pleasant evening." Smiling, the guard pointed them toward a door on the right wall.

Wait a minute. Kari frowned at her bare feet, then looked at the man. "Excuse me, but why is Buck allowed to keep his shoes on?"

The guard blinked. "Did I make a mistake? Which one of you is the Dom or Domme?"

"I am." Buck gave her a disgusted look. "Just be quiet, Kari. Don't talk at all."

She bit back her first response—and the second—and settled for a nod. Buck might look like Prince Charming—tall, slim, blond—but his manners needed a little work. Still, she should give him a break. If he wasn't Mr. Perfect Dominating Man, she wasn't exactly a ten on the Gorgeous Submissive Woman scale, right? In fact, considering her conservative upbringing, this whole evening was probably doomed to failure.

Before they reached the door, Buck yanked her to his side, his fingers digging into her skin. "There will be other Doms here and other beginners. Remember you're with me. Don't talk to anyone else. Don't look at anyone else."

"Got it. Now let go of me." With an exasperated sigh, she pried his hand from her arm, then followed him into a large office with lush dark brown carpeting and creamy white walls. An antique desk and office equipment took up the far side of the room. In the right corner, several big men and two women, all dressed in gold-trimmed leather clothing, eyed her and Buck before returning to quiet conversation.

The center of the room held a sitting area occupied by two men. One was a tall, broad-shouldered man with silvering dark hair wearing European-tailored black slacks and a black silk shirt. His dark gray eyes had focused on her and Buck the minute they walked through the door. Now, he tilted his head toward the couch across from him.

"That's got to be Master Z," Buck hissed as they crossed the room. "All this is his. You watch your mouth and don't speak unless I give you permission."

She did exactly that, closing her mouth over her impulse to tell him where to go. He meant well, and she wasn't going to leave before she found out more about this bondage stuff and why it excited her so much.

In black leathers, the other man looked downright dangerous: hard-faced with an equally hard body, open vest stretching over broad shoulders. Black hair slightly curling to the nape of his neck, potent brown eyes, the shadow of a beard along a stern jaw. If Buck was the golden prince, this man was the dark one.

When the men rose, Kari froze, feeling like a mouse confronted by lions. Mouth dry, she managed to move forward and smile.

"Buck," the gray-eyed one said in a smooth, deep voice. "Welcome to the Shadowlands. I am Master Z." He shook hands with Buck and then Kari. His warm hand engulfed her cold fingers as he studied her for a moment. "Welcome, Kari."

She opened her mouth, remembered not to speak, and smiled instead.

Master Z nodded to the other man. "This is Master Dan."

The man nodded, shook hands with Buck, and then took Kari's hand, his grip much gentler than she'd expected. When she looked up, his dark brown eyes trapped hers. He didn't leer or do anything other than look at her, yet she felt a flush rise into her face. She pulled her hand back and looked down. She could still feel his penetrating gaze.

"Please be seated," Master Z said. He waited for everyone to sit, then resumed his seat. He tapped the coffee table where their medical records and questionnaires were spread. "Your papers are in order. You're both free of any disease."

He glanced at her and Buck. "The rules of the Shadowlands are simple. Don't touch anything or anyone that doesn't belong to you without permission. Do not interfere in someone else's scene. The equipment is here for your use, and after your introductory class tonight, there are private rooms upstairs, also for your use." He nodded to the men in the corner. "Dungeon monitors—DMs— supervise activities and are available to answer questions or even to help as needed. Watch for the gold trim or an orange badge."

His gaze turned to Kari. "Here at the Shadowlands, use the term 'Master' for those in authority over you: me, the DMs, and possibly, your Dom. When in doubt, address any Dom as Sir or Ma'am."

"I understand. Thank you," she said without thinking and winced at Buck's glare.

Dan Sawyer half listened to Master Z while he sized up the two people who would be in his charge. The bland-faced man with pale blond hair and blue eyes. About five-eleven and a lanky one-seventy in a black suit. He had a narrow mouth with more frown lines than laugh lines and checked his date frequently as if afraid she'd disappear.

The woman wasn't beautiful, but compellingly pretty. Midtwenties. Wide blue eyes and hair the rich brown color of Guinness. A soft pink mouth bracketed by faint lines, showing she knew how to laugh and did it often. She was little, about five-four, and definitely not slender. Her long dress couldn't conceal her very lush curves despite being buttoned right up to the top.

Interesting choice of attire for the club. Was she modest? Probably. He studied the way she'd pulled her hair into a tight French braid. Modest *and* conservative. Huh.

He rubbed his chin and studied her further. Had she wanted to be in a BDSM club, or had her date dragged her? Maybe he had, considering the way she was rubbing her arm.

Shaking his head, Dan leaned back in his chair. Looked like this couple would bear watching.

She'd be a pleasure to watch. To see tremble. To see helpless need in those big eyes. To see... He set his imagination aside. Wherever those thoughts had come from, they were out of place. He was a teacher tonight.

A roar of laughter from the corner caught his attention, and he glanced at the other DMs for beginners' nights. All had been Dominants for years, all trustworthy men and women. Some with their own submissives, some, like Dan, without. A few were looking for a new sub to train. Dan wasn't.

There were plenty of subs begging for his use, and he frequently enjoyed one for an evening, but his interest in long-term commitments had died with his wife three years ago. No one could replace his Marion.

"Then you're ready to start." Master Z's voice broke into Dan's thoughts.

Lecture was over; time to get the puppies moving. Dan rose. "Come with me. I'll show you around the club and answer questions until your class begins."

And like puppies, they followed him across the room, obediently at first. Then Dan heard the man whispering and turned. He caught a few words: "...stay right beside...guys trying to grab themselves a woman...saw how he looked at you. You belong to me...I'm in charge."

"Uh-huh." The woman rolled her eyes and tried to move away.

Buck grabbed her arm hard enough that she winced. His voice rose. "Are you listening to me?"

Having once been married, Dan could have told him those were fighting words.

And yes, Kari's face turned pink with anger. She yanked her arm away and stepped back. "Yes, I'm listening, and I don't like what I hear. I'm going home."

Buck's face darkened. "Don't be childish. You knew this was going to—"

She spun on her heel, headed for the door.

He grabbed her wrist. "Look, honey, I'm sorry. Maybe I—"

"Let me go!" She tried to pry his hand off and failed.

Oh, hell, Dan thought. The guy apparently didn't understand the basic *fuck off!* she'd put so politely.

"Let her go." Dan set his hand on the wannabe Dom's shoulder, tightening his fingers until the man flinched and released her.

"If she doesn't want to continue, you can't force her," Dan said. He glanced at the girl. "Kari, do you want to leave?"

"Yes. I do," she said. From the pissed-off look in her big blue eyes, she'd crossed the dude off her date list. *Smart move, sweetie.* Did she have a ride home? "Did you come together or—"

"Separately," she said.

"Then I'll walk you to your car." And prevent any altercations in the parking lot. "Buck, if you want to continue, go on in."

The man stood there for a minute, then scowled at his date. "Fine. I'm going to take the class, since I already put out the money. I'll call you later, and we'll talk. I would have taken good care of you. You're not being reasonable at all." Straightening his suit coat, he headed for the door to the main club room.

"Well, then." Dan looked down at his charge. She was rubbing her arm again. "Are you all right, sweetheart?"

Startled, she looked up and he caught his breath at the hint of pain in her eyes, at the vulnerability. The *need.* His body responded as if she'd been stripped and tied to his bed. *Damn.*

"Um. Yes, thank you very much. I'm sorry about this," she said, her voice was melodic, a little husky. And so very polite. What would it take to break through the politeness to the woman beneath?

"No problem." He nodded toward the front door.

But as they passed the sitting area, Z lifted a hand, stopping them. "Kari, sit down, please."

She took a seat and folded her hands in her lap, all prim and proper except for the pink toes peeking out from under her dress.

"I see you and your date have parted ways," Z said. "But you obviously had an interest in this lifestyle or you would not be here. Am I correct?"

Her eyes dropped, and she nodded slightly.

"Excellent." Master Z continued, "Since that is the case, Master Dan, could you secure her a drink and see if she would like to continue tonight's class with you?"

The woman's head jerked up. "Continue? But…"

Z's glance at Dan was filled with amusement before he said, "Indeed, continue. Master Dan has far more experience and is far more gentle than your…other choice." Z's voice lowered, commanded, "Look at him now."

Instant compliance. *Submissive. Innocent. Temptingly lovely.* Before he could stop himself, Dan held his hand out. "We'll go discuss it, Kari. Come."

Again, that appealing obedience.

As he curled his fingers around the cold little hand, he could only think about the next time he would order her to come. With his fingers inside her and his mouth on her clit, yes, she would most surely come.

Chapter Two

Oh God, what was she doing?

The man's grasp enfolded her hand. *Master Dan.* She didn't even know his last name.

They crossed the room, heading toward a heavy wooden door. She halted abruptly.

"Kari?"

She looked up. Good grief, he was even bigger than Buck. Somewhere over six feet, but when you're short, anything over six feet was hard to judge. His shoulders were beyond broad. Like the other men in the room, his gold-trimmed black leather vest had nothing under it. Well, nothing except muscles and more muscles and a sprinkling of black chest hair.

His biceps bulged, and his forearms appeared almost as thick. The leathers he wore for pants were—wow, really tight.

When her gaze managed to move back up to his face, he smiled, laugh lines crinkling around his eyes. Her face heated, and she knew her pale skin reddened.

"You're allowed to look, sweetheart," he murmured, running a finger down her hot cheek. "I enjoy having your eyes on me."

His eyes were a dark, dark brown, his face tanned and hard looking until he smiled. But when he didn't... She remembered the hard look on his face when he had grabbed Buck. She bit her lip. Go home, she told herself. Now.

He started to push the door open.

"No. Wait, please." She held up her hand. "If it wouldn't inconvenience you, might I take a minute to think?"

"Take all the time you need." Crossing his arms, he leaned one shoulder against the wall, amusement in his eyes.

Just standing here beside him wasn't going to work. Shoot, even Madame Curie wouldn't be able to think with that man looking at her. Kari turned her back and paced across the room.

Stay or not? That was the basic question for tonight. So check the facts.

If she simply went home, nothing would change. Her life would go on. She'd never know if she might have learned something that would make a difference in her sex life. Nothing else had. How many relationships had failed due to her lack of interest in sex? She'd thought her basic personality or body created the problem. But the excitement she felt hearing about domination—heck, just the word itself—had been amazing. A revelation in a way.

She could definitely get aroused.

But this BDSM stuff appeared very, very strange. Kinky. And she wasn't a kinky person in the least. Shoot, the school nuns had used her as an example of model behavior. "*Why can't you be more like Kari? She's polite. She follows the rules.*"

Well, following the rules in the bedroom wasn't working too well for her, now was it?

She reached the end of the room and turned around. Master Dan hadn't moved, his patience apparently inexhaustible. Nonetheless, she needed to figure this out, pros and cons, and reach a decision.

In the Go Home column: First, she didn't know nearly enough about this stuff. She scowled as she paced back. Her home computer had died last month—stupid technology—and she couldn't afford to replace it yet. She sure couldn't research BDSM on the school computer. So she only knew the tidbits Buck had doled out. Her mouth tightened. She *hated* being ignorant.

Second: She didn't know this man at all. How dangerous was that? She could just imagine, all her friends and family mourning around her grave. The tombstone would read *Kari Wagner, Died of Sheer Stupidity.*

In the Stay Here column: It would be almost as bad to have her grave marker read *Died of Terminal Bedroom Boredom.* Unmarried and childless. There was a darned good reason she wanted to try this stuff, after all.

As for knowing the man? She glanced at Master Z. The owner had leaned back in his chair, fingers steepled, watching her pace. He was no dummy, and he'd basically recommended Master Dan.

And Master Dan sure wasn't anything like Buck. She pursed her lips. She considered that a major bonus, right there.

What about being ignorant? Well, she might be, but she had a feeling that Master Dan knew *all* about the subject of domination.

She stopped in front of the door to the bar, could hear the sounds of classical music and muted conversation. If she left now, she'd never have the courage to return. Her head said no. Her heart said go for it.

Master Dan straightened.

She placed her hand in his. Go it was.

"Nervous?" he asked softly.

"A bit." No point in hiding the truth. Considering her heart was trying to pound through her chest, he could probably hear the noise.

"Let me make it easier. Right now, all we will do is go into the club room and talk. Can you trust me that far?"

Just talk in a bar. She could handle that. "Okay. The bar."

"Good girl." His eyes softened.

Opening the door, he escorted her through, setting a warm hand low on her back.

Once inside, Kari paused to look around. The huge room boasted a circular bar in the center, and wrought iron circular stairs in the corners. Groups of plants sectioned the tables and overstuffed couches into secluded sitting areas. Flickering wall sconces and glass chandeliers hanging from low rafters provided shadowy light and made the hardwood floor gleam.

A scattering of people occupied the couches and bar stools. To Kari's relief, no one was doing weird things or having sex on the floor. Leathers, latex, and skimpy dresses seemed the attire of choice—nothing too outlandish.

He followed her gaze. "Beginners tend to dress conservatively. You'll see a big difference when the regular club members are here on Saturday."

As they crossed the room, Kari spotted Buck at the bar. Her step faltered.

He noticed her, and his face lit up. Then he saw Master Dan with his arm around her, and his mouth compressed so hard his lips disappeared.

To her relief, he didn't approach. She would hate to be the cause of a scene, or even the center of attention.

Without speaking, Master Dan slid his hand up to her waist and moved her closer, his nearness comforting.

Once past the bar, he found an unoccupied sitting area. Taking the very center of the couch, he pulled her down beside him. He smelled of subtly dark cologne, of soap...of *man*. And she was way too close. She tried to shift away, only to realize he'd wedged her between him and the arm of the couch.

"Does it bother you to sit beside me?" he asked, leaning back and studying her. His leg against her thigh was hard, ungiving.

Did he expect her to be rude? "Um, no, of course not." Trying to ignore the feeling of being crowded, she tipped her foot up, wiggled her toes. Why was she barefoot anyway?

"Look at me." He put gentle fingers under her chin, forcing her to meet his level gaze.

"Kari, part of the adventure is being honest with each other. When I ask you a question, I want an honest answer, not a polite one." He smiled slightly. His fingers were warm as his thumb traced little circles on her cheek. "Let me show you what I'd like."

He pitched his voice a little higher and said, "Master Dan, when I realized I was between you and the couch arm, I felt trapped. Like I can't retreat if I want to." His voice returned to its natural subterranean deepness. "Is that about right?"

How did he know that?

He kept watching her with those intent eyes, and each stroke of his thumb across her skin left heat in its wake. He lifted his dark brows. "Kari?"

"Yes," she said almost inaudibly. "That's how I feel." The admission left her feeling as if she'd undressed in front of him, and she tried to look away. He tipped her head back, let her see the pleasure on his face.

"Good girl. I can tell that wasn't easy for you." He brushed a kiss across her lips.

Her lips tingled although the touch had been fleeting, a tiny hint of pleasure.

Dan studied the little newbie. Nervous as a burglar who'd tripped an alarm. And so polite. Her hands lay in her lap, laced together.

"May I ask you some questions?" He massaged her cold little fingers as he waited for her reply.

"Of course. May I ask questions also?" She fidgeted. He watched her fidget. His deliberate intrusion into her personal space definitely set her off balance.

"I hope you will since that's my job tonight, being an instructor. So what do you do when you're not in a wicked house of sin?"

"I'm a—" She hesitated, stiffening a little.

Smart girl, not blurting out too much personal information. Caution wasn't a bad thing. "Ah. Never mind that. Why don't you tell me about the assh—about Buck? I'm assuming he's not your husband."

"No!" Obviously horrified, she frowned at him. "I wouldn't have gone with you if I were married."

"Good to hear. Just a boyfriend, then?" And hadn't the man looked steamed there at the bar. Dan automatically checked his surroundings. All clear.

"I was dating him." She studied her fingers. "He's usually a nice man. I'm not sure why he was like that tonight."

The idea of dominance brought out more than just true Dominants. Perverts, control freaks, and general assholes were plentiful. "You need to be careful about who you trust when you're getting into any kind of power exchange. That's why the class is restricted to this room tonight. No one goes anywhere private." He put his arm across her shoulders, pulling her closer. Curves and softness. Delightful. "Have you ever been married?"

"No. Engaged once, but it didn't work out." The muscles around her eyes tightened...a past hurt? Before he could quiz her, she asked hastily, "How about you? Are you married or involved?"

The unexpected question stabbed through him, and he forced his voice to stay even. "No. My wife died a few years ago. A car accident."

"I'm so sorry." She laid her hand on his cheek. "Do you have children?"

He shook his head. "She wanted to wait. She said she was having too much fun to want to slow down." At times, he could be grateful he wasn't responsible for a child; other times, he ached for someone to love.

"I'm sorry," she repeated.

"Thank you." Her sympathy touched him inside, lightened the heavy feeling in his gut. He took her hand and pressed a kiss to the center.

She smiled at him, her eyes gentle…and pulled her hand back.

Her retreat returned him to the present. So the little miss might be shy, but not when someone needed comfort.

"Um—Mas—"

"So many worries. If 'Master Dan' feels awkward, call me Sir. Any other designation here will get you in trouble."

She frowned. "All right, but—"

He interrupted, taking her hand. "So, Kari. We get a variety of people on beginners' nights. Some have used bondage and such at home, sometimes for years. Do you have any experience at all?"

"Not really. I…we…Buck wanted to tie my hands, and I wouldn't let him." Her muscles tensed, and she tugged at her hand. "I probably don't belong here. Not really. I'm not—"

He chuckled but didn't release her hand or move his arm from her shoulders. "You know, if someone like Buck tried to tie me up, I'd run for the hills. All that shows is your body has better taste in men than your mind."

She blinked. Relaxed a little.

"What does your body say about being with me?" he asked. "Do you feel safe?"

Glancing away from him, she considered, and her brows drew together. "Pretty much. Yes." She sounded surprised.

"All right then. Now tell me about your fiancé. Did you two try anything?"

Her lips curved up. "Oh, no. The thought would have appalled him."

He traced a finger over her plump lips, and her gaze darted to him. "So no experience at all. Why are you here?"

She looked down, pulled in a long breath, and raised those gorgeous eyes back to his. "Buck told me about domination and bondage, and I didn't realize real people do…it. I've never been that interested in sex, but when I heard about this, I was…"

"Turned on?"

She nodded. "But honestly, I don't think this will work for me. I'm very… I'm not the type of person who—"

"You're modest. Polite. Obey the rules."

Relief at being understood showed in her eyes. "Yes. Exactly. My father was quite devout and very strict with my sister and me. Catholic girls' school, no dating in high school, no makeup. She rebelled; I was the good daughter." She gave him a sidelong look. "I'm very repressed."

He laughed. Not so repressed that she'd lost her sense of humor. Still, that explained a lot. Dan fingered her tight French braid, glanced at the dress buttoned to her neck. She wouldn't find this easy.

"So you see, I'm probably wasting your time. I'm very sorry."

Now he knew about her background, he thought she'd been brave just to come here. Should he let her go? He thought about the way her eyes had heated at just a simple command. "Let's talk a little longer and see."

Her foot pointed to the door, but her fingers still gripped his hand. She wanted and didn't want. Did she have any idea how that type of dichotomy could entice a Dom?

"All right." She raised her chin.

"All right," he echoed. "We've established you have no experience. How about fantasies?"

Chapter Three

Kari felt herself turn red.

"Well, she has fantasies." He grinned. "Good. A gorgeous barbarian chasing you down and taking you against your will? Have you had that one?"

"I—" She bit her lower lip. Was she wearing an I-have-kinky-dreams brand or something?

"I would enjoy chasing you; I wonder if you'd enjoy being caught?" His hand cupped her cheek, turning her head so he could kiss her. Ever so lightly, his mouth teased hers, coaxing her to respond. He had firm lips, but smooth, and she moved closer, wanting more. He traced her lips with his tongue, nibbled on her bottom lip, and when she opened for him, he swept inside, sending her senses reeling.

When he pulled back, her fingers were clamped on his upper arms. She fought to catch her breath. A furnace seemed to have started in her body. God, she wanted to kiss him some more.

He smiled and traced her wet lips with his finger. "Save our place," he whispered.

Kari blinked, realized a woman stood beside the couch, her gaze on the floor. She wore a red latex corset, a short black skirt, and wrist cuffs. How long had she been standing there?

"Tabitha."

"Master Dan, may I bring you and your companion something to drink?"

"Kari, what would you like? No, let me see how close I can get." He studied her, and a crease appeared in his cheek with his smile. "It would have to be like you. Sweet. Not exotic, but straightforward. Honest. A screwdriver or perhaps rum and Coke?"

Her jaw dropped. "Rum and Diet Coke. How did you know?"

He nodded at Tabitha, and the young woman disappeared. "Yes, let's talk about that. Part of a Dominant-submissive relationship is—" His eyes glinted with amusement. "Ah, even the words make you blush. Such a lovely pink."

And she could feel her face turning redder with the compliment, darn him. She'd taken her turn at teaching sex education classes and never blushed once. Why now?

"Dominant. Submissive," he said clearly. "Say the words for me, Kari."

Well, that wasn't asking too much, considering where she was. "Dominant. Submissive," she said, managing to speak a little louder than a whisper—maybe not much.

His smile was like a reward. "Good. Shall I give you a harder assignment? *I* am a *Dominant.*" He tilted his head at her to finish.

"I—I—" But she wasn't. Not really... Was she? It was one thing to be thinking about being, well, *controlled* in bed, and quite another to apply an actual label to herself. Labels had meaning. And made everything far too real. This was just supposed to be...an *experiment.*

"Mmmph, that *is* a hard admission, not one you are ready for. Let's put a limit on it then. For the next hour, until nine o'clock, I am a Dominant."

She could do an hour. In fact, that's exactly what she wanted to do. "For the next hour, until nine o'clock, I am a submissive," she said firmly.

And she shivered.

That smile again. "Brave girl."

Tabitha arrived with their drinks, set them on the table quietly, and departed without a word. "Is she a submissive?"

He handed over her drink, took his. "Yes. In training here."

Training. You had to train to be ordered around?

The skin around his eyes crinkled with humor. "You're here for three evenings of classes." He stroked his knuckles along her jaw. "Training is for those wanting to go deeper into the lifestyle, not something you need to worry about."

"Okay. Good." She sipped her drink, blinked at the strength, and sipped again. "How many people end up drunk?"

"None." He drank some of his, clear as water, and set it back on the table. "Master Z limits everyone to two drinks."

Now how could they enforce that? Then she remembered how Sir's big hand had gripped Buck's shoulder, and she felt a tickle of laughter. Enforcement obviously wasn't a problem. And she should pay for her own drink. She fumbled at the pocket of her dress where she'd tucked her key and some money. "The barmaid didn't say what my rum and Coke cost."

"No cost. Drinks are included in membership fees, or for you, the price of the class."

Oh. She put her hands back in her lap. "What happens now?"

"Now we simply talk about what suits your needs."

She stared down into her drink, watching the bubbles. His silence had her looking up, right into his observant eyes.

"Needs is another word that bothers you," he said. "Talking about sex isn't something you do, is it?"

What, did he have some sort of view into her head? "It wasn't an acceptable topic of conversation when I was growing up, no." Her father could expound for hours on purity and innocence without ever saying the sex word.

"Mmmph, in that case, let me run through some options, and we'll take it from there."

Options sounded good. Were there options that were the equivalent of sticking one toe in the water? She took another sip of her drink. "All right."

"I have one request first."

A request in this place might involve just about anything. She eyed him warily. Nodded.

"Can I get you to sit on my lap while we talk?" He ran a finger over her lower lip, slowly, and she grew aware of how soft her own lips were. His mouth curved up in a wicked smile. "I promise not to put my hands anywhere you don't want them."

"But why would I sit on your lap?"

"Sweetheart, it will make it easier for you; sex isn't something to be discussed at arm's length, now is it?"

Sex. With him. She might consider this evening an experiment, but sex wasn't that way. It was personal. He'd be touching her. Intimately. But she wanted this; she really did. "All right."

She set her drink on the table and rose to her feet, smoothing her dress down. He slid into her place. Reclining back against the armrest, he put his legs up and pulled her into his lap.

With her feet still on the floor, she sat stiffly until he laughed and pulled her down against his chest, her head in the hollow of his shoulder. Sit on his lap? This was more like snuggling...and pretty nice. After a moment, she let her hand rest on his bare chest where the vest had fallen away. She ruffled the crisp hair, tracing her fingers over the hard contours of his chest. He was so darned big, she actually felt tiny next to him—well, on top of him—like her weight was nothing to him.

His voice rumbled through his chest. "There we go. You fit into my arms very nicely—a nice, soft armful."

His obvious enjoyment warmed her, made her feel feminine and attractive, something she'd been missing for a while now. For two years, actually, since Curt had left her for some hot, skinny artist.

"What was that thought?" Dan asked. She could feel his fingers in her hair, unpinning the French braid.

"Noth—"

"Kari."

She could hear the warning in his voice, and somehow she didn't want to disappoint him. "I was thinking about my ex-fiancé."

"And?"

"And how fat and frigid he made me feel, okay?" she snapped and tried to sit up, but he tucked an arm across her waist and held her in place. Easily.

"Stay here, little one." He laughed, a low, growling sound. "You have a temper buried under all that politeness. I wonder what else is buried down there."

"I'm sorry." He'd only been nice to her, and she'd lashed out.

"I'm not. You know, with both the temper and the worries about your size, you remind me of Z's sub. Personally I like women with some padding. I like lush." He stroked up to just under her breasts, and she froze.

"And curvy." He ran his hand across her hip, squeezed her bottom, continued down her thigh. Everywhere his hand touched, her skin wakened like spring after a hard winter, and warmth washed through her.

"You have the loveliest fair skin," he murmured, trailing his fingers down her arm. "Soft and creamy, and those pillowy lips of yours would tempt an angel to sin. I'm no angel." His hand tangled in her loose hair, tipping her head back, and his mouth settled on hers. His lips were firm, demanding, opening hers and taking possession without mercy.

When he pulled back, she was breathing hard, her hand fisted in his vest. God, the man could kiss.

"And only an idiot would call you cold," he murmured. "Now, back to business. First of all, I need to find out what kind of a submissive you might be. I think I know, but let's be sure."

"Submissives come in different types?" How could she know so little? When she got home, she was going to take a hammer to that stupid dead computer. "I'm afraid I don't know what you're talking about. Can we try multiple choice?"

He laughed. "All right. *A:* You want to serve a master, making him meals, doing whatever he wants, around the house or in bed. *B:* You want to play a role for a short time, be a schoolgirl or a secretary, but you'd set up your own rules with your top—ah, the person in charge. *C:* You want to give up control for sex but not especially for anything else. *D:* You like pain and want someone to deal it out."

That was quite a list. "People really want all those different things?"

"Oh, definitely. That was just the short list." He tugged on her hair. "Give me a letter, sweetheart."

Well, she knew what she wanted. Why the heck couldn't she be as blasé about sex as her friends were? She wet her lips. "*C.* We—I came here—" She sighed. "*C.*"

"Good enough," he said easily. "Choice *C* for sex."

At least he hadn't jumped up and yelled, *You want what?* in horror. She realized her fingernails were digging into his side and made her hand relax.

Taking hold of her hips, he moved her lower on his lap and slid his arm tighter around her until his hand settled under her breasts. His other hand stroked her neck, her collarbone. She sighed in pleasure, squirming a little to get even closer, and froze when she realized what she was squirming on. He was not only hard; he was huge.

"Sorry," she whispered.

"Don't be sorry about giving someone pleasure, sweetling." His fingers played with her hair that spilled down her front. Somehow several buttons on her dress had come undone, and his hand dropped to rest on the beginning swell of her breast with his other hand just below. One above, one below, like he was holding her breasts captive between the two. Why did that seem erotic?

"How do you feel about being told what to do in bed?"

She caught her breath as the image sent a wave of heat through her. "Um."

But he didn't wait for her answer, just murmured, "That's a go."

A second later, he moved his hand from below her breasts and slid it into her dress where more buttons had come undone. His hand settled back to where it had been before, only now his warm palm lay directly on her naked skin, grazing the lower edge of her breasts. She stiffened and then forced herself to relax. She was here for sex, right?

"Some people like being tied down, kept from moving while their partner pleasures them."

She managed not to squeak.

"Your body likes that idea."

Another pause and she realized she was rubbing her thighs together and stopped immediately. *Tied* up for sex. Being ordered around was one thing, but restrained with ropes or handcuffs? Too much. She hadn't liked the idea at all when Buck had tried it. "No," she said shakily. "I think you're wrong."

"Let's see." He touched his lips to hers, kissed her sweetly, thoroughly, his tongue tangling with hers. When he drew back, she smiled with pleasure.

"That's called vanilla sex," he murmured.

Suddenly he gripped her wrists with hard hands, holding her so she couldn't move. "And this is nonvanilla sex." He took her mouth again, plunging deeply, possessing her ruthlessly. When she tried to move, his grip tightened on her arms, holding her in place.

She couldn't *move*. Every nerve in her body shocked to life as if lightning struck her. Arousal seared through her. She bit back a moan.

He released her, quirking a cynical eyebrow.

Deep inside, her body shook like a palm tree in a tropical storm. What was happening to her? She pulled in a breath. "That didn't…" Her voice trailed off. She was lying to herself and to him. "You're right."

"I like your honesty." Wrapping his arms around her again, he stroked her back. Her cheek rested on his bare chest. His heart beat in a slow, relaxing rhythm, and her own pulse slowed as the claws of desire unhooked from her.

"On your last night, you'll have to take a look at the costumes the members wear," he said conversationally. "It's pretty amazing some of the things people put on. Of course, since it's beginners' night, tonight's attire is pretty sedate." As he talked, he slid one hand into her dress again, nestling up against her breasts, the other resuming its place just under her collarbone.

"You know, some people like a little pain now and then: spanking, pinching, tiny punishments."

It was as if he were having this conversation with himself, except the images he was putting into her head were just... A man spanking her bare bottom? *Jeez, no.* And yet, she actually felt herself dampen.

"Mmm-hmm, yes, I think you'll need a little reprimand now and then."

Her breath hitched. He wouldn't really, now would he?

He rubbed his chin against the top of her head. "You smell good, little sub. Like soap and flowers and...woman. And your hair is as long and silky as any man could want."

Okay, she'd just lie here all night, snuggled into his naked chest, and let him talk to her with that low, low voice. Listening to him was better than having sex with—with anyone she'd ever been with before.

"You know, some people like more pain: being whipped hard, pins inserted under their skin, hot wax dripped on them."

She froze. That... He wouldn't. She shoved against his chest, tried to get free.

"No, that's not for you. Definitely not."

Body stiff, she tried to slide off him.

One arm held her tight against him as his other hand stroked her hair as if he were petting a cat, settling her down. "Truthfully, Kari, I don't like the hardcore S and M either. Real pain doesn't turn me on, and I can see you feel the same."

She took a breath and let herself relax. A little. "Do people really do that? Here?"

"Yes. You'll see some of that, maybe on Wednesday, definitely on Saturday. It's not something you need to do if you're not into it."

"Well, that's good. Thank you." He was so warm and his arms so comforting that when he tilted her head back for another kiss, she didn't resist at all.

Pulling back, he looked her in the eyes and said, "If anytime, anything I do or we do goes beyond what you can stand, then you say 'red,' and everything stops. That's your safe word, sweetheart. Red. Make sense?"

Cool. She could stop everything when she wanted. The sense of relief mingled with confusion. That didn't seem like she was giving up much control.

He kissed her again, and his big hand slid up to cover her breast, his thumb brushing across her nipple. Each touch sent zings of intense sensation spearing through her until she was squirming again.

"Kari, the safe word is for pain. Or something you absolutely can't stand. You use it for anything less, and the night is over. I pack you up, and you go home." His intent gaze trapped hers. "I am going to give you what you want, not what your mama told you is proper. I'm going to push your limits, sweetie."

He nuzzled her until his lips were against her ear. "And you're going to scream as you come over and over again."

She gasped, could feel her nipples harden, and so could he, considering his hand was right there on her breast. He chuckled, sucked on her earlobe, and sent chills chasing across her skin.

"Ahem." Behind them, a woman cleared her throat. Kari jerked to a sitting position, embarrassed at her behavior in public. What had she been thinking?

A DM in a gold-trimmed black bustier and black latex leggings stood by the couch. "Sorry to interrupt," she said, her lips curving up.

Sir sighed. "Olivia. You, as always, have a crappy sense of timing. What?"

"Z said you are to participate in the newbie class. Both of you. Raoul's waiting for you."

"Well, hell. We'll be there."

Sir looked at Kari. "Up you go," he said briskly, pushing her to her feet. "You'll enjoy this, I think. At least the last part of the class." He buttoned her dress, his fingers sliding into the gaps, teasing her sensitive skin, making her regret the interruption.

When he was finished, he ran his knuckles across her breasts, up and down over her jutting nipples. He grinned and murmured, "Guess you're just cold, huh?"

She couldn't keep the laugh bottled up.

They joined the thirty-or-so beginners milling around at the end of the bar. To Kari's surprise, the couples included not only male-female, but also gays and lesbians. With one heterosexual couple, the *man* wore cuffs and a collar. So men could be submissive? Too strange.

Then a gleam of blond hair caught Kari's gaze, and her eyes met Buck's. Grinning, he started toward her and then spotted Master Dan. A scowl darkened his long face, but he stopped.

Even as Kari breathed a sigh of relief, guilt welled within her. She'd arrived with him; she should still be with him.

"All right, people, let's get started." The dungeon monitor teaching the class was an inch or two shorter than Sir, but so thickly muscled he looked like he could pick up her car without breaking a sweat. "Master Dan," he said. "I've got a shy crowd here, and I want to run through some basic bondage. Bring your sub up here."

What?

Sir's arm tightened, and he swept her along, despite her attempt at planting her feet. "Don't worry, sweetling. This is show-and-tell with all your clothes on and no sex."

Well, she *was* used to being in front of people, if teenage students counted as people, something she rather doubted. She shouldn't have a problem with this.

Master Dan nodded at the teacher. "Kari, this is Master Raoul."

She smiled at the man. Was she permitted to talk? Sir hadn't said.

As if he'd read her mind, he murmured, "Say hello, sweetheart."

"I'm very pleased to meet you," she said.

"Hello, Kari." The DM gave her a slow, appreciative look before frowning at Sir. "You always were Z's favorite."

"I know." Master Dan flashed a wicked grin. "So get moving. I have other things to do tonight."

"I bet." Turning back to the class, Master Raoul picked up a pair of metal handcuffs from the bar top. "This is the basic handcuff. Adequate, but if you get your sub excited and she yanks on them, she'll have nasty bruises for a few days. And it's easy to get them too tight. With these, as with all restraints, be sure you check the circulation frequently. Doms, this is a biggie; if you restrain someone, you never leave them alone."

He set the handcuffs down and held up leather wrist cuffs with buckles. "Much more comfortable and safer for circulation. If your sub deserves it, you can even buy lined ones. Master Dan, if you would demonstrate."

Master Dan took the cuffs and held out one hand. "Give me your wrist, Kari," he said.

Her heart gave a hard thud, and she hesitated.

His eyebrows rose. "Now, Kari."

Her hand plopped into his before she'd come up with all the reasons she should say no.

He buckled first one, then the other cuff on, running a finger under to be certain they were snug but not tight. Pulling her wrists in front of her, he hooked the cuffs together. The commanding look in his eyes and the feel of his firm hands on her arms made her stomach quiver and heat pool in her lower half.

When he finished, he stepped back, studying her face. His lips curved in a hard smile.

Trying to ignore the dampness seeping between her thighs, she yanked at the cuffs. She definitely couldn't get free of them, but still, this wasn't all that scary. Her hands were in front of her; she could defend herself.

Master Raoul nodded. "Basic restraint. Hands in front, but not very intimidating. Leaves a lot of room for evasion. Dan?"

To Kari's shock, Master Dan set his hand on one breast, cupping her firmly. Even as a thrill rushed through her, she instinctively knocked his fingers off with her cuffed hands and glared at him.

"Not a very obedient sub you have there," Master Raoul commented dryly as the group laughed.

Oh, heavens, had she embarrassed him? She shouldn't have reacted without thinking. Kari risked a glance.

Although he didn't smile, his cheek creased, and his eyes were amused as he unclipped her wrists.

"Hands behind the back will help solve that little aggression problem," Master Raoul said.

Master Dan stepped behind Kari and clipped the cuffs together at the small of her back. This time, she yanked at them unsuccessfully, and a shiver ran through her at the helpless feeling. With her hands behind her back, she could do nothing to—

"And as you see, your sub is much more manageable," Master Raoul said.

Master Dan's hard chest pressed against her back as he reached around her, one arm securing her waist. His other hand closed on her breast. She jumped, squeaked, and couldn't move, couldn't get free as he caressed her, his fingers sending erotic sensations swirling through her.

Chapter Four

Dan felt Kari's heart pound as his fingers stroked her full breasts. He could also feel the way her nipples tightened. Arousal flushed her neck. No question, the little miss was submissive.

But so new. Just as well she had no idea how much control it took to not open those tiny buttons, slide his hand under her bra, stroke her soft skin, and roll her nipples between his fingers. And that would be just the beginning. Bending her over one of the couches, exposing her ass, and—

"There's a small problem with this type of bondage, however," Master Raoul stated.

Wrenching his mind back to business, Dan responded to the cue. He scooped Kari off her feet, enjoying the tiny squeal she gave. Kneeling, he laid her on her back on the floor and straddled her thighs. Her eyes were huge as she stared up at him.

"As you can see, she's lying on her arms, an uncomfortable position for a sub, especially if you plan to be on top of her." Raoul grinned.

Dan rose and set Kari back on her feet. The deep breath of relief she took made him chuckle.

"Thank you, Kari and Master Dan," Raoul said. "Now someone may volunteer for the next demonstration, or I will pick two people myself." A middle-aged couple stepped forward, and Raoul talked them through leg restraints.

Dan put his arm around Kari, enjoying her tiny squirms as she tested the cuffs every few seconds.

"You can take these off now," she whispered, giving him an annoyed look.

Those flashes of temper could drive a Dom crazy thinking of the various enjoyable ways to punish them. Again, she was too new, no serious disciplining allowed. But since she was still frowning up at him, her mouth was perfectly positioned, and he didn't resist. Tightening his grip on her waist, he kissed her. After a second of resistance, her lips softened, and his tongue plunged inside. He took her mouth thoroughly, as he wished he could take the rest of her before the night ended. Her quivering response made his blood boil and his cock strain to be set free.

With a regretful sigh, he pulled back, moving to stand beside her. One hand rested on her shoulder, strategically placed to feel her body's responses to the rest of the toys Raoul brought out. By the time Raoul finished the lesson, every beginner Dom had restrained a sub in one way or another, and Dan had discovered Kari was turned on by leg restraints also. Good to know.

Now the single students paired off, and everyone wandered through the club to practice what they'd learned. With beginners locked out of the private rooms upstairs, he and Kari were stuck down here too.

He remembered a relatively isolated area, though, near the back of the room and well hidden behind a bunch of foliage. He beckoned to a trainee. "Sally, run over and put a RESERVED sign on the sitting area to the left of the theme rooms."

The trainee laughed as she shook her head in disapproval. "Shame on you. That's cheati—" She shut her mouth quickly, several words too late.

Kari frowned as the barmaid dropped to her knees before Master Dan. The pretty brunette looked mortified and a bit frightened as she whispered, "I'm sorry, Master Dan."

Master Dan's expression hardened into stone. "I've lost patience with your lack of control over your tongue. Show me your bands," he snapped.

Sally held out her arms. Each wrist held a narrow leather cuff wrapped with yellow, blue, and green ribbons.

"First, do as I asked. Then report to Master Cullen and inform him you are to be given to a DM for spanking and his use. Are my instructions clear?"

Sally's eyes widened, and her outstretched hands trembled. "Yes, Sir."

"Go."

After pushing to her feet, the brunette escaped, almost tripping in her haste to get away.

Kari stared up at Master Dan, horror chilling her body. "Did you just give her to a stranger? Just like that?"

He turned. The coldness disappeared from his expression as if it had never been. "Ah, Kari. Sally is another sub in training. This is part of her instruction."

"But a spanking? And...use?" She had a pretty good idea what *use* meant. Dear God. Kari stepped back. She really didn't know this man at all.

Her hands were still cuffed, she realized with a jolt of fear.

"Dan—oops—Master Dan, I mean." A pretty blonde in tight jeans and an emerald green, low-cut blouse hurried up. "Z wants you to join him for a few minutes, if you could. Something about a club membership."

"Of course." Master Dan turned to Kari, and she took another step back. His eyes narrowed before he turned to the blonde.

"Jessica, I disciplined Sally for mouthing off, and now Kari's terrified. She's probably convinced I'm a white slave trader. Can you stay with her and reassure her while I'm gone?"

"Only if you'll agree to join us for supper next Friday."

"Works for me. Sure." Pinning Kari in place with a hard look, he closed the distance between them. He stroked a finger down her cheek, sending a thrill through her.

She swallowed hard, unable to look away from his penetrating gaze. The man had just scared her spitless, so why did his touch still make her all quivery inside?

He smiled, as if he could feel her response. After unhooking her hands from behind her back, he strode off toward the front of the room. Tall, straight shouldered, gorgeous—and more frightening than Hannibal Lector. She was in way over her head here.

"Ready for some female company?" the blonde asked, following her gaze.

"I would be very grateful." Kari stuck a hand out. "I'm Kari, and what you'd call a newbie, I guess."

The woman took her hand, gave a strong squeeze. Like Sally, she wore leather cuffs. Fur-lined, but lacking any ribbons. "I'm Jessica, and I'm past newbie status, but I haven't been in the scene very long. Let's have a drink and talk."

The circular bar was nearly deserted with only two beginners hovering at one end, and three dungeon monitors at the other. Kari slid onto a wooden stool beside Jessica.

In the center, the giant bartender concocted a fancy drink, humming to the soft music of Pachelbel's "Canon." In dark brown leathers that matched his thick hair, he had a rough face of blunt angles and a solid jaw. After delivering the drink to a newbie, he sauntered over to Kari and Jessica.

Leaning a big arm on the bar top, he gave Kari a long, slow look that made heat rise in her cheeks. "Little subbie, do you want another rum and Diet Coke?"

Would speaking get her in the same kind of trouble as Sally? What were the darned rules in this place? "Just Coke, please."

He didn't yell at her. Instead, he turned to Jessica. "Margarita?"

"Yes, thank you, Master Cullen."

His laugh boomed through the bar. "So formal. Setting a good example for your friend?"

Jessica grinned.

Master Cullen set the drinks in front of them, gave Kari another of those *looks*, and left to take another order. Her face heated. Jeez. With a rueful smile, she glanced at Jessica. "I swear, I've spent most of my time here blushing. And sometimes I'm not even sure why."

Jessica laughed. "If you mean Cullen, some of the more powerful Doms can make you turn red just by looking at you."

"Well, no wonder then." This place was obviously littered with strong Doms. Her mind turned back to what had caused the worry gnawing away in her stomach. "Tell me about Sally. When she messed up, Master Dan gave her to some Dom—any Dom—to *use*. That seems like almost rape."

"But it's not." Jessica held up her wrist. "Did you see the ribbons on her cuffs?"

Kari nodded.

"They show what kind of activities a trainee is into. Red for serious sadomasochism, yellow for milder pain like spankings, blue for bondage, and green for sex. If she had a green ribbon, she was all right with being given to any Dom here."

"Oh." Wow. What would that be like, to be just handed over to someone? Kari took a hefty gulp of her drink, wondering if she should have had the rum.

"This place can be overwhelming. The first time I was here, I just wanted shelter during a storm. I didn't know it was a BDSM club. There was all this *stuff* going on." She rolled her eyes. "I got in so much trouble…"

Kari grinned. "Tell me more."

"Next class, I'll give you the full story. For now, how do I convince you that Master Dan's not a white slave trader?"

"Uh. It helps knowing he didn't do something that Sally wasn't expecting, I guess." Kari frowned. But now that he wasn't touching her, looking at her, she was starting to have second thoughts. Did she really want to continue? All the other beginners were off in dark corners practicing that bondage stuff, and Master Dan would be expecting to do that with her. And he wasn't any beginner. A little thrill ran through her at the thought of his big hands on her, and she squashed it down. "But I don't know him, and to let him tie me up or something seems insane."

"I understand completely. What can I tell you about him…" Jessica tapped a finger against her chin as she thought. "He and Master Z are friends, and he's been a club member for years. He used to come with his wife, but she died, and he hasn't been seriously involved with anyone since. Z said he's changed; apparently he used to laugh a lot more. He helps with the beginners, and you certainly aren't the first new sub he's taken under command. Oh, and the subs say he's one of the best Doms in the place."

Kari breathed out. Was she pleased or unhappy with this information? Knowing he was a respectable Dom—and didn't *that* sound like a contradiction in terms—meant she had no excuse to back out. And she both wanted to and didn't want to stop, before anything got more intense. She sighed and finished her drink.

"It's scary stuff when you're not used to it." Jessica pursed her lips and gave Kari a wry look. "And even when you *are* used to it. If you have a good Dom, that sense of uneasiness can be pretty exciting."

Kari glanced toward the front and saw the group of dungeon monitors reentering the room. Master Dan's gaze scanned the room. When his eyes came to rest on her, the floor seemed to drop a few inches, leaving her dizzy. Apparently, his look was even more potent than the other Doms.

He strode over to the bar, his gait long and powerful, and stood so close she could feel the heat radiate off his body. He smiled at Jessica. "Thank you for staying with her," he said. "Kari, did she answer your questions?"

Kari nodded.

His hand tilted her chin up so he could look directly in her eyes. "Do I have your trust? Do you want to continue?"

She bit back the yes that wanted to escape from her lips. *Think, Kari.* But she knew the answer, and it wasn't changing. "*He's one of the best,*" Jessica said. That must be better than blundering around with beginners. "Yes," she said. "Continue." Oh God, was she insane?

She glanced at Jessica, and her uncertainty must have shown.

Jessica gave her a sympathetic look. "I'll get back to Z then." She shook her finger at Master Dan. "You be nice to her."

Master Dan frowned. "If you were mine, I'd beat you more often."

Appalled, Kari sucked in a breath and then saw a smile pull at his lips, the gleam of laughter in his eyes.

And Jessica only laughed as she slid off the stool and moved away.

Grasping Kari around the waist with hard hands, Master Dan lifted her off the stool and set her on her feet. Startled, she clung to his arms for a second, getting her balance. "All right, Kari. Here are the rules for the rest of the evening. You do what I say. Immediately. Without arguing. You don't speak unless I ask you a question. If you say anything, it had better be 'yes, Sir.' You will address me as either Sir or Master Dan."

His voice roughened. "What do you say to me, little sub?"

Startled, she jerked, then bit her lip before answering slowly, "Yes, Sir."

"Very nice. Now let's see if I remember where we were before the lessons started." He pulled her closer. And closer until she was plastered against his body, her breasts flattened on his wide chest. He bent, taking her mouth gently, tipping her back until she grabbed his shoulders for balance. He held her easily while he plundered her lips, his tongue plunging into her mouth until her head swam. When he pulled back, her hands were buried in his hair. With a laugh, he set a hand on her bottom to press her against a hard erection. "This is what that soft, hot mouth of yours does to me," he whispered in her ear.

Her insides flared with heat.

Clamping an arm around her waist, he led her to the back of the room. They passed roped-off areas along the wall, each with a different piece of ominous-looking equipment: benches, something that looked like a sawhorse with a shelf on each side, a massive wooden X against the wall. Some had shackles and cuffs, and Kari's eyes widened as she tried to imagine how a person would be attached.

Master Dan smiled slowly. "Next time, you will see more of the equipment. And use some of it."

Oh...my. She imagined herself cuffed to the bench or on that thing against the wall, and her lower regions actually tingled. "Um. Where are we going?"

They went past a small island of plants, and he turned into a sitting area with a couch and chairs. A coffee table had the requested RESERVED sign on it. "Right here. This is as private as we're going to get tonight." He pulled her down onto the couch beside him and gripped her shoulders. "All right, Kari. What's your safe word?" he asked.

Kari looked up at him. His face was serious, the humor gone. And she was alone with him.

Chapter Five

Dan smiled as she looked at him with wide eyes. She had no idea how those helpless looks could affect a Dom.

"Red," she whispered. She bit her lip again, and he couldn't stand it.

"If anyone nibbles those lips, it will be me," he murmured, licking over the plump bottom one. He tilted his head and took her mouth, then delved deep inside. She tasted of rum and Coke and something that was essentially Kari.

She sighed, her muscles softening as need overcame her fears.

She was a challenge, and he hadn't enjoyed anyone so much in ages. He could see the passion in her, locked deep inside all those habits and rules. Even more, he could see she was sweet down to the bone, much like Marion had been. But different. Marion had enjoyed her passions; this little sub had definitely been raised by nuns.

Enfolding her in his arms, he pressed her back onto the couch. Her arms wrapped around his neck, pulling his lips back to hers. He nuzzled her neck, enjoying the light fragrance—softly floral with a woman's subtle musk beneath. He wanted to explore further, to find all the places on her body where her scent was strongest.

He would get there, step-by-step.

As he deepened the kiss, she gave him anything he asked for, sucking his tongue into her mouth, giving him hers in return.

When he drew back to lean on his elbow, she made a little sound of disappointment. He studied her for a moment. A pulse beat fast in her neck; her lips were appealingly swollen and red, and her eyes heavy lidded with passion.

She was ready for more. Keeping his gaze on her, he set his hand under her long dress, slowly stroking up and down her leg, ever more upward, until he could set his palm on her crotch. She jumped a little, but he didn't move. He could feel the warmth from her pussy radiating outward. Her panties were damp, and he had to smother the urge to strip them off and bury himself inside her heat.

First things first. He wondered if she'd ever remember the hour limit they'd started with. Nine o'clock was long past.

He caught her gaze—a little dazed, fully aroused. But if he didn't keep her off balance and moving forward, all that modesty and restraint would return. Time to let her discover the joy—and anxiety—of vulnerability. "Lower the top of your dress."

Her breath hitched, and she tried to look around, but he caught her chin and lifted his eyebrows. "What do you say to me?"

"Yes, Sir." Her delicate fingers undid the buttons down to the waist. He watched with a steady gaze as she glanced at him before sitting up and pulling her arms out of the dress.

He enjoyed the sight of her, his pleasure increasing as she flushed. So modest. Stripping would be one of the hardest tasks he could set her. But well worth it for him. She was a visual treat with her breasts almost overflowing the lacy white bra.

"You have lovely shoulders, Kari." He leaned forward so he could kiss his way across the pale white skin. She had little freckles scattered across her shoulders. He licked them and could swear they tasted like sugar. Since he was in the right place, he obligingly undid her bra. "Remove this."

She slid it from her arms and leaned forward to place it, neatly folded, on the coffee table.

There were reasons he loved women who were bigger than stick figures, and here were two of the finest reasons: abundant, lovely breasts with pale pink nipples. Under his gaze, those nipples contracted. He touched them with just his fingertips, watched them tighten even further. "When I'm through tasting these, they will be as hard as pencil erasers and a lovely dark red."

He waited for her blush, grinned, and stroked her heated cheek.

"Yes, exactly that color." He let his hand slide down—not like he was able to stop it—under one breast, savoring the heaviness. With his fingers, he swept in a circle around one breast, then the other, never touching either nipple, tormenting until she arched her chest forward for more.

"You are still overdressed, sweetheart. Remove your panties."

This time the hesitation was longer. He lifted her chin with one finger and gave her a firm look. "What do you say to me?"

"Yes, Sir," she whispered and stood. Her fingers trembled as she pulled up the dress. Her briefs were white, but low cut and lacy. Soft and innocent and sexy like Kari herself.

He knew she was no virgin, but she might as well be, given that her deeper passions had never been explored.

She pushed her panties to the floor, stepped out. The folded panties joined her bra on the coffee table. Tidy little sub.

"Good girl." He grabbed a fistful of the dress she still wore and pulled her between his knees. Trembling and soft, lush, and sweet. *Submissive.*

And all his for the moment.

Kari shook inside, feeling far too vulnerable. He was still dressed; she was half-naked. Yet every time he ordered her to do something with a voice that would accept only compliance, she got more excited. Wetter.

Now his knees pinned her in place as he gazed at her body. His eyes were so hot, so hungry, that she brought her hands up to cover her breasts.

He caught her arms, gave her a disapproving look, and pulled her hands down. "This is my body to play with this evening, little sub. Keep your hands down at your sides. In fact, put them behind your back and lace your fingers together." His rich baritone deepened. "What do you say to me?"

"Yes, Sir." She complied. Her hands behind her back made her breasts arch forward, almost right in his face.

He hummed in pleasure, leaned forward, and took one nipple into his mouth. His mouth was hot, lips firm, and as his tongue swirled around the nipple, she moaned, shocking herself.

When she tried to move back, he put an arm behind her. Fastening his grip over her laced fingers, he pulled her closer. His mouth tightened and his tongue rubbed her nipple against the roof of his mouth. Heat stabbed straight down to her core.

Then his free hand possessed her other breast, rolling the nipple between firm fingers.

"Oh, God." Her vision blurred. She needed to move, to do something as an ache of longing burst in her lower body.

His grip tightened.

"You have magnificent breasts, Kari. I'm going to enjoy them tonight." His dark brown eyes looked at her, studied her.

She looked away. This was a bar room, not a bedroom. No doors, no bed. That just wasn't right.

Even worse, she was taking a man's orders and…she liked it. Oh, she did. Each time he set those dark eyes on her, her insides softened until now her lower half felt like warm Jell-O. She didn't seem to have any control over her own body.

Releasing her, he moved to the chair. "Come and sit on my lap. You look like you need a hug," he said softly. He pulled her onto his lap and leaned her against his big chest. His heart thudded beneath her ear, slow and steady, as his arms snuggled her tighter. His hands were gentle as he stroked her back and arms until she relaxed against him, feeling like a pampered pet. She rubbed her forehead against his chest with a sigh.

"Not so bad, is it?" he murmured.

"Guess not."

"Good. Then we'll continue." Before she could respond, he tilted her back until her shoulders rested on the chair arm with her bottom on his lap.

"Hey!" She struggled to sit up, but he set a hand between her breasts.

"You stay where I put you, little sub," he growled, mouth flattening.

She froze. Her heart sped up as she got that strange, melting feeling again.

The corner of his mouth turned up. "You like being bossed around, don't you."

It wasn't a question and required no answer, thank heavens.

His eyes glinted with amusement. "We'll talk about that later. For now, you are in a very nice position." He set his hands on her breasts, stroking and massaging, teasing her nipples until they were tight and swollen and aching.

And that was before he put his mouth on her. He sucked on each nipple, rolling the peaks. He nipped one, and she gasped as a current of heat shot from her breast to her groin. Her private areas were wet, embarrassingly wet, and throbbing.

"You taste sweet," he murmured, then shook his head. "And you're making me forget my job here. Give me your wrists."

Her heart thudded hard. Setting her cuffed wrists into his broad palm was exceedingly difficult, but she managed. He reached into his pocket, pulled out a two-foot length of chain, and snapped each end to the cuffs.

"I'm being gentle with you, little sub," he said. "Your hands can be in front as long as they stay where I put them." He took her arms and pushed them over her head, making her back arch. "Do you understand?"

Why was her body almost shaking with need? "Yes, Sir."

"Very good."

He played with her breasts for a few more minutes until she had to press her lips together to keep from begging him for more.

Then he ran his fingers up under her dress. She gave him a wary look even as her core heated in anticipation of his touch. His hand felt huge, pushing her legs apart as his fingers teased her pubic hair, never quite touching her mound.

She stiffened as footsteps approached their sitting area. Three men walked around the corner. A DM and two newbies.

One was Buck. *Oh, no no no!* Her breasts bare, his hand under her skirt... What had she done? Kari made a grab for the top of her dress.

Master Dan glanced over at the men, then said to her, "Put your arms back where I placed them, sub."

He pinned her with his gaze, and she couldn't keep her arms from moving back over the arm of the chair. Her breath almost sobbed.

His gaze softened slightly. "Better." He looked at the men again and deliberately cupped her breast with his free hand. She stiffened, bit her lip to keep from moving.

Buck's hands clenched into fists, and he took a step forward. "She shouldn't—"

The DM grabbed his arm. "Buck, did I explain about interfering between a Dom and his sub?"

"Yes, but—"

"Go." The DM pushed the other two back around the plants and paused long enough to smile. "Pretty sub, Dan. Doesn't look like she enjoys being displayed."

Master Dan shook his head. "Not this time, not with the asshole here." A grin flashed over his face. "Next time, though…"

With a snort of laughter, the DM followed after the men.

Sir's gaze returned to Kari, and he stroked her cheek. "I'm proud of you, little sub," he said, his eyes as warm now as they had been cold before. "I know you don't like being exposed like that."

The approval warmed her inside, at least until she remembered the shock on Buck's face. How the men had looked at her, and Sir had let them. "You should have covered me, or—"

His jaw hardened. "No, Kari. We discussed your interests earlier. Now that we've started, as your Dom, I decide what is correct or proper or desired. Aside from your safe word, you have no say, no opinions, no control."

Her mind seemed to split, one part going, No, that's wrong. The other half whispering, Yes, this is what I want.

He waited quietly, his fingers playing with the curls in her long hair.

Finally she sighed.

His lips turned up. "Come to any conclusions?"

"Only that I'm confused."

"Good answer for a beginner." He kissed her, taking his time, nibbling on her lips, sucking her tongue into his mouth, giving her his. His hand circled her breast, his fingers toying with her nipples until heat spread through her again, and she arched uncontrollably.

"There we go," he murmured. "Now, I want you to stand up for me." He helped her to her feet and turned her to face him. "Sit down. Ride my legs."

As he lifted her dress, she lowered herself so she straddled his knees. The dress bunched around her legs. What was he going to do?

"Good. Now put your arms around me."

After a moment, she dropped her cuffed wrists over his head, sliding her arms down until her hands rested on his ribs. Her face was almost even with his, her breasts jutting toward his chest. When he cupped one of her breasts, she inhaled sharply at the heady feeling, the punch of increasing need. Could he tell how wet she was? The thought sat uneasy in her chest, and she tried to pull back, but the chain between her wrists was behind his back. Her heart gave a thud. Then she realized if she lifted her arms, she'd be free. Okay, she was good. She settled a little more comfortably and looked at him.

He smiled at her slowly. "Give me your right foot." He held his hand out.

She frowned. Lifting her foot that far would be really indiscreet considering she wore no panties.

"Kari," he growled, and her foot rose before she could tell it no. He grasped it in a callused hand and pushed it down between the seat cushion and the arm of the chair. "Now—" He gave her a hard look. "If that foot moves from where I put it, I'll tie it in place. Is that understood?" He waited.

The warning sent a rush of arousal through her, fully as intense as when he was touching her. "Yes, Sir."

She frowned as cool air touched her private areas. But the dress still covered her adequately. Thank goodness she'd worn a long one today.

Watching her intently, he leaned back and slid his left hand under her skirt to press against her mound.

Startled, she jumped and tried to lift her chained wrists back over his head. She couldn't. He'd trapped her chain behind his back. She tugged at her hands, and her breath sped up. She couldn't move her hands, couldn't do anything, and he had his hand between her legs. Fear shot through her, followed by a disconcerting wave of heat.

He still watched her. Now he smiled slowly and pulled his hand out from under her dress. "You like being restrained," he said softly. He showed her the wetness glistening on his fingers. "You're aroused, sweetheart."

She blushed from her breasts to her forehead, and he chuckled.

As he slid his hand back under her dress, she tugged again, feeling the world tilt at her helplessness, at the carnal feel of his fingers between her legs.

At knowing she couldn't stop him.

His free hand wrapped around the nape of her neck, pulling her forward. His mouth settled on hers, hot and demanding, and as his tongue took possession, he slid one hard finger into her. She inhaled sharply, tried to pull back, but his hand behind her head didn't release its hold.

His kiss deepened. Down below, his finger slid in and out, and she felt hot, needy, out of control. Exposed. She started to move her foot, to bring her legs together.

He lifted his head and gave her a hard look. "You don't want to do that, Kari."

She left her foot in place, her breathing heavy. His finger never stopped, and her vagina tightened around the invasion. Her raised leg trembled. And then his finger slicked out and up over her clitoris.

Her hips jerked uncontrollably. "Uhhhh." She bit down on her lip to keep from more betraying noises.

He stroked over the sensitive nub, spreading her slickness around her folds until her entire center tingled with need.

"Open more," he said and moved his legs apart, spreading her, exposing her further to his touch. "You have a soft pussy, sweetheart. And you're very tight." With his words, he slid his finger back up inside her, making her insides clench. When his thumb circled and stroked her clit, her hands curled helplessly against his sides.

With a low laugh, he pulled her forward, pushing her forehead against his hard chest. She needed the support as he stroked inside her, curling and hitting a sensitive spot, one that sent blood roaring through her veins like hot lava.

She could hear herself panting. Her hands closed into fists, unable to move from where they were pinned against his sides. She could only take what he was doing to her. His free hand stroked across her breasts, sending sharp, spiking lines of heat through her as he rolled her nipples between his fingers.

Her thighs quivered uncontrollably. Everything tightened inside her. Each stroke inside and each flick of his thumb on her clit sent her closer, until her breathing stopped and the pressure built. Waiting, waiting... He pulled his hand back and then pushed two fingers into her, the thickness stunning, and she broke as devastating pleasure burst inside her, as her vagina convulsed around his impaling fingers, as her hips bucked to his thrusts, over and over.

Chapter Six

She was absolutely beautiful when she came, Dan thought. Her lips parted, cheeks flushed pink. Her chest heaved as she panted, jostling those luscious breasts. Her response was so honest.

After he'd induced the last few spasms, he removed his hand, enjoying the heady fragrance of her arousal. Releasing her wrists, he repositioned her so she could rest in his arms. He could feel her heart pounding when he cupped a breast.

Exhausted, she lay against his chest, limp as overcooked spaghetti. Damn, she was a comfortable armful. Little and round, fragrant and responsive. And sweet. He kissed the top of her head.

When her breathing slowed, she lifted her head. "Um...I...well...thank you."

He chuckled. Her cheeks were even pinker now than when she'd come. "You're welcome, little sub."

"But what about you? You didn't..." Her whispered words were muffled, her face pressed against his chest.

Sweet. "I'll survive."

"But..."

He tilted her chin up so she had to look at him. "You know, I would like nothing better than to tie you down, open you up, and bury my cock in that wet pussy."

She inhaled sharply and quivered.

He stroked her cheek with his thumb. Silky smooth. "And you would like it too, little sub, wouldn't you?"

Another wash of red across her face. Her pulse picked back up. She was unable to meet his eyes as she nodded.

"But you aren't ready for that tonight, sweetie, and the time for your beginner class ends about now. I don't think you want to have a dungeon monitor find you with your legs over my shoulders and me deep inside you." The thought made him harden. "Right?"

Her spine straightened. She shook her head. "I think I'd better go now."

He stroked her breasts, watched the nipples move from after-climax softness to hard points again. He hadn't had enough time with those breasts; they weren't nearly pink enough. But hell, it really was time to stop.

With a sigh, he grabbed her bra and helped her into it, covering the dual temptations. He buttoned her dress, nudging her hands out of the way when she tried to help. "I enjoy dressing you," he murmured and grinned. "Of course, I enjoyed undressing you more."

Having her entirely naked would be even better. An image of her in bed, arms chained over her head, squirming under his mouth, his fingers, his cock, made him harden even further, as if he hadn't already been in pain since the moment his fingers touched her damp panties.

But a beginner deserved a gentle first experience, just enough to learn what being restrained felt like, but not enough to scare her.

With one hand along her jaw, he held her for his kiss, his grip tight enough she could feel his strength and her helplessness. Reminding her of what domination meant. When he released her, that succulent little body trembled.

"Now, you have an idea of what submission means," he whispered. Was there anything headier than a woman quivering in his arms? Knowing he could take her in any way he wanted. Knowing he could make her come, over and over, by his touch.

And knowing his words alone could send her into total confusion. "Did you like being restrained, Kari?"

She wanted to shout at him. The man knew full well how embarrassed talking about sex made her, and he asked her that deliberately. Shoot, every time he held her in place, her insides went all soft and liquid, and he knew that too. Annoyance flared inside her.

"Kari. I asked you a question." His voice had that edge of command. Deeper, harder.

"Yes, dammit." He'd made her swear. She glared at him. And what kind of slutty woman was she to like being cuffed and ordered around and... Her body remembered the overwhelming feel of his fingers moving in her, on her, and she clenched inside. She wasn't going to get into a discussion about this. Absolutely not. "I liked it. Okay?"

One eyebrow raised, and his lips flattened into a hard line. He tilted her suddenly, back against his left arm, pinning her right side up against his chest. He secured her left wrist with one hand. As his arm tightened around her, his right hand slid under her skirt, between her legs, and he pushed a finger right into her.

She gasped, struggled. "What are you—"

"Be silent." He set his thumb on her still-sensitive clit, pressing firmly.

She gasped against the shock of awakening need.

"Now, I can keep you here, just like this, finger-fucking you until you're screaming for release, until the entire club can hear you."

His graphic words widened her eyes with horror.

"Or you can apologize and remember how a sub addresses a Dom in this club." His finger started moving in and out, his thumb making circles on her clit, and she realized he could easily make her lose control. She pulled at her hand and got nowhere; his grip was tighter than the cuffs, and the feeling of helplessness sent arousal soaring within her.

His finger moved within her, slow and sure, then fast and hard, circles and strokes. She burned, her hips rising into his hand. He stopped suddenly, leaving her throbbing, his dark eyes on her face.

She realized she was breathing hard and pressed her lips together. Okay, so no problem. She'd cool down and—

He started again, plunging in and out, and she let out a cry, her hips thrashing uncontrollably. Oh, God, he could do just what he'd said. "I-I'm sorry, Sir. I'll be more careful. Please—"

His grin was a flash of white, then gone. "Apology accepted." When he removed his hand, her whole lower half ached with need. "And how you feel now will remind of you this lesson in the future."

She started to glare at him, got a level look, and managed to give him a tight-lipped smile.

He laughed. "Sweetheart, I hope you don't play poker."

With his hand—she could smell herself on his fingers—he turned her head and took her lips. She tried to push him away, realized her hand was still gripped in his, and again the heat rose within her. His kiss was hard, thorough, and long. It left her head spinning and her body aching even more.

When he lifted his head, she couldn't move, could only manage a shuddery breath. With a soft chuckle, he kissed her cheek and cuddled her against his big chest. She rolled her head against him, contented and a little confused.

When he held her, controlled her, she got so aroused, but when Buck did almost exactly the same things—ordering her, wanting to restrain her—she felt repelled. That didn't make any sense.

Of course, any woman with a functioning ovary would see Sir and want him. Oh, yes. But it was more than that. Part of what made her so hot and needy was the aura of power around him. No, more than that…*controlled* power.

He didn't let his body lead him around. He didn't let her lead him around either. And he was honest. She didn't have to guess if she did something right. If he wasn't happy, she found out right away. If he wanted her to do something, he said so.

And he liked her body. Liked *her.* She really liked him too. Especially right now. Getting off—when she did—always left her feeling a little lost. Vulnerable. But the way he held her so firmly against him made her feel safe. Cherished, even.

Even if she had more questions about herself than when she started, he'd given her an evening to remember.

She set her hand on his cheek, feeling the roughness of beard shadow. "Sir," she whispered and pulled his head down so she could kiss him and show him how much she appreciated his consideration.

When they broke this time, his eyes were soft as he looked down at her. "Kari," he murmured. He pulled her tighter against him, his hand stroking her shoulder. "Sweetheart, you are…"

He stopped, and his hand froze against her arm. For a moment, he looked at her as if he didn't know who she was.

"Sir?"

His brows drew together, and his arms loosened. Then he pushed her to her feet. "It's time you went home."

When he stood, she lifted a hand toward him but let it drop. "Are you mad? Did I do something wrong?"

His mouth smiled, but his eyes didn't. "No, you did nothing wrong. You're a very nice woman, Kari."

Well, talk about damned with faint praise.

Silently, he walked her back to where the DMs had herded the beginners into a group. Master Raoul appeared to check if anyone had questions and remind them the second beginners' class was Wednesday.

As the others dispersed, Kari turned to Master Dan. "Thank you for the...um, lesson." How awkward this was. She wanted to touch him, but he looked so cold.

He nodded, his face unreadable, his eyes without warmth. It was as if he'd pulled himself behind some impenetrable wall. "I'm glad you came, Kari. I hope you enjoy the next couple of lessons. Be careful with your next choice of Dom." He nodded to her and walked toward the exit.

Staring after him, she rubbed her hands over her arms, feeling a distinct chill. What had she done wrong? She had smarted off earlier, but he'd obtained his revenge for that.

She'd kissed him. Was that against the rules? Shoot, whatever she'd done, he obviously wasn't going to have anything to do with her in the future. But he could have been a little nicer about it.

She tried to work up a good anger instead of feeling lost. What a jerk, walking off like that. "Fine then," she muttered to his back. "You have a nice life too." Turning, she almost ran into Sally.

The trainee had obviously overheard everything. Her gaze was full of sympathy.

"So what was that all about? Did I do something wrong?" Kari asked.

"No, girlfriend. That's just Master Dan; only he's not usually that abrupt." Sally stared after him, her brows together. "But it's not you. He never uses a sub more than one night."

"Oh." The unhappy lump in Kari's stomach grew bigger. So she was just another submissive to him. Here she'd thought there was more than that between them. God, she could be stupid about men. "Got it. Thanks, Sally."

"No problem. We subs stick together."

"Miss Kari?"

Kari turned to see the security guard. Oh, great, had she done something else wrong? "That's me."

"I'm Ben. Master Dan asked me to walk you to your car."

"I don't need an escort," she said, then hesitated. Buck lingered near the room exit. "Then again, I'd love the company. Thank you."

As they walked past Buck, he gave her a sheepish smile. "Kari, I wanted to apologize. I was nervous and took it out on you." He glanced at the guard. "I don't want to keep you from leaving. How about I call you later this week and we'll talk? I hope you can forgive me."

What could she say? After the way Master Dan had brushed her off like a nasty bug that had gotten into his soup, Buck's eagerness to be with her was comforting. She moved her shoulders and gave him a weak smile. "There's really nothing to forgive. We'll talk later this week."

"Great." He nodded at Ben and strode away, his step with a bounce in it.

Well, at least one person thought she was nice. A shame Master Dan didn't feel the same.

* * *

Dan stalked into his apartment, stripping off his leathers on the way to the bedroom. He threw them into the corner. *What a crappy evening.*

In the kitchen, he grabbed a beer and sucked half of it down before dropping into his chair in the living room. The cold brew helped, but he was still pissed, and he thumped his head against the back of the chair. What the hell was wrong with him, anyway?

Like he didn't know. He saw her again, like he'd been seeing her every few minutes on the drive home: Kari soft and round in his arms, her eyes glazed with passion, her lips swollen from his mouth. He hardened further, if that could be possible. Hell, he'd been hard all night.

He should have grabbed Sally or one of the other trainees and obtained some relief before leaving. So why the hell hadn't he? Because Kari would have felt betrayed? He wasn't married to her, involved with her; why should her feelings matter?

And there… That was the problem, the reason he felt like shit right now. The little sub had gotten to him. She didn't look like Marion, and her personality was very different, but she sure as hell brought out his possessive nature. *She's mine, her body is mine, that laugh is mine. That swollen mouth is mine, and I made it look like that.*

But she wasn't Marion. No one could be.

He opened his eyes, his gaze falling to the photograph sitting on an end table. Marion on a spanking bench, leaning so far forward her lovely breasts spilled out of the black corset. Laughter filled her face as she dared him to take her.

She was dead. All that life, that passion gone.

His fault, dammit. After being called back to the station that night, he'd canceled the evening they'd planned. She'd yelled at him and then gone out to party without him. It had been raining…

Too much alcohol, too fast, too wet.

The highway patrol had called him at the station that night. He hadn't believed them. Fuck, he hadn't accepted her death for a good year after.

If he'd stayed home, she wouldn't have died. He knew that. Even though his grief had finally eased, the guilt had become part of him. Sometimes he felt as if he'd already joined her, become just another cold, gray body in the morgue.

He studied the photo. She'd loved him, truly loved him; he'd always known that. But she would have moved on by now.

He couldn't. And so, no matter how that little sub made him feel, he wouldn't see her again.

Tipping his head back, he finished the beer. Considering how rude he'd been when he left her, she'd undoubtedly gotten the message that she was on her own. Why didn't that make him feel better?

* * *

Dressed in her robe and pajamas, Kari picked up the cup of herbal tea and took it out to her small backyard patio. The wide swing rocked gently as she curled up and leaned her head back on the cushions. What a very strange night.

The phone had been ringing as she walked in the door. Buck, calling to check that she got home safely. He'd apologized again before hanging up. She frowned. Sometime in the next day or so, she'd have to decide if she wanted to see him again. Her first few dates with him had been fun, so maybe she was being oversensitive about his behavior at the club. He'd probably been nervous, and some people became hypercritical when stressed.

Then again, he hadn't been stressed last week. She giggled, remembering how he'd instructed her on the proper way to fold hand towels. Talk about nitpicky. Perhaps this would be a good time to call it quits.

She took a sip of tea. The chamomile scent drifted up from the cup and mingled with the fragrance of her roses. Her tiny tiered fountain gurgled pleasantly, the water glinting in the moonlight. A breeze rustled through the bushes and flowers, lifting the muggy heat.

As she rocked the swing, the soft pajamas chafed her breasts, her nipples so tender the thin cotton fabric felt like sandpaper. Her thoughts drifted back to the club. How could she ever process all her impressions?

That BDSM stuff had put her into a constant state of arousal, and everything Master Dan had done only increased it. From holding her arms down and kissing her, to the helplessness of having her hands cuffed together, to being pinned in the chair with his fingers—his *fingers*—inside her. That memory made her entire private area ache and dampen.

He'd called that area her *pussy*. Since starting to teach high school, she'd heard the oddly descriptive term a time or two, but it certainly never appeared in any biology textbook

She set the swing to rocking again. Although his fingers, his mouth—heck, everything he'd done had been stimulating—the huge difference had come from feeling helpless, from having no control.

She'd never been so excited in her life. Had never had an orgasm like that...ever. And God, she wanted to do it all over again.

But she wouldn't have Master Dan with her next time. The thought made her stomach twist, so she sipped more tea. He had been...overwhelming. She couldn't get him out of her mind, how his face had looked when he'd touched her. The way he'd watched her so intently. How he'd pushed her, controlled her.

Jessica said there were other experienced Doms. Would she feel the same with one of them? Would they have the same deep laugh, firm hands...? She sighed, remembering the hard, clean line of his jaw, the corded muscles in his neck. Would they have those?

No, probably not. But she'd discovered something about herself tonight. The way her body reacted to domination was what she'd been looking for all her life. Master Dan's control had filled a need inside her. Scary as the thought of returning to the club alone might be, she wasn't going to stop now.

Chapter Seven

The warm tropical breeze lifted Kari's hair as she hurried up to the Shadowlands on Wednesday evening. She scowled at the setting sun. She was late. The stupid car had overheated, forcing her to drive slower. She really needed to get it to the repair shop.

She'd always hated being tardy, but it was far, far worse tonight. Her stomach churned, like she'd eaten worms for lunch instead of her usual tuna sandwich. And she probably should have eaten supper instead of changing clothes fifteen times; she still had not found anything appropriate.

What if everyone was here already? This was just so not like her, going someplace alone. At least Buck had accompanied her on Monday, even if that hadn't lasted long. She grinned briefly.

Her smile faded as she remembered who had taken his place. And how unhappily the evening had ended.

But if she didn't attend this class, she'd feel like a coward, like Master Dan had driven her away. She wiped her damp hands on her dress and raised her chin. To heck with Sir anyway; she'd darned well have fun with someone else.

The tall oak doors were open. Sucking in a breath, she walked inside. Behind the desk, the big guard rose, and a smile lightened his battered face. "Welcome back, Miss Kari."

"Thank you, Ben."

He flipped through the file box on the desk, found her name, made a check on the card. "Give me your shoes and socks; then you can go right in." He pointed to the door on the far wall, not the one that led to Master Z's office. Apparently she didn't have to go through the screening process again.

After setting her blue-striped sneakers and pink socks on his desk, she looked at the door and hesitated. *Last chance to escape.* Her feet didn't want to move. After a minute, she glanced at the guard.

His brows drew together, making him look just plain mean. "Did you have trouble here last time?" he growled. "Something I should know about?"

Oh heavens. "No, not at all. Everyone was very nice." Did putting cuffs on a woman fall into the nice category? "I'm just..." She sighed and confessed, "I'm working up my nerve. I'm not used to going places like this by myself, you know?"

"Gotcha." Ben grinned at her. "You don't have the look of a loner. Hang on just a sec." He pressed a button on his desk.

"No, wait!" *Too late.*

"What?" The bartender's voice barked out of the intercom.

"If Jessie's in there, can you ask if she'd escort one of the newbie subs inside? She's feelin' a little lonely."

A snort. "If she's a sub, she won't be lonely long." A pause. "She's on her way out."

Kari felt like a kindergartner refusing to walk into school on the first day. "I would have—"

"Nah." Ben sat back down at the desk. "Don't worry. You're not the first novice to get scared, won't be the last."

The inner door opened, and the woman who Kari had met on Monday trotted out, her blonde hair bouncing. "Hey, I was hoping you'd be back."

Kari smiled, pleasure mingling with relief. "Thanks for rescuing me. I'm not sure why I froze."

"Been there, done that." Jessica grinned at the guard. "Right, Ben?"

He shook his head. "You were trouble from the beginning. Get a move on. I think she's the last to arrive."

"In that case, let's get you in before Raoul gets all huffy." Jessica pushed Kari through the doors and into the club room.

Trying not to be obvious, Kari looked around for Master Dan. His tall figure didn't appear, and disappointment grew inside her, making her chest ache.

As they passed the bar, the bartender, Master Cullen, grinned at Kari. "Now if I'd known it was you, I'd have gone out myself to hold your hand."

She gave him a tentative smile, unsure if he was joking or not.

At the end of the room, they found the class. Jessica patted her shoulder, whispered, "See you later," and headed away.

"Well, everyone has returned for more. I'm pleased." Master Raoul rested his hip on the back of the couch. "On Monday, we covered safe words, basic restraints, and safety issues. Now you've had a chance to practice, does anyone have questions?"

As the students shook their heads, Kari took the time to look them over. About half were obviously couples, standing beside each other, holding hands, mostly man-woman sets, with an occasional guy-guy or woman-woman. The singles divided fairly evenly between the two sexes.

"You came back." A whisper behind her and she thrilled, thinking Sir had found her. She felt his breath on her neck and glanced over her shoulder. Buck. Oh joy. He stood too close, his thighs brushing against her bottom.

"Hi, Buck." She hadn't returned his message on her answering machine. She tried to edge away without being too blatant.

"I've missed seeing you," he whispered. He ran his hand down her arm, then turned his attention to the instructor. She let out a relieved sigh.

Raoul went through the basics of domination and then talked a woman named Linda through a slave posture. Kari winced. *Slave* didn't sound as harmless as *sub*, somehow. He explained the club dress code and about the "private play" rooms upstairs. The penalties for interrupting a scene. Cleaning the equipment.

And then he started on a tour of the room, explaining the furniture in each of the roped-off areas. He shackled one of the gay men to a big wooden X called a St. Andrew's cross. Then came a spanking bench, a bondage table, an exotic lacing table, a sawhorse, a whipping post, two cages in a corner, a spiderweb thing, a stockade. He used a different sub to demonstrate each piece of equipment.

"Kari, your turn," he called, motioning to something called a bondage chair.

She swallowed and moved forward. At least he didn't strip anyone, just demonstrated the various restraints and how each piece could be used. She seated herself on the chair. After Master Raoul fastened her ankles to the chair legs, her wrists to the chair arms, she realized the center of the seat was cut out, leaving just her buttocks perched on the edge. With legs shackled open, and the missing chair bottom, a naked person's private parts would be on display. She shivered, relieved when the instructor unfastened her.

After two more pieces of equipment, Master Raoul said, "That's it for the formal lesson. All the equipment down here is duplicated in various upstairs rooms if you prefer private play. Remember that gags are forbidden at this point in your classes. DMs will be in the hallways upstairs and down here to answer questions or intervene if there's a problem."

He looked at each sub in turn, his expression serious. "Subs, no matter what safe word you agree on between your partner, the club safe word is red. If you shout that out, a DM will come to see if everything is all right. Remember, 'safe, sane, and consensual' are the operative words here. Got that, everyone?"

People nodded.

"Remember, you discuss what you will be doing first and reach an agreement. Establish trust before you jump in. Class is dismissed. Pair up as you wish." He frowned as he counted the single newbies. "Anyone left without a partner talk to me over at the bar."

As he walked away, the singles began talking. One couple headed out, then another. Kari saw two men watching her, one with a cruel look in his eyes that made her stomach twist, and the other would probably run if she said boo. She thought about what Master Dan had done to her, tried to imagine letting either of the men do *anything* with her, and couldn't.

"Kari, honey. How about we try using that spiderweb?" An easy smile on his face, Buck approached and set his hand on her shoulder.

Without thinking, she stepped back and shook her head. Her instinctive reaction reminded her of Master Dan asking how her body felt about something. Maybe she'd listen to her body for once. "I'm sorry, Buck. I don't want to—" *Let you have any control over me.*

That would be rude. Oh, she just wasn't comfortable saying no to people or hurting their feelings. She glanced at the diminishing group of singles and realized she didn't want to be with any of them. That solved her problem nicely. "I'm afraid I'm not staying for the practice part. But thank you for the offer."

Nolan strolled into the club room and smiled at the underlying scent of sweat, fear, pain, and sex that Z's fancy cleaning crew could never remove. Muscles he didn't know had been tight started to loosen.

As he crossed to the bar, he checked out the changes. A few new pieces of equipment—a lacing table, a spiderweb. There'd probably be a few other things in the theme rooms. Z liked toys.

"Hey, Nolan, welcome home!" Rising from a bar stool, Raoul shook Nolan's hand, a grin on his swarthy face. He glanced at Nolan's gold-trimmed vest. "I see Z already tagged you for DM duty."

"Nolan!" Cullen's yell set his ears ringing as the bartender leaned across the bar to thump his shoulder. "Damn, dude, where have you been?"

Nolan thought on it for a minute. "Here and there. Mostly Baghdad."

"No alcohol there, I bet." Cullen slid a cold Corona over.

Nolan stared at it. Nobody else drank Corona around here. "That beer over a year old?"

"Nah. Z told me you were back. I stocked up," Cullen said.

The welcome made Nolan's chest tighten. "Thanks."

"You still look like a nasty bastard," Cullen commented, ignoring a couple of newbies signaling for his attention. "You're gonna have the subs all scared and clamoring for your attention. How's your pretty slave doing, by the way?"

"I uncollared Felicia before I deployed," Nolan said. And although he'd missed her, he hadn't realized how much of a strain being a master twenty-four/seven was until she was gone. "So it's been a while. I'm looking forward to playing again." He sucked down half the brew, something else he'd missed. "Anything new?"

"Z has a sub now, a cutie. Grabbed her before she even made it through the door," Cullen said. "Hell, he had her before she even knew she was submissive, but she hooked him right back."

"Z? Hooked?" Nolan set his beer down. "Seriously?"

"Looks like. Good match," Raoul said. "I thought for a minute Dan was going to follow in his footsteps. He took on a beginner Monday, a sweet little sub, and looked pretty involved, but he chilled out again."

"That the pretty sub Jessica was talking to? Kari?" Cullen asked.

"Yep." Raoul nodded toward the group of beginners. "Little, round, really polite."

"I like her." Cullen scratched his cheek. "And Dan needs someone to kick him out of his rut. When Marion died, seems like she took him with her. The asshole hardly laughs anymore." He studied the beginner class. "Yeah, she might be good for him."

"Z must have thought so. He asked Dan to take her on."

Nolan listened idly. Dan'd had a rough time there, losing his wife like that. It was time he came out of that dark shell. Turning, he checked out the class. The singles had dwindled until only a few remained. He identified the sub whom Raoul and Cullen had mentioned, watched a wannabe Dom brace her, try for her. She not only turned the guy down but left the group entirely, heading toward the bar. Very pretty, short, and curvy like he preferred.

"Heads up," he warned Raoul. "Incoming."

Kari walked away from the other newbies, feeling like a failure. She'd made it here, attended the class, but she'd basically blown the final by not practicing what she'd learned. But she just couldn't. Not with them. Face it, she'd been hoping Master Dan would be here, would have changed his mind. *Dumb, Kari.* He'd made himself quite clear.

She started toward the door and then stopped. She should be polite and tell Master Raoul she was leaving. For all she knew, he might do a head count at the end of the night.

Master Raoul was at the bar like he'd said, talking with Cullen. Next to Raoul, another DM, a big, darkly tanned man around forty, leaned on the bar, listening. With a white scar across one cheekbone and cold black eyes, the man just plain looked dangerous. She gave him a wide berth and stopped on Raoul's other side.

Cullen broke off in midsentence and smiled at her. "Little Kari, how are you?" The look he gave her warmed her right to her toes.

Ignoring the quiver in her stomach, she nodded back. "I'm fine. And how are you?" *Oops.* "Ah...Sir."

Cullen and Raoul chuckled. The other man didn't even smile.

"Very nice," Cullen said. "Can I get you something to drink, or is someone waiting for you?"

"No, thank you." She turned to Master Raoul. "I'm going to call it an early night, but I enjoyed your class very much. Thank you." She nodded and moved toward the door.

"Stop." Master Raoul's command had a snap in it.

Kari's feet froze before her brain had processed the word. She turned.

"Are you having a problem with one of the other beginners?" Master Raoul's eyes narrowed as he inspected the class.

"No, not at all. I just am not—" She couldn't think of a way to say this politely. "I feel uncomfortable with—" *With beginners.* She shrugged rather than finish. "I see no need to practice, so I'll head out. I appreciate your concern."

He'd been studying her face. "Going from Master Dan to a beginner... I see the problem. I'll find you an experienced Dom."

"No, really, I'm—"

"You know, I've had a little experience," Master Cullen said mildly.

Raoul snorted. "Like fifteen years or so?"

"About that." Cullen lifted his head and shouted toward the front of the room, "Dan! Man the bar. I'm taking some playtime." He ducked under the bar and towered over Kari. "I'll top you tonight."

She managed to close her mouth. "Well…" Experienced, for sure. More easygoing than Sir—or at least more talkative. The set of his jaw, the way he watched her expressions made her think he might be as intimidating as Sir.

There wasn't the same sense of connection with him or the trust she'd felt with Master Dan. But so what. Her reasons for being here were still valid. "Thank you. I'd like that."

Kari heard footsteps behind her, then Master Dan's voice with a hint of laughter. "You and your damned playtimes. I'll babysit the bar for a couple hours, but that's it, Cullen."

Sir's deep, rough voice singed through every pathway in Kari's body, and her insides melted like a sun-warmed chocolate bar. She stiffened but didn't turn around. Cowardly, but she didn't want to see his face turn cold again.

Cullen looked down at her, and a smile flickered over his hard-hewn face. He put a heavy arm across her shoulders and mashed her against his side. And then, hand gripping her shoulder so she couldn't escape, he turned them both to face Master Dan.

"Well, Dan, I'm not sure I'm going to want to stop at two hours." Cullen rubbed his knuckles gently across her cheek. "Little Kari looks like she's got more stamina than that."

Master Dan saw her, and his face turned to stone. Even as his gaze dissected her like a bug, his mouth thinned. His anger hit her like a fist to the chest.

Kari pulled in a shaky breath and tried to back away, despite the restraining arm around her shoulders. What had she done to make him so mad at her?

"Dan, buddy, you got a problem?" Cullen asked, his voice as easy as if Sir didn't look murderous. Raoul's eyes narrowed.

Sir's gaze never left Kari as his jaw tightened. He inhaled slowly as his iron will imposed control. When his eyes released Kari, she almost staggered.

Sir's gaze rested on the bartender and then a corner of his mouth curved upward. "You asshole. Your fucking sense of humor is going to get you killed one of these days. Maybe today."

Kari wrapped her arms around herself. She'd seen quite a bit of fighting in the schools, but these two guys were huge. They'd destroy the whole bar.

"I haven't enjoyed anything so much in days." Cullen's laugh boomed in the quiet room. "But you know, you're scaring *my* sub." His hand squeezed her shoulder, pulled her a little closer.

Chapter Eight

Dan's hands fisted as possessiveness burned through him in a red-tinged wave. One more word and he'd knock his fucking *friend* across the room. "Don't push me."

Cullen grinned.

Dan moved closer. When Kari's big blue eyes lifted to meet his, his breath was sucked away. He couldn't keep from touching her long, wavy hair, running his fingers down her soft cheek. She trembled. He'd scared her, dammit.

Cullen cleared his throat. "Dan, I think—"

Dan kept his eyes on Kari. "Go away, Cullen. Playtime's over. She's mine." He sucked in a breath and corrected himself. "Mine for this evening."

"I should make you work a little harder, but okay." Cullen dropped his arm. "Kari, I'll be here if you need me." He moved away.

Dan held out his hand. How badly had he damaged her trust? She couldn't possibly understand his behavior, considering he didn't understand it himself. "Let's talk."

Her eyes wary, she chewed on her lip, and he hardened at the memory of how soft those lips had been. She shook her head, and his mouth tightened. He'd never forgive himself for—

"I must be crazy," she muttered and set her hand in his.

The relief almost swamped him. He led her to a nearby couch and pulled her down beside him. She wore another long dress, but this one was silky and a true blue color that matched her eyes. The top dipped low enough to display the beginning curve of her breasts, and with her full figure, it was provocative as hell.

His plans had definitely changed for the night, from wanting to avoid her to wanting to strip her naked. If he could talk her into it.

Having regained her composure, she tapped a finger on his arm. "I got the impression that you were a one-night stand sort of guy."

"I am." He laid his hand over her delicate fingers, realized her hands were chilled, and clasped them in his. "To be honest, Kari, I don't get involved with anyone. I've found that if I keep encounters to one night, there're no hurt feelings."

"Then why did you take me from—" She glanced toward the bar and Cullen.

A flare of jealousy bit into his stomach like acid for the second time in five minutes. *Dammit.* "I'm here; you're here," he said, keeping his tone light.

He paused. Honesty was essential between a Dom and sub; if he wasn't willing to bare his thoughts, how could he demand the same from her?

"No, it's more than that," he said. He pulled her closer, slid an arm behind her back. "I don't know what's going on between you and me, but it's not finished yet." He looked away from her, and Marion's face rose in his mind, more shadowy than normal. "When I lost my wife, I lost everything. I don't have anything to give. Only sex for a night." He didn't have more. He didn't *deserve* more. "So I can't offer you a commitment other than I want you tonight."

"That's no commitment at all." She stared across the room, her gaze on someone using the bondage table. After a minute, she shook her head like a dog shedding water. "But it's enough. That's all I want too. Just sex."

"Well, that I can give."

"I know," she said under her breath, then looked at him with a smile. "I was looking forward to exploring more of this BDSM stuff, but the other beginners…" She frowned, obviously searching for the right words. "It seemed too much like the blind leading the blind."

"Now that *would* be frightening." He took her chin, looked into her eyes. "Are you afraid of me?"

She tilted her head. "Not…exactly. I trust you, but I'm a little scared of what you might do."

"Well, little sub, that *is* the point. Do you remember your safe word?"

"Red."

"Good." He unclipped something from a metal ring on his left side. "I almost forgot your jewelry. Give me your wrists."

She hesitated, then laid her wrists into his hand.

He buckled on fleece-lined leather cuffs. "What the well-dressed sub wears in the Shadowlands. Master Z would have been displeased if he'd seen your wrists naked."

As she frowned at them, he pulled her onto his lap, his arms holding her against his big chest. She felt just right. "Now, let's run through what might happen here tonight."

"Okay." Dropping her cuffed wrists to her lap, Kari leaned her head against his shoulder. Cullen probably would have been nice, but he wasn't Master Dan. She really did trust Sir to keep her safe. His solid arms felt good—just right—around her.

At least until his fingers pulled down the zipper on the front of her dress. His hand slid under her bra and closed over her left breast.

"Wait." She tried to pull away, but his other hand gripped her hip, holding her in place. God, she'd forgotten how strong he was, how big. Her insides quivered as her breathing increased.

"The restrictions for a beginner's first night are gone, Kari," he murmured, his thumb stroking her nipple to a hard peak, the controlled power of his grip making her shake. "Tonight, I can—and I will—take you, with my hands. My mouth. My cock. Any way I want. As many times as I want."

With his hand on her breast, he could undoubtedly feel her breathing increase, her pulse speed up. "Your body likes that idea," he whispered. "Your body is mine to play with, to restrain, to show off. Your only response to anything I want will be, 'yes, Sir.'"

Need clawed into her as her insides turned liquid. She dampened.

As if he could tell—and he probably could, the jerk—he whispered, "Are you wet for me now, little sub?"

Her body didn't feel like her own anymore. Yes, she'd wanted to explore sex here, but this was too fast. Too much.

When she didn't answer, he removed his hand from her hip and tilted her head to meet his gaze. His eyes crinkled as he studied her face. "You're flushed. Your pulse is hammering. Your breathing is fast. Kari, either answer my question, or I will check for myself. Right here."

She gasped and closed her legs tightly at the thought of his hand under her skirt, right in the center of the room. This wasn't at all like that isolated spot he'd found for them last time. Didn't he understand anything about privacy? Discretion? Politeness? She pushed at his hand and gritted out, "Fine. I'm wet. Okay?"

The minute the words left her mouth, she remembered his response the last time she'd snapped at him, and her world tipped sideways.

His eyes went cold. "No, that answer is as far from okay as it can get. Open your legs for me now."

"I will not." She tried to move from his lap, and his grip tightened.

"Since you like multiple choice, here you go. *A:* You can be an example for the other subs when I drag you to the bondage table, strap you down, and let everyone see how wet you are."

Her breath choked in her throat as horror filled her.

"Or *B:* You may apologize for your tone, and I'll let you open your legs for me here." He gave her a hard look, and she knew he'd do just what he said. "Which is it, little sub?"

"Here," she whispered. "I'm sorry, Sir. Please stay here."

He pulled her dress up to her knees, set a hand on her bare leg, and waited.

She tried to look around, to see if anyone could see her.

"Do it now, sub, and keep your eyes on me," he ordered in a glacial voice. His command sent disconcerting heat washing through her.

Biting her lips, she eased her legs apart. His right hand stroked up between her thighs, forcing her to open farther until his palm pressed against her mound. She glanced down and turned red. Her dress was pushed up, barely covering her, and anyone could see the location of his hand.

People walked past the couch. A woman in a black bustier, fishnet stockings, and high heels glanced over and grinned. Over by the spanking bench, Buck stared at Sir, his mouth twisting into an ugly line. Then there were Master Raoul and Master Cullen at the bar…

With a low moan, Kari shoved at her skirt.

Master Dan sighed, lifted his left hand from her hip. "Give me that hand."

Darn it, she knew what he planned—one arm pinned against his chest, the other in his grip. She'd have no choice but to let him do what he wanted.

He chuckled. "And that just made you wetter." Oh, God, he had his fingers pressed into her crotch.

"Hand, Kari."

Giving up, she set her hand in his. He closed his fingers around her wrist and set both their hands against her hip, holding her wedged in one place. She had a moment to feel her helplessness, and then he slid under the edge of her panties and pushed a finger inside her. Her hips jerked at the suddenness of the entry, at the flaring arousal that soared through her.

"Yes, you're very wet." His finger moved inside her, sent jolts of sensation through her. "Makes me want to bend you over the couch and bury myself in you."

He could undoubtedly feel the way her vagina clamped down as well as she could. Oh, God.

"But I think we'll go upstairs so I can take my time exploring your body." His eyes crinkled. "You like that idea too, don't you? Answer me, sub."

"Yes, Sir." His finger moved, stroked the walls of her vagina in erotic circles.

"Afterwards, I'll bring you back down here." He glanced at the St. Andrew's cross. "I could strip you and bind you up there."

She stiffened, the thought exciting. Appalling.

"Ah, not quite ready for that yet, are you?" He nibbled on her ear. "Even if I left your clothes on, I could put you in the stockade, lift your skirt, and take you there."

His finger moved within her. "Not that yet, either, although the interest is there, isn't it?"

She had no answer for him, confusion and fear and arousal so mingled inside her that she couldn't think at all. The way he had her restrained with just his body, his hands, made her feel so strange. So needy. She looked at him, unable to speak.

His smile was hard, satisfied. "I like that look on your face." He bent his head and took her lips ruthlessly, satisfying himself. His finger thrust in and out of her below, the twin assaults swamping her mind in desire. She trembled as urgent need coursed through her.

When he pulled away, his eyes were heavy lidded with passion, dark with promise. "Let's go, sub. I have things I want to do to you."

He gave a low laugh, and she knew he'd felt the clench of her insides around his finger.

He removed his finger, making her jerk, leaving her throbbing. Pushing her to her feet, he wrapped a hard arm around her waist. "If you talk fast, I'll let you choose the room."

He kept her hand firmly in his as he led her up the spiral stairs in the front corner of the room. At the top, at the sight of doors running down a long hallway, she pulled back. *Sex.* She was going to have *sex* this time. This was—

"Little sub, you worry so much your head must ache." He pulled her into his arms, and his embrace turned comforting. Warm. "You're aroused. And scared." He nibbled on her neck, then kissed her until her knees sagged and the world spun.

Pulling back, he looked at her. "Blue is definitely your color. Let's go with that."

Halfway down the hall, he opened a door to a small room. Candles in sconces on the gray-blue walls provided a soft, flickering light. Classical music came from speakers somewhere in the room. The room had a bed with a dark red velvet cover and a big armoire. Velvet ropes dangled from the headboard; more ropes with leather cuffs were tied to the foot of the bed. A chill crept up Kari's spine, followed by excitement. Would he really use those on her?

Placing his hands on her shoulders, he steered her to stand beside the bed. Running a hand down her front, he chuckled, realizing she'd raised the zipper. With a firm hand, he pulled it all the way down. As her dress gaped open and the air hit her overheated skin, she shivered and her nipples peaked, showing through her thin lacy bra.

He touched one breast, stroking over the hard bud. His gentle finger sent little ripples of need through her.

After a second, he nudged her dress off, letting it pool at her feet, leaving her in her white bra and panties.

"Your underwear is very much like you," he said. "The white for sweet, sheer lace for sexy." One hard hand held her upper arm as he ran a finger across the top of her bra, his finger warm, slightly abrasive, the touch sensitizing her skin. There was something erotic about being forced to stand still, not being able to move as a man played with her body, pleasing himself.

"Remove your bra, Kari," he said, stepping back and watching her with narrowed eyes.

She fumbled with the catch, embarrassed, yet wanting his hands on her so badly her mouth was dry. The flickering lights weren't bright, but she still felt awfully exposed as her breasts spilled free. He cupped his hands under them, squeezing slightly, enough to make her suck in a breath. Enough for heat to flow through her. "Now the panties can go."

Feeling awkward, she pushed them off and let them slide to the floor. His eyes on her felt hot. He smiled slowly. "You're a lovely woman, Kari. I'm going to enjoy taking you."

The blunt words, so openly carnal, thrilled her. Confused her.

Gripping her upper arms, he raised her onto her toes and took her lips in a hot, wet kiss, exploring her mouth until her hands fisted with the need to touch him. He drew back and traced her swollen lips with his finger.

"Up on the bed with you." He patted behind him.

Oh, God, she really *was* going to do this.

As she crawled up onto the bed and turned to sit, he tossed his vest on the ground, opened his leathers. Oh heavens, he was even more muscled than she'd realized, and he was...huge, his erection past his belly button. Thick and hard and... "I don't— um—You're awfully big," she ventured.

He grinned as he sheathed himself in a condom. "We'll fit, sweetie." Joining her on the bed, he pressed her down onto her back and covered her with his body, his heat unbelievable. She ran her hands over his shoulders, amazed at the contoured muscles of his back, how they tightened to rock hard with each movement.

He bit her neck, licked the spot, bit again, the pain sharp and erotic.

"Open your legs for me."

She hesitated despite the arousal urging her on. He was so big...

He chuckled. "Don't worry, by the time I enter that sweet pussy, you'll be begging me." He kissed her hard, forcefully. "Open your legs, Kari."

She parted her legs, and he slid between them. She could feel his penis against her entrance, the feeling exciting. Making her shiver.

"You know, I wasn't planning to do this until later, but I tire of repeating each command," he murmured, and he kissed her again, taking her mouth deeply. When he pulled back, she realized her right arm was fastened above her head, a thick rope securing her cuff to the headboard.

"Hey!"

He lifted her other arm and secured the wrist cuff to a rope before she'd gotten past the surprise of the first.

"Wait. I don't—"

One knee on each side of her hips, he sat up. His balls bumped against her pussy, making her jump. As his weight on her legs pinned her to the bed, she pulled on the ropes; her breathing increased. She was tied to the bed. *Tied.* Before, she could at least move; now her cuffs were fastened to something. She couldn't even run.

He tilted his head, studied her as she pulled at the ropes. Leaning forward, he held her face between his two hands, his eyes a rich brown. She stilled, feeling like a trapped animal, a shivering mouse held in someone's grip.

His rough voice was quiet. "Are you in pain, Kari?"

"No, but…"

"No, what?"

He wasn't serious, was he? She was tied up, and he was sitting on her. And yet, she was horrified to feel herself getting wetter and wetter.

His hands left her face to stroke her breasts, circling the sensitive nipples until she pressed up for his touch. "No, what?"

His hands lifted, waited.

She was breathing hard and her answer huffed between her lips. "No, Sir."

"Very good." His fingers closed on her nipples, pulling, rolling, each movement just one tiny step short of real pain, each squeeze sending zings of sensation straight to her groin. "Such sensitive breasts." He bent to suck one nipple into his mouth, working it, the feeling so intensely pleasurable, she cried out. He switched to the other.

"Look, Kari," he said, his fingers pulling gently. "See how beautiful."

Her breasts were swollen, tight with the nipples darkened to deep rose and spiking upward like tiny pencils. "Say, 'My breasts are beautiful.'"

"My breasts are beautiful." And they were too.

His eyes warmed with approval before he slid down her body, pressing kisses to the undersides of her breasts, nuzzling her stomach. He nipped next to her belly button, making her squeak with surprise. And then he was *there*. Just looking at her most private of places. Her pussy.

Totally embarrassed, she tried to close her legs.

He pushed back to lean on his heels and narrowed a gaze at her. "My body to play with," he repeated. "Open your legs for me."

She slid them out, feeling the flush working its way up her chest. She was so wet, he'd see, know she was—

"Farther." And he just sat there, waiting. In charge. *Dominant.*

She slid her legs farther apart, feeling her...her *everything* open. Totally exposed.

"Very nice. You have a lovely pussy, no matter how you try to conceal it. And I'm going to enjoy it in so many ways." He pressed his hand to her there, right between her legs. "I'm going to lick it all over."

She could feel herself dampen and so could he. "Maybe I'll use a vibrator, pushing it deep inside you." Her vagina actually clenched, and he grinned wickedly, his eyes crinkling. He felt every little involuntary movement she made.

He positioned himself between her legs, his shoulders between her knees. She could feel his breath on her inner thighs, and her legs started to close against the intimacy.

"Keep them open, Kari, or I will tie them open." And they both felt her wetness increase.

"You are a surprising woman, little sub." He chuckled as he rolled off the bed, one ankle already in his hand. Grabbing the fleece-lined cuff roped to the footboard, he buckled it on and tightened the rope, imprisoning her leg at an angle. He snatched her other ankle as she was trying to decide if she should fight, and there she was, spread-eagled. Just like her fantasies, only this was real. Maybe too real.

The instinctive need to be free had her pulling at the ropes holding her wrists. Her chest squeezed with fear as she tried to kick her legs, and the restraints held. He stood at the foot of the bed and watched silently. Waited until she stopped.

He lay down between her legs. With her legs pulled outward, everything was open for him.

"You have a pretty, pretty pussy, Kari. Hidden within those little brown curls"—he pulled her pubic hair lightly, tantalizingly—"everything is pink." One finger slowly slid down the outer labia. "You're very wet for me, can you tell?" He touched her right over the entrance, swirled a finger inside just long enough to make her squirm with pleasure.

When he took his fingers away, leaving her aching, she whined like a child.

"We have time, sweetheart, and I'm going to take my time."

She almost blurted out a protest. *Take me now; put your hands on me now.* She managed to close her lips.

He stroked down her thigh, his hand so big that his fingers could curl underneath. His knuckles traced the path back up, across her tender, sensitive inner thigh, lightly over her pubis, and down the other leg. Almost to the right spot. Exquisite torture. Her fingernails dug into her palms as he stroked her legs, the curls on her pubis, the soft crease where her hip met her leg.

Her clitoris throbbed more with each pass, with each time he didn't touch her where she so needed to be touched. "Please," she whispered, aching with longing.

"What do you call me?" he asked, touching her with just one finger, so close, edging so close.

She arched up. "Please, Sir, please."

"Nicely said, sweetheart," he murmured approval. And he slid the finger right into her.

"Aaah." The nerves inside her vagina flared to life with the intimate invasion.

He lowered his mouth to her clit, a touch like butterfly wings. She arched again, tightening around his finger, needing more than the light flicks on her clit. She was so close. The world narrowed to just the feel of his hands, his mouth. One more touch…

He pulled his finger out, emptying her, and lifted his head.

Nooo. She whimpered a protest.

"You don't have permission to come."

"What?" she whispered shakily.

"You come when I say, not before."

"You can't—"

"Kari," he warned in a hard voice. "I've been patient, but my patience is at an end. Did you get taught about punishment in your class?"

Not really. But the way he'd sent Sally off to be punished… She didn't want anything like that to happen to her. Her thighs shook with her need. "Sir, I'm sorry."

"Very nice." He lowered his head, licked up her labia, sucking one into his mouth, then the other, the sensation like hot velvet.

His tongue laved right there in the center. *Oh God, almost.* Not far enough, she needed more.

Then one finger opened her, sliding in ever so slowly and back out. She tightened around him, her legs quivering uncontrollably. In again, his finger large, pressing down to add friction, out.

Two fingers. She moaned at the added sensation as his fingers drove into her, faster, harder. Her whole pussy was afire, wanton hunger burning through her. She strained against the restraints as his mouth came down on her. His tongue slid over her clitoris and around it, swirling and rubbing as his fingers plunged in and out.

She panted, her bottom pushing off the bed, closer, closer. "Ah, ah—"

And he stopped, took his hands away. "Not yet."

"But—"

"Silence."

Her groan came from deep within her, her entire lower half too tight. Throbbing with need. She'd never felt so out of control. Never begged before. She *hurt.*

He licked the tender skin of her inner thigh, and she shuddered. His shoulders rubbed against her legs, and she trembled against the restraints.

She pulled at her wrists, wanting to touch him, to force him to touch her; she'd even touch herself if she had to. Over her head, her hands closed into fists as the feeling of helplessness roused her further, making everything worse.

He slid a finger into her again, shooting urgency through her, her arousal higher and harder than before. She moaned, her head rolling from side to side. When her hips lifted, he ruthlessly pressed her back down, holding her for his use.

He pushed his finger in, pulled out, and added another finger. Her tissues were so swollen each thrust shoved her closer and closer. His tongue flicked across her clit, and she went rigid as her muscles tightened, as her vagina clenched around his fingers. She neared the peak, held there...

"Come now, Kari," he ordered, his voice deep. Sucking her clitoris into his mouth, his tongue rubbed it hard and fast.

Her world flashed white, splintering around her, and she shattered with it. Spasms in her vagina rippled against the hard fingers impaling her, and her hips jerked uncontrollably. Her legs thrashed against the restraints, her arms pulled against the ropes, and the sensations went on and on.

When her climax started to slow, he'd move his fingers, slide his tongue across her again, and she'd arch back up as the exquisite tremors shuddered through her again. And again.

Finally, she lay limp, drenched in sweat, her heart pounding so hard her ribs must be bruised. "My God, no wonder people like being tied up," she murmured.

His hand slapped her thigh hard enough to sting.

She jumped. "Hey!"

"Did you speak, little sub?" He lifted his head, his stern eyes holding a warning.

She started to say something, thought better of it. "Sir. I'm sorry, Sir. I thought we were done. Sir."

He chuckled. Then he rose onto his knees, his big hands roved up her thighs, massaging the cramped muscles. He slid his hands up her stomach, and with a smile, cupped her breasts, squeezing just hard enough to make her breath hitch. His fingers lightly pinched her softening nipples back into attention.

"Kari, sweet, we're just getting started. In fact, I think you should come again before we move on."

No. Wait.

And he slid back down. With fingers and mouth and tongue—and teeth this time—he brought her to another orgasm. A screaming one.

Oh God, oh God, oh God. Her heart was thudding so fast it felt like a galloping horse, and her lungs labored to find enough air.

He moved back and unfastened her ankles. "Kari."

She blinked at him.

He gently pushed the sweaty strands of hair off her face and then moved on top of her, holding his weight on his elbows. "Bring your legs up," he whispered before he took her mouth, plunging his tongue in.

She could taste herself, another shock in itself. Managed—eventually—to remember what he'd said. *Legs up.* Her legs were free, and she slid them up to settle beside his hips. His penis slid in the wetness of her folds; each brush against the swollen, sensitive tissues sent tremors through her.

When his hand dropped down and pressed the head of his penis to her entrance, she moaned, shivered.

Without any more warning, he drove into her, all the way to the hilt.

"Oh!" Impaled on him, she tried to jerk away. "Oooh…" Her insides pulsed around his intrusion, and her arms futilely yanked at the restraints.

Chapter Nine

"Oh, sweetheart, you feel good," Dan murmured, taking her mouth again for a kiss. So good she was liable to kill him dead as her pussy squeezed his cock like a hot, pulsing fist. She was tight, slick with her own juices.

From the tightening of her muscles, the slight cringing away, he was bigger than she was used to. He got a deplorable sense of satisfaction from knowing that.

He kissed her while he waited for her body to adjust, plunging his tongue into her mouth in slow strokes, imitating what he'd be doing to her shortly. With one hand, he toyed with those sensitive nipples. The little whimpers she made could harden a dead man.

When he felt her hips start to move upward in response, he grinned and slid out—in—her moans as addictive to him as gin to an alcoholic. As he increased the speed, he released her wrists from the restraints. Her arms wrapped around him convulsively before her hands started stroking his back, adding to his pleasure.

He surged deeper, and her silken pussy contracted around him. With every hard thrust, his balls slapped against her soft buttocks, sending an inflaming vibration through him. He could feel her thigh muscles tremble as she awoke again to pleasure and moved right into true need.

What idiot could have possibly thought she was cold? Gripping her hips, he yanked her up against him with each stroke and then rubbed his pelvis down her clitoris as he withdrew. Her moans transformed into hard panting, and her fingers clenched his shoulders like miniature vises. Her little fingernails dug into his skin, arousing pinpricks of pain.

Faster, harder—she was almost there. He could feel his cock swell as he kept himself from coming. Reaching down between them, he swirled his fingers in the wetness from her pussy, then stroked up and over her clit.

She broke with a scream, spasming around him so hard his own climax engulfed him. With a roaring growl of pleasure, he buried his length within her and let her milk him dry.

Kari was still shuddering from the shock waves of pleasure when Master Dan rolled them over and nestled her to his side, her head on his chest. She could hear his heart drumming under all that muscle. His arms kept her against him, and she—she needed that right now, somehow.

He'd tied her up.

And she'd not only let him but had enjoyed everything he'd done. What was happening to her?

"You're thinking again, little sub," he murmured, kissing the top of her head. "What about?"

She'd be doing a lot of thinking, she had a feeling. Instead of answering him, she ran her fingers over his rock-hard biceps. "You're so strong," she whispered.

"You're so soft," he whispered back. His fingers slid down her waist to squeeze and stroke her bottom.

"I should be all muscular like you."

"You sound just like Z's sub. Listen, sweetling, and I'll tell you again. I know it's not politically correct, but I like my women soft." He pulled her closer. "And curvy." He skimmed a hand over her waist and then teased her breast until she sighed with pleasure. "And responsive. I love your body, little sub." He pressed a kiss to her fingers.

His women—and she was one of them? The thought made her warm inside.

And he liked her the way she was—God, how awesome was that—someone who looked like him lusted after her body. Tilting her head, she watched him fondle her breasts, his lips curved in a smile, his eyes half-lidded.

She really did have nice breasts, didn't she?

And if he kept up his attentions, she was going to get all turned on again. How did he *do* that? She ran her fingers down his neck, tracing along his jaw.

Cupping one breast, he rubbed his thumb over the nipple. "Now tell me"—his voice changed from lazy indulgence to a deeper, firmer timbre—"how did you feel when you were tied and opened for my pleasure?"

Her hand stopped midstroke. *Talk about it?* He wanted to talk about...that? Men weren't supposed to be so verbal, were they?

"Shy, little sub? After all that I've done to you? I've had my fingers buried in your pussy, my mouth on your clit, my cock rammed inside you. If you can let me do that, surely you can talk to me."

Heat seared her cheeks, and he chuckled. "Did being tied up scare you?"

She nodded, turned to hide her face in his shoulder.

He rose on one elbow. Grasping her shoulder, he pressed her flat, securing her even further with a leg across her hips. "You don't hide your feelings from yourself or from me. Tell me how you felt when you were tied up."

"Vulnerable," she whispered. "Like I couldn't help what you were going to do."

"And it aroused you even more." His hand played with her breasts, circling the tightening nipples. "Kari? Did being so securely restrained arouse you? Did you like it?" He pinched one nipple, a tiny flash of pain-pleasure.

"Yes." She looked away from him, her face hot. "Yes, darn it."

"Yes, what?"

"Yes, Sir. I liked it."

"Brave girl." He kissed her gently, nibbling on her lips. "It's not easy to admit enjoying something so different from what our mamas said we should enjoy. Why they think everyone should be alike in making love when no one can even agree on what ice cream they like, I'll never know."

He rose, disappearing into the tiny bathroom in the corner. When he returned, he brought back a warm washcloth. Standing beside the bed, he wiped the sweat from her face.

"Thank you. That feels good." It also felt strange to have this giant guy being so nurturing. Especially since his leathers were still open and displaying everything.

He put his knee on the bed and leaned forward. What was he...? He parted her thighs, stroking between them to clean her...there.

Blushing furiously, she tried to close her legs. "I can do that."

"I enjoy doing this sometimes." His knee settled on her ankle to keep her legs apart. He was very thorough. She was squirming and everything down there tingled before he was done.

As he walked into the bathroom, the leathers molded to him, showing every hard curve of his butt and thighs.

She pushed herself up and sat on the side of the bed, her head whirling. How very different this was from anything she'd done before. His control of her was what she'd wanted, and so far past what she'd expected that it scared her. Had she really begged? Screamed? Come over and over?

He returned with another warm washcloth and handed it to her. "Since you feel left out, you can join in. Wash me, Kari." He stood in front of her, totally unselfconscious, totally gorgeous, his sex framed in the V of the opened front.

Wash him. She could do that. Would even enjoy doing that. Kneeling on the bed, she started with his testicles, so soft, so heavy in her hands. When done, she moved forward. His penis, even nonerect and wrinkly, was still huge. Thick. And under her fingers and the washcloth, it started to grow.

"Your hands feel good on me, little sub," he said. He lifted her chin and gazed down into her eyes, and his voice changed, deepened and hardened, much like his penis was hardening in her hand. "Put your mouth on me now." *His master voice.* "What do you say to me?"

He wanted her to—well, okay—she'd done it before. In bed. In the dark. He'd be able to see her. Watch her. *Oh God.*

She licked her lips. "Yes, Sir."

She dropped the washcloth onto the floor and then took his penis into her hands. Even as she held it, it hardened, lengthened. *Wow.*

"See what just your hands can do to me?" he murmured. "My body wants yours. My cock wants those sweet lips around it, your mouth sucking on it."

The thought was empowering. Exciting. Hauling in a breath, she licked up his erection like an ice-cream cone, letting her tongue trace the big veins running along the outside. The skin was all softness wrapped over an iron bar. She slid her lips over the velvety-soft head. He growled in pleasure when her tongue swirled around its edge, so she concentrated there for a while. Then she moved on, trying stuff, seeing what reactions she could get.

When she sucked all of him into her mouth, his breath stopped.

Her tongue up the underside of his penis made his stomach muscles jerk.

He stroked her hair. "You are very good at this, sweetie.

Pride surged through her. *Sex.* She could do it.

He murmured, "Tighten your lips just a little—no teeth, please. Now, up and down, fast, and hard."

She did, and did it darned well, she knew, as his hand closed convulsively in her hair.

"Damn, but you have a wonderful mouth." A minute later, he said, "Stop now."

She looked up at him in surprise. He smiled down at her, traced her wet lips with his finger. "Don't worry, sweetheart, we'll finish later. For now, it's time to return downstairs. Master Z asked a few of the regulars in to demonstrate the equipment. Of course, compared to a normal bondage night, the scenes will be relatively mild."

She nodded.

"Go use the bathroom while I pick out your clothes."

Him pick out her clothing? *No way.* She'd seen pictures of what people wore in fetish clubs. "No. I have clothes here, and I'll—" At the sight of his darkening eyes, she stopped, closed her mouth. *Too late.* She'd seen that look on his face with Sally, with herself.

"Little sub, you have exceeded my patience. Five swats." Gripping her wrists, he pulled her off the bed and took her place. He didn't release her. "Bend over my knees."

She tried to back away and got nowhere. "No." She shook her head frantically, her heart starting to hammer in her chest.

"No?" He lifted his brows in surprise. "Seven swats." His mouth set in a straight line, and the humor and gentleness disappeared from his face.

"Sir, please. No. You can't."

"I can. Ten."

No. She didn't resist—much—as he positioned her beside his knees. His grip unyielding, he laid her across his lap until her top half dangled on one side, her legs on the other. Her head spun, and she gasped. This wasn't happening, couldn't be—

"Farther, little sub," he said and shifted her until her bottom stuck up in the air. One of his legs pinned hers, and his left hand pressed her shoulders down. Trying to squirm, she realized she couldn't.

She felt his warm hand on her bare bottom, massaging, stroking. This wasn't a spanking, she thought, confusion running through her as her skin grew more sensitive to his touch. She felt the reawakening of desire.

And then he spanked her.

The first slap stung, and she jolted in disbelief. "No!" She wiggled, trying to escape.

He held her in place easily. "One."

Another slap. The sound echoed in the room as she jerked, the burning on her bottom intense and painful. "Two."

The third and fourth came almost together, hard and fast. Then slower, alternating cheeks. By eight, tears dripped from her eyes.

"Ten. There, little sub, all done." He didn't release her as he stroked her stinging cheeks. His hand was cool against the heat, bringing pain—and unexpected pleasure.

She lay limp, head hanging down, letting him pet her. Soothing her, she thought.

Slowly the strokes became longer. His hand cupped her cheeks, delving between her buttocks. One finger slid down into the crack, then farther, and animal hunger roused within her.

"Wa—" She clamped her mouth tight, her hands fisting in the carpet.

"You're learning, little sub, you're learning." He sounded infuriatingly amused.

Then he slid her legs apart, opening her to his touch, and his fingers moved through her tender, sensitive folds, swirling over her clitoris. His fingers slid easily—she was very wet—awakening every nerve ending to a burning arousal.

She moaned. The stinging pain of her bottom somehow increased the need flaring in her.

As she squirmed under the onslaught, he chuckled and, pinning her hips with one hand, plunged two fingers inside her.

"Ahhh!" An unbearable storm of sensation exploded inside her, and she came hard, bucking uncontrollably against his thrusts.

Before she had recovered, he picked her up off his knees and turned her into his embrace, handling her as if she weighed nothing.

"Shhh," he murmured, his cheek pressed to her hair. He kissed her wet cheeks and took her mouth so gently and sweetly that she started crying again. Not speaking, he just held her, stroking her with the same hand that had spanked her and then given her an incredible orgasm.

Exhaustion claimed her. Her muscles went limp. He held her firmly against his chest, and there was a strange security in his powerful arms.

She finally pulled in a shuddering breath. "Sir?"

He kissed the top of her head. "Learn to think before you speak, little sub. Not every Dom is as easygoing as I am."

She stiffened. Easygoing?

He chuckled and stroked her hair. "Of course, some subs mouth off just to get punished. Amazing how much fun a good spanking can be, isn't it? I sure don't remember that being covered in my college classes."

A gulping laugh broke from her, and she took a breath as the world returned to normal. "Um, Sir? What do you do for a living? You never said."

"Neither did you."

Well, they were definitely better acquainted today. "I'm a biology teacher. High school."

"Lucky kids. I'm a cop. A detective, actually. Want to see my handcuffs?"

She shook her head no and then rubbed her cheek over the springy hair on his chest. "No wonder you intimidated Buck so easily."

A growl rumbled through him. "He's lucky he got off so lightly."

"Sir?"

"Um-hmm?"

His arms never loosened, she was still snuggled up against him, held so firmly she couldn't move. The fact she found that reassuring was a little frightening. "When Buck grabbed me, you told him it was my choice whether to leave or not. But you didn't give me a choice now. You grabbed me…and spanked me."

"Ah." He rubbed his chin on the top of her head. "Your wannabe Dom lost his temper and tried to make you do something you didn't want. You didn't have a safe word arranged, did you?"

"Well, no. But—"

"Now I could be mistaken, but on your first night, we talked about what you might enjoy. Did I mention spanking? Punishment?"

"But I didn't say yes."

"Ah, sweetie, what I heard was that you didn't say *no*." His fingers cupped her cheek, raised her face to look at him. His brown eyes seemed to bore right into her. "I felt your body's response. First in the bar and again here. Was I mistaken?"

Heat flooded her cheeks. "No," she whispered. He'd barely touched her down below and she'd climaxed. Hard.

"Brave girl." His voice was warm, lazy, as comforting as his hands stroking her shoulders. "One other thing. Did I lose my temper?"

"Well." He'd been...displeased, definitely. But his voice and actions had been carefully controlled, she realized with surprise. Her lesson had been very deliberate. "No, Sir."

"Ah." He ran his fingers down her arm to her hand, massaged her palm. "Being under someone's control and punished... Some people find that very erotic, especially if you're already aroused." He lifted her hand, sucked on a finger, and the feeling of his mouth anywhere on her body made her womb clench. "You are one of those people who find it erotic, Kari. If you didn't, you'd have used your safe word."

She stayed silent. Nothing in her life was ever going to be quite the same again, was it? What she'd found out about herself these two evenings... She had some hard thinking to do. Soon.

When she didn't answer, he hugged her tightly, then set her on her feet. He steadied her as her knees wobbled. When his hands rubbed across her still-stinging bottom, she hissed.

He actually chuckled, the jerk. "You won't forget again, now will you? Because I could grow fond of seeing your pretty ass turn red under my hand."

"No, Sir, I won't forget."

"Very good." His eyes roamed over her body. From the heavy-lidded stare, the flush on his skin, and the thick wedge of flesh bulging under his leathers, she could tell he had enjoyed punishing her.

He moved a little closer. He was close, very close. His vest hung open, exposing a hard six-pack of abdominal muscles. "I could easily... No, I better not. Use the bathroom and take a quick shower." He grinned. "You need it now, I'm afraid. I'll pick out your clothes."

Her mouth opened, closed quickly, and she just nodded.

Pleased, he pressed a quick kiss to each breast, making her breath catch. "Go."

Chapter Ten

Dan listened to the shower as he opened the armoire door and surveyed his choices. Z kept a nice variety of fetish wear in each room. He eyed a French corset and then shook his head. She wasn't ready for that one—not yet—although those breasts would look sensational pushed up and overflowing. His cock twitched in agreement.

Maybe a maid's outfit? No. She was a modest woman, and he'd pushed her hard. He could relent with the clothing. *A bit.*

He pulled a dress out, soft and clinging, with a halter top that tied behind the neck. Anything that tied was fun. And the midthigh length was long enough to give her a sense of security. He grinned. That wouldn't last.

Perhaps he should keep her up here? But no. She'd come to the Shadowlands for an introduction to the lifestyle, so she really should see some of the regulars play. Considering how she'd reacted so far, it might be interesting.

She was so sweet.

He smiled, remembering her wide-eyed look when he told her to suck him, the tears on her cheeks after her spanking. *Sweet. Innocent.* Some men liked battling with sarcastic, angry subs. He wasn't one of them. Although he appreciated her courage and sparking temper, her modesty and nurturing nature drew him even more.

Her responses were so compelling, so honest, that he found himself wanting to wring more from her. But he needed to control himself to keep from pushing her too fast and far. She wouldn't stop with this visit. She might retreat after this, but her true nature was submissive. Now that she'd discovered the depth of passion inside her, vanilla sex would be even more tasteless to her.

She stepped out of the shower, rosy pink from the heat, her shoulders a confection above the blue towel. *Yum.* Crossing the room, he bent his head to nibble the curve where her neck met her shoulder. He tilted her head back and kissed the softness of her neck. "You taste wonderful and smell divine."

"Thank you," she said. She'd obviously recovered her composure in the shower, and her little shivers were gone completely.

Back in control, was she? Hmmm.

"I found something you'll like," he said, stripping the towel from her. "It slides right over your head."

* * *

Kari paused at the top of the stairs. The noise from the bar washed over her, bringing back a semblance of reality.

Why was she still here? She'd achieved her goal, to see what this BDSM stuff was all about. Now she really wanted to think about what had happened, what she'd done—what he'd done—for a while. A long while. She needed to be away from here to do that.

Time to go home. Her body was satisfied. Oh yes, more satisfied than ever in her life.

She turned to look at Master Dan and caught her breath when the soft material of the dress rubbed against her tender nipples.

No bra. No panties. She would have horrified the nuns. Then again, considering the other clothing in the armoire, she should be grateful this dress covered her fully. She'd seen a sheer lacy gown in there with the breasts and groin cut out. Good grief.

Yes, she appreciated this dress. This amount of indecency was enough for her. And Master Dan had refused to allow her underwear. She'd never gone—what did they call it?—*commando* before, and the cold air touching her nether regions made her feel very naked down there.

A little excited too, but she'd die before admitting that.

"I think I'll go home now," she said as he moved closer and tucked a firm arm around her waist.

He tilted his head and studied her silently. Unexpectedly, his fingers stroked across her breasts, and she sucked in a breath at the tingling, inside and out.

"No, little sub, your body isn't ready to leave yet." He held out his hand. "Take my hand."

It was an order, and her fingers were in his grip before she thought about saying no.

His eyes softened, and when he smiled approval, she had to smile back. He was right, darn him. The part of her that knew better, that followed the rules, wanted to leave. All the rest of her wanted to stay, to have his arm around her waist, to do what he ordered her to do.

He led her downstairs to the bar. Boy, things had livened up. Men and women nodded at him, greeted him by name. Not all of them, though. Where there were couples, only one would speak. The dominant one, whether man or woman. A few people were at the bar; others occupied the couches, occasionally with a man or woman at their feet. An older woman in an evening gown sat at a table with a male sub kneeling beside her.

She noticed the roped-off areas near the walls had been brightly lit, standing out in the shadowy room. She frowned and tugged him in the direction of one. "What—" At his narrowed gaze, she gulped. "Sir?"

"Good catch." And when he grinned, the flash of white in his tanned face was mesmerizing. "You have questions for me, Kari?"

"Yes, Sir."

"Ask."

But her questions disappeared right out of her mind when the roped-off area came into sight.

A naked woman squirmed on the St. Andrew's cross.

Kari's mouth dropped open. Good God. In the class, Master Raoul had put a clothed man up there; this was so very different. She took a step back, came up against Master Dan's hard frame.

His arm came around her, his hand just under her breast. He whispered in her ear, "Imagine yourself up there, unable to cover yourself, open to every man's gaze, available to every man's touch."

She could...she could see herself, and the thought was terrifying. *Erotic.* Her pussy dampened, and he rumbled a laugh in her ear. "Yes, the thought excites you, doesn't it?"

No way, no way would she let herself be put in that position. She shivered as he set his hand almost on her pubis, pressing her back against his erection.

"I would like to see you there too. But not yet, my sweet."

Hand against her back, he moved through the room. They passed a naked woman on the spiderweb, and then a man on the bondage table. A hooded Domme in a red latex corset stood beside him, wielding a switch.

When they reached the back wall, Kari stopped again. Her hands closed convulsively on Sir's hard biceps.

"What are they...she...?" But she could see. A woman lay on her stomach across the sawhorse, her wrists cuffed to the front legs. Her bent knees were strapped to the short cushions on each side, and she showed…everything, even more than the woman on the wall frame.

A man stood behind her, his jeans open, fully erect. He thrust into the woman with one stroke, and she screamed in pleasure.

Master Dan had to pull Kari away, she was so outraged. "Sir, he just took her right there. In front of everyone."

He stopped, lifted her chin, and looked her right in the eyes. "Call me Master Dan or Master. I tire of being nameless. I want to hear my name and my title from your soft lips, little sub."

"Bu—"

His eyes darkened, his mouth tight. He was really, really serious. *Call him Master.* To actually say that *aloud* felt like she'd be giving him too much power over her.

He waited, fingers unyielding, his other hand clamped on her shoulder. People swirled past around them. A woman somewhere broke into a cry of rapture, a man shouted in pain.

She had let him tie her and take her, punish her. Her body recognized his title, even if she didn't want to admit it. "Master."

"Again."

"Master Dan." As she feared, saying the words relinquished something inside her, some control she'd still been holding on to.

"Sweetly done, little Kari." He took her lips gently, lovingly even, his tongue rubbing against hers, slow and sensuous, until she was pressing up against him for more. His arms tightened around her. He was hard and ready, and she wanted him again. When she rubbed her breasts against his chest in invitation, he growled a laugh, and his hands reached under her skirt to massage her bottom.

The air on her butt hit her like a cold shower; she pushed away and opened her mouth to scold him. Shut her mouth.

"Nice save." He held her against her chest, stroking her hair. "What should you see next?" He glanced over at the other side of the room and shook his head. "Mmmph, not that."

She stood on tiptoe and still couldn't see.

"Perhaps next time." He stroked her cheek and smiled down into her eyes. "There will be a next time, will there not?"

Oh my God. Come back? This was so much more intense than just that first lesson. And seeing the equipment in use... Just look at what might be done to her. "Uh—"

His eyebrows drew together. "The answer is, 'yes, Sir.'"

"Yes, Sir." He wanted her to come back. More. Oh God.

"I think we both deserve a drink, don't you?" he murmured and pulled her to the bar.

"Daniel, how're things at the station?" A white-haired man, his hands knotty with arthritis, nodded at Sir. "Did I hear Bonner is retiring?"

"End of next year, he says." Sir shook the old man's hand with obvious care. "Master Gerald, this is Kari, here for the newbie classes."

"Pleased to meet you, Kari." Gerald wrapped an arm around the tiny woman standing next to him. "This is my wife, Martha."

Probably in her seventies, Martha wore a collar and cuffs that matched her bright pink bustier. Her long black skirt had pink studs along the waist and hem. She nodded at Kari, her aged eyes dancing with humor. "Master?"

"Go ahead," the old man said.

"Welcome to the club, Kari. We enjoy seeing young faces."

Was she allowed to talk? Kari glanced up at Sir, received a nod. "Thank you. I'm pleased to meet you."

"Kari, you're still here!"

Kari turned to see Jessica break away from a group of people. "May I borrow your sub for a moment, Master Dan?" she asked, taking Kari's hand.

Sir frowned, pointed to a spot about ten feet away. "Go no farther than that."

Jessica dragged her over to the spot. "How on earth did you end up with Master Dan again? I heard what happened Monday when you left."

Gossip. Like cockroaches, it survived in any climate and apparently any kink. Kari grinned. "He decided he wanted another night. Go figure."

Jessica pulled at her lip and watched Sir talk to the old man for a moment before turning her gaze back to Kari. "Well, that's interesting. Are you doing all right?"

Kari sucked in a breath. "It's so different. I like it and I don't want to like it, and I feel like I'm going straight to hell, you know?"

Jessica laughed. "I doubt we'll get a chance to chat tonight. Your last class is Saturday, right? Why don't you come early, and we'll have time to talk."

"I'd like that very much."

"See you then." Jessica grinned and darted away, heading for the front of the room.

As Kari rejoined Sir, Cullen walked over, his grin breaking the hardness of his face. "How's your sub, Dan?"

Master Dan stroked his hand down her cheek, his approval of her so obvious that she unconsciously leaned into his hand. Both men smiled. "How do you think?"

Master Cullen studied her, his eyes lingering on her mouth, and she realized her lips were swollen from Master Dan's kisses, from sucking on his... She flushed hot.

"She looks nicely used." He set two drinks on the bar top, and Master Dan handed her one.

She sipped. Rum and Diet Coke.

"Master Cullen never forgets a drink." Sir's finger traced over her wet lips. When she closed her lips around his finger and sucked, he chuckled, though his eyes heated. "He rarely forgets a sub's reaction or needs; he's very popular." He tapped her drink. "Enjoy it while you can."

That sounded ominous, and she edged away from him as she sipped. The strong drink gave her a slight buzz. No supper. Oops.

When she'd finished about half, Master Dan smiled at her and pulled her a little closer. She realized his eyes weren't smiling... No, he had that look in his eyes, the one that made her quiver inside. "I have decided your lessons are not over for the night."

She froze, then remembered to swallow.

"Your body is mine for tonight. Is that what we agreed, little sub?" He waited. "Kari?"

"Yes, M-Master."

"I use your body as I please." He waited for her nod, then leaned forward and whispered, "And give it where I please."

Her eyes widened, but he already had her hands in his. "One of the reasons that subs wear cuffs in here is this—" He hooked the cuffs together, then pulled a chain down from the low rafter over the bar area. Lifting her arms up, he hooked the cuffs to the chain. And stepped back.

Her arms were fastened straight over her head. She yanked, couldn't move. Her breath came fast, and her heart pounded. "Master?"

"Oh, very good." He smiled, nuzzled her face, his jaw abrasive with a day's whiskers.

"I don't—"

"Kari, a few minutes ago, you showed me that being looked at by strangers is arousing to you. Even being touched..." He tugged on the strings holding her halter top up.

The top dropped, leaving her naked above the waist. In a roomful of people. Many—heck, most—of whom were men. Cool air wafted across her breasts, and she shivered.

She shook her head. "Master Dan. No. Please, no," she whispered frantically. She pulled again at the chain.

"You'll only hurt your wrists," Master Dan murmured and bit her chin, the little nip almost painful. "If you damage those pretty wrists, I'll punish you." His hand reached under her skirt, right in front of everyone, and rubbed her naked bottom as a reminder. "I think you should stop pulling."

She stopped, hoping he'd take his hand away, but he continued to play with her butt, sliding his finger into the crack, squeezing her sore cheeks. At his teasing touches, pain, then pleasure surged through her.

Her nipples tightened, attracting his attention. He moved his hands up to fondle them, pulling gently, pinching until the nipples stood erect. Embarrassment vied with growing arousal within her.

"There. I think you're ready for visitors, don't you?" He turned her so she faced the room rather than the bar. Her legs shook, and the chains chimed softly over her head. He exchanged a look with the bartender.

"I do enjoy that sound," the bartender commented. "She has gorgeous breasts; you must be pleased."

Master Dan nodded. "I am. She's incredibly responsive." He rubbed his knuckles over one breast, and it tightened again to a hard, almost painful nub.

As Kari felt heat rush into her face, Master Cullen laughed. "A beautiful reaction. Love the way she turns red."

After kissing the top of her head, Master Dan moved a couple of feet away to sit on a bar stool, leaving her standing by herself. When he turned his head to talk with a friend, she tried to shift around to face the bar.

"Stay where I put you, little sub."

She did. Even when a man walked right up to her. He wore black leathers with gold trim like Sir's—another dungeon monitor. He glanced at Master Dan.

"Good to see you, Sam." Sir nodded at him. "She's one of the beginners."

Despite his silvery gray hair, the man had muscles like a young man. He looked at her and his eyes were pale blue in a stern, leathery face. "I couldn't help but admire your tits. What's your name, girl?"

If she didn't look at him, didn't answer, maybe he'd go away. Instead he caught her chin just like Master Dan and leaned down. His eyes were piercing. Unforgiving. "Subs answer questions put to them. What is your name?"

"Kari. Sir," she whispered.

Without releasing her chin, he stroked one hand over a breast, squeezing it, pulling on the nipple hard enough that she had to catch her breath. She didn't know him at all, and he was playing with her. He could do anything to her right now, and he knew it. The thought was horrifying. *Exciting.* She felt herself moisten down below and pressed her thighs together. *Oh God.*

He'd watched her face as he touched her, and now he smiled. "There's a good girl." Running a finger down her cheek, he walked away, leaving her confused. *Needy.*

Master Dan studied her, and his hard lips curved in a faint smile. His gaze softened, but when she looked at him in appeal, he shook his head. "Not yet, Kari."

He turned back to his conversation. She closed her eyes, felt the trickle of her own arousal down her leg. This was so... She couldn't...

A hand grabbed her breast, and she gasped and opened her eyes. A man her age dressed in a black suit, the cruel-eyed beginner. His fingers twisted her breast.

Biting back a cry, Kari tried to pull back.

She heard a low growl, and Sir ripped the man away from her.

Hands fisted in the man's suit, Master Dan held him up in the air as if he were a child. Sir's face was furious. Terrifying. "Did you ask permission to touch my sub?"

Not waiting for an answer, he shook the man. Hard. The man's head bobbled as he gasped, "Sorry, sorry. I—"

With a snarl of disgust, Master Dan dropped him onto the floor. A DM ran up, and Sir scowled at him.

"Sorry, Dan. He got away from me while I dealt with another newbie." Grabbing the suited man by the scruff of his neck, the DM pulled him away. Quickly.

Kari didn't blame him. When Master Dan turned to her, she cringed at the look in his eyes, the threat in his pose.

He stopped. Taking a deep breath, he visibly relaxed his muscles. She could see the violence flow out of him. Suddenly he was back to the Master Dan she knew—well, didn't know—but at least he didn't look like he'd tear people apart anymore.

Very gently, he unhooked her from the chain and wrapped his arms around her. She nestled there, feeling small, scared. *Comforted.* He simply held her, not moving, just letting her quiver in his arms.

When she stopped shaking, he ran his hands up and down her back. "I'm sorry, sweetie. Some beginners don't remember the rule that no one touches a sub without their Dom's permission."

He cupped her face, his gaze intent. "I should have been more careful with you. Can you forgive me?"

The man took her breath away. Did he know how rare it was to hear an honest admission of fault and apology? "I forgive you, Master."

He gave her a warm smile, but his eyes still held remorse. He felt horrible about what had happened, and that just seemed wrong. He'd grabbed the man within a second. He shouldn't feel so bad.

She put her hand on his and wrinkled her nose at him. "But I forgive only if I get a kiss to make it all better, Sir."

The remorse lifted from his eyes like fog from a mountain. Mischief took its place, and he grinned.

She gave him a wary glance. He had an appalling habit of ignoring respectable behavior.

His hand traced across her breast. "He touched you here, I think." He bent to kiss the spot. His lips feathered against her skin. "And here." He lifted the other breast for his lips to nuzzle.

Her nipples tightened into hard points as she started the slow glide back into need.

He touched her lower, cupping her mound. "I'm beginning to regret he didn't lay a hand elsewhere."

Right there in front of everyone, he had his hands on her…her private parts. But even as she flushed and scowled at him, her pelvis tilted into his hand.

His brows lowered, his mouth flattened. "Did you just frown at me?"

Chapter Eleven

She froze. *Oh no no no.*

He waited, tilted his head.

"Yes, Master. I'm sorry, Master. Very sorry, Master."

Amusement glittered in his eyes, even though his face remained stern. "Well, now, I can't have a sub giving me frowns. My reputation will be ruined." His hands closed around her wrists, and a second later, he'd hooked her cuffs to the overhead chains. Again.

She barely kept the scowl from reappearing on her face, and he could tell. The jerk.

He chuckled, then hauled her into his arms long enough to take her lips so thoroughly she sagged from the chains when he released her. "Ah, now that's better."

He resumed his seat, but he didn't take his eyes off her this time. No one was going to sneak up again without him noticing. And somehow, that just wasn't helping her feel much better. People stared at her, much like she'd looked at the woman on the cross. The men's eyes ranged down her body, lingering on her breasts.

She tried to keep her attention on Sir, watching as he talked quietly with the club members and other DMs. He discussed sports with one, advised another on disciplining a sub, argued politics.

Everyone liked him, obviously, although he certainly wasn't as gregarious as Cullen or Raoul.

No one came over until… Her eyes widened.

The owner of the Shadowlands, Master Z, approached, strolling through the crowd like a lion walking through a forest of prey. Shoot, *all* the dungeon monitors moved like that, had that aura of power and self-confidence. And Master Z was coming here.

Her breath hitched. She was all but naked.

He stopped beside Master Dan. "You didn't break him into pieces, Daniel. I appreciate your restraint."

"Came close." Master Dan's frown was intense. "My fault. I should have been more aware."

"Indeed. A lesson for all concerned." Master Z's gaze turned to Kari, and she felt a flush sweep all the way from her breasts to her face. He glanced at Master Dan.

Sir not only nodded, he actually grinned.

Master Z moved close enough she could feel his warmth, see the pleasure in his silvery eyes when he looked at her. "You are as lovely as I had thought, Kari." His smile made her feel warm, welcome. *Beautiful.*

"And I see you have found favor with our Master Dan." He stroked a hand down her cheek. "He didn't know it, but he has been looking for a gentle heart, a caring spirit, one who needed his control to discover the full depth of her passion. You are well suited."

Her head spun as she tried to comprehend his words, but when he rubbed his knuckles over each breast in turn, studied the way they hardened, he derailed her thoughts completely. "You'll be the envy of the Doms, Dan," he said. With another smile for her, he strolled back into the crowd.

"Bloody matchmaker," the bartender said with a grin, refilling Master Dan's glass from a bottle of spring water.

Two lines appeared between Master Dan's brows, and his mouth tightened. "He's full of it and wasting his time to boot. I'm not looking for any matches." His mouth thinned when he looked at Kari.

Kari felt cold creeping into her. Even though he was still right there, the man she'd been with earlier had disappeared. She felt abandoned and very vulnerable with her hands chained over her head. She bit her lip and looked down, away, anywhere but at his cold eyes.

"Hell." Something thumped on the bar, and then boots appeared in her line of sight. A hand lifted her chin, warm against her skin. "I'm sorry, sweetie. I might be annoyed with Z, but that has nothing to do with you." He kissed her gently, and tears burned her eyes. "You've brought me only pleasure tonight."

"Are you sure?" she whispered. He hadn't frowned at Master Z, only at her.

"I'm a cold bastard inside." He ran a finger down her cheek, his eyes crinkling at the corners when he smiled. "And you're very warm. Yes, I'm sure." His hand stroked down her body to circle her breast, lower still to cup her mound. With his other hand, he raised her skirt and touched her intimately, sliding his fingers through her wet folds. She gasped as pleasure surged through her. He kissed her neck, then bit her sharply. His finger pressed against her pussy, undoubtedly feeling it clench in reaction to the erotic thrill. "Definitely warm," he murmured, licking the bite. "Hot might be a better word."

She flushed. Although it was a heady feeling being called hot, she knew everyone could see where his hand lingered. To her relief and disappointment, he kissed her nose and settled himself back on the bar stool. "I'll finish my drink and then let you down."

He took a small sip—way too small; they'd be here all night—and smiled at her.

She managed, barely, not to glare at him.

He lifted his eyebrows, lips quirking in amusement, then turned as another man in gold-trimmed leathers walked up. The mean-looking one she'd seen with Raoul earlier. "Dan."

"Nolan, I heard you were back. Welcome home," Master Dan said, shaking the man's hand. "The place wasn't the same without you."

"It's good to be back in the States." The stranger tilted his head at Kari, and Sir nodded permission.

Nolan approached and looked down at her. Did all these dungeon monitor guys have to be so big? Black hair and black eyes as if he had Hispanic or Native American ancestry. His cold, hard gaze and the threatening set of his mouth made her want to flee. Involuntarily, she yanked on her restraints, tried to back up.

He didn't move, just watched her futile struggles. Her breath kept getting faster.

"Do you like being touched?" His voice was low and harsh with a hint of a Texan accent.

Her hands clenched on the chains. She couldn't answer that, not out loud. She licked her lips, glanced sideways at Sir.

Master Dan's eyes narrowed. "Answer the question, Kari. Honestly."

The man's eyes were so scary that she dropped her gaze to the floor. "Yes, Sir, I do," she whispered miserably. How could she want Master Dan's hands on her so badly and still be turned on by someone else's touch?

"Well, I'd hate to disappoint such an honest sub," the man drawled. She looked up. His mouth curved slightly, amusement in his eyes. Maybe, maybe he wouldn't hurt her—

He did worse. He tormented her, fondling her breasts with callused hands, circling around the edges of her nipples until the nubs burned with need. He finally relented and expertly squeezed each nipple to just the edge of pain and pleasure.

Her back arched, and she couldn't muffle a moan.

At that, the man actually smiled. He tapped her on the cheek with a scarred finger, slapped Master Dan on the shoulder, and walked away.

To her horror, Kari felt wetness running down her inner thighs, and she pressed her legs together.

Master Dan studied her. Nodded. "Looks like we need to go upstairs again."

He released her hands with a quick twist, and she staggered against him. Her lower half actually ached with need.

But rather than walking toward the steps they'd used before, he headed toward the back. Past the sawhorses.

A new woman was on one, her bottom poking up and out. Kari slowed, inhaled sharply. The woman's crotch had been completely shaved. *Oh my.*

Master Dan wrapped his arms around Kari from behind, held her in place when she would have hurried to get past. He set his chin on her shoulder, seeing everything she was seeing. "Shaving your pussy makes it more sensitive. To everything," he whispered in her ear. "And the spanking bench puts that little pussy where all of it can be reached. Touched. Played with."

His hand dipped down, stroked her folds right through her dress, his fingers knowledgeable. Between his seductive words and his penetrating fingers, she couldn't control the tremor of arousal that ran through her.

"Yes, I think you would like that position, little sub."

Her breath stopped entirely. *No—not in front of people.*

Just then, a man walked up to the woman on the sawhorse. He pulled her cheeks apart farther, slid two well-lubricated fingers into her anus, in and out, and everyone in the area heard the woman's moan.

Kari's knees gave out, and Master Dan swooped her up with a laugh. "Upstairs for you."

And without even breathing hard, he carried her upstairs and into a different room. Candlelight flickered over dark gray walls and black carpeting. No bed, only an armoire in the corner and a big easy chair in the other corner.

Still carrying her, Master Dan turned a little farther.

Kari stiffened in his arms. *A sawhorse.* Straps everywhere.

"You enjoyed looking; let's see if you enjoy riding." He put her on her feet and wrapped an arm around her, setting his big hand on her stomach to steady her. Grabbing her dress with one hand, he yanked it over her head, leaving her naked.

Her anxiety increased as his hot gaze slid down her body. "Spread your legs, Kari."

Staring into his eyes, she eased her legs apart.

"More." When she complied, he anchored her in place with a firm hand on her bottom, then touched her intimately, sliding his fingers through her wetness, caressing her clitoris with long, slow strokes. She grabbed his arms, her fingers digging into his skin as he drove her higher and higher, until her anxiety disappeared under the surging need.

"There we go," he murmured. He turned her to face the sawhorse. Pressing her hips into the edge, he ordered in her ear, "Bend over." His erection pressed into her buttocks as she bent, and she shivered, wanting him inside, thrusting…

His chest hard against her back, he flattened her onto the bench. The cold leather chilled her bare stomach, shocking her back to reality. When he clipped her wrist cuffs to the rings on the front legs, she felt like a trapped animal. Panicking, she jerked at the restraints.

He closed his hands on her arms, holding her firmly. "Stop now, sweetie. Are you in pain? Use the safe word if you need to."

She panted, pulled at her wrists.

"Kari, answer me."

His words finally registered. *Safe word.* She could make him stop anytime. The reminder helped, and she hauled in a slower breath. "I-I'm okay."

"Of course you are." Releasing her arms, he eased back. His hands settled on her back, warm against her cold skin. Gently, he massaged her shoulders until she sighed and relaxed.

"That's better, little sub," he murmured and kissed her cheek. "I like you a little anxious, but not scared."

She'd barely decided she wasn't too anxious. Then he set her knee on the attached padded bench and strapped it down. Then the other leg, securing her in an almost doggy position. With her knees set more forward, more of her showed.

When air slid like chilled fingers against her moist private places, she tried to move her legs. Nothing happened. *Everything* was on display, and she couldn't move.

As if he could read her mind, he said in a low, husky voice, "Now you're open to me. Fully. To my eyes, my fingers, my lips."

She shivered, and yet the burn of arousal inside her heightened.

He was behind her, and she couldn't see what he was doing, no matter how she twisted. A door creaked open.

"Master?" Her voice shook. "Are you there?"

"I'm here, Kari. I'll never leave you alone if you're restrained." Something rustled, and she realized the creaking sound had been the armoire door.

"Let's see if I can't get your mind off all these worries." He knelt behind her, his hands rough on her bottom, spreading her as his thumbs roamed up and down her labia. She squirmed, made a noise, and he laughed.

And set his mouth on her.

"Ahhh!" She jumped, her legs wrenching against the straps.

Rubbing her folds gently between his fingers, he exposed her clitoris completely. He swirled his tongue around it so hard and quickly, she cried out again.

"You feeling a little warmer?" He inserted a finger, and her tissues were so swollen from his previous use, she could feel every inch going in. She clenched around him.

"I like how my finger feels inside you," he murmured, "but I know you'll enjoy something longer. This should fit about right."

She felt so vulnerable, unable to see or move, as he pushed something into her. Not his cock; this thing was cold. Her vagina spasmed around it, tried to push it out. He held it in place and then moved it slowly in and out. She was so wet, it glided easily.

All the way out, then back in, filling her fully until she moaned. But it wasn't enough, not quite. When he took it out, her legs quivered uncontrollably.

He chuckled, and then she felt his tongue lick up and over her clitoris, over and over. He lapped at her like a dog, his tongue flat. Her insides tightened; her clit hardened. Every little cell in her waited, waited for each excruciatingly arousing slide of his tongue.

"More," she moaned. "Please, Master."

As if in response, she heard a *click* and a buzzing sound. When he touched the vibrator to her swollen labia, she gasped.

With a firm stroke, he slid it all the way into her vagina, and everything inside her burst into fiery pleasure. And then he pulled her clitoris into his mouth, rubbing it firmly with his tongue. With her legs strapped down, she couldn't move her hips, and the exquisite sensations grew even stronger, building into a fireball of ecstasy exploding out from her center. She screamed as the convulsions engulfed her.

When he wiggled the vibrator inside her, another climax rolled over her before the first was even done.

With a sensual hum of satisfaction, he removed the vibrator, making her vagina spasm again and her legs jerk.

He stepped away, and she heard the crinkle of foil as he sheathed himself. She tried to tip her head to see but couldn't. Her wrists and legs were still shackled. His hands on her bottom made her jump. Rubbing her buttocks, he murmured, "Still a little pink from your punishment. Such a pretty ass. And your pussy is wet and pink and ready for me."

Before she realized what he intended, he thrust into her, thick and hard. She felt herself stretching inside as he speared all the way to her cervix.

She yelped, pulling against the straps, the cuffs. "Too big, Master. Please…"

He chuckled. "Compliments from my sub?" His shaft moved inside her. Painfully. He pressed one hard hand down on her bottom, holding her in place. "Don't move, sweetling; your body will adjust."

Her whole lower half throbbed as if he'd shoved all her insides over for his possession, filled her to bursting.

Ignoring her little whimpers, he leaned over, his chest hard and hot against her back as his hands cupped her dangling breasts. "They just fall into my hands like ripe fruit," he murmured, squeezing gently, and she shivered.

Strapped, impaled, flattened from his weight, and now her breasts pressed upward from his hard hands. Surrounded entirely. Something opened in her mind. As she surrendered completely to his will, brutal arousal shocked through her and every nerve in her body violently awakened. "Master." She panted. "Master, I need—"

"Shhh. Soon, little sub." His breath seared her shoulder as his rough fingers abraded her sensitive nipples. When he pinched the points between his fingers, jolts seared through her until she squirmed uncontrollably, trying to rub her clit against the table. *More, please, more.* She rolled her forehead on the leather.

Murmuring something against her back, he bit the nape of her neck, holding it between his teeth, sending chills down her arms.

And then he finally, finally started to move, sliding his cock out of her so gradually, it seemed to take forever, then back in, an excruciatingly slow, circular motion. Her hands fisted on the straps as her body shook with unfulfilled need. Moaning, wanting more, faster, harder. She wiggled uncontrollably.

He pressed an unyielding hand against her butt, holding her in place and eliminating even the tiny movements she could make. "Little sub, you're so tight and slick, you're threatening my control."

His speed increased slowly, too slowly, and she tried to raise her butt, but she couldn't do anything. Whatever he wanted to do to her, she had to take it.

The thought sent her over, and she came with a fast rush, writhing against the leather of the sawhorse.

His hand stroked down her back as he straightened a little. "No, that was an inadequate climax, sweetie," he said, massaging her buttocks.

He wanted more from her. She wasn't sure whether to cheer or cry.

"You'll give me a better one," he said with certainty. Then he pressed his hips against her, thrusting deeply, and she moaned, his size no longer painful, just incredibly pleasurable.

With a low laugh, he pulled out, then rammed into her and continued, withdrawing, then burying himself. Hard, fast. His balls slapped against her swollen labia. His thickness inside her was thrilling. Sensation built on sensation until her vagina tightened around him.

He shifted slightly, and suddenly his fingers were on her, sliding in her wetness all over her oversensitized clitoris. The overload was too much and everything contracted and convulsed inside her, and she was coming so violently that she screamed over and over.

With a final thrust so hard that he actually moved the sawhorse, he came too, and the hot jerks of his penis spasmed against her insides again and again until only twitches remained.

He rested against her, his breathing controlled and hard. She could feel his heart pounding against her back.

"Now *that* was a worthy climax," he said, his voice even deeper than normal. He kissed her shoulders, her neck, before pulling back.

As he withdrew, sliding out of her acutely sensitive tissues, she shuddered. After disappearing into the bathroom briefly, he undid her restraints, then removed her wrist cuffs. With careful hands, he helped her dismount and held her up when her legs wouldn't work.

"There now," he murmured in his rough voice. A soothing voice. Why did she feel so...so vulnerable now, like she'd break into tears any minute?

Cupping her chin with his hand, he tilted her face up. She blinked frantically against the burning in her eyes.

"Ah, baby." He picked her up, cradling her like a child, and oh, she needed that so badly. Cuddling her close, he sat down in the chair with her pressed against his chest.

She let her head drop onto his shoulder. Heard her breath hitch as she tried not to cry.

Holding her firmly, he rocked the chair and talked to her, his voice a low, soothing murmur, filling the empty spaces that had opened inside her. "You are a beautiful woman, Kari... I love that soft, rosy body of yours... You have such a gentle spirit... I am grateful that you trusted me enough to give in to what was inside you. All that passion, sweetheart, you shared with me... Do you know how beautiful you are when you show me your need and when you come without hiding anything?"

Not asking her for any response, he just continued talking, telling her of his pleasure, his pride in her, until the horrible feeling of vulnerability dissipated and she felt like she was herself again.

When she sighed, his arms tightened around her, and he kissed the top of her head. They rocked quietly for a few minutes, the silence warm. She'd never felt so close to anyone in her life.

Eventually her brain turned back on with an almost audible click.

Her brain wasn't happy.

She felt...funny. Like too much had happened, like the world wasn't what she'd thought. *She* wasn't who she thought.

"Tell me," he said quietly, cupping her face. He kissed her temple, ruffling the tiny hairs with his breath. He snuggled her closer, his body warm where she was starting to feel cold. "Kari?"

"This isn't me," she whispered. "I'm not like this."

"Like what, sweetie?"

"I'm a teacher. I'm educated and smart. People don't boss me around."

"Ah, that. Being smart, educated, even having authority at work has nothing to do with what you like to do in private or in bed, sweetheart." He stroked her cheek, tucked her hair out of her sweat-streaked face. Wiped the tears running down her cheeks. She was crying?

"In your case, I figure you have three reasons that vanilla sex doesn't work for you. First, you really are submissive, for whatever reason. Some think it's just part of a person's personality, like being an introvert or extrovert. Others say it's upbringing. Doesn't really matter. You are what you are; you need what you need."

His words hit her almost like a sentence of doom: *You're submissive. There's no escape. Live with it.*

"Second, you, little nun, have guilt added into the mix. Your father's lectures, your religion disapproving of anything carnal— all inside you." He put his big hand between her breasts. "Right there."

She put her hand on top of his, could almost feel the big lump of judgments, criticism, scorn right under her ribs.

"And third, since you're an intelligent woman, your body wants to enjoy sex, but your brain never stops working and worrying." He rubbed her shoulder, stroked down her arm to take her hand. His fingers rubbed her knuckles. "Is that true, Kari?"

So true it was frightening. She could never stop thinking about what she should do, what he could do better, how hot the room was, what music was playing…

His dark brown eyes studied her face. When she sighed, he nodded. "It's hard for an educated woman to turn her head off. That's part of the joy of being a submissive. None of the decisions are yours. When you can't refuse anything and can't even move, those voices in your head go silent. All you can do, and all you are permitted to do, is feel. And you felt everything, didn't you?"

She nodded, but he didn't need her answer. He'd known every little twitch she gave. She rubbed her cheek on his chest gratefully. Understanding why she'd reacted so strongly helped a little. A little.

She listened to the slow beat of his heart. Surrounded by his arms, his scent, her body relaxed into him. Something about his strength, his understanding, his concentrated focus on her and her needs, was almost too overwhelming. Refusing to think further, she burrowed closer and let herself float away.

Sometime later, a chime sounded. Master Dan shook her gently. "It's midnight, Cinderella, and the dance is over."

"What?" She blinked at him.

He helped her to her feet. Her legs shook. She looked up at him, feeling lost. His eyes softened, and he hugged her, kissing her deeply. Gently.

"I wish we had more time," he murmured. "But the DMs will be around soon to drag slowpokes out." He kissed her again, this time with his hand curled around the nape of her neck, holding her in place. "I'm going to go find your clothes. I'll be right back."

By the time she'd used the bathroom to freshen up, he had returned. After she dressed, he escorted her down the stairs.

"Hey, Dan!" Standing by the front door, a familiar-looking woman in a black bustier and leggings waved them over. Kari recognized the DM from Monday.

"Olivia," Master Dan said.

"Nice to see you using the private rooms again." Olivia gave Kari a disconcertingly slow and appreciative look before she turned back to Dan. "If you're interested, I'm throwing a dungeon party Sunday afternoon. Bring your pretty sub and come play."

"Ah—" Sir started.

"Don't say no. It's been far too long since you partied with us," the DM said. "We miss you."

Kari looked up. Surprise and what looked like guilt flickered in Master Dan's eyes. His muscular arm went rigid, then dropped away from her waist.

"I can't make it. Sorry." His voice sounded as if the life had drained out of it.

"Oh, honey, I'm sorry too." Olivia patted Sir's arm gently and moved away.

"Let's go," Master Dan said to Kari.

As she stepped out into the night, the humid air blanketed her, the scent of tropical flowers and swamp almost overpowering. The loss of Sir's touch created an ache inside her as he silently walked beside her to the tree-lined parking lot. Others were leaving also, faceless figures in the shadows and moonlight. Cars moved down the drive in a slow string of lights.

Taking her keys, he unlocked her car and opened the door. She looked up, hoping for a kiss, a hug...something...but his gaze was as remote as the distant moon.

"Thank you for the evening, Kari." His fingertips brushed her cheek, featherlight.

Her lips tightened. No more *sweetheart* from him. The ache increased, and she tightened her lips against a betraying quiver. He had only promised an evening. The evening was over, and she never caused scenes. All those etiquette lessons from the nuns hadn't gone to waste. She slid into the car, then forced a smile and a cool tone, "Thank you for the lesson, Master Dan. I do appreciate the time you've spent with me."

His eyes were distant, but sadness lingered in the lines of his face. "Drive carefully." He put her keys into her hand and closed the door softly.

Chapter Twelve

Dan's chest ached like he'd cracked all his ribs. He rubbed his sternum as he walked back to the Shadowlands. Why Olivia's invitation had hit him so hard, he didn't know; after all, he'd been fending off well-meaning friends for three years now.

Fending off subs too. He remembered Kari's expression a minute ago, how her big eyes had filled with confusion, then hurt. His mouth tightened, and the frozen feeling inside him increased. Being with her a second time had been a mistake. For both of them. It wouldn't happen again.

Not bothering to knock, Dan walked into Z's office. "Got a minute?"

Z set down the paper he'd been reading. "Daniel. Did you have a good evening?"

"Fine." Dan raised his hand to run it through his hair, stopped halfway, and lowered his arm. Subs weren't the only people who Z could read like a grade-school primer. "Just wanted to give you a heads-up. I won't be able to make the dinner on Friday or be here on Saturday."

"Is there a problem?"

"No." The terse answer with no explanation was rude, but he had no damned explanation. Just that he needed to not be here for a while.

Z studied him for a minute before asking, "Was little Kari a disappointment to you?"

Damned mind-reading psychologist could be like a cat with a cornered mouse. "She'll make someone a wonderful sub, I'm sure. I'm not in the market for one, though, and you fucking well know it." He winced at the raw sound of his own voice.

"I hear you," Z said mildly. "Well, then. I'll tell Jessica about Friday. We'll miss you on Saturday, Daniel."

"Right." Mouth set tight, Daniel headed out, resisting the urge to slam the door behind him.

Outside, he scowled up at the moon, remembering how Kari's pale skin had glowed in its light. He shook his head. Real fucking romantic. He pulled his keys out, headed for his truck. No traffic, he'd be home soon enough.

Home. He sighed, rubbed his face. The thought of his cold, empty apartment made his guts twist. *Fine then.* He'd hit the station instead, put in some time on his unsolved cases stack.

* * *

Early Thursday morning, Kari wandered through her quiet neighborhood, a basket of warm muffins over her arm. Around five in the morning, she'd finally given up on any sleep and put the time to good use.

Tail waving in the air, her German shepherd, Prince, trotted in front of her, guarding her from evil field mice, stray cats, and other dogs. Especially the aggressive poodle that lived three houses down. A cool breeze brushed against her skin and sent droplets from last night's rain pattering off the leaves onto the pavement.

After getting home last night, she'd sat out on the patio, trying to come to terms with Master Dan's behavior. She'd felt so close to him, and he'd acted like he'd felt the same, and then he'd just shut down. But he'd warned her, after all, said he didn't have anything to give. She shook her head. He'd given her more than any man before, but apparently she wasn't enough for him, not compared to his dead wife.

Kari stopped, closed her eyes at the despondency the thought created. But she couldn't see a way to fight a dead wife's memory. She opened her eyes and took a deep breath of the clean air. Life was what it was; she'd just have to move on and cherish the wonderful things she'd learned from him.

She walked up to the Jernigans' porch and left the basket of blueberry muffins on the table beside the mail slot, knowing Mr. Jernigan would find it when he went to get the newspaper. His elderly wife had been discharged from the hospital yesterday, and everyone knew Mr. Jernigan could burn canned soup.

Back on the sidewalk, Kari trailed after Prince, who knew the route as well as she did. Her sneakers slapped against the pavement, reminding her of the sound of flesh against flesh...of Master Dan plunging into her. *Lordy.* She shook her head, trying to forget that image before she got all heated up again. Impossible task. Too many parts of her ached: her pussy; her swollen mouth; her breasts, almost too sensitive to tolerate her softest bra; her wrists, sore despite the lined cuffs he'd used. She had scrapes on her legs from the straps and a bite mark on her stomach.

Oh, she'd been used and used well. She tried to frown, but her arms wrapped around herself in a do-it-yourself hug, and she laughed instead. Hadn't it just been great?

She danced two steps, then stopped to push little Annie's skates and tricycle off the sidewalk into the grass. Some of those joggers just didn't watch where they were going even in the daylight, let alone at night.

At night...last night, she'd been so aroused that she'd screamed...actually screamed when she came. So many times too. That was just... Wow.

From across the street, a bird warbled a spring song and received an answer from Debra's yard. For the birds, it was nesting season; for her, it was a time to reexamine her life. She wasn't some frigid, passionless person after all; she just needed something more than other people. Something different. *Exotic*—she'd call it that, since *kinky* didn't sound very respectable.

Seeing Mrs. Jones hadn't retrieved her newspaper, Kari left it on the cushioned chair next to the front door. The frail woman pushed her walker as incompetently as she drove her old Suburban. An accident waiting to happen.

Prince waited for her on the sidewalk and gave her his humans-are-so-slow look before continuing on. Didn't he realize she had thinking to do?

Last night, Master Dan had changed something in her. Her inability to control what happened and his sure knowledge of how far to push her had broken through some barrier she hadn't known was there. She felt like a beginner's chemistry experiment. Add a little sodium bicarb to vinegar and suddenly she bubbled and fizzed with the best of them. Wasn't that just awesome?

Prince trotted back. She stopped to pet him and frowned at the ugly gray sleeve of her sweatshirt. As a new fizzy person, she really should shine up her test tube. She looked down at herself and her baggy gray sweats, then thought about the ankle-length dress lying on the bed for school. Pretty pathetic. Maybe if she didn't dress like an escapee from a nunnery, she would stop thinking of herself that way. Time to go shopping.

* * *

On Friday evening, Kari picked up the ringing phone. "Hello."

"Kari, this is Buck."

"Oh. Um. Hi." She sighed. There must be people who enjoyed going out on Friday evenings, but all she wanted to do was curl up in jammies, eat popcorn, and enjoy a mindless movie. After a week of attempting to teach teenagers, the last thing she wanted was to have a conversation, especially an awkward one. "What's up?"

"We've never had that talk you promised," he said. "How about I come over? We can discuss what's going on."

"Ah, that won't work, Buck. I'm beat." All right, the polite thing would be to say she was sorry, but she wasn't.

A pause. "Are you still mad at me for Monday? I said I was sorry."

Apparently the discussion would be now. She sat down at the kitchen table and tried to prepare herself. "I'm not mad."

"Well, good. Then I'll pick you up for the last class tomorrow around eight."

Maybe she needed to learn to be less polite. Submissive to one man didn't mean that everyone else could walk all over her. "No. Um. I like you, Buck, but I don't want to date anymore." There. That was plenty blunt. She immediately felt guilty.

"Are you dating that Dom from the club? Is that why you don't want to see me anymore?" His voice held a thread of bitterness.

"I'm sorry, but that's not your business," she said, striving for the gentle-but-firm tone she used with nosy students who wanted to know about her personal life.

"Kari, that guy's not good for you. I can tell," he said. "I don't like the way he's got you behaving."

"I appreciate your concern, but it really is my business." There had to be a way to get off the phone. *Lie.* "Sorry, Buck, but I've got another call coming in. I have to go. Bye."

She punched the End button. Hopefully, he'd never remember that she didn't have call waiting. *Bad, bad Kari.*

* * *

Saturday evening, Kari set the phone down with a loud sigh. Darn it. No—*damn* it! The auto mechanic had been very apologetic, but the part for her car wouldn't be in until Monday morning. No car till then.

She dropped onto her comfy floral couch and leaned her head back. It wasn't a total disaster. Carol could take her to school on Monday, and she didn't have any place she needed to be this weekend.

Except the Shadowlands.

"Well, Prince, looks like it's you and me tonight."

Setting his head on her knees, the shepherd looked up at her with big brown eyes, perfectly content to have her at home. She stroked his soft ears and sighed. She'd been off and on about returning to the Shadowlands, but now that she couldn't go, she felt a definite letdown. No BDSM stuff. No Master Dan.

Rising, she paced across her living room. She looked at her wrists, remembering the weight of the cuffs and the erotic feeling of helplessness when Sir had strapped her onto that sawhorse thing. How he'd pinned her hips down as he thrust into her, so big and hard... She shivered as her body roused, craving that sensation again. All those sensations.

Still, she needed to be practical. Over the past couple of days, reality had slowly crept back. Although bondage might be interesting, it wasn't exactly something a person did forever...was it?

She reached the end of the room and turned. How long could a person indulge in...*exotic* sex? Hmm. When Jessica had talked about Master Dan being a member of the club, she'd said *years*. And that older couple, Martha and Gerald, had been together for twenty years. They looked perfectly content. Not depraved or anything. So, people *could* do it for years.

Would she want to? Heat ran through her at the thought. What would it be like to be actively interested in sex instead of putting up with it? What if, after an evening of reading or watching TV, her man ordered her to strip and bend over the arm of the couch for his use? Would that change her life? The instant dampness of her pussy gave her the answer.

Master Dan said she was wired to need domination for true satisfaction. A sexual submissive. She wrinkled her nose. That submissive word still sounded awfully distasteful. But facts were facts. She'd gone to the Shadowlands to test the hypothesis that bondage and domination aroused her. Her experiment, although not done to anything resembling scientific standards, had proven exactly that.

Knowledge gained, new problems discovered. Did she want to pursue this further?

She snorted. *Darned right.* Not that she could do anything about it tonight.

Ruffling Prince's fur on the way past, she kept pacing. Couldn't do anything about Master Dan either, now could she? Her introduction to the lifestyle might have been completely different if she'd had a different instructor. Sir was...something. All those muscles to run her hands over, the firmness of his grip on her body, the assured authority. His deep, rough voice. Just thinking of him made her burn.

Would he wonder why she wasn't there tonight? Would he miss her? She shook her head and sighed. Doubtful. With all those subs around, he didn't lack for female attention. Yeah, he wouldn't give her a second thought when she didn't show. Even if she had been able to attend the last class tonight, he'd made it clear their time together was over. The jerk.

He didn't want anything permanent; he wanted his dead wife. So it was just as well that her car was hospitalized. *Really.*

Darn it.

Look on the bright side. By staying home, she wouldn't run into Buck.

Prince whined, reminding her of her petting duties, and she slipped to the floor to hug him. "Buck won't be coming back here again." Prince hadn't liked Buck at all. "I should have listened to you about him, huh?"

In total agreement, Prince licked her face and leaned against her, leaving hair all over her new red tank top and jeans.

She planted a kiss on top of his furry head. "So did you notice? I've got cleavage. And my legs are pretty good too, for that matter." Instead of trying to hide her body, she was finding ways to showcase it and enjoy it. Yesterday, the other teachers had been surprised, then effusive with compliments over her new look. *Thank you, Master.*

"Well, buddy, let me get you some supper and—" Kari stopped. Oh, heck, how could she have forgotten? Jessica expected her to show up early so they could chat. Sir might not miss her, but Jessica would. Kari grabbed the phone again and carried it to her desk. Pulling out a copy of the Shadowlands forms, she found the phone number. Would someone be in the office now?

"Shadowlands." A man's voice. Low. Familiar. One of the DMs?

"Um. This is Kari Wagner. I was supposed to meet Jessica there tonight. Is there any way I can get a message to her?"

"She is here, Kari. Allow me to call her to—"

"No, there's no need. Can you just tell her that I won't be able to make it?"

There was a pause. "Is there a problem, little one? Can I help?"

Her breath caught. This was no DM; it was Master Z. "No. No, really. My car's in the shop, that's all."

"And is your lack of transportation good…or bad?"

The insightful question silenced her. "I…" She sighed. "A little of both, I guess. It's all so different, you know?"

"Kari." His deep voice sharpened. "Did you have a problem with Master Dan?"

Just hearing Sir's name sent blood surging into her face and elsewhere. "No," she managed to say, her words husky. "No, he was—" *Wonderful. Scary. Intimidating. Too much for an inexperienced schoolteacher.* "He was fine."

A chuckle. "I am happy to hear it. I'll give Jessica your message, that you'll be enjoying a quiet evening at home."

"Thank you," Kari said glumly and clicked the phone off. Just hearing a Dom's voice with that edge of command brought back all the reasons she wanted to continue. She yearned to hear Sir tell her what to do, to feel his hands holding her, to struggle and get nowhere.

But he wasn't for her.

She shook her head. *Get over it.* She'd done what she'd set out to do, seen what it was all about. Returning to the Shadowlands would just give her pain, at least until Master Dan had lost some of his appeal. After that, she'd go back and meet someone else.

Until then, maybe she should return to her normal life and normal men. The thought was as appealing as planning to eat oatmeal for three meals a day. Forever. *Darn it.*

* * *

Dan drove out of the police station parking garage and turned toward home without any sense of pleasure. His body sagged against the car seat, his mind equally tired. Three hours waiting to be called as a witness, and then the perp settled, a new form to fill out for snitch money. Dan's partner wanted to go on vacation for a month, and who the hell would he end up with then? Some kid fresh from patrol?

Why hadn't he chosen to be an accountant? A quiet office and numbers. No blood, no violence. Far fewer lies. *The paperwork would still suck.*

His cell phone rang, and he pulled off to one side of the freeway. Flipping the phone open, he glanced at the number displayed. The Shadowlands.

"Z? What's up?"

"Not Z, Dan. This is Jessica."

He blinked. Z's sub? "What can I do for you?"

"Well. You know the beginner you were with this week? Kari?"

Knife-edged fear tightened his hand on the phone. "What happened? Is she all right?"

A huff of laughter. "Cops. You always imagine the worst. She's fine. But her car isn't. It's in the shop."

"She called for a ride?" That didn't seem like the little sub. Unlike most women, she didn't beg for release until he tormented her to the point where her brain shut off. Very doubtful that she asked for help often, at least for herself.

"No, you idiot. She called to say she wouldn't be coming. We were planning to meet early, and she wanted me to know."

"Well, that's good she called then." Maybe he'd go tonight then, since she wouldn't be there to mess with his emotions, to lure him into taking more, *giving* more than he wanted.

"Oh." A pause. "Right. It's good. Sorry to have bothered you."

Dan frowned. Had Z's little sub just said "stupid asshole" under her breath?

After pulling back into the heavy traffic, he flipped on the radio, tapping his fingers on the steering wheel to Emmylou

Harris. The air off the gulf was briny and warm, the sun setting in a clear blue sky. He'd have time for a shower, maybe a fast bite, before leaving for the club.

She wouldn't be there tonight.

Dan turned the music up louder, ignored the bastard who cut in front of him to make an exit. Tampa drivers terrified the nation: macho Cubans mixing it up with aggressive East Coast drivers tailgating retired snowbirds going twenty miles below the speed limit. Driving was probably the most dangerous part of his job as a cop.

She wouldn't be on the road; she didn't have a car. *She wouldn't be there tonight.*

Good. Very good. He didn't need to see her again. Didn't need any more reminders of her little whimpers right before coming, or the way her hot, soft mouth closed over him, or how her pussy would tighten around him, or—

He slowed to let a bus onto the freeway, breathed in the diesel fumes. Busload of kids, probably some sporting event at the school.

She was a teacher. She'd be a wonderful teacher. He remembered how she'd tried to ease his mind about his carelessness: "*I forgive only if I get a kiss to make it all better, Sir.*" The tender look in her eyes when she kissed him that first night. And—

Fuck. She just wouldn't stay out of his head. He pulled off the freeway, flipped open the phone, and punched in the number.

"Shadowlands." Z's voice. Good thing it wasn't Jessica.

"Give me her damn address, you sadistic bastard."

Chapter Thirteen

Number thirty-three. Dan pulled into the driveway.

The twilight showed a two-story house, sky blue with sparkling white trim. Bright red and white flowers bloomed along the fence with more in pots on the wide porch. Stepping up to the front door, he rang the doorbell.

When light footsteps sounded from inside, Dan berated himself again. He should stay away from her; she deserved better than what he could give. Dammit, he didn't want anything more from a woman than some mutual satisfaction. Definitely no emotional involvement.

Yet something about her pulled at him. He should never have taken her under command, and he damned well shouldn't be here today. Fuck, he was an idiot.

Hell, she might not even want to see him. He'd behaved like a real asshole on Wednesday. For the second time. What if she didn't want to return to the Shadowlands? Or be with him?

He set a hand against the door frame. Only one way to find out. Any Dom worth his leathers could read a sub's face. He'd soon know if the no-car reason she'd given Z was an excuse.

The door opened, and he had his answer in the big blue eyes.

Surprise, delight, wonder, delight, worry. "What are you doing here?"

He ran a finger down her cheek, unable to keep from touching her. "Jessica said you needed a ride."

"I… You're here to take me to the club? Really?"

"Do you want to go?" He watched her face, her open expressions. She was honest, inside and out. Did she know how rare that was? After years on the force, he'd grown cynical, begun to believe everyone lied. But not this little sub.

"Yes. Mostly." A wrinkle appeared between her brows. "It still doesn't seem real, like something a person should do. But—" She smiled. "Oh, yes, I want to go."

"With me?" He tilted her chin up so she couldn't look away.

The look of longing told him everything he wanted to know even before she whispered, "Yes."

As satisfaction roared through him, he grinned. To hell with his misgivings. He could manage one more night. "In that case, you need to change. Jeans aren't allowed, although…" He ran his gaze down her body. Red top displaying ample cleavage and gorgeous shoulders. Jeans so tight he wanted to bite that sweet ass. "I like what you're wearing."

Her face lit up. "Thanks."

"Definitely my pleasure. I could use a shower, if you don't mind. Jessica caught me on my way home, and I detoured here."

"Of course."

"I keep spare leathers in the truck. Let me get those."

A minute later, he walked into her house and stopped short. A German shepherd blocked his path. As a cop, he approved; as the man planning to strip Kari of those jeans, maybe not. He knelt and held out a hand. "Hey, boy."

A thorough sniffing later, he had a new friend. Ruffling the dog's soft fur, Dan said, "He's a beauty. What's his name?"

"Prince."

"Like the musician?"

"Like, someday my prince will come," she said under her breath, adding aloud, "Something like that, yeah. C'mon into the living room."

Cops have keen hearing, and the longing in her words struck Dan like a hard punch to his gut. He froze for a moment until Prince nudged him with a cold nose. "Right, dog. I'm moving."

Escorted by Prince, Dan followed Kari into a living room done in soft pastels with overstuffed chairs and a couch in flowery print. A small white brick fireplace conjured up images of how beautiful Kari would look in the firelight. Tied and helpless and whimpering her need. He shook his head; damn, he was impossible.

"Hello there." A thin woman in her midtwenties rose when he entered the room. Brown hair, brown eyes, maybe five-six.

"Jennifer, this is Mas...um...Dan," Kari said, giving him a flustered look.

He crossed the room, stuck his hand out. "Nice to meet you. I'm sorry for the intrusion."

Jennifer shook his hand. "No intrusion. I'd just come over to ask Kari for some advice on teenagers." She grinned at Kari. "I'll try that and see what happens. Thanks, hon."

She kissed Kari on the cheek and headed for the front door. "You two enjoy yourselves." The door shut quietly behind her.

"Well." Kari glanced at Dan. "My towels are in the dryer. Give me a second."

While she was gone, Dan prowled around. The right side of the living room led to an old-fashioned kitchen with light oak cabinets to match the big round table and chairs at one end. There was a colorful braided rug on the floor, plants in the window over the sink, the scent of cinnamon in the air. Oatmeal cookies were spread on waxed paper. Flour, sugar, and a bottle of vanilla sat on the counter.

She made cookies from scratch? Unable to resist, he took one. Warm and chewy, it brought back memories of weekends at his grandmother's house in the country. Like Kari's home, Gran's place had been cheerful and filled with friends and family. The contrast with his bleak and lonely apartment was chilling.

"Where are—" Towels over her arm, Kari came around the corner into the kitchen. She tried to frown at him, but laughter lit her eyes. "Bad Master! Those are for the children."

"And they're very good." He touched the dimple that appeared in her cheek as she tried not to smile. "You can call me Dan, you know. Formality can be saved for the club. And sex." He smiled as she flushed. "Definitely for sex.

"Well, okay. Thank you." She waved her hand at the counter. "You really can have more, you know. I made plenty. Or can I fix you some supper? Maybe a sandwich?"

A born nurturer. "No. I—" His stomach growled, giving him away.

She laughed and pulled out bread and meats from the refrigerator. "Mustard? Mayonnaise?"

"Just mustard." He leaned against the door frame, watching her bustle about for him. Marion had rarely cooked; she'd assumed he could get his own meals as well as she could. But they—

"What's the matter?" Kari touched his cheek with soft fingers. "You look so unhappy."

"Nothing." No. The cop was taking a cop-out, and a Dom must be honest with himself. And his sub. "I was thinking about my wife. She didn't like to cook."

"Oh." Kari stroked his cheek with light fingers and then returned to making his sandwich. After a minute, she handed him a plate with his sandwich on it, poured a glass of milk, and led him to the big oak table. "Sit. Eat while I put the cookies away."

He'd just finished the sandwich when she joined him at the table and dropped two more cookies on his plate. "You read my mind," he said lightly.

"Men seem to love sweets."

And sweet women like Kari. Damn the way she pulled at him. He shouldn't get involved. Couldn't.

She nibbled on a broken cookie. Then her blue eyes swept up. "Tell me about your wife's death, Dan. How did the accident happen?" she asked softly.

His stomach clenched as the food inside turned to a hard lump. "She skidded off a road into a tree."

Kari tilted her head. Asking more questions would be like deliberately poking at his pain. Horribly rude.

Yet he reminded her of her sister. When Hannah's baby had been stillborn, everyone said she was handling it, only she wouldn't talk to anyone. But Hannah normally shared every little thought or pain. Arriving a week later, Kari prodded until Hannah screamed at her, burst into tears, and finally shared her tangled mess of emotions. More than just grief, Hannah felt guilty over the dumbest things: taking a puff of a cigarette, bouncing too much when she walked, eating something unhealthy. And she'd been envious of every mother with a healthy baby, hated them, hated God, hated her husband, who somehow hadn't prevented the death. Hannah had talked and cried and talked some more.

And after that, she'd been able to simply mourn for the loss of her baby.

Dan's eyes held the same torment. Kari clenched her hands in her lap, her heart aching as she decided to push him. "Were you there?"

His head jerked back as if she'd slapped him.

She waited. "Dan?"

"Dammit!" He slammed his hand on the table so hard the dishes jangled. Pushing to his feet, he stalked across the room. "No. I wasn't there. I got called into work. I could have refused, but I didn't. And she went out partying. Drinking. By herself. If I'd been there…"

"You think if you'd stayed home, she wouldn't have died."

"She'd be alive." At his sides, his hands opened and closed, over and over. The stark lines on his face were deepened by pain. "I protect people; that's my job. And I let my wife die."

A nun once told Kari that guilt has no logic. She kept her voice low the way she did when trying to pet the Garretts' pit bull. "So if I decide not to go tonight, and you get drunk and run off the road, will it be my fault?"

He glared at her, but after years of teaching sneaky little children, she knew how to offer up wide-eyed innocence. "That's not the same at all," he snapped.

"Isn't it?" Kari rose and put her arms around him. His body felt like a stone pillar. "Unless you promised to be at her side every moment of every day, you didn't do anything wrong. People make their own decisions, and sometimes bad things happen. Not your fault, Dan, any more than it would be my fault if you went out tonight and got in an accident."

He didn't move.

Remembering Hannah's anger, Kari added softly, "You know, if you got drunk and killed yourself driving, I'd not only be grieving, I'd be furious with you for doing something so stupid."

He growled, but she ignored that and just held him, her cheek pressed against his chest, feeling his pain, sharing his pain. Had she gone too far? Would he ever talk to her again?

After a minute, he took a ragged breath, and his muscles loosened. Wrapping his arms around her, he held her gently.

She could have nestled there all evening, but the phone rang. He stepped away from her. Feeling like cursing, she went to answer it, after pointing at the table. "Finish your milk."

His huffed laugh relieved her immeasurably.

His legs felt rubbery, as if he'd run a marathon, so Dan took a chair at the table. After a minute, he did as the little sub ordered and drank his milk. The first swallow caught on the tightness in his throat, but the rest went down well enough after that.

Her voice was like a melody of happiness and caring as she talked with some friend about a play rehearsal. Prince padded over to lean against Dan's leg, a comfortingly warm weight. He stroked the soft fur, thinking about Kari's words.

She said she'd be furious if he died being stupid. Was he mad at Marion? He'd loved her, mourned her. But anger?

Now the possibility had been raised, he could almost feel the heavy mass of rage inside him. She *had* been stupid, not for going without him, but in getting drunk and then driving. They'd fought about that before, and she'd laughed at him, called him a hidebound cop. His jaw tightened. And then she'd died…died and left him alone.

Feeling guilty. Feeling angry.

His eyes burned as the unsettling emotions swept over him, uncontrollable as waves hitting the shore. The room felt suffocatingly hot. He had to leave. He walked out into the night air, leaving Kari staring after him.

* * *

Kari heard a tap at her front door and jumped to her feet. *Oh, thank God.* The last half hour had seemed like an eternity. Every few minutes, she'd gone to the door and stood there, wanting to go after him. Then she'd return to the couch and sit down again. After the third time, Prince just stretched out and watched her.

Now she ran to the front door and pulled it open. "Are you all right? I'm so sorry, I should never have said—"

He kissed her firmly. Briefly. "I'm fine, and yes, you should have said everything you did." He ran his finger down her cheek. "I'm sorry I left so abruptly."

"It's all right." She watched him walk into her living room, reassured to see his prowling gait had returned. "Do you still want to go? I'd understand if you didn't."

"Yes, I want to go." He glanced at his watch. "We still have time before Ben locks the doors. Can I take that shower?"

The guest bathroom lacked a shower, so Kari led him down the hall to her bedroom and the master bath. He followed silently—a good thing since she couldn't figure out anything to say. She could talk fine when he'd needed her, but he was back to normal.

And having Master Dan here, in her home, was disconcerting.

Before she'd only seen his Dom side, but there was more to him. The depths of his pain and guilt over his wife's death broke her heart. But it was the little things that she hadn't been prepared for. The way he'd stolen a cookie. How he looked completely at home in her kitchen. How friendly he'd been with Jennifer; he hadn't whipped out cuffs or expected to be called Master. How normal—*gorgeous*—he looked in black jeans and a short-sleeved shirt. How he talked to Prince like a person.

And Prince liked him.

In leathers and at the Shadowlands, Master Dan was like a dream. A fantasy. This Dan was real. Frighteningly real.

"Here you go." She set the towels on the counter.

"Thank you. I'll be quick." He unbuttoned his dark brown shirt and tugged it out of his jeans, before reaching in to turn on the shower.

"Right." Her gaze got trapped at the sight of his muscular chest, his broad shoulders. When he undid his pants, she glanced up and saw the amusement in his eyes. The disconcerting heat that matched her own.

"I'd better change," she muttered and fled.

In the bedroom, she couldn't concentrate. He'd be naked by now. In her shower. If she had any courage, she'd go in there and join him. Yes. She'd do just that. She took two steps toward the door and heard his voice.

"Kari, I need…" The last part of his sentence trailed off.

What could he need? The shower had soap and shampoo. Steam billowed in the bathroom as she entered. Feeling like a voyeur, she hesitated outside the shower curtain, trying not to stare at the outline of his big body. Or at least to not be obvious about it.

"Dan?" Saying his name still felt so strange. Nice, but strange. "Did you need something?"

"I did." He pushed the curtain back, grabbed her around the waist, and set her in the tub. "I need *you*."

The water and his deep laugh drowned out her startled yelp.

With ruthless hands, he stripped her out of her clothes and started washing her, his hands running over her arms, her back, her breasts. He gave extra attention to her breasts. "Cleanliness is next to godliness," he informed her, holding her firmly in place despite her squirming.

"I had a shower earlier." His touch was making her hot, needy. Abandoning modesty, she ran her hands over his chest.

"But I guess another one is good." She slid her arms around him and pushed her belly against his erection.

His eyes kindled. "As long as you're there, wash my back." He handed her the soap. Arms around him, she scrubbed his back and butt, each movement rubbing her breasts against his chest. The friction from his chest hair sent tingles running through her.

He took the soap back and returned the favor, although he spent far too long washing her bottom, massaging her cheeks, and running a finger down the crack.

Stepping back, she washed his front, lingering on his chest, searching out the flat nipples and playing with them. His contoured muscles moved under her touch. Where had he been when she'd studied muscle groups in college anatomy? His biceps hardened when he ran his hand up her body; his pectoral muscles flexed when he put his arms around her. Slowly, she worked her way down his front to his—not a penis—he called it his *cock*. The velvety texture seemed incongruous over the iron rod underneath. She washed his balls, firm and heavy. His legs were apart, his hand stroking her hair as she bent to the task. When she finished and looked up, his eyes were black with passion.

She swallowed hard.

"My turn." He plucked the soap from her motionless fingers. His foam-covered hands slicked over her breasts. When he rolled her nipples between his fingers, her legs weakened. And then he touched her between her legs, sliding over her clit, washing her folds until her knees buckled. He grinned, steadied her, before turning her so her back was toward him.

He removed the flexible shower hose from the overhead clip and dropped it to spray on the tub floor. Taking her hands, he set them low on the shower wall, bending her forward. Her breathing increased.

The curtain slid aside, and a second later, she heard the crinkling sound of a condom wrapper. "Don't move, little sub. I'm going to take you hard and fast," he said. Just his voice sent a shudder through her.

Securing her in place with an iron arm around her waist, he entered her with a hard thrust that raised her up on her toes. She gasped as the shock sent waves of sensation searing through her.

"You feel incredible," he murmured in her ear, one hand caressing her breasts. His chest was hard and hot against her back as he pushed even deeper.

And then he stopped. "Hmm."

Her heart skipped a beat. That sound from him was as ominous as a doctor saying, "Oops."

"Sir?"

He ran a hand down the shower hose and pulled it up. "Seems a shame to waste all this water, doesn't it?"

"What do you mean?" Confused, she glanced at the shower handle. She wiggled her hips a little. He was thick and long inside her; why wasn't he moving? "You can turn it off."

"Oh, no, sweetie, I have a better idea." He twisted the adjustable head to a single stream. With a hum of satisfaction, he positioned it in front of her breasts. She sucked in a breath at the erotic, brutal sensation.

He moved it down her front slowly, down and down, until the fierce droplets struck her already sensitive clit.

"Master!"

He chuckled, murmured, "Bingo," and held the spray in place, held her in place as he eased his cock out of her. He drove back into her hard, filling her completely. In, out. Each thrust moved her hips forward, changing where the pulsing water struck her clit. Her hips jerked with each assault, her legs trembling so badly, his arm around her waist was all that held her up.

Her clit was on fire, so sensitive that the force of the water throbbed through her whole body. His rhythmic thrusts merged with the sensations, and everything in her tightened. She went onto tiptoes, pushing back against him, needing...needing. He moved the spray suddenly, back and forth, hitting all sides of her clit, and the shock threw her over the peak. Her climax roared over her in a devastating wave, exploding outward as she thrashed in his hard grip.

With a deep laugh, he dropped the showerhead, and grasping her hips in hard hands, he pounded into her, each thrust sending more and more spasms through her. His fingers tightened on her hips and his roar echoed through the small room as he came.

Wrapping his arms around her from behind, he held her through the after-shudders and when her legs went limp. She curled her fingers around his forearms, wanting to hold him tighter. The happiness she'd felt when he climaxed had startled her and worried her a little.

When she could finally stand on her own, he turned her around, kissed her hard on the lips. "There, little sub. Don't you feel better now that you're all clean?"

Chapter Fourteen

An hour later, Dan walked with Kari up to the front of the club. He stayed far enough behind to enjoy the view of her wearing his shirt...and nothing else. Good thing he carried spare clothing in the truck. He should have guessed that the woman wouldn't own anything a nun wouldn't wear.

He'd considered having her change into the soft cotton pajamas in one drawer, imagining how her breasts would have made SpongeBob dance.

But his hands had ached to play with her butt some more, so he'd put her in one of his spare shirts. The dark blue brought out the color of her eyes and set off her rich brown hair. Even better, the material was thin enough to see each movement of her full breasts. She was so tiny that the shirttail completely covered her ass with a few inches to spare.

Of course, since it was so long, he'd refused to allow her any underwear. Her face had reddened with anger and embarrassment, and her eyes sparked with blue fire. He'd hoped she'd lose her temper, but she remembered her spanking too well... *Dammit.*

He grinned, anticipating his revenge. Sometime tonight, he'd ask her to pick up something from the floor.

She looked back at him, saw where his eyes were focused, and shot him an evil look. "Do you pick out your sub's clothing all the time?"

He closed the gap between them, ran his hand over her bare butt. *God, she was soft.* "No, sweetie, this is just for my pleasure so nothing's in the way when I *take* my pleasure."

Pink washed over the nape of her neck.

At his usual station behind the guard desk, Ben glanced up as they entered. "Kari, good to see you. Jessica hoped you'd make it tonight. Just in time too. I'm closing the doors in a few minutes."

Then he saw Dan, and his mouth dropped open. He glanced at Kari, then Dan again. "I'll be damned."

"Probably so," Dan bit out as the unsettled feeling he'd managed to calm on his long walk reared back up inside him. *Marion. His anger, his guilt, his loss...* All that was bad enough. How he felt about Kari added a different guilt.

And yet he'd wanted to be here with her.

"Well..." Ben rubbed his jaw. "Good. Go on in, folks."

Dan pushed the feelings back down inside him, managed a thin smile. "Thanks, Ben." He nudged Kari toward the inner door.

Kari made it three steps into the club room before she stopped, stunned. Two steps farther than Dan had figured she'd get. The quiet beginners' nights didn't prepare a newbie for a normal Saturday. Tonight, people crowded the small dance floor to the right, dancing to the raw, throbbing music. Across the room, Doms and Dommes, with subs kneeling at their feet, filled couches and tables. The dress code was in force, leather and latex predominant, corsets and loincloths not unusual, the odd disobedient sub wearing only cuffs or collar. They were late enough that the scene areas were in full use, and the slap of a flogger on bare flesh, wails, screams, and moans of arousal sounded over the music.

Kari edged closer to him, looked up with wide eyes, the look on her face so dazed, so innocent, that he had to pull her up against him so he could take her mouth. Damn, but he already wanted her again.

Kari sagged in Master Dan's arms, her body rousing as if she hadn't just gotten off less than an hour ago.

"You're addictive, little sub," he murmured in her ear, biting her neck hard enough to make her shudder with need.

"So are you," she said under her breath. "Dammit." The way he overwhelmed both her body and emotions was frightening.

He frowned, tilted her chin up. "What did you say?"

Oh, spit.

"Kari?"

She huffed a breath. "I said," she muttered. "So are you."

He arched an eyebrow.

"Dammit."

The amusement in his eyes made her want to punch him, but the feeling of his body as he yanked her up against him again wiped the notion out entirely. The warmth of his hands went right through her thin shirt. His leathers brushed her bare thighs, and the feeling of air against her private parts was almost as worrying as the interested looks from everyone walking past. Next time she'd just take the spanking and wear what she wanted.

Or maybe not. She eyed his solidly muscular chest, exposed by the open leather vest, remembered the glint of laughter in his eyes when she'd balked at the no-underwear decree. He'd not only have enjoyed spanking her but would still have stuffed her into his choice of clothing.

The memory of how he'd stripped her clothing off in the shower, pushing her hands away as easily as she'd have brushed away a fly, sent a wave of heat through her and she shivered.

His eyes narrowed. When he rubbed his knuckles against her breasts, she realized her nipples had turned to hard nubs.

"And what are you thinking about, little sub?"

She flushed, didn't answer.

His arm around her tightened. His fingers caught one nipple in a sharp pinch.

When she squeaked, a few people turned to look at them. He didn't even notice.

"Sir!"

"I asked you a question, Kari."

Muffled laughter sounded around them, and she felt her cheeks turning hotter and hotter. "The shower," she whispered. "That's all."

"Ah." He grinned. "Good to know it has such an effect on you." His hand on her butt pressed her against him. He was fully erect. "Thinking about that has the same effect on me. I have a feeling you're going to be a very clean submissive," he whispered in her ear.

She sank against him, loving the feel of his body. Loving the feel of his hands until she realized he'd pulled the tail of the shirt up to her waist so he could touch her bare bottom.

She tried to shove back, but his arm around her waist only tightened. His fingers moved slowly over her buttocks, massaging her cheeks. "Did you forget the rules, sweetling? For tonight, your body is mine to use."

He continued as her outrage passed, as his fingers started to arouse her. The knowledge that people could see made the heat even worse. He tightened his grip, rubbing her against his erection until her pussy throbbed.

"Daniel." Master Z's voice behind her.

Kari stiffened, tried to pull away. Sir's arm didn't loosen, and he held her in place until she stopped pushing. Finally, finally, his point made, he released her.

She turned and looked up at Master Z, her face probably as red as a tomato. To her surprise, he had his arm around Jessica. Was Jessica his sub?

"I'm so glad you made it here." Jessica frowned as her gaze swept over Kari. She shook her head at Master Dan. "I wanted you to give Kari a ride, not to ride her."

Sir barked a laugh, then said, "Z, your sub's getting mouthy. Called me an asshole earlier."

Master Z tilted his head. "Did she now? If she sets such a bad example for our beginners, she will need to demonstrate what follows." He paused, said reflectively, "I haven't given a lesson on discipline for some time."

Jessica froze, her eyes widening. A tremor shook her body.

Smiling slowly, Master Z looked down at Jessica and murmured, "Thank you for the suggestion, Daniel."

Chuckling, Sir pulled Kari away.

Kari rose up on tiptoe to whisper, "What did he mean by 'demonstrate' and 'a lesson'?"

"Master Z teaches by demonstrating how something should be done."

Discipline? Oh God, poor Jessica.

Moving through the crowd, Sir kept a hard arm around Kari, and she loved how feminine and protected his strength made her feel. When they reached the bar, she snuggled even closer.

He glanced at her and ran a finger down her cheek. "I like touching you, little sub," he said, his eyes gentle.

Her breath seemed to stop inside her chest.

But then he grinned and his hand trailed to where the shirt gaped open over her breasts. His voice lowered. "And I also like spanking your ass until it's a glowing red. And fucking you hard against a wall."

She put her fingers over his mouth to silence him, but his amused look said he knew how his carnal words sent hunger through her and wet seeping between her legs.

Cullen wandered over and set drinks in front of them. His gaze lingered on her heated face. "A sub for three nights, Dan. That's gotta be a record."

She felt Sir's body stiffen against her as his muscles turned iron hard. "Don't jump to conclusions," he growled. "I'm just helping out with beginners' nights like I promised Z. Nothing else." His arm dropped.

His words sucked the air right out of Kari's chest.

Again. Nothing had changed. She turned her face away, her gaze coming to rest on Martha and Gerald across the bar. The old Dom nuzzled his wife, the caring so obvious in his actions that Kari's lips tightened. Their affection made her realize she'd hoped for that with Dan. Especially after he'd come to get her, and they'd shared so much.

Well, obviously that wasn't going to happen. How could she keep forgetting he didn't want anything more than an occasional fucking? She deliberately used the *f* word, squeezing her hands together so hard the joints ached.

How had she been so delusional? This place wasn't about love; it was about domination. Pain. Sex. She'd been stupid.

"The sub you're with tonight isn't adequately dressed." Cullen's lazy tone had turned mean. Was he mad at her or at Sir?

Master Dan glanced at her, his gaze shuttered. "Very true. Got a spare set of cuffs?"

Cullen crossed the bar, opened a cupboard, and returned to thump down leather cuffs.

"Give me your wrists, Kari," Sir snapped.

She hesitated. Did she even want to be with him tonight? How much of this high and low stuff could she take? Then again, she was just here for the sex. Just the sex. Nothing more.

Mouth tight, she slapped her wrists into his broad hand, ignoring his narrowed eyes.

He buckled the cuffs on, checked for the tightness automatically, his gaze not leaving her face.

She looked away. *Just the sex, nothing more.*

"Interesting attire, Dan," Raoul said, sliding onto the bar stool next to where Kari stood. He nodded at the shirt she wore. "Amazingly provocative on her."

"I like it," Sir said. He didn't snap at Raoul, she noticed. "She wasn't happy."

"Like anyone would be." Kari yanked the bottom of the shirt lower and scowled. Damn him anyway. She should have just stayed home. "You can see right through it, and it hardly covers my—"

Raoul raised his eyebrows, and Kari's breath strangled in her throat. *Oh dear Lord.* Holding her lip between her teeth, she ventured a look at Master Dan and tried not to cringe at the expression on his face. This wasn't the hurt man whom she'd hugged in her living room. This was Master Dan, and her fantasy of him had just taken on a nightmarish tinge.

His gaze chilled her right to the bone. "Apparently your modesty weighs more heavily with you than my will. Rather surprising you have any modesty left, considering how you spent a good portion of Wednesday night." He glanced up at the chains on the rafters.

"I'm sorry, Master. Very sorry." She lowered her eyes, heart hammering in her chest. Would kneeling help?

"I am sure you are," he said quietly and started unbuttoning her shirt. Her hands rose instinctively to stop him. His hard look made her drop her arms back to her sides. "Toss me a towel, Cullen," he said.

He used the towel to cover a bar stool, lifted her onto it, and flipped the shirt open. With unyielding hands, he moved her legs apart until her private parts showed, her brown curls blatantly dark against the white material.

"Please, Master," she whispered.

"Please is the right word, sub," he said. "And that's what you'll do. Please both yourself and me." He took her hands, placed them over her breasts. "Play with your breasts until your nipples are as swollen and red as I had them three days ago."

She shook her head.

"What do you say to me?"

Her fingers flinched as he moved her hands, massaging her breasts, ruthlessly plucking her nipples until fire streaked toward her groin. "Yes, Sir," she said, unable to look away from his lethal brown eyes.

He stepped away. She tried to move her hands like he wanted and ended up covering her breasts with them instead.

His jaw clenched. "Kari, do what I said, or I'll lay you out on the bar and use my mouth to do it myself."

Even as she recoiled, heat flooded her insides, and the towel dampened under her. Sir's lips curved up mockingly, even though his eyes remained frozen.

Gritting her teeth, she touched her breasts, stroking, pulling on the nipples, pinching them. Club members stopped to watch with appreciative looks before smiling at Master Dan. Eyes half-lidded, Cullen propped an elbow on the bar, acting like he was at a movie. Kari raised her chin and looked away.

When Master Dan turned his back on her, she continued, her hands trembling as embarrassment seared her again and again with each laugh and half-heard comment. Buck—oh, God, Buck—started to approach, then stopped. He shot Dan a nasty look and moved away.

When Master Dan finally checked on her, he frowned. Nudging her hand away, he took a nipple between his fingers, pinching and rolling with increasing force until pain, then pleasure, shot through her, hammering into her clit. Her breath sucked in.

"That hard," he said coldly. "Last warning, sub."

She nodded miserably. Closing her eyes to shut out the world, she touched herself. Harder, faster. To her shock, her body roused; her pussy ached as her breasts swelled and tightened. Her nipples moved past sensitive to throbbing need.

Hands closed on her wrists, held her immobile. She opened her eyes. "Master?"

"You can stop now, Kari."

Her hands fell to her sides, shaking. Her lips quivered.

He studied her, and the hardness eased from his face. His brown eyes warmed. He rubbed his knuckles over her jutting nipples, and she sucked in an audible breath at the gentle abrasion. "Now that's a very pretty color," he said. His smile sent pleasure through her, melting the lump in her chest and almost making her forget why she'd been so mad at him.

He tilted her chin up to pin her with his gaze. "Whose body is this tonight, sub?"

"Yours, Master."

"If this body is mine and I want to show it off, should you be embarrassed?"

"No, Sir."

He nodded. "Good enough for now. You did well." After buttoning her shirt, he cupped her cheek so gently that her eyes puddled with tears. "Kari, I should let you go. I know that, and you know that. You deserve a Dom who can give you more than a night here and there."

If she'd been standing, she would have fallen. Instead she firmed her spine and curled a hand around his wrist, resting her fingertips on the hard tendons. "I'm here tonight for the sex. Nothing more."

He could undoubtedly read the lie in her face, but he didn't challenge her. "So be it." He turned her bar stool to face the bar and tucked an arm around her waist.

The warmth of his touch made her tremble inside fully as much as she shook outside.

Cullen appeared, removed her untouched, watery drink, and set a fresh one down.

Master Dan handed it to her and asked Cullen, "Anything interesting happening tonight?"

"Looks to be a good night. Raoul plans to scene with his sub. Flogging, I think, then the cane. Mistress Anne brought in some new toys and was going to demo them on her sub later. Cock cage, ball crushers."

"Anne is usually a good show."

"True." Cullen's fingers tapped the bar as he thought. "Ah, Z's opening the Capture Gardens. Said he'd save you a spot."

"Well, now." The change in Master Dan's voice whipped Kari's head around. Anticipation and amusement. One side of his mouth curved up as he looked at her. She knew that expression, and it made her insides quake.

"In that case, give me another set of cuffs, small plug, and lube," Sir said. "And what time?"

"Anytime now." Cullen looked at Kari, his eyes filled with the same amusement as Sir's. "Kari. You may want another drink."

Kari choked on the sip she'd just taken.

Chapter Fifteen

The jerk hadn't bothered to explain anything. Fuming, Kari had barely finished her first drink when three chimes sounded over the music. Heads lifted all through the room.

"Wha—" She closed her mouth quickly, earning herself a frown from Sir, but nothing more.

"The Gardens are open." He led her to an open door on the right wall and into a room with a stone floor and darkly paneled walls. About twenty members congregated there. On the far side, a door leading outside stood open. The scent of night-blooming jasmine and newly cut grass wafted in.

An older DM, one of those who'd touched Kari's breasts on Wednesday, faced the crowd. His light blue eyes met Kari's, and he winked.

She flushed, then wondered if she'd ever lose that response. Probably not. Really, modesty should have been her middle name.

"My name is Sam," the DM said. "I'll be your contact for any problems during this role-play. There are rules, and as Master Z has decided upon the punishments, you want to listen closely. He can be a sadistic bastard." A ripple of laughter ran through the crowd.

"For those who haven't participated before, the game is this. Your sub is released into the Garden with a head start. You search for her or him," he added, nodding at a gay couple and a Domme with a male sub. "Once found, take whatever satisfaction you and your sub have agreed upon, either right in the Gardens, inside on the equipment, or upstairs in private."

Kari's eyes widened. On the first night, Sir had asked her about her fantasies. "*A gorgeous barbarian taking you against your will? Have you had that one?*" Her insides quivered. Was this real?

Sir leaned over to whisper, "When I catch you, I will take you right then and there." His hand slid over her bare butt, squeezing possessively.

She bit her lip against the surge of arousal.

Sam continued, "Resistance is expected, but serious fighting is forbidden; no deep scratching, punching, or hard kicking for either subs or Doms. Subs, the club safe word is red, and DMs will be in the Gardens."

"Doms, you may only capture the sub whose band matches yours." Motioning the gay couple forward, Sam fastened bright green glow-sticks around the Dom's wrist and matching ones on his sub's ankle and wrist. "Chasing anyone else's sub is forbidden. Of course, if one blunders right into you, feel free to cop a feel and then swat her to get her running again. Anything more than that…" Sam's smile was pure evil. "Well, the last Dom who tried for more was flogged by Mistress Rachel until her arm wore out, and then his membership was canceled. Pissing off Z isn't smart.

"The game lasts two hours, and three chimes mean the game is over. Subs, a few idiots have managed to hide by removing their glow-sticks. This is your warning. At closing, the DMs search the Gardens. Any sub still outside is considered available for use by any and all DMs who join the search."

As Sam finished his lecture, Dan realized Kari had pressed so close to his side, she almost melted into his skin.

She looked up at him with big eyes. "I don't think I want to do this."

So modest and so passionate. Why did the discrepancy bring all his Dom urges to the forefront? He rubbed his cheek against her silky hair and whispered back, "I know you really do want to. I can see...smell your arousal."

Her eyes widened, probably from his language. And then, brave little sub, she nodded.

The line moved forward as Z vetted the players; mind games like this brought out his overprotective nature. Now Z shook his head at the couple in front of them. "Sorry, Adam, but Beth isn't ready for this yet. She's terrified."

"But—" Adam scowled and shrugged. The bunched muscles in Beth's bared shoulders eased as she and her top for the night stepped out of line.

Dan smiled at the slender redhead and received a fleeting smile in return. He'd once considered topping her before realizing she only chose weaker Doms. Sub or not, she wasn't about to give up much control. Something nasty must have happened in her past to make her so wary.

He and Kari stepped up to face Z.

"Little one, do you understand how the game works?" Z studied Kari. "You'll be running away from Master Dan. When he catches you, he gets to do whatever he wants."

Kari shivered, then nodded.

Z glanced at Dan. "She has a nice mixture of fear and anticipation." Smiling, Z nodded to Sam, who fastened a bright pink glow-stick around both their wrists and another around Kari's ankle.

"Pink, huh." Dan shook his head at Sam. "Thanks a lot, you bastard."

"But you're so *pretty* in pink, Master Dan."

Fighting was forbidden in the club, so Dan just thumped Sam in the chest on the way past. Sam barked a laugh.

Once clear of the line, Kari tugged on Dan's arm. He leaned down to hear her whisper, "But you *do* look pretty in pink, Master."

"Just keep it up, sub, just keep it up," he warned.

When she giggled, his brain went stone-cold dead. He'd never heard her laugh, not like that. He grinned, wanting more. He needed to... No, he didn't need anything. No more evenings, dammit.

They walked a few more paces while he subdued his emotions.

"Master?"

He nodded permission for her to speak.

"I run, and you catch me. I understand that. But I'm not much of a runner, you know."

Dan tipped Kari's face up. "I enjoy a good chase, so I'll add an incentive. If you don't try hard—say, if I catch you within fifteen minutes—then I'll show you how the spanking bench works in the bar room. Do you understand?"

If her blue eyes got any bigger, they'd take over her whole face. "Yes, Master."

He could hardly wait to get his hands on her. "I'll even be nice and give you a fighting chance." He removed her cuffs.

"Dan." Nolan strolled over.

Damn, it was good to have him back. "We got fog tonight?"

Nolan nodded. "Z went all out. There's dry ice in every fountain."

Dan smiled at Kari's puzzled expression. She'd understand soon enough. "You doing the subbie preps?"

"My favorite job, especially since returning. You wouldn't believe how overdressed women are in Iraq." Nolan nodded at Kari. "Clothing? Oil?"

Dan studied the little sub. Her eyes were wary but bright, her breathing fast. Not too scared. He could have her prepped in his favorite way. "No clothes, lots of oil."

"Well, now, that will be my pleasure." Nolan turned to Kari, his faint smile fading. "Sub, hang your shirt on the hook over there and return to me to be prepared."

Her eyes whipped up to Dan's.

"Kari, go with Master Nolan."

"But…"

Nolan scowled, his voice cruel. "What do you say to me, sub?"

She flinched and gave Dan a look of betrayal before dropping her eyes. "Yes, Master." She unbuttoned the shirt and pulled it off slowly.

Nolan smothered a grin as Dan's sub hung her shirt on a hook and tried to act nonchalant. She looked around, obviously hoping no one saw her. Of course, everyone did. Grins appeared on the other Doms' faces; even Master Z's lips curved up before he turned to the next couple.

Nolan remembered this little one from last Wednesday. No man with a dick would forget those lush and responsive breasts. Considering Dan's preference for voluptuous and sweet, Nolan figured the Dom might end up keeping this sub. A good thing. He'd been alone too long.

Nolan stomped on the envy rising within him.

As Kari approached, he looked her over slowly. Coldly. Part of prep included increasing a sub's anxiety, and with his scarred face, he was damned good at it. Odd how a man could enjoy scaring a sub and simultaneously want to cuddle her up and reassure her. Just one of those oddities of being a Dom.

He set a hand on her curvy ass just to feel her recoil and pushed her outside. The night air was warm and humid, perfect for playing in the Gardens.

Behind them, a sub in a lacy corset and tight latex pants let out a high shriek, then darted out the door and into the Gardens. Nolan glanced down at Kari. She chewed on her lip, obviously dying to ask why that sub got to keep her clothes and she didn't. Dan had trained her a bit, since she managed to keep silent.

A few feet to the right of the door, another DM, Jake, leaned against the wall, the sprayer at his feet. The DM's appreciative gaze ran over Kari. "Who's this?"

"Dan's sub."

"Oh, yeah, a newbie. I saw her on Monday. Very cute." Jake gave her another approving look, then straightened. "Don't move, *chica.*"

Nolan stepped back as Kari froze in place like a terrified rabbit. After pumping up the sprayer, Jake opened up. She flinched as the fragrant oil hit her, covering her shoulders, above her breasts, across her back, drizzling down her skin.

After one complete circle, Jake stepped back. "Been thinking. We should change jobs."

"Nope." Seniority had its rewards. Nolan stepped forward and closed his hands on the sub's soft shoulders.

"No!" She jerked back and put her hands up.

Damn, but the shy ones were fun. Nolan growled, "Stand very still, subbie, or I will chain you to the door and let everyone have a turn. Or do you want to use your safe word?"

Even with the patchy moonlight, he saw her face pale, but she shook her head. Mouth pressed into a tight little line, she lowered her hands.

Taking his time, he stroked the oil over her body, down her arms, her hands, her shoulders, and back, enjoying the satiny skin and curves under his hands. No wonder Dan liked her.

"Spread your legs, sub." Her hands fisted, but she complied. Kneeling, he spread oil over her legs, smoothing down and then back up. A pity he couldn't do her cunt too, but oil wasn't good for pussies. When he stopped at her upper thighs, her tiny exhale of relief made him grin.

He heard Jake chuckle.

Unfortunately for her, he wasn't done yet. Rising, he gripped her upper arm to secure her—the little rabbit looked ready to scamper—and massaged the oil into her breasts, taking his time. His father always said, "*If a job is worth doing, it's worth doing well.*"

He'd seen Dan force her to play with herself earlier and figured she'd be pretty sensitive now. And yes, her breasts swelled all too quickly under his hands. *Damned shame.* So he concentrated on her nipples until her muffled whimpers became audible. Until pink arousal showed in her cheeks.

He rubbed the back of his hand over the brown curls of her pussy. Very, very wet. She closed her eyes in humiliation. Well then, his job here was done. "Sub."

Her eyes opened, and a tremor ran through her as she stared up at him with huge blue eyes.

"Looks like you're ready to give Master Dan a good time. Off with you now." He pushed her toward the Gardens and smacked her bare bottom hard enough to make her yelp.

She ran. Once past the first tall hedge, fog appeared, pooling on the grass, curling upward like white fingers, giving the area a surreal atmosphere. Slowing, she moved past curving flower beds, heady with fragrance. Tall bushes and trees formed secluded nooks.

In the eerie mist, small fountains glimmered with soft lights, the only illumination in the gardens other than faint moonlight and the glow-sticks that darted here and there like colorful lightning bugs.

Okay. She needed to evade Master Dan for at least fifteen minutes, but how could anyone hide in here? The bushes were too thick to burrow into, the fountains too small to hide behind. Swings and flat lawn chairs offered no shelter. Even the soft grass was cut golf course short.

And look how the other subs' light sticks danced. Way too visible.

Suddenly a man's voice rose. "Masters, the chase is on. Find your slaves and make them pay for trying to escape."

Kari shivered. This might be just a game, but knowing Sir hunted her, planned to take her, made her insides feel funny. Scared. *Aroused.*

Spotting a pink glow that matched her bracelet, she ran across an open space and dodged behind more bushes. She stopped next to a gurgling fountain and saw white mist boiling from the water, spilling over the concrete sides like a volcano erupting. The fog suddenly turned silver, and Kari glanced up. Slow-moving clouds revealed the moon before hiding it again, darkening the world.

A sub ran past, her master in full chase. A squeak like a captured rabbit sounded a minute later, then high-pitched begging. Slaps of a hand hitting flesh and cries of pain.

Kari put a hand over her mouth. The sub hadn't yelled out a safe word, so she didn't need help. Did she?

Hands behind his back, a DM strolled toward her, obviously listening for trouble. Kari relaxed slightly.

He spotted her. His gaze ran over her, lingered on her breasts, and stopped on her bracelet. With a grin, he pointed to the left. Kari saw a pink glow heading closer, and she gasped.

"Run, subbie," the DM said, amusement in his voice, and waved her off.

Breasts bouncing, she ran, weaving through the clearings, trying to find a barrier to block the glow-stick light. She ran some more. Had it had been fifteen minutes? She turned a corner and froze at the sight of a pink bracelet moving across a clearing. Master Dan. His shadow reached toward her like a monster from underground, the cuffs clipped to his leathers rattling.

What if she hadn't used up all the time?

Struggling for breath, she fled, sprinting past more fountains, veering one way, then another. Past a man pounding into a woman on all fours, past a man with arms chained to a low branch.

A hand grabbed her wrist. She squeaked, yanked, and Sir's fingers slid off her oil-covered arm. She dashed away, but he seized her within a minute and again lost his hold.

A couple of yards farther, his body thudded into hers from behind, and his arms wrapped around her waist, securing her.

She struggled, trying to push his hands away. No success. Then she lifted her feet and dropped, sliding right out of his arms. She rolled, pushed to her knees.

With a laugh, he flattened her under his heavy body, knocking the wind out of her. "Sneaky little sub."

With implacable hands, he flipped her onto her back. She started fighting again, instinctively trying to escape the hard hands holding her in place. His grip slipped, and he cursed, then straddled her, pinning her to the ground with his weight. Using his knee, he trapped one arm long enough to buckle a wrist cuff on. He did the other wrist and secured the cuffs together in front. He sat back on his haunches.

"Sweetheart, you're faster than a rabbit." His eyes heated. "And very slick." His hands stroked down her neck and her shoulder.

Holding her cuffs over her head with one hand, he kissed her hard, taking her mouth slowly. Thoroughly. His fingers played with her breasts, erotically slipping and sliding over her oily skin, toying with her nipples until her hunger grew overwhelming. When her hips tilted up toward him, he sat back and grinned wickedly.

The look in his eyes boded ill for her comfort level. What was he thinking? She glanced around the small, way-too-open clearing where fog drifted in small patches of white. No equipment, no benches, or crosses. *Good. That was good.*

When he rose to his feet, she made her move, rolling over and away. He snatched an ankle before she could rise and then wrapped a cuff around it. The other ankle got a cuff too.

She squirmed harder, and he chuckled. "Fight all you want, little sub. You're doomed." Pulling her to her feet by the wrist cuffs, he led her across the clearing to a picturesque grouping of three trees. Trees, wrist cuffs—this didn't look good.

"This looks good," he murmured. "Kneel."

"Sir," she whispered, bracing her feet. "There are people here."

"How about that?" he whispered back. Grabbing her around the waist, he laid her flat and threw a leg over her to keep her in place. She pushed at him. Got nowhere.

"Put your hands over your head."

Was he insane? "No." She shook her head frantically. "Not here."

He sighed and rolled her onto her side, pinning her legs between his own, and smacked her bottom, a hard, stinging blow. She barely managed to muffle her yelp.

"Put your hands over your head, Kari." His hand stroked over her burning skin. "Or don't. I would enjoy spanking you first."

He would too.

When he pushed her onto her back, she lifted her hands over her head, horrified at how vulnerable she felt. Outside. In public.

And yet, when he snapped the cuffs to a chain wrapped around the base of the tree, her breasts tightened and she dampened. As he rose to his feet, a quiver of panic went through her. Why had he put ankle cuffs on her? She looked around and realized chains circled the tree trunks with the ends dangling.

He grabbed her right ankle, lifting her leg into the air and snapping it to a chain that was waist high on the tree.

"No, Master. No." She kicked at his hands. He laughed, snatched her other foot, and secured her left ankle to a chain on the other tree. Her legs now formed a narrow V in the air.

He rubbed his cheek and studied her. "Wider would be good." Shortening the chain on the left tree, he reclipped her ankle cuff, pulling her legs farther apart. The misty air struck her wet labia like a shock of ice.

"I love being outdoors, don't you?" he said in a normal voice, kneeling between her legs.

"Shhh," she whispered. "There are people around."

"We're in the shadows. Mostly." Then he chuckled, traced a finger through her wet folds, making her squirm. "However, if I'm any good at all, the entire garden will hear you scream when you come."

Oh God. "I don't want to do this," she hissed, glaring at him.

Chapter Sixteen

Dan tried to smother his laugh. She couldn't get much wetter or more aroused. "Poor Kari. I can tell you're turned off by the whole thing." His finger circled her clit, and she wiggled like a worm on a hook. "You're lying to me, sweetheart. Have we talked about honesty?"

Her eyes widened.

Lying down on top of her, he braced himself on one forearm. Her soft breasts cushioned his chest; her soft thighs cradled his hips.

Grasping her chin roughly, he frowned down at her. "How many times did you tell me no in the last five minutes? And now you're lying. You're racking up the punishments you have coming. I'd suggest you confine yourself to 'yes, Sir' before I decide to make some of them very, very public."

Those big eyes. He could never describe the way they pulled at him, the satisfaction he got from seeing the nerves revving in them, the wariness, and the trust when she let him drive her to the heights. He took her mouth hard, pulling a response from her. When he squeezed her breast, he felt her nipple's hard point of arousal. Her trembling increased.

There was nothing more gratifying than a sub's sweet yielding.

Or a sub's squirming when being punished. He pushed back onto his knees, kneeling where he could see her pussy, a dark triangle in the misty shadows. Pulling the toy, lube, and condom from his pocket, he opened his leathers and sheathed himself. With the lube, he prepared the plug. "You might find this a bit different, little sub, but I think you'll like it...eventually."

He was holding something the length of her finger, shaped like a rocket with a flat base. It glistened with lubricant, and now he ran his hand down her thighs to her bottom. He spread her cheeks apart. When his fingers touched her rectum, horrifying realization hit.

"No! Don't." She jerked at the restraints futilely.

A second later, something slid into her rectum, hard and cold, sending shivers through her at the sheer unfamiliarity of it.

"Take it out!" she whispered, moving her hips, trying to escape.

"No."

She gasped as he plunged a finger into her vagina, moving it against the swollen, sensitive walls. He lowered himself in the grass. His hair brushed her inner thighs, and his hot breath skimmed over her folds.

"Master." Her voice cracked. "Please."

"Try the plug this once, Kari, and we'll talk about it afterward." He touched the thing again, making it move inside her, and she gritted her teeth at the raw, carnal feeling. His fingers moved and then it started to vibrate inside her, an almost soundless buzz that set unfamiliar nerves to firing. Her hips lifted off the ground as waves of increasing pleasure ran through her from the unfamiliar direction.

And then his fingers pulled back her folds, opening her farther, exposing her engorged clit. He licked up and over the nub, and she bucked in his grip at the feeling of his hot, wet tongue. She almost climaxed right then.

He pulled back. "Not yet." Waited as her body ached for him.

Finally he lowered his head again. The thing in her vibrated away as his tongue slid and flicked over her clit.

She panted, shot back into hard arousal.

When he slid a finger up inside her, she moaned at the exquisite sensation. He added another finger, moving slowly in and out, circling the walls of her vagina. The thickness of his fingers pressed the walls against the anal plug, sending vibrations coursing through all of her, until every nerve between her thighs throbbed intensely.

Her thighs, her stomach, her whole body tightened as he played with her. She sucked in a sobbing breath. She was close, so close—

His tongue moved away from her clit, his fingers stopped. "No, you don't have permission to come."

She moaned. "Please, Master."

He didn't answer. When her breathing slowed, he started again, brought her up and up...and stopped.

Her head rolled back and forth, her hips raised to him. She whined as everything inside her throbbed.

After a minute, he restarted and ruthlessly teased her until her clit was on the excruciating edge of climax and her need was so great that the world narrowed to each touch of his mouth, his fingers.

He lifted his head and removed his fingers from inside her.

"Oh, no, please..." Her legs shook as she sobbed for release, her voice rising uncontrollably. "Please, Master. Oh, please, please, please."

Chuckling, he pushed himself up and, a second later, plunged his cock deep inside her, impaling her so hard that she screamed at the exquisite feeling. Her tissues were so swollen, so sensitive, that each slide of his shaft increased the storm of sensation assailing her. His thick cock pressed against the vibrating thing in her bottom, and her body shuddered.

The feelings grew overwhelming, and she stiffened, every muscle tightening as she hung on the precipice. Even her breathing stopped.

"Come now, Kari. Come," he ordered in a deep voice. His hard fingers pinched her jutting clit, and her world went white. She screamed, screamed again as he thrust in and out of her, her mind in splinters and her vagina convulsing around him.

An eternity later, she blinked up at him, her body still giving little shudders. His corded arms planted beside her shoulders, and his eyes dark with passion, he waited, unmoving.

Her legs were still in the air, her arms over her head. "Let me free," she demanded, her voice husky.

His lips curved in a smile. "Little sub, you're going to regret being so bossy," he murmured. Ignoring her demand, he pinned her hips with one hard hand so he could pound into her even deeper and harder. The steady rhythm took her past her climax and started building another. As arousal flared in her, she tried to lift her hips to meet his, but his hand held her just where he wanted her. His thumb slid in circles over her clit.

She whimpered at the building need, at the sensations shooting through her.

He was merciless, his cock massive. Her hips jerked uncontrollably within his grip; her trembling legs made the chains chime. Each plunge of his shaft, each sweep of his thumb over her sensitive clit sent her further out of control.

"Sir?" Unable to think, only to feel. "I can't—"

"Come again, Kari. Come now." His thumb pressed down as he thrust deeply into her, and she exploded, feeling her blood boiling from her pelvis to her fingertips. Short screams escaped her as she shook like a breaking doll in his grip.

His fingers tightened, and his cock drove deep, reaching far up inside her. He groaned as his release jerked inside her, making her buck and shiver.

She roused a minute later. He pulled out, leaving her hollow, and then removed the thing inside her. When he stood and moved away, she shot awake. "Master!"

"Easy, sweetheart, I'm right here." He returned from across the clearing. His hands were gentle as he released her restraints, lowered her legs. She groaned as her joints and muscles protested.

Lying down beside her on the soft grass, he pulled her into his arms, the embrace so comforting, so welcome, that her breath shuddered. She'd dropped every barrier she had under his hands, his body. He'd seen her at her most vulnerable, and when he held her like this, she felt closer to him than she had to anyone before.

He tucked her head into the hollow of his shoulder. One arm kept her close while his hand stroked her hair, her arm, her side, and the tenderness of his touch, the care he took with her, made her heart swell.

After a minute, she remembered where they were. She was naked; her legs had been in the air. Everyone in the whole county had probably heard her screaming her release. *Oh, God.*

"Now what was that thought?" he asked. In the wavering light from the fountain, she could see his dark eyes crinkling in a smile.

"I was...loud."

He laughed, deep and satisfied. "You certainly were. You know, you sound different when you get off." He kissed the top of her head.

"How so?"

"You normally have a soft voice. Careful and polite." His finger circled her breast, teased the nipple until it budded. "But when you climax, your voice is raw. Carnal. Nothing held back." His pleasure was obvious.

She groaned and hid her face against his chest. *She could never face any of those people again.*

He rubbed his chin on the top of her head and chuckled.

As she breathed in, his scent surrounded her, mixed with the fragrance of oil on her body and their lovemaking. Sighing, she hitched an arm over his chest and pulled him closer. "I wish we could just lie here and never leave," she murmured.

She knew the words were a mistake the minute they left her mouth.

His muscles stiffened, and his arm around her loosened. She closed her eyes as grief hollowed her chest. Withdrawing again? How could he keep doing this to her?

"Kari." He sat up, pulling her with him. His hand cupped her chin. Even in the dim light, she could see his face had that...that *damned* cold look again. "Don't get attached to me. It can't—"

The lovemaking and then his tender attention had lowered the shield she'd put over her heart, and now his coldness stabbed into her chest. The anger she'd bottled up surged out of control. She slapped his hand away from her face. "Can't, don't, mustn't."

A muscle in his jaw tightened.

She shoved to her feet and glared down at him.

"You big jerk. You tell me there should be honesty between a Dom and his sub. It goes both ways, you know." Her voice rose to a shout; she couldn't control it any more than she could her temper. "There's more between us than just sex, and you *know* it. But you're afraid of me. You're afraid to live."

She unbuckled her ankle cuffs and dropped them onto the ground. He sat silently, watching her with unreadable eyes, his jaw tight. Rage swelled inside her until she choked with it. She fumbled with the wrist cuffs. They came off finally, and she threw them at him, watched them bounce off his unmoving chest.

"Damn you." She choked on the words, pain growing inside her. "I d-deserve more than this. I'm going to find someone who will appreciate me."

Silence.

Furious, she sliced at him one last time. "You know, you're not mourning her anymore; you're just too scared to move on."

Hand over her mouth, trying to keep the sobs inside, she ran from the clearing. Ran until she discovered a fence at the far end of the Gardens. Wrapping her arms around herself, she slumped against the rough wood. Tears slid down her face onto her bare breasts as the angry fire inside of her faded, then died, leaving only ashes behind. She wanted to go home, home where her life was safe and normal, where Prince loved her.

Finally she took a shuddering breath and shook her head at whining like a child not getting something. *Someone.*

God, how pitiful. She pushed off the fence. Walking through the mist-filled Gardens, she caught glimpses of others, flashes of bare skin, eyes watching her. The whole place had probably heard her yelling. She didn't care. Didn't care about this place, this lifestyle, or about him either. Especially not about him. He was so stupid, so dumb, so cowardly, and she…

Wanted him. Damn him. How had she gotten so… attached…as he called it, despite all his warnings?

But she had. And he didn't return the sentiment. *Fine.* She wanted to spit at the bitter taste in her mouth. Spit at him. She'd find someone who did want her. There must be other clubs in Tampa.

But the thought of someone else touching her made her—

"Kari." Dan's deep voice came from across the secluded glade. He stepped out of the shadows, the moonlight carving shadows across his muscular chest. "You're right, sweetheart. I didn't—"

Growling like an animal, someone slammed into him, knocking him against a tree. Kari heard the *thud* of his head against the trunk. He dropped, stunned.

She started to run to him, then stopped. The attacker was tall. Blond hair glinted in the moonlight. "Buck?" Kari whispered.

"You leave her alone, you bastard," Buck yelled. Straddling Dan, he punched him in the face.

"No!" Kari yelled, running across the clearing. She kicked Buck in the back of his head, her bare foot bouncing off his skull.

He turned. "Kari, honey. I heard you yelling. I'll—"

Dan hit him hard, knocking him completely over. And then Dan was on his feet, legs spread, waiting for Buck to stand.

"You hurt her," Buck spat out, his face contorted with hatred. He pushed himself to a kneeling position, fog swirling around his thighs and hands. "I'll take better care of her than you ever could."

Dan's face tightened. "Just leave, you idiot, while you can."

Buck jumped up, holding a heavy branch from the ground. He swung, clubbing Dan's upper arm.

Dan jerked back. Blood oozed, black in the dim light becoming a trickle running down his arm. "Hell, you're persistent." Dan crouched and moved sideways, staying just out of reach.

"Buck, stop," Kari yelled. He ignored her. "Red, red, red!" she screamed at the top of her voice. *Oh, God, somebody. Please come.*

Buck jumped at the sound, then turned his head. Dan slapped the club aside and slammed a fist into his face, then punched him in the stomach, folding him over. Bringing his hands up, he caught Buck's jaw and tossed him backward. The man hit the ground hard.

Relief flooded Kari. *Thank you, thank you, thank you.* She released the breath she'd been holding.

Master Nolan burst into the clearing, skidded to a stop. His glance flickered over Kari, Dan, and then Buck. He shook his head. "Didn't know you were into ménages," he said in a dry voice.

Dan snorted. Frowning down at his arm, he shook his head in disgust. "I'm getting slow."

Kari had moved to help him when Master Z appeared. He put an arm around her and pulled her against his side. "Are you hurt, little one?"

"I'm all right." She attempted a laugh. "I even got a kick in."

"Indeed."

As Master Nolan tied something around the gash on Dan's arm—a silk cloth he probably used for restraints—Kari took a step forward, wanting to make sure Sir was all right. She stopped herself. He didn't want her. She had to remember that.

Dan rubbed his jaw, glanced at the makeshift bandage. "Thanks."

"No problem." Nolan nudged Buck with his foot and got a groan. "I'll even take the garbage out."

Master Dan motioned to Kari. "Let's get you out of here before anything else happens. I'll find someone to take you home."

She considered arguing. Could they maybe talk this out? Then she shrugged. What was the point?

He put his hand against her lower back, the warmth against her bare skin reminding her she was naked. "Let's go."

Master Z and Nolan came behind them, half dragging the stunned Buck.

Just before they reached the door of the mansion, Master Z called, "Kari, I want to speak to you. Dan, please help Nolan with this idiot."

Master Z stepped to one side so Dan could take Buck's other arm. As the men moved away, Kari joined Z in the shadows.

Z studied her face. "Did the violence leave you shaken?"

"Not really. Not now." She looked at her hands. Not even a tremble. "I've seen fighting. I teach high school, and I swear there's a brawl or two every lunch period."

He chuckled. "No wonder you kept your head so well." He turned his head to watch the men. Another DM ran out to help with Buck. "Do you still want Dan?"

The unexpected question shocked her, and a wave of longing welled up in her, tied her tongue.

"Well, that emotion is clear enough; you definitely want him." Smiling, he rubbed his knuckles over her cheek. "He wants you too, Kari, much as he'd like to deny it. And between your walking away and then Buck wanting you back, his defenses have been shaken. But if he goes home now, he'll shore them back up."

"What can I do?" she asked, frowning at Sir's broad back as he handed Buck over to the other men.

"Kitten, if you run, he'll chase you. He won't be able to help himself after fighting another man for you. Once he catches you..." Z sighed and shook his head. "I can't predict how he'll react at that point."

He'd catch her. Probably be pretty angry too. She bit her lip. "He'd never hurt me. Not in anger."

"You know him well then." Z tilted his head and waited.

He might hurt her heart, though. Again. The jerk. "I'll do it. Who knows, maybe Master Nolan will catch me first."

He barked a laugh. "You've got a mean streak, little one. Go now while you have a head start."

Chapter Seventeen

Having disposed of the asshole, Dan walked back out into the Gardens. He felt strange. Lighter. Probably from pounding on Buck. A fight was a damn good way to unload emotion. He'd enjoyed the hell out of planting his fist in the guy's gut. God knew he'd needed to punch someone and—his step stalled—and Marion wasn't around to yell at. Much of that anger he'd expended had been at her.

But he wasn't angry anymore. How could he be? She'd paid horribly for her mistake. Oddly enough, his guilt had disappeared with the anger. Someday, he'd have to thank Kari.

But right now, he wanted to take her home. He might feel better, but he still had no intention of getting involved or... He frowned. Z stood alone in the shadows of the trees. "Where's Kari?"

"Went back in." Z jerked his head at the Gardens.

"What the hell do you mean she went in? You let her go back in the Gardens?"

Z shrugged. "She wanted to play some more. Said maybe Nolan would find her before you."

"Did she now?" Nolan walked up behind Dan. "Guess I'll have to—"

Dan growled. "You take one fucking step farther, and I'll take you apart."

The corner of Nolan's mouth tipped up, and Dan let out a breath. Hell of a lot of control he was showing. "Sorry, Nolan."

But hearing that asshole Buck say he'd take better care of her, when Dan had been trying to find her to apologize, and now to have Nolan doing the same...

"I'll go get her," he told Z. "And then I'll beat her ass for a while."

"Indeed."

Her curved bottom, soft under his hand. Her mouth quivering. Her eyes warming at the sight of him. "I'll find her," he repeated.

She ran.

One corner, then another. He was going to be... The word *annoyed* wasn't nearly descriptive enough. The thought increased Kari's speed. Her glow-sticks shone too brightly, beacons in the eerie fog. She whipped around a fountain, circling toward the right. How had she let Master Z goad her into this?

She shook her head, knowing the answer. Stupid Kari. How many times was she going to let him hurt her?

At the right corner of the Gardens in a wide clearing, the grass hadn't yet been cut. The cool strands brushed over the top of her feet. She slowed and dropped to her knees. If she sat on her ankles, only a faint gleam from her ankle bracelet escaped through the higher strands. She tucked her glowing wrist between her legs and scowled when the light lit her pale skin faintly pink. But if he didn't get too close, he wouldn't see it.

He wasn't the only one in a bad mood after all, and she felt like making him work a little.

From the right, a man shouted in victory. Kari hunched closer to the ground. A panting fight from another direction ended in a woman's shriek and a man's rumbled satisfaction. The minutes passed. Her legs started to cramp.

Had he given up? Maybe he didn't even want her, hadn't even come after her at all.

Then she saw a thin pink light moving steadily closer, flickering through the intervening bushes.

She could hear him now, his footsteps even and slow. Stalking her. Her heart started to hammer, her fingers closing around strands of grass. He wouldn't hurt her; her head knew that, but her body...her body felt like prey and wanted to run.

Closer. He knew she was hiding for he checked each small clearing. Her area came next. *Oh, God.* Her nerve broke. She scrambled to her feet and darted away.

He gave a grunt of satisfaction. Heavy footsteps thudded behind her. Risking a glance back, she saw him, bare chested and heavily muscled with the determined, cruel face of a predator.

Ignoring caution, she ran faster.

He closed on her. Out of breath, she stumbled, her heart hammering so loud she couldn't hear him. His hand closed on her arm, pulling her around. She yanked, and his hand slipped off.

She sprinted away. Glancing back, she saw he'd disappeared. She slowed.

He charged her from the side, huge and overpowering, bringing them both down onto the grass. He rolled at the last minute, taking the fall on his back, protecting her with his arms.

Panting for breath, she fought him instinctively, still covered in enough oil that his grip couldn't hold her. She kicked at him, and he laughed. His hard hands slid over her breasts, her waist. She slid free and pushed to her feet.

He grabbed her ankle and yanked her down on top of him. Rolling, he pinned her under him, his weight inescapable.

She squirmed frantically as he flipped her onto her stomach, sitting on her as he loosened his leathers, applied a condom. She tried to crawl away as his implacable hands hauled her onto her knees, his arm securing her in place.

Fingers parted her folds, probing, sliding into her, her wetness a stunning betrayal.

A second later, he rammed into her, burying himself so hard, she cried out in shock. She tried to crawl away from the impaling shaft and from the treacherous pleasure.

"God, no, sweetheart. You're not getting away." His fingers dug into her hips, holding her immovable as he hammered into her, over and over. "You're mine, Kari," he growled. "My sub. My woman. Mine." Each word was punctuated by a hard thrust.

He'd called her his woman? A thrill ran through her. *But it wasn't true.* Shaking her head frantically, she tried to pull away.

With a low snarl, he shoved her knees farther apart and lifted her bottom higher, rendering her more helpless.

As she strained against the grip of his big hands, arousal shot through her, every nerve in her body flaming to life. His thick shaft plunged in and out of her sensitive tissues ruthlessly, and she tightened around him, the need becoming unbearable. She keened, unable to stop the sound.

A ripple started inside her, like a tidal wave, carrying everything before it, intensifying until she convulsed around him, until her whole body shook with the strength of the exquisite spasms, her voice lifting in high cries of bliss.

And then he buried himself deep, deep inside her and came with a low roar.

Her arms gave out, and she landed on her forearms, dropping her heavy head in the grass. He still held her hips in the air, breathing in heavy gasps.

She felt battered inside and out. Taken. Possessed. His words rang in her ears. *"My sub. My woman. Mine."*

Dan's words rang in his ears. *"My sub. My woman. Mine."*

Her body trembled in his grip, her pussy giving intermittent twitches of satisfaction. He'd used her hard, reacting to Buck's attack and her taunting like the alpha he was. He'd had to possess her, to brand her with his scent, his body, his cum.

Mine.

He couldn't move. His fingers wouldn't release their grip on her soft hips.

He didn't want to release her. Ever. No matter how often his mind told him to retreat from her, his emotions and his body kept forcing him back.

His own expression came back to him. *"Your body likes that idea,"* he'd told her, trying to teach her to look past her inhibitions. Hadn't done a hell of a job following his own advice, had he? He'd been too busy looking to the past.

She'd hit him over the head with the truth, shown him that he was both blind and deaf, and then she'd walked away.

He'd already been coming after her when the asshole attacked. Dan's jaw tightened. Should have punched the bastard a few more times, loosened some teeth.

Then again, maybe he should have thanked him. All-unknowing, the asshole had finished the awakening of Master Dan, the biggest idiot on the planet. But his ears were open now, and his body was telling him that he'd found his mate.

His heart agreed.

Beat a man over the head hard enough, and he'll eventually figure things out.

Dan leaned forward and pressed a kiss to the nape of his little sub's neck. Slowly he pulled out of her. The whimper as she was emptied made him smile. He patted her soft ass. "I'll be right back, sweetheart." He disposed of the condom.

When he returned, she let him pull her into his arms, all her fight fucked right out of her. That shouldn't have felt so gratifying. With a sigh, she snuggled close like a milk-fed puppy. Having her there, fitting against him as if she'd been designed for him…his world seemed to jerk and spin and suddenly right itself. Yeah, she was his.

Now all he had to do was get her to agree to take on a cynical cop with a penchant for kinky sex.

Piece of cake.

Kari rubbed her cheek against Sir's skin, wanting to take his scent with her when she left. And she needed to leave. Now. Before she burrowed farther into his arms. Why had Master Z thought Sir chasing her would make a difference? Why had she even tried? He'd used her and now held her…just like every other time. Had she really thought he'd blurt out some romantic nonsense?

She had to get out of here. At the thought of standing up and walking away *again*, she wanted to cry. "Let me go, please." She pushed away from his body. "I'm going home. I want you to leave me alone."

"No, you don't." He pulled her closer, his fingers tightening on her hip like a steel trap. "Did you hear me say you're mine?"

Just hearing the words tugged at her heart. And yet, in a minute, he'd turn that cold face on her. "Just now?" she said, trying for a polite, indifferent tone.

"Mmmmh, just now when I was buried so deep inside you I never wanted to leave."

The rumbling words made her shiver. Still, she knew what came next. She struggled up and braced herself with a forearm across his chest. She'd take the news looking at him, not huddling like a child.

His hand cupped her cheek. "I meant that, sweetheart. You're mine." He smiled slowly, his cheek creasing. "And I intend to keep you."

"Keep me?" Her heart bounced inside her, choking her words into incoherence.

His eyes were intent, and she realized he'd been studying her face. A satisfied smile crossed his lips.

"You can't keep me."

"Oh, but I can." His finger traced her lips, and the look in his eyes was one she hadn't seen before. "Your body says it likes the idea."

Keep her? She shoved the hope down. *Don't be silly.* He meant he'd see her at the club, use her as a sub. "You mean here at the club?"

"Here, Kari. And everywhere else."

Her brows drew together. There had to be a catch. "Does that mean I get to keep you also?"

"Oh, absolutely." He kissed her, his lips demanding. "I'm a firm believer in equality at all times—"

"At all times?" She glanced at the cuffs clipped to his leathers. "Why do I find that hard to believe?" And why the heck was she arguing with him. *Mine, mine, mine.*

"At all times," he repeated. "However, in the bedroom or in the club, I am a lot more equal than you." His grin flashed white before he rolled her onto her back. Pinning her between his knees, he buckled her cuffs on.

"Jerk," she said, the joy impossible to contain.

"That would be me. But I'm *your* jerk." He lifted her hands over her head, trapped them there. Leaning down, he stopped with his mouth an inch away from hers, his breath warm on her face. "We'll discuss this later, but you're at the club right now. So what do you say to me, little sub?"

She barely managed to whisper, "Yes, Sir," before he took her mouth and kissed any thought of defiance right out of her head.

THE END

Cherise Sinclair

I live in the west with my beloved husband, two children, and various animals, including three cats who rule the household. I'm a gardener, and I love nurturing small plants until they're big and healthy and productive...and ripping defenseless weeds out by the roots when I'm angry. I enjoy thunderstorms, playing Scrabble and Risk and being a soccer mom. My favorite way to spend an evening is curled up on a couch next to the master of my heart, watching the fire, reading, and...

Over the years, I've lived in many states and worked at a multitude of jobs before settling down to writing. You wouldn't believe how wonderful it was to meet other authors and discover I'm not the only person to have a mind populated with characters talking, arguing, and having hot sex. *Did I mention the hot sex?*

Cherise

Visit Cherise Sinclair on the web at www.CheriseSinclair.com

CPSIA information can be obtained at www.ICGtesting.com
Printed in the USA
BVOW032208141212

308246BV00001B/39/P